Love & Cherish

Till Death Do Us Part

Love, Murder,
Suspense and Surprise

Terry Rajan

CCB Publishing
British Columbia, Canada

Love & Cherish: Till death do us part

Copyright ©2007 by Terry Rajan
ISBN-13 978-0-9784388-7-6
First Edition

Library and Archives Canada Cataloguing in Publication

Rajan, Terry
Love & Cherish: Till death do us part / written by Terry Rajan.
ISBN 978-0-9784388-7-6

I. Title. II. Title: Love and cherish.
PS8635.A455L69 2007   C813'.6   C2007-907182-1

United States Copyright Office Registration # TXu 1-022-090

Publisher: CCB Publishing
             British Columbia, Canada
             www.ccbpublishing.com

Prologue

Diary Excerpt:

Why is he doing this? I don't understand. He was so wonderful before. Taking me to dinner, the opera at the beautifully remodeled Paramount, the trip to Vegas. His hands always so gentle and knowing afterwards. I would have done anything for him. What happened? He's treating me so hatefully now! On top of everything else, I thought at least he, a doctor, would understand what I'm going through. Well, I've made my plans. They'll all get what's coming to them! Soon.

Chapter 1

Dickson Street, on a far corner of northeast Seattle, was one of those older streets where ancient, gnarled maple trees spread their immense root system beneath the sidewalks, lifting the concrete up in uneven segments and creating a challenge for the inattentive jogger or casual passer-by. This only added to the charm of this middle class neighborhood, and although the residents grumbled, nobody had taken any steps to contact the City to have the sidewalks repaired.

The homes were a fair eclectic mixture of turreted Victorians mingling with low-slung ranches. The maples were shedding their foliage now and the red, gold, and rust-colored leaves swirled around in little gusts, piling up against curbs, covering lawns, and creating a pre-Halloween atmosphere on this crisp, early-October day.

The Martin's home, a modern ranch-style in white, was situated about midway down Dickson Street. Arnold Martin, known as Arnie to his few close friends and family, was a research scientist with the University Hospital in Seattle. With his broad shoulders and six-foot frame, it was easy to see why some people mistook him for one of the assistant coaches at the University of Washington, a nearby college.

Also sharing the house was Arnie's wife of 12 years, Sondra, and their two daughters, Ashley, a rambunctious ten-year old, and her twelve-going-on-thirty older sister, Heather. Both girls had been born and raised in this house and were well known in the neighborhood, especially Ashley, who tended to have many more misadventures than her sister.

The sun was perched on the horizon like a large red basketball as Arnie pulled into his driveway. Turning off the ignition of his new Lexus, Arnie sat there for awhile, scrutinizing the house and surrounding property. He could remember the day he moved into it twelve years ago. In retrospect, it seemed like it had been the happiest day of his life - baring the birth of his two girls, that is. Back in those happier times, he loved to walk through the front door after a hard day at work, proud of the new home he was able to provide for his growing family. Now, though, it was a totally different story. He often felt as if he had to talk himself into returning home lately. If it wasn't for the girls, he wondered if he would even bother to make the effort. He knew his relationship with Sondra was sinking further every day, and wasn't sure what to do about it.

He absently noticed that the yard needed mowing again. Thankfully, the cold weather would soon settle in to stay and the lawn would go dormant, giving him a nice reprieve until spring.

In comparison to the metallic, midnight blue of the car, sparkling in the waning sunlight, the house appeared drab. No life in the fading white paint, a few places where it had started to wear thin from the weather, the siding almost visible underneath. *Just like my marriage is starting to wear thin*, Arnie thought. With a new coat of paint, Arnie knew he could soon have the house back into tiptop shape. But could he repair his failing relationship with his wife? Restore their once congenial life together? This had been weighing heavily on his mind for quite some time.

The house itself was fairly large for a rambler. Four bedrooms, a spacious living room with two huge picture windows that kept the house bright, and two bathrooms, one of which was in the master bedroom, a big selling point at the time he and Sondra were house hunting. The only thing he regretted to this day was that it had not come with a guesthouse, as a few of the houses along this street had. Then he could just live there, close enough to his kids to keep an eye on them, while far enough away to avoid having to deal with Sondra more than necessary for the well-being of his daughters.

He realized he had put off fixing a lot of things over the years, not just his marriage. Plans to add a carport or garage had never panned out. And now, Arnie had to admit, he was used to parking either out on the wide street, or in the roomy driveway, which boasted plenty of room for two cars and a game of Hop Scotch, which he saw drawn on the concrete with colored chalk.

Looking up, he saw that the roof tiles had developed a light tinge of green over the winter. Probably moss. Nothing unexpected in a state where rain had more descriptive names than any other state he could think of. From light drizzle, to intermittent showers, to downpour, Washington had it all. It was rather ironic that the new term going around for natives of Washington was now "Moss Backs." In better times, his heart filled with passion and hope, he would have approached the job with a contented energy. But nowadays, he seemed to have lost that intensity and settled into a more passive train of thought.

"I guess I'm going to have to get somebody to go up there and clean it off," he said to no one in particular.

He started to open the car door, then changed his mind. He wanted to enjoy a few more minutes of peace before facing whatever awaited him inside. Adjusting the car seat to a more comfortable position, he fiddled with the radio and got a smooth jazz station. He listened to the gentle rhythm of the song, the sweet notes of the saxophone bringing up memories of some of the good times he'd spent with Sondra. There were speakers in every corner of the vehicle, knobs and levers to adjust the bass, treble, and who knew whatever else. Arnie could manipulate cells and operate expensive lab equipment, but he had yet to figure out how to operate most of the controls on his car stereo. He reached out and turned the volume up a notch.

The Lexus was a very nice, quiet luxury car, with all kinds of fancy gadgets inside to control everything from seat positions to power windows. But it didn't give Arnold any happiness. He would gladly have traded those 'good old days' for the luxury now surrounding him. He still missed his '92 Taurus, despite its longer warm-up time on cold, winter mornings, its rear window that would only open two inches. It used to be a nice car, back when he and his little family had spent so much time riding around in it. But he had put more work into it the past couple of years than he cared to think about. And the girls had each added their own unique signatures of scratches and dents to it as they grew up. Rather like the marks some families carved into a doorframe as their children grew taller. He didn't know if he would have kept it much longer or not, but the accident a few months ago had made that decision for him.

Arnie leaned back against the headrest, closing his eyes. He was feeling tired. Too much stress, he knew, not all from his job. On top of all their other problems, he knew Sondra was going to be angry to hear that he had to leave on business again. Something he seemed to be doing more than usual lately since Dr. Murray Evans, his new supervisor this past year, had taken over as head of the Science Research Department.

It seems Dr. Evans loathed traveling by air, as well as public speaking, and since the terms of their government grant required periodic seminars to keep the public informed of their medical progress, he was more than willing to pass it on to the assistant field director, Arnie himself. This latest trip was to a conference on cell manipulation, something that might prove helpful with their work in the lab. He actually didn't mind going; he just didn't want to face the anticipated reaction from his wife, having just returned from another seminar only a few weeks before. And as soon as Sondra hears he is going back to Los Angeles, he knows she will be bringing up Judy's name, and that is probably going to cause another ugly scene.

Seeing a movement out of the corner of his eye, Arnie looked up. His youngest daughter, Ashley, was peeking through the lacy, front curtain. Hearing the car drive in, she was impatiently waiting for him to come into the house. Arnie, noting her big brown eyes studying him with concern and the way the afternoon light reflected off her brown hair in golden highlights, felt his heart lighten. He gave her a grin and a little wave, unable to remain in the car after seeing his beautiful little girl waiting for him.

Feeling all of his thirty-six years, and then some, he climbed out of the car, grabbing his bulging briefcase from the passenger seat. He swung the door shut, not bothering to lock it. As far as he was concerned, in his present mood, somebody was welcome to come and steal the darn thing!

He skirted an array of bicycles and abandoned toys as he headed for the front door, reminding himself to give the girls the "put away your toys" speech one more time. He was fairly tight-lipped these days, and with thoughts of work weighing heavily on his mind tonight, his lips had all but disappeared.

Arnie broke the subject at dinner as casually as he could. "I have to go on a business trip again." He avoided eye contact with his wife, as he moved vegetables around on his plate. He missed seeing her sit up straighter in her chair, but he could *feel* her instant displeasure at the news.

"Again?" Sondra questioned disbelievingly. "Where to this time?" she asked, shaking her head in annoyance. She pushed her plate away, having lost her appetite, and picked up her wineglass.

"California," he said, with all the nonchalance he could muster. "Pass the rolls, please." And waited for the storm. He didn't have long to wait.

"You just got back!" She protested, taking a long sip of her White Reisling. "How long this time?"

Sondra frowned at their youngest daughter, Ashley, who was chewing with her mouth open, taking pleasure in hearing herself grind up a carrot from her salad. She had a swath of spaghetti sauce across one cheek. Sondra reached over to pick up Ashley's unused napkin from beside her plate and placed it on her daughter's lap. Ashley, oblivious to her mother's silent message, proceeded to stab another carrot and stuff it unladylike into her mouth, wiping the sauce with the side of her hand, then onto the leg of her jeans, earning a scowl from her mother.

Her older sister, Heather, already acting more like the teenager she would soon become, nibbled on her own vegetables, deciding to ignore her little sister's eating habits for once, more interested in the conversation about to take place between her parents.

"Only about three days. It's a conference in Los Angeles." Sondra said nothing to this. Thinking it was going better than he expected, Arnie relaxed a little and started to enjoy his meal. He may not miss the stress occurring more often between him and his wife, lately, but she was a good cook. He didn't get food like this in the hotels he stayed at when away from home.

Ashley, swinging her legs in time to a tune only she could hear, piped up. "Can we come, too? We want to go to Disneyland, don't we Heather?" She slurped up a long spaghetti noodle, leaving an orange trail where it hit her upper lip. "We don't have any school this whole week 'cause they have to fix the leaky pipes so we don't all drown!" She looked imploringly at her father, hazel eyes wide and innocent as she dangled another piece of sauce-laden pasta from her lips. "Can we, Daddy?" She finished her plea with a noisy sucking motion and the spaghetti disappeared.

Heather watched her sister's disgusting behavior, but before she could say anything, her mother sharply reprimanded Ashley to behave at the table and eat like a lady or she would have to leave.

Ashley pouted and stabbed a tiny piece of meatball, placing it into her mouth with slowly exaggerated movements. Then she continued to chew noisily, keeping pace with her swinging legs, and giving her sister a "So there!" look.

Heather turned towards her father. "Yes, can we, Dad? I have all my allowance saved up from this summer, and," she added, her blue eyes hopeful, "we never go anywhere fun anymore."

She glanced over at her sister, who was using her finger to make a spaghetti smiley face on her plate. "Will you stop being such a pig!" she exclaimed. "Mom, stop her, will you? It's disgusting!"

"Shut up, Dipwad!" Ashley retorted.

"Girls!" their mother warned. "Do you both want to spend the rest of the evening in your room?" She eyed them sternly. They shook their heads and quietly resumed eating.

Arnie's grin was genuine, but he had to disappoint them. "Sorry, girls. I'm not going to be anywhere near Disneyland, and this is a business trip. And, "he added, "There isn't enough time to make arrangements for all of you on such short notice. I'll take you the next time, okay?"

He watched their faces fall, and feeling bad, became once again very interested in the food on his plate. He could almost hear Sondra's disapproval. He knew he was letting them all down - again.

With sarcasm far beyond her years, Heather intoned, "Next time? And when might that be? I'll be graduating in a few years and I won't want to go anywhere with you then!" Arnie thought she sounded just like her mother, but he felt bad about the whole thing just the same.

"How about we try to go in a month or two, okay, girls?" He compromised. "I promise. I'll miss both of you while I'm gone," he added, tilting his head to the side and batting his eyes at them to make them smile.

"I'll miss you, too, Daddy," said Ashley, coming around the kitchen table to give him a big bear hug around his neck, leaving a little orange smear on his cheek to match her own. Heather just rolled her eyes and left the table, going to her room without finishing her dinner. This earned Arnie a scowl from Sondra, and the rest of the meal was eaten with only occasional small talk between Arnie and his daughter, Ashley. Sondra, deep in thought, chose to remain silent, with only a token nod or response when absolutely necessary.

Later, after the girls had gone to bed, Arnie and Sondra relaxed at opposite ends of the living room. After perusing the local paper for several minutes, Arnie set it aside and looked over at his wife. "Why didn't you tell me the girls would be out of school for a few days?" he asked.

Sondra frowned, marking her place in the novel she was

reading with the corner of the TV Guide she'd torn off the day before. "Why didn't you tell me earlier that you would be going to Los Angeles?"

"Touché," joked Arnie, trying to lighten up the situation.

Not in the mood to be talked out of feeling put out, Sondra set her book down on the coffee table with a dull thud. "When do you go?"

"Tomorrow morning."

Sondra curled her legs up underneath her and folded her arms across her chest, not a good sign. "How long have you known? I'll bet you told your girlfriend, Judy, didn't you," she questioned, with a hurt look.

Arnie tried to hide his smile and replied, "She is *not* my girlfriend. How many times have I told you, she's just a friend. Why are you bringing her into this?" He received a glare in response.

Arnie tried to move the conversation forward, to get it off of Judy. "Murray just informed me this morning that I was taking his place at this conference. Murray was going to go himself, but he claims he's feeling under the weather or some such nonsense, and since I'm next in line, I *have* to go. I've told you before that he hates flying." He watched her carefully for signs of relenting - or the start of an argument, which he dearly wanted to avoid tonight.

Sondra stood up, her eyes furious. "I don't believe you," she snarled. "And I think you're probably taking that Judy woman with you!" Arnie was wondering why she was over-reacting to this, but he knew better than to ask her. It would only make things worse.

Arnie sighed deeply. "Sondra, this is ridiculous," he said. "We are arguing about nothing. Judy is *not* coming with me! She doesn't go anywhere with me, let alone business trips. I have tried to explain this to you over and over. Why do you hate her so much when you haven't even met her!"

Sondra looked at him like he'd grown two heads. "Do you honestly expect me to *like* the woman my husband is fooling

14

around with!"

Arnie, surprised by the vehemence in her voice, insisted, for the hundredth time, that he was *not* having an affair, with Judy or anyone else. "I keep telling you, we are just friends. I enjoy talking to her, is all."

"You used to do that with *me*," Sondra pointed out. "You don't even bother, anymore!" She walked over to the window and looked out at the dark street a moment or two, then angrily pulled the drapes shut.

"What," she asked, walking back to the couch to stand in front of her husband, "do you get from this stranger that I can't give you?" She stood with her hands on her hips. Arnie looked up at her and sighed. There would be no peace tonight until this was dealt with.

"I can't exactly say. It's like she's my best friend, that I can tell her anything." Arnie could have kicked himself the second the words were out of his mouth. *Bad choice of words, Arnie,* he told himself. Seeing the hurt flit across her features, he quickly stood up, intending to give her a hug, but Sondra shrugged off his touch, as well as his attempts at an apology and walked away from him.

"Arnie, what did you say at our wedding day? Let me remind you 'Love & Cherish till death do us part'. Do you remember? *I'm* supposed to be your best friend, Arnie! Remember, 'To have and to hold'? There are no percentages of commitment you give to something, Arnie," she said, eyes watering, a miserable expression on her face. "Not in your job, not in raising a family, and definitely not in a marriage." She wiped her cheek, a tear slowly traveling down its length. "You, yourself always said that. Either you're going to be one hundred percent committed to this marriage, Arnie, or you're not." she said brokenly. "I know we haven't had the best marriage lately, but I need to know if it's worth fighting for, or if we're both just wasting our time! You need to decide, right now, who you're willing to give up, me or your friend, Judy."

Sondra watched him intently, a strange expression on her face - almost like the one Arnie got when he was close to seeing the results of one of his cell experiments under a microscope.

Arnie, confused and surprised at the turn the night had taken, couldn't say anything for a moment. Sondra, her anger coming back, crossed her arms again and glared at him. "Yeah, that's what I thought! Well," she sniffed, eyes getting watery, "You just go to your little friend Judy. We'll do just fine here, the girls and I, by ourselves. After all," she added forcefully, her face red with more than the wine she'd had at dinner, "We've been managing for a long time while you have been flying all over the country!" With that she turned and stalked out of the room.

"Sondra, I..." But he realized it was too late, as he heard their bedroom door slam shut behind her.

Knowing it would be impossible to get Sondra to listen to anything he had to say when she was so upset, Arnie decided he'd better find something else to do until she cooled down. Afraid he would find the door locked against him, he would try later to pick up the paperwork he had left on the dresser earlier.

If Arnie could have foreseen the devastation that was about to take place in his life, maybe he would have chosen to risk facing that locked door. And perhaps he would have been able to lead history into an alternate direction. One that could have possibly prevented the events that would forever change the lives of so many people.

Instead, falling back onto the couch with self-loathing, he picked up the TV remote and flipped idly through the cable channels.

Chapter 2

In the bedroom, after a good cry, Sondra mopped up her tears with a soggy Kleenex and decided to call her sister, Libby, in Portland, Oregon. As soon as Libby picked up the phone, Sondra blurted, "Guess what? Arnie's going on a business trip to Los Angeles tomorrow!" She tried to sound cheerful. "The girls don't have school for a few days, so I thought we'd come down and spend a couple days with you." Sondra paused, then added, "That is, if it's all right with you?" She swiped at a tear that escaped, hoping her sister couldn't tell she'd been crying.

Sounding a bit surprised, and wondering what was wrong, Libby replied, "No, that would be great! When are you coming?"

Relieved, Sondra leaned back against the headboard, "Well, I thought we'd drive down the day after tomorrow, Wednesday. We should be there in time for lunch." She used a corner of the bedspread to dry her face, already feeling better at the thought of going to see her sister.

Libby was warming up to the idea. "Great! My girls will be thrilled to have a day or two of playing mother-approved hooky from school! See ya when you get here!"

*   *   *

The next morning Arnie got up early, being very careful not to wake up Sondra. He peeked into the girl's room before he left and saw their innocent, sleeping faces, wishing he *was* taking them to Disneyland instead of going to a business conference. He looked at his watch, saw it was getting late and left quietly to catch his taxi for the airport.

Sondra heard him leave, but waited until he was gone before going straight to the girls' bedroom to wake them up. "Hey, sleepyheads!" she said, bouncing on the side of little Ashley's bed. "Wake up! How'd you like to go visit Aunt Libby tomorrow?" The girls bounced out of bed, Ashley giving a little shriek of excitement at going on an unexpected adventure. "Yeah!" she screamed, hopping up and down, and flapping her arms like a baby chick. "Can we go today? I'm gonna pack!" She raced over to her dresser and started tossing clothes onto the bed, not at all concerned that she might be taking all underwear and nothing else.

Heather, a little more thoughtful, asked how long they would be at their Aunt Libby's. "Well," her mom replied, getting up to put half of what Ashley had strewn about back into the drawer. "I figured we would stay a couple days, at least, while your father is gone. What do you say to that?"

After thinking about what the alternatives would be if she stayed at home, like hanging out with her friends doing the same old thing they did every weekend, she gave her mom a big grin and agreed it sounded like a great plan.

Sondra spent a major part of that day making important phone calls, chasing the girls out of the room if they happened to be within hearing distance. Not usually bothering if the housework was done or not, she now organized the house and got it so spick and span, that both girls were wondering if there was a big family holiday coming up they didn't know about because their mother was acting like she was expecting company. Questioning their mom did no good, as it ultimately meant they were sent to "go do something useful", which, translated, meant chores. So they ended up staying in their room or visiting with their friends to stay out of her way.

The next day, Wednesday, dawned crisp and clear - a perfect day for the four-hour drive to her sister's. Sondra woke the girls up just as it was beginning to get light and instructed them to get dressed and bring their overnight bags into the entryway. After a quick breakfast, Sondra went across the street to the Chapmans. Laveen and her husband, Jake, both in their early 60's, were like grandparents to the girls, having known the Martins since before the girls were born.

Mrs. Chapman was still in her nightgown, and Sondra couldn't help but admire her trim figure and only a hint of gray in her otherwise auburn-colored hair. Laveen was enjoying a cup of steaming coffee, the rich aroma making Sondra yearn to try it. She knew Laveen made one of the best brews in the neighborhood. Her friend insisted it was because she kept the beans in the freezer and freshly ground just enough for every pot.

"What are you doing up so early, Sondra?" she asked, holding the door open in welcome. "You beat Jake up, he's still in bed sawing logs! Come on in where it's warm, there's plenty of hot coffee in the pot," she said, as she stepped to the side to allow her neighbor to enter.

Sondra was more than tempted, but knowing she couldn't, she backed away a step and told her, "Not this time, Laveen. The kids are waiting at the house for me. We're going to my sister, Libby's, place in Portland to visit for a couple days while Arnie's out of town on a business trip. I was wondering if you'd keep an eye on the house for me? I should be back early tomorrow."

Laveen, shivering in the brisk wind that occasionally brushed past her bare legs, gripped her coffee cup with both hands and said, "Don't give it a second thought, dear. We'd be happy to do it. I hate to run you off, but I'm freezing my tush off! So drive carefully, okay? I'll see you when you get back and we can have that cup of coffee and catch up on things!"

Sondra stepped closer to give Laveen a hug, something she normally reserved for holidays or after too much alcohol at the occasional dinner party. Then she turned and went back across the street. "Give those girls a big hug for me, will you?" she heard her friend holler, just before the door was closed against the cold, fall air.

An hour or two later, as they drove towards Oregon, the girls were entertaining themselves with the childhood games most children played: license plate bingo, "99 Bottles on the Wall", and trying to make the big semi-trucks that roared by in the other lanes honk their horns by pulling their own invisible air horns with an up and down arm motion. When that was unsuccessful, although they got a couple of friendly waves, they switched to finding the alphabet on passing road signs.

Sondra, thankful that she had a couple of kids that could handle long road trips without killing each other, turned briefly and looked into the back seat. "I know you're having fun," she said, "but I expect you to be on your best behavior when we're at Aunt Libby's house. I'll have to go out tomorrow to do some errands, so you need to be nice to your aunt and cousins." The girls exchanged puzzled looks, but nodded their assent, deciding it was probably not a good idea to question the errands their mom spoke of when she was in such a good mood. When their mother had nothing further to tell them, they went back to their game. "I see a D on that sign . . .!"

*   *   *

As the miles dropped away, Sondra went on autopilot, her thoughts drifting back to her childhood. Her sister, Libby, was only a year younger. They used to fight a lot growing up - over boys, who borrowed what without asking - nothing more serious than the usual teen-age crisis, and were not always the best of friends. Their parents, and later their stepmother after their mom died and their dad re-married, were of the belief that children should be seen and not heard. So they usually had to rely on each other for company. Once their stepmother had come to live with them, Sondra resented having to take care of her younger sibling, often having to forego a special school event or fun with her friends. But, as they grew older, they had become close friends, and had spent more time together, willingly.

Libby got married one year after Sondra did, they both had been blessed with two little girls around the same time periods, so the girls were very close in ages. But then their paths diverged into two entirely different directions.

Libby got divorced, the circumstances still not entirely clear to the family, and had remarried a much more mature man who, Sondra had to admit, treated her sister and his two step-daughters a lot better than *their* real father ever did. And here *she* was, thinking she was happily married to a wonderful lover and provider, when all this time she'd been living with a no-good adulterer! Sondra sighed, more sad than angry, wishing things could be different between Arnie and her. At least, she told herself, he is a very good father, and would do anything for his girls. Well, she amended that thought, except for taking them to Disneyland! And had to smile to herself.

*   *   *

Sondra and the girls arrived early in the afternoon and were greeted warmly by Libby. Her two girls burst out the front door, greeting their cousins with high-pitched screams. After all the hugs and excited outbursts were over with, all four girls dashed around the house to the back yard to see who could get to the swing-set first. Once the girls settled down to play, Sondra and Libby went inside and sat down at the kitchen table with some fresh iced tea. "Great timing," Libby said, "We're almost ready for lunch. Thought we'd have to eat without you."

Sondra, not really paying attention to what her sister was saying, abruptly announced, "I have something very personal I want to tell you. But you have to keep it a secret." She watched her sister's reaction, rubbing her finger around the rim of her glass.

Libby listened for a moment to the sounds of the girls playing out back, then said, "You know I never told anybody about all the times you used to sneak out of the house to smoke! I'm sure glad you came to your senses and quit, too! Now, what is it? Is this why you decided to come out here so suddenly? Are you in some kind of trouble?"

"I think my husband is having an affair!" Sondra blurted out.

Her eyes wide, Libby was speechless for a few moments. "What!" she exclaimed, incredulous. "Arnie? Can't be, he loves you and the kids too much to risk something that stupid! Where did you get a crazy idea like that?" Her sister scoffed, getting up to refill her glass.

Taking a deep breath to steady herself, Sondra admitted, "Yes, he loves his girls, but he doesn't love *me* anymore!" She choked down a sob and took a quick sip of cold tea.

Her refill forgotten for the moment, Libby sat down again and asked what made her come to this conclusion.

Sondra stood up and went to the sink, looking out the window to where the girls were climbing on the swing-set, listening to their infectious giggles before answering. She turned back towards her sister. "Do you remember the car accident he had a couple months ago?" Now she felt she had to sit down and pulled the chair out opposite her sister. Her sister nodded. "Well, he was with this certain woman that night. I was a little suspicious when he had the accident in downtown Seattle so late at night, so I asked him to be straight with me about it. He admitted he'd been with this woman, but insisted that she was just a friend! We've had a lot of nasty fights over it since that night!"

Libby still didn't seem convinced. She truly liked her brother-in-law, and wanted to give him the benefit of the doubt, even if his own wife wouldn't. "He may be telling the truth," she said.

"Oh, right!" Sondra scoffed. "Spending time with a young girl in her apartment at midnight just to talk!" She slammed down her glass angrily, tea sloshing onto the table. She couldn't believe her sister was taking her husband's side on this. "And I noticed another thing - he often comes home from work late at night now. This started just shortly before he had the accident and it's still going on! Arnie's supervisor, Murray, told me all about this little affair!" She tapped the side of her glass anxiously.

Libby shook her head, "Why would you take his boss' word over your husband's? What exactly did he tell you?" She leaned back in her chair, prepared to hear the worst.

"He told me that Arnie met this Judy person on a plane that day he went to Los Angeles on a business trip. And that he's been seeing her ever since," Sondra said, her eyes welling up with unshed tears, a stricken look on her face. She took a deep breath. "Murray says he saw her one time and she's beautiful and very young. Arnie takes her to dinner all the time and they go to her apartment to *talk*! So Arnie says anyway! What other proof do I need?" She blew her nose with her napkin, giving herself time to calm down. Her sister, still not ready to believe what she considered lame evidence, remained silent. "Well," Sondra exclaimed, "I'm getting back at him!" She sat back with a smug expression.

Arching an eyebrow, Libby asked, "And what exactly does *that* mean?" Afraid to hear the answer, she waited. She was seeing a side of her sister she hadn't seen before, and wasn't sure she liked it.

"I'm going out with his *supervisor*," she whispered, as if afraid somebody else would hear her terrible confession. She waited for her sister's reaction to this news, holding her glass tightly.

Leaning in closer, responding in a like whisper, Libby exclaimed, "You're dating another man?" Sondra shook her head, looking down at the amber liquid in her frosty glass. "What?" Libby's mouth suddenly hung open. "You mean you're sleeping with him? With Murray Evans?" She looked totally skeptical. "No way!"

Eyes gleaming, Sondra said triumphantly, "Yes! Murray's very handsome and smart. He has short, dark wavy hair, gorgeous brown eyes, and large hands. He's a wonderful kisser and...he knows how to please a woman in bed, if you know what I mean!" She blushed and looked away, anywhere but at her sister.

Skeptical and yet finding herself amused, Libby tried not to laugh. Thinking about her own two marriages, not to mention the several other men she had dated over the years, she agreed, "Oh, yeah, I know exactly what you mean!" Steering it back to a more serious note, Libby asked her sister if she knew what she was getting into. "An affair is nothing to be taken lightly, Sondra. What if Arnie or the girls find out?"

"They won't." Sondra responded defensively. "We have been very careful, we meet only when Murray can arrange for Arnie to be out of town, or when Arnie has a big experiment going on and can't make it home until late in the night.

"Murray has never been to my house, we always find a hotel somewhere away from town. And the girls are always happy to stay over at their friends houses, or Laveen, my neighbor takes them for a few hours. You know she loves those girls like her own grandkids. She thinks Arnie and I meet somewhere for a quickie," she admitted. "I just let her think what she wants to, it's not going to hurt anything. Arnie rarely talks to the Chapmans, so I have nothing to worry about there." Libby could only shake her head at the thought process that had gone into this whole thing.

Sondra continued, "If I'm lucky, I might get to see Murray before Arnie gets back from L.A. Although," she added dryly, "he'll probably stop at *Judy's* house on the way home, anyway!"

Libby walked over to the stove to stir a pot of soup she had simmering on the burner, her movements sending the rich, mouth-watering aroma around the room. Happily married now herself, she was deeply disturbed by her sister's illicit activities. She couldn't believe that she hadn't seen any of this coming. Replacing the lid onto the pot and turning it off, she returned to the table and sat beside her sister.

"Sondra," Libby said gently, "you and Arnie were once very happy together. I can remember a time when neither of you could leave each other's side long enough to go to the bathroom! What happened to you? Both of you? To your wonderful marriage?"

Sondra looked down at her hands, and seeing them turning white from being clasped so tightly together, released them and tried to relax. "It's all been an illusion. I know he's never loved me. He married me because Heather was on the way. For a while we were doing well, Arnie was starting to love me. Then Ashley came along, and I don't know what happened. Maybe Judy happened!" She let herself fall back against the chair and looked sulky, reminding Libby of the girls when they didn't get their way. Sondra looked a lot like Ashley when she was pouting, she thought, hiding a smile.

Libby, now more comfortable with the subject, reminded Sondra that there was quite a few years unaccounted for between Ashley's birth and Arnie meeting Judy. "There's got to be more to it than that. Something that's been changing between you two for quite a while. If you don't mind me asking, how has your sex life been with Arnie?"

Sondra was taken by surprise at the question and raised her eyebrows at her sister. Libby reminded her that *she'd* started all this. "It's...well...it's just that...It hasn't been very good, I guess. He stays up reading all those stuffy research papers in bed, late into the night. It's not uncommon for me to find him sleeping sitting up, papers strewn all over the bed, the bedroom light still on. It gets pretty annoying, so we don't even sleep together anymore. He started sleeping in the guestroom months ago so he wouldn't wake me up, and eventually, he just stopped coming into my room altogether. We rarely make love nowadays, and then it's like he's just going through the motions, like he feels he has to. I stopped trying to attract his interest. He doesn't even notice what I'm wearing or if I cut my hair. So why bother!"

Libby listened intently before moving on to her next concern. "Okay, so what about communication between the two of you," realizing she was starting to sound like Dr. Phil on Oprah.

Sondra thought about it before replying, "Just normal, I guess. Although we used to talk a lot more than we have been. And lately we do more arguing than talking."

"So, what are you going to do about all this? Are you going to approach Arnie and demand some answers? Or are you going to keep seeing this Murray guy?" Libby stopped, a sudden thought occurring to her. "Are you leaving him - is that why you *really* came here?" Libby asked, worried for her sister and the two little girls outside.

Sondra shook her head. "No, I hadn't thought that far. And, it's not what *I'm* going to do, it's 'what is *he* planning to do?' That's the real question here." She drew designs in the wet ring left by her iced tea, wondering how much she should tell Libby. "There's one more piece of this puzzle I need to find out. Arnie's little friend, Judy, called me last night and told me she knows that Arnie - not 'Dr. Martin', mind you - has gone to Los Angeles again, and she wants very much to meet with me." Sondra raised an eyebrow towards her sister.

Libby went to the cupboard to get soup bowls. "So, what did you say to her? Are you going to do it?" She placed the bowls on the table, pausing to hear Sondra's response.

"Well, I asked Judy what she had in mind and she said she just needed to explain a few things that I didn't know. I asked 'Like what?' and she said, 'About Arnie and his plans." No idea what she has in mind, or what *plans* my darling husband might have going, but I agreed to meet her at my place at 2:00, tomorrow. She probably already knows where we live, but I gave her the directions anyway," Sondra commented, crossing her arms over her chest like she does when she's upset.

Libby looked stunned. "Is that 2:00 *tomorrow*?"

"Yes, no sense putting it off, and anyway, I have a lot of questions to ask Arnie's girlfriend!"

"You don't think she's going to tell you that Arnie is leaving you for her, do you?" Libby asked, appalled.

"I don't think so," Sondra replied. "She didn't sound triumphant or anything. You know, like she'd won or something." She got up to help Libby with the place settings. "She actually sounded rather pleasant."

"What, now you like her?" Libby teased.

"No! I'm just saying she didn't sound threatening like a mistress should. Wow, there's an ugly word - *mistress*. Puts a whole new meaning on it when it involves your own family. I guess, if I'm honest, I'm one, too, aren't I?" Libby was glad to see that at least she had the decency to look humiliated as the truth finally hit home. Even though she'd gotten herself into this mess, she felt sorry for her sister, who looked ready to burst into tears.

"What did you plan on doing with the kids?" Libby asked, already knowing what the answer would be.

Looking slightly humble, Sondra asked if they could stay with her sister for two days. "They have so much fun with your kids, and they won't cause any problems - even Ashley can stay out of trouble for a couple days! What do you say, please?" she coaxed, looking up at her sister pleadingly.

Libby reached over and took her sister's hand in her own. "Are you sure you want to meet with this girl?" she asked earnestly. "You might hear things you don't care to hear."

Sondra shrugged. "Why not, what else is there to lose? I feel like I've already lost my husband to her, and now my marriage, thanks to my own petty revenge with his supervisor! But this will give me the chance to find out what she and Arnie are *really* up to. I can't go on without knowing, it's killing me!" she exclaimed, feeling like her heart was about to tear in two.

Libby, sharing her sister's pain, told her the girls were more than welcome to stay with them as long as it took for her to straighten things out, and that Ken wouldn't mind having two more bodies to wrestle around with. "He *really* needs a dog," she said, smiling. "Are you going to stay the night tonight?"

"Yeah, if it's all right with you, I'll stay here and leave early in the morning after the kids get up, okay?"

"Hey, time for some of that primo soup I made before it turns to mush! You call the girls in to get washed up and I'll finish setting the table."

*   *   *

Sondra didn't sleep at all that night, too busy tossing and

turning, unable to stop thinking about Arnie and Judy together, and what was going to happen tomorrow. What would she say to her husband's girlfriend? What would Judy look like? What was her husband's taste in other women? She tried to think of other things, the girls, even Murray, but with no luck. Her thoughts kept returning defiantly to the upcoming events of the next day. She sighed deeply and rolled onto her other side. It was going to be a very long night.

Chapter 3

The next morning, the sun just peeking up over the foothills, Sondra was up and ready by 7:00. Since the girls had giggled and played until long past their regular bedtimes, Sondra had to wait until 8:00 before they started showing signs of life. She explained to them that she was leaving them with their cousins for two days, and that they needed to be very good for Aunt Libby and Uncle Ken. She hugged them, gave everybody kisses, then gave her sister an especially tight hug, and headed back to Seattle, wondering all the way what she had gotten herself into.

*   *   *

Stopping for coffee at a little roadside diner, Sondra had a few minutes to think about how she might approach the meeting coming up with Judy. She thought about different approaches she could use, from friendly - *not!* - to hostile, while she watched the tired waitress scurry around the crowded room completing orders before finally reaching the counter to take her own order "to go". She remembered what it was like trying to keep up with all the orders, scrambling to get people their food while it was hot, hoping a lull would come so you could slow down and take a breath. Sondra tried to catch the weary waitress' eye to give her a smile of gratitude, but the waitress wouldn't make any eye contact with the patrons, too busy trying to just do her job. *I sure don't miss this lifestyle!* She reminded herself, taking her coffee and leaving the bustling diner.

Back on the highway, Sondra thought to herself: *You need to stay calm. No matter what she tells you, be cool.* "At least until you find out exactly what the hell is going on!" she said aloud, beating on the steering wheel a few times with the palm of her hand, not so much frustrated as keyed up at the coming events. Then guiltily, she looked around, as if the spirits of her daughters might have been tagging along in the back seat and witnessed her childish behavior. "Get a grip, Sondra," she chastised herself.

She pulled her silver Volvo wagon, a gift from Arnie less than a year ago, into her driveway about 12:45 that afternoon. She had been glancing at the clock on the dashboard periodically on the drive back, nervously keeping track of how much time remained before her 2:00 meeting. Parking in her usual spot on the right side of the driveway, she glanced up at the dark clouds looming overhead, waiting to drop their heavy burden. *That's how I feel, too,* she silently told the clouds.

Hoping her emotions were not apparent, she went directly across the street to the Chapman's house and rang the bell. Mrs. Chapman, now in jeans and an old white T-shirt of Jake's, opened the door, a pleased look appearing on her face. "You're back already!"

"Yes, I just got here a few moments ago. I'm tired - the drive seems extra long when you're all by yourself!" she said with a little smile. "Say, I have a friend stopping in for a bit around two o'clock, why don't you come over for tea or coffee later, maybe about three? She'll be gone by then and we can play catch up."

"That'll be fun. Where are the girls? Didn't they come back with you?" Laveen asked, looking over Sondra's shoulder. She loved those little girls, although she had to admit that the youngest one, Ashley, who always seemed to be getting into trouble, was her favorite. You never knew what was going to come out of that girl's mouth!

"No," replied Sondra. "Since they don't have school for a few days, I thought it would be fun for them to stay with their cousins.

I'll pick them up later in the week." Exchanging good-byes, Sondra went back across the street to her house to get ready for her visitor. Time seemed to slow down to a crawl, but, at last, it was time.

*   *   *

Laveen, sitting in her living room reading the latest People magazine, glanced up as a movement caught her eye. A yellow taxi was pulling up in front of the Jensen's house, next door to the Martin's. Normally, Laveen, a creature of habit - as are most humans - would have dozed off by now, as she usually did sometime after lunch, but a particularly interesting article had caught her attention and she had fought her drowsiness to try to finish it. Now, her fatigue forgotten once more, she pulled her recliner upright as she watched the taxi to see who would come out, thinking perhaps one of the Jensen's sons was visiting from Idaho. A woman got out and bent over to pay the driver. Laveen squinted to see what she looked like, but the lady was on the opposite side of the taxi and the vehicle was blocking much of the details. As the woman stood up, Laveen saw that the woman was very pretty, in her early twenties, with a slender figure. She was nicely dressed in a long, black leather coat and matching slim-heeled shoes. Looking at her long, black hair swaying across her shoulders, Laveen got the impression that the young woman might be of Native American decent. Before she could make out anything further, though, the young woman opened a big red umbrella, as it was beginning to sprinkle, effectively covering any further facial features.

Laveen watched the young stranger turn towards the Jensen's walkway, then hesitate and look around, as if not sure she was at the right place. Turning back to the taxi, she bent down as if speaking to the driver. Laveen couldn't tell what the driver looked like from inside the dark interior of the cab, but he seemed to be a fairly burly guy.

After a few moments, the woman straightened up, looking around as if to get her bearings, then started to walk in the direction of the Martin's house. Laveen was very curious when she headed up the Martin's walkway towards their front door. Reaching the doorstep, the woman shook the moisture off the umbrella and folded it up, turning her back to the street as she did so. Frustrated, Laveen muttered to herself, still unable to figure out who it could be. Glancing at her watch she recalled, however, that Sondra had mentioned expecting a visitor around two o'clock. It was now a few minutes after.

Being a self-confessed snoop, Laveen felt no qualms about continuing to watch what was taking place next door. She could clearly see the front of the Martin house through her living room picture window, especially from the recliner. Being an avid reader, it had been placed just so to catch the bright light, especially since her aging eyesight had recently started to worsen – and refusing to acknowledge even that bit of aging, Laveen had thus far resisted the glasses that could have made reading a little easier.

"But", Laveen told herself, "There's nothing wrong with my long-distance vision!" and she continued to scope out what was taking place across the street, her magazine long forgotten.

She watched the young lady reach out to ring the doorbell, shifting her weight nervously from foot to foot. Laveen tried to see what she was holding. It looked like a small handbag, but the distance was too far to see any details, and the light rain was making it even harder to see.

As Sondra answered the door, the woman took a step back, then seemed to catch herself and stepped closer, stretching her hand out to the other woman. Sondra ignored her hand, causing Laveen to wonder about that, since she felt Sondra was always a polite, if not overly welcoming person for as long as she'd known her. They appeared to engage in a few seconds of silent conversation before Sondra stepped aside and allowed the stranger to enter her home.

When nothing further was to be seen, Laveen yawned and decided she would take that nap after all. She put her magazine on the coffee table, and reclining her chair to its fullest, closed her eyes.

*   *   *

The loud thud of the garbage truck, followed by the beeping of its back up signal woke Laveen up from her heavy doze. She glanced at the clock above the TV set. "Well, that was a quick forty minutes!" Adjusting her chair to upright, she looked out the window, wondering to herself if Sondra's company was still there. "I wonder if that was a high school friend Sondra hadn't seen in a while? Her visitor looked pretty nervous." She recalled the ignored handshake, then shrugged. "Guess I should start getting ready to go over there. I can find all that out later."

But just as she was starting to get up she saw the door of the Martin's house open. She watched as that same young woman quickly closed the door behind her, and hurried down the walkway. The woman paused, looked to her right and left, then rushed down the street to where the taxi was still parked, almost running in her apparent haste to get away.

Laveen didn't see Sondra show the young lady to the door or come into view to bid her good bye. "Now that's odd," Laveen murmured. "I wonder if they had a fight over something?" She watched the woman jump into the back of the taxi and it drove off, leaving her to wonder why the taxi was still in the same spot all this time. "Maybe it came back." she reasoned.

She looked at the clock, almost 2:45. She headed for the door, then, hesitated, wondering if it was wise to go over there now, or wait until three o'clock. "No, I'd better wait, she might need time to get herself together. I can ask her later what was going on." With that thought, Laveen left the living room and went into her bedroom to fix her makeup and change out of Jake's old shirt.

By three o'clock Laveen was ready to head out for her "tea"

appointment with Sondra. She rang the doorbell and waited, hoping Sondra remembered she had asked her to come over, wondering if she should have called first to make sure it was still all right. Seeing that Sondra had not come to the door yet, Laveen almost turned away to go back to her house to make that phone call, but changed her mind. "She's probably trying to get her face together before she greets me so I can't see how upset she is," Laveen told herself.

And, with that thought, she rang the bell again. Still no answer.

Cautiously, not wanting to disturb her friend if she was asleep or in emotional turmoil over what had undoubtedly been an unsuccessful visit, Laveen opened the door and quietly entered her friend's house. She softly called Sondra's name, then, coming in further, called her name a little louder.

The short entry hall opened into a rather large living room, well lit from the two impressive picture windows to the right, with another hallway to the left that led to the bedrooms and kitchen. As Laveen slowly entered the living room, she looked around, calling Sondra's name again, then suddenly stopped, putting her hand to her mouth, her face losing all its color. There, in front of the row of bookcases holding Arnie's medical journals and research books, was Sondra, lying in a pool of dark fluid that could only be blood!

Shocked, in a panic, Laveen fought the urge to throw up. She knew she should go over and feel for a pulse, some sign of life, but she just couldn't make herself go any closer to her friend's body. Surely she couldn't still be alive with all that blood around her! It looked like an awful lot to her – *Just how much blood could a person lose and still survive?* she thought to herself.

Wait, she thought, *maybe it's not Sondra at all!* She took a few steps closer. The face was covered by a piece of white material, but Laveen could see plenty of dark blond hair peeking around it. The body was clothed in a pair of jeans, navy-colored slip-on pumps, and a long sleeved, robin's-egg-blue pullover. Unfortunately, it was one that Laveen had seen Sondra wear dozens of times. There was no further doubt in Laveen's mind that it was Sondra lying on the floor.

She looked around the room - for what, she wasn't sure. Her line of sight landed on a picture of the Martin family propped up on a corner of Arnie's desk at the far side of the room, not too far from where the body lay. Laveen remembered when the photo was taken, shortly after the girls started school last year. The girls...!

Laveen called out the girls' names, "Heather, Ashley!" She listened, no answer.

She called again, louder this time. Still no reply. She briefly thought about going into the left hallway to check the bedrooms, but, being honest with herself, there was no way she was really going to do that! What if she found two more bodies! Then, with a ragged sigh of relief, she remembered that the girls were still in Oregon with their cousins.

Chewing on her thumbnail, she stopped to think for a minute. "Okay, Laveen," she encouraged herself. "What have you learned from all those hours you've spent sitting in front of the TV?" Spotting the telephone on the lamp table at one end of the sofa, she quickly grabbed it and, wondering at the same time if she was obliterating important crime scene evidence by picking it up, she dialed the police department.

"This is 911, what is your emergency?" asked a lady's voice.

"Somebody just killed Sondra!" she yelled. She kept her back to the body, trying not to remember all the horror movies she loved to watch late at night where the dead body of the best friend suddenly sits up!

The lady on the other end of the phone told her, in a reassuring voice, to calm down and state her name and where she was calling from.

"This is Laveen Chapman. I'm at 1101 Dickson Street. My neighbor, Sondra Martin is dead!" She paused, glancing briefly at the body, then whispered; "Somebody killed her!"

"Are you sure your neighbor is dead, or just unconscious?

Have you checked for a pulse? What is the cause of death, ma'am?"

Laveen looked at the pool of blood, noticing for the first time a large knife next to her friend. She shivered and replied, "I'm pretty sure she's dead," she said softly. "There's a big old knife next to her and she's not moving!"

"Is there reason to believe the killer might still be in the house?" asked the dispatcher. "Are you in any immediate danger?"

Her heart jumping at this question, she looked wildly around, expecting to see a masked man sneaking up on her. Then she remembered the woman leaving the house earlier. "No, I'm pretty sure nobody's here but me and Sond... me and the body." But she decided to keep her back towards the wall just the same.

"Okay, ma'am, please wait outside for the police to arrive. They're on their way. Don't touch anything, and don't let anybody go into the house."

Laveen said all right, replaced the handset of the phone, and went to stand outside on the steps, closing the door gently behind her.

Chapter 4

A police car drove up four minutes later, lights flashing, but siren silent. It parked in the driveway, behind, but to the left of the Volvo. It was soon followed by a second squad car, which parked at the end of the drive, effectively blocking any further traffic in or out. Two officers stepped out of the first car, nodding to the second pair of men, who had been called in to block any curious neighbors from getting a closer look at the crime scene, and ultimately destroying any possible evidence.

They approached Laveen, who was standing nervously just below the front door step, feeling cold and frightened. Her arms were wrapped tightly around her midriff, partly from the chill wind that had risen to mix with the light drizzle, but mostly from sheer anxiety and fear that had set in shortly after she'd made the emergency call.

The first man, Officer Dave Patton, asked Laveen if she was the one who had found the body. Laveen nodded. After asking what her name was, Officer Patton called the information in. Then said, "Okay, we're going to go in and take a look. We need you to show us where the victim is, Mrs. Chapman."

"Do I have to go back in there?" Her eyes began to shine with unshed tears, and she clutched herself even tighter." I don't think I can see it...her, without getting sick." She hung her head and they heard a very low "I'm sorry."

Patton told her she could stay outside while they checked it out. After asking her to describe where she found the body, along with a brief description of the inside of the house, he waved one of the other officers over from where he was standing, talking to a second officer. So far, in this quiet neighborhood, crowd control hadn't been needed. If anybody was curious, they were containing it within the safety of their own homes, discretely peeking through lacy curtains.

Officer Patton explained what was happening, then asked the officer to stay with Mrs. Chapman while he and his partner went to check on the body.

It had been only a few minutes since the 911 call and the officers had arrived and went into the house, but to Laveen, it seemed to take an interminable amount of time for it all to happen. A deep tremor went through her body, partly from fear. Seeing the witness shivering from the change in the weather, he thought, the new officer asked her if she lived nearby.

"I'm just over there," she said, teeth beginning to chatter from more than the cold. "Across the street," pointing to the tan two-story house, green trim around the eaves and windows.

The officer gently suggested she go back to her home and get warm. "Somebody will be over soon to get more information from you."

After six minutes or so, Patton and Lotze came back out, having checked and found no signs of life, the house otherwise empty of potential suspects. They called into the station to cancel the extra paramedics, that they would be needing the medical examiner instead. Being told where they could find the witness, the two officers crossed the street to finish their interview.

Seated in the living room, Patton, now reached into the pocket of his police jacket and brought out a small spiral notebook and pencil. Flipping it open, he wrote the date and time they had been called, a brief run-down of what they found in the house, and the time of their interview with the witness.

"You're the one that made the call to 911?" Patton began. Laveen nodded, hugging a couch pillow to her breast, knowing her friend really was dead now. He asked her for her address and phone number, and Laveen complied, stumbling over the phone number in her anxiety.

"Can you give me an idea of the time you found it?"

"The...The body, you mean?" It was Patton's turn to nod. She told him about arranging to meet her friend at three o'clock.

"Did you touch the body, ma'am, or anything in the room?"

"Oh, no!" Laveen was horrified at the thought. "I didn't even get close to it!" Then she added. "Except for the phone. But it wasn't close to the...it wasn't close to anything."

The two officers exchanged a glance, feeling concern for the woman, who was obviously distressed. They didn't like this either, but for them, at least, it was just an unpleasant aspect of their job.

Laveen excused herself for a few moments and returned with a box of Kleenex.

"Do you know where the husband of the victim is? Did you see Dr. Martin or his car around this morning?" asked Patton, chewing on the end of his pencil. The elder of the pair, he had picked up the bad habit during his rookie days, then never bothered to stop. Occasionally, despite himself, Lotze, the younger cop, found his pencil sneaking into his own mouth during times of stress – a habit he definitely worked hard at not acquiring!

"No, he's been gone since Tuesday morning. He usually leaves the car here and takes a taxi to the airport. He just got a new one recently, and he's afraid somebody will steal it while he's gone. She pointed out her front window at a dark blue Lexus sedan parked out along the curb, in front of the Martin house. "That's his car, right there. It's been there the whole time."

Officer Lotze went outside to take a closer look at the car while Patton continued the questioning. "Did you see anybody hanging around the Martin house, anybody acting suspicious, anything out of character?"

"Well, I did see a woman visit Sondra earlier that I'd never seen before." This caught the officer's attention and he looked up from his notepad, pencil poised halfway to his mouth.

"What time was this?"

"About two o'clock. I didn't really think anything about it

because Sondra told me earlier that she was expecting a visitor. But the woman came running out of the house later like her hair was on fire!" Laveen crossed and re-crossed her arms nervously, feeling the chill in the air despite her light sweater. She got up to set the thermostat to the next level.

Patton, nibbling on the eraser end of his pencil, noticed movement, and looked out the window at his partner, who was returning from Arnold Martin's car.

As Lotze entered the house, making sure to wipe his feet as he did so, he shook his head.

"Nothing I can see," he said, with a nod in the general direction of the car. "It's locked up tight, nothing on the seats except some papers."

For his partner's benefit, Patton briefly restated what Laveen had said about the unknown woman. "I'd like you to describe the woman and her behavior. What seemed unusual, the taxi, whatever you can that might help us locate her."

"Well," she began, "she came in a yellow taxi. "I'm sorry, I didn't pay any attention to the name of it." Patton waved his pencil at her to continue, busy taking notes.

"I thought it was a little strange that she got out next door at the Jensen's house, although she was visiting the Martin's. She walked up to their door and..."

"Mrs. Chapman, can you describe her?" Patton interrupted.

"Oh, sure! She seemed young, had very long, black hair down to about here," she used her index finger to make a sawing motion just below her shoulder blade. At first I couldn't get a good look at her face because she was holding an umbrella - it was raining a little at the time. But then she turned and I was able to see her. She was very pretty."

"Okay, continue. Anything else about her you can recall?"

"Well, she was wearing a long leather coat. A black one. I think she must have money, those don't come cheap, not the ones that go all the way down to your ankles!" Getting a raised eyebrow from the cop, Laveen realized she was blathering and continued. "I thought she acted a little scared or nervous."

"What makes you think that?" asked Lotze, surprising Laveen, since he'd been so quiet up to now. He was usually content to let the more experienced officer handle the questioning.

"She kind of hesitated once in a while as she was walking towards the Martins'. It was like she was trying to talk herself into going there or something. I didn't give it a thought at the time. And," she added, "Sondra didn't seem very friendly when she opened the door. At least she wouldn't shake hands with the woman when she held her arm out."

She felt pleased that her nosiness had finally paid off, wait until she told her husband Jake! He was always telling her to mind her own business. Then she remembered the terrible cause of all this attention, and her euphoria deflated like a balloon with a slow leak. The sadness welled up and she felt herself wanting to have a good cry - again.

"Is there anything else you need," she asked, choking down her tears in front of the officers.

"No, I guess that'll do it for now," said Patton, flipping his notebook shut. "I think we have enough information at this time. But we may need to contact you for further information if something else turns up." Patton and Lotze got up and started to leave, then Patton stopped and turned back. "Oh, I called the homicide detectives earlier. They'll be wanting to talk to you, too." Seeing her eyes widen, he smiled reassuringly. "It's procedure. Just tell them what you told us, you'll be fine. Good night, Mrs. Chapman."

*   *   *

Ten minutes later two plain-clothes detectives drove up in an unmarked, gray Buick sedan, parking behind Arnie's Lexus. The two men, looking as if straight out of a Spielberg movie in their neat suits and shiny dress shoes, got out of the newer-model car and walked over to where the first two officers on the scene, Patton

41

and Lotze, were standing.

Briefly speaking to the two men, they then entered the house, asking the officers to remain outside. Looking around the crime scene before approaching the body, the lead detective, John Ward, tall, blonde and with a hint of gray found only if you looked closely, commented on the placement of a small white cloth draped over the victim's mouth. He stepped closer, still not entering the crime area, and examined the arrangement of the cloth and knife.

He observed that one corner of the cloth was caught in the victim's right earring, and that it was partially obscuring her face. He surmised that she may have fallen backwards, her face then falling over towards the left, which allowed the cloth to remain in place on her face. The knife, next to her had a thick, leather-bound handle. The leather itself, once brown, had aged into a dark shiny patina. The knife looked worn, but still strong. And deadly. He figured the knife blade itself must be fairly wide, and estimated its overall length to be around twelve inches, give or take a couple of inches. Despite the presence of the weapon, Patton wondered if the woman had bled to death, given the copious amount of blood present around the trunk.

"What do you think, Neil," he glanced at his partner over his shoulder as he squatted down to get a different perspective. "Look like the guy used some type of inhalation drug on her first? Maybe to get her easier to handle?" He already had his own opinion of what might have occurred, but he liked to throw it out to his younger protégé. Sometimes he got perspectives he hadn't thought of.

His younger partner, Neil Cawston, twenty-six, was shorter, average in height and looks, and had the physique of one devoted to attending the gym on a more-than-usual basis. He was new to the detective department, only recently paired up with the more experienced detective over the last few months to learn all he could about the field.

Freud would undoubtedly say Neil was compensating for his lack of stature and looks by building his muscles to immense proportions. Neil, however, would admit that he started working out to attract the ladies, plain and simple. His hard work and time spent in the gym, albeit time consuming, had already rewarded him with the delightful company of a long string of young ladies over the years. Not ready to commit to a "real" relationship, Neil looked forward to many more encounters of the female kind.

John, on the other hand, being a man of simple pleasures despite his surfer-boy appearance, was content dating his long-term girlfriend of four years. They had recently talked about making it a permanent relationship, as they had several times within the past couple years. But now, with this new case, that might have to be put on hold once again – the reason his first wife divorced him many years ago after a tumultuous six-year marriage. He regretted not having had any children, but he supposed that was for the best, seeing how the Department had consumed most of his time over the years.

Despite being almost fifty years old, John, at forty-eight, good looking, with blue eyes, had a classic California-tan look, not obtained in the usually wet Washington weather. If asked, he would tell you he came by it naturally, his mother being of Greek descent, his father being responsible for his pale, Norwegian locks.

Needless to say, the two detectives made quite an impact whenever they entered a room. The men resented their looks, while, at the same time, grudgingly respecting their talent in the field. The women admired those same looks and fantasized about the two men, being no age limit to admiration and sex appeal, while also respecting them for their sleek ability to solve the most difficult crime.

"With just the cloth to go by, I'd guess whoever did this probably used some form of anesthesia, maybe chloroform or something like it." said the younger man. He stayed behind the older detective, taking mental notes on everything he observed. "It's also questionable whether the knife or the drug actually caused the death. My bet's on the knife."

John pointed to an empty glass bottle on the rug near the still head of the body. "Maybe," he shrugged. "We need to get somebody out here to go over the crime scene, take samples. Let's call the boys in," he said as he stood up, dusting the knees of his black slacks off despite not having knelt down on the carpet.

The "boys" showed up several minutes later. The police photographer, Denise Lansing, a small, cheery black woman in her thirties, as well as several forensic crew members. Chasing everybody out of the way so they could take their samples, measurements and photographs, they got busy with smooth, practiced skill, having worked as a close group long enough to do their jobs while staying out from under each others feet.

Denise, as used to these gruesome sights as a person could be, carefully walked around the crime scene, taking pictures of the body from various directions. Very careful not to disrupt the scene, she took close-ups of the knife and facial area covered by the piece of material, as well as distant shots depicting the relationship of the body to the surrounding room. When she was finished here, she would go outside and take photos of the victim's car, having already worked the entrance of the house when she first arrived.

Meanwhile, both cars were being dusted for fingerprints, and the Volvo would eventually be towed to headquarters for a more thorough search. The interior of the vehicle would be combed over for strange hairs or other clues to the crime. Then a physical search would take place, with seats removed, if needed, in hopes of finding something that would lead to the killer, an altogether too rare event.

A few minutes later the Chief Medical Examiner, Robert "Bobby" McDaniels entered the room. He carried the traditional black medical bag, in which he carried his "tricks of the trade" used to gather evidence – envelopes, zip-lock baggies of various sizes, pocketknife, rubber bands, shoe covers, masks, and a multitude of other "tools".

Pulling on a pair of latex gloves, Bobby waited until all the pictures were taken, and the room measurements completed, before moving in. He began by taking a close look at the body, touching nothing, recording all he saw on a small portable dicta-phone he carried everywhere he went. Then he began the real work – bagging the hands to preserve possible skin samples from under the nails; using a small vacuum around the site to collect any hairs and other possible evidence; placing the cloth, the bottle and other items found, into re-sealable baggies, as well as the many other time-consuming tasks required on a crime scene. There was much to be done before the body could be bagged and taken to the ME's lab for a closer examination, followed by the actual autopsy.

Feeling in the way amidst all the flashing and bagging of evidence, the two detectives decided it was time to visit the witness. They went across the street, picking up the pace as the earlier drizzle began to turn into a steady downpour. Shaking themselves off once they reached the small porch, they knocked on the Chapman's door.

Laveen, looking frazzled, pale, and closer to her true age of sixty-two, answered the door and ushered them in once they had identified themselves.

"We're sorry to bother you at a time like this, John apologized. "But there are a few things we need to clear up. We'll try to keep it brief."

"Yes, I know you have to do this, I've seen it on every mystery show I've ever watched! I just didn't know I'd be one of the star players in my own production!" She asked them if they'd like some coffee, or something to eat. Accepting the offer of hot coffee, they followed her into the warm, aromatic kitchen and sat at the table where she waved them into padded, oak chairs.

Being one of Laveen's favorite rooms to spend time in, trying out new recipes, sharing gossip with friends, the place had a homey, comfortable feel to it. Both men couldn't help but feel a little more relaxed in the country-styled kitchen, with its jars of homemade jams and canned vegetables on shelves, the racks of spices, and the checkered tablecloth where they were seated.

Laveen poured them all a cup of her famous brew, offered the men cream and sugar, and then joined them at the table, dropping heavily into her chair as if the weight of the day's experience was too much to carry.

The younger man, Neil, asked if it would be all right if they recorded the session, placing a small black recorder in the center of the table. John once again had his notebook out to take notes.

Giving a nod of consent, Laveen gave a choked sigh and stared at her hands, wrapped tightly around her cup. The two men waited, sipping their coffee, giving her a few moments to collect herself. John noted the University of Washington logo on the woman's cup. He also noted that the coffee was some of the best he'd ever had – and in his profession, first as police officer, then as homicide detective, he'd tasted coffee from all around the Seattle area. And some had left questionable doubts as to its true identity!

"I can't see why anybody would want to harm such a wonderful person as Sondra," she finally said. "She liked everybody, had so many friends, had two beautiful girls..." She fell silent, thinking about what would happen to the girls now, with no mother. "Does Arnie know yet?" she suddenly wondered out loud, looking up and making eye contact with the detectives for the first time since they entered her house.

"Arnie?" asked John. "That's the victim's husband?" he asked, referring to his earlier notes he'd gotten from the police officers. "Can you tell us where he might be right now, Mrs. Chapman?"

"Oh, call me Laveen, please. I'm not sure. I know Sondra said he was going to a convention or something in California. Let me think..." She twirled the liquid in her cup thoughtfully, holding her bottom lip between her teeth. "Oh, Los Angeles! But I don't know where. You can probably call his office for that." She told them the name of the hospital where he worked. "I'm sorry I don't know any more than that, like a phone number or something." Looking very distressed, she added, "They seemed to be such a great family. I loved Sondra so much, it just seems so unreal!" Hands shaking, she brought her cup to her lips, but partway there, she suddenly stopped, remembering something.

"The girls! Did anybody notify the girls?"

Both detectives looked up at this; John flipped through his notes. "Nothing was mentioned about them to me. They are with their aunt, a Mrs. Libby Steel, is that correct?"

Laveen looked up at the clock on the wall, noting that it was now almost four o'clock, the girls would have been home from school an hour ago. Telling the detectives this, she added, "It's a blessing that Sondra left them with her sister. Thank God they didn't have to see what happened to their mother, poor babies! Do you think Libby has been called yet?"

"We'll look into that, but I'm sure they've tried to contact her by now." John made a note to look for an address book at the Martin home. "Can you tell us what line of work Mr. Martin is in? What exactly he does at the research hospital?" asked John.

"Well," said Laveen thoughtfully, "I'm not exactly sure *what* Arnie does! I know he does a lot of experimenting and developing to find cures for diseases and such. I never did really ask specifics. Being research and all, well, I found it kind of boring, to be honest. I was more Sondra's friend than Arnie's, especially after the girls both started going to school and Sondra had more time on her hands. That's when we really started to become friends. I'll miss her." At that she started to cry, covering her face with her finely manicured hands.

Neil, fishing a handkerchief out of his jacket pocket, handed it to her before getting up to pour all of them a fresh cup of coffee. John nodded his approval, thinking to himself that growing up with three sisters had definitely not hurt his partner any in the sensitivity department.

Once Laveen had regained control of her emotions somewhat, John began asking the tougher questions.

Pen and notebook ready, he asked, "Can you tell us what time you discovered the body of your friend? And how you happened to go over there just after the incident occurred?"

"Well," she began with a sniff. "I've known the Martins about 12 years, ever since they moved in across the street. Sondra and I get together once in a while to have coffee or tea, I bring her something I baked that day, we share the local gossip going around about our other neighbors, problems Arnie's told her about his job, things like that. Normal friend stuff, you know?" She sighed, realizing what she'll be missing.

"Before Sondra left, yesterday morning, she came over to ask me to keep an eye on the place. She also invited me over for tea about three o'clock after she got back – I guess that's today." Laveen fiddled with her coffee cup, tracing the logo with a finger.

"Did she seem scared? Or act out of character at the time you saw her last?" asked the young detective.

"No, I didn't think so." She thought briefly, then added, "Although, she's never asked me to watch her house before. But then again, Arnie's always been home any time she went to her sister's or was gone more than a day. They usually time these things so one of them can stay with the girls, or they take them with them."

Neil, having grown up around several younger siblings, asked why the girls hadn't been in school. "There's no holiday that I can think of until Thanksgiving."

Laveen had to say that she didn't know. John made a note in his book to call the schools in the area to find out if the girls periodically missed class, was there a special holiday being celebrated, or was there another reason altogether for the girls being absent during a normal school week.

"So, when did you go over to visit Mrs. Martin?" John continued.

"Well, she told me to come over about three because she was having company at two. I saw a young lady show up in a taxi about that time. I thought it was strange because she was dropped off down by the Jensen's, but walked up here to go to the Martin's." She paused. "I told all of this to the other cops, do I have to repeat it all over again?"

"I'm afraid so. Sometimes, if you're asked the same thing again, you remember things you didn't think about the first time."

John explained.

Laveen nodded her understanding. Even if she didn't like it, she could see the reasoning behind it.

The detectives asked her go to the living room to point out the Jensen's' house and where the taxi had parked, then they returned to the kitchen to complete the questioning.

"When did you actually go next door, Mrs.....Laveen," asked John.

"I thought about going over there early, like a quarter to three after the woman came running out of the house, but I didn't. Maybe I could've saved Sondra if I had! She might still be alive!" She choked back a sob. Neil reached out and patted her hand, and Laveen gave him a tiny smile in gratitude. She noticed how large his shoulders were under his gray suit jacket.

John asked her to describe what the woman had looked like, and how she was behaving as she ran out. Laveen described what she had seen. "She seemed scared when she came out. Like somebody was chasing her. She didn't even have her coat on - and you know this rain can be cold this time of year. She ran back to where the taxi was still parked and jumped in, and they left."

"Why didn't you go over to see how Mrs. Martin was doing after the girl ran out in obvious distress?" asked John, hating to ask when he knew Laveen already felt guilty for not doing that very thing, but needing to know just the same.

"I figured she needed time to calm down. I wasn't sure I'd be welcomed just then, since Sondra might have been very upset about the visit. Sondra has never been one to share her feelings with me when she's been upset, you see. She's a very private person, and I've always respected that." She dabbed her eyes with Neil's handkerchief.

Seeing John about to speak, Laveen continued. "I went over there at exactly three o'clock, like she asked me to," she said, lifting her chin up defiantly. "That's when I found it...Her." She once again slumped down in her chair.

"Can you tell us exactly what you saw?"

"I walked into the living room – I called out several times, but nobody answered. I found her lying on the floor, by the bookcases. She was on her back, and there was a lot of blood around, although I wasn't sure that's what it was. I never saw the knife until later, when I was talking to the 911 lady on the phone. It was so horrible!" she cried, once again burying her face in her hands.

"So", John wanted to clarify, "you figure the woman left about two-forty-five? Is that right?"

A muffled "yes" was heard. Then Laveen got herself together, wiped her face with the handkerchief, and looked at the two detectives. "Am I a suspect?" she finally inquired, the possibility just occurring to her. Her eyes were wide as she waited for the answer, looking from one detective to the other before settling onto John's handsome face. *It's amazing*, thought Laveen, *I can still find someone very attractive even after finding my best friend dead! I must be one sick puppy!* She shook her head at herself.

John cleared his throat, genuinely liking this poor woman, but needing to be honest with her just the same. "Yes, I'm afraid you are. But the good news is that you are not our main suspect."

"The young woman?" asked Laveen, semi-relieved.

"Yes. Well, I think that about covers it. Will you be remaining in the area in case we need to contact you?"

Laveen said she would, and showed the detectives to the door, thinking that, if you had to be interrogated, it was a bonus to have two such hunks doing the "honors"!

John turned back, "Oh, would you happen to know if Mr. Martin knew anyone who had a grudge against him, somebody that would want to harm him or his family? And the same for Mrs. Martin, anyone we might need to talk with?"

Laveen said no, she couldn't think of anybody, that both the Martin's were quiet people and seemed to be well-liked.

John looked up at the gray sky. The rain had stopped, for now. He gave her one of his cards and told her to call if she thought of anything else they might need to know. Then they said good-bye and left, going back across the street to look for the address book to call Sondra's sister, Libby Steel, the school and Arnold Martin's place of employment.

They were in time to see the Medical Examiner, McDaniels, coming out of the Martin house, waving his hands in the air to emphasize everything he was saying to his assistant. The paramedics, called to the scene as part of routine procedure, were loading the black bag-encased body into the back of their vehicle under his watchful eyes. They would drop it off at the county morgue, where McDaniels would take over its care.

"Hey! Bobby!" yelled John. Meeting up at the end of the driveway, the three men shook hands. John introduced the old ME to Neil, referring to him as "one of the best" in the city. Bobby, as he was commonly known to the "death squad," the cops, medics and others who answered the calls whenever a body showed up, was short, pudgy and sported a droopy gray mustache to go with his straggly, graying hair. He was constantly jerking his head back to get a stray hair off his forehead, and behind his back his assistants liked to joke that the technique he used to flip his bangs back would make any cheerleader proud.

He did so now, causing a drop of rain to hit John in the eye. "Shit, Bobby!" he protested, rubbing his eye with exaggerated motions. "Why don't you get that mop cut one of these days!"

"No time." Bobby pulled the collar of his heavy coat closer towards his ears, a vain attempt to keep the cold rain from trickling down his neck.

"Well, hell, let me find my pocket knife!" John pretended to search through his pockets, earning a scowl from the ME.

"Don't bother, can't afford the medical insurance I'd need after you finish with me!"

Turning serious, John asked the ME, "What you got for us, Bobby?"

"I'm declaring this a death under suspicious circumstances. I'm having her taken to the morgue for an autopsy."

Looking grim, John asked him when he thought he could get

started on it.

"Probably in the morning. I'll get on it first thing." He turned and started to leave, wanting to get out of the chill, damp weather, tossing a wave of his hand at the two detectives over his shoulder.

"Hey, Bobby!" yelled John. When Bobby stopped and turned towards him, John taunted him with, "Try to stay dry, would ya!" Which earned a different kind of hand signal as the ME crawled into his beat up Suburban.

*   *   *

Finding the address they needed to locate Arnie's workplace minutes later, John suggested they head out to the University Hospital to see if they could find out where the convention was being held before trying to track down the taxi that had brought the young woman here.

After showing their ID badges, they were led to the Staff Manager's office. They were given the address and pertinent information about the conference in Los Angeles by a highly agitated, thin man who repeatedly bemoaned the fact that the Hospital did not need trouble or they would lose their research grants.

Finally able to get away from the tense man with the bad comb-over, the two detectives returned to their office downtown. John placed a call to the convention center, and after being transferred around several times, he was finally informed that Dr. Martin would be difficult to locate at this time, as there were several places he could be. So, while not liking the option available, John had to leave a message requesting that Dr. Martin return home immediately for a family emergency once he was tracked down. He also placed a call to the Los Angeles police department regarding the matter, and they promised to send an escort to the Convention Center to pick up the husband and get him to the airport as quickly as possible.

Next, finding the number easily in the address book, John had the dubious honor of placing the call to Libby Steel and informing her of her sister's death. Being reassured that the Martin girls were, in fact, at the Steel residence and that they were more than welcome to remain there for the duration of the investigation, if needed, John signed off, telling Mrs. Steel that they would be contacting her soon for further information on the case.

John hung up the phone with a sigh. He disliked this part of the job, where he had to discuss deceased family members with the survivors. He rubbed a large, smooth hand over his eyes and yawned. Shaking his head to get the blood flowing in his brain, he pulled a phone book closer and began looking up numbers for local taxi services. His partner, sitting across the desk from him, grabbed another book, and they began the lengthy process of locating the driver that dropped off the lady in question.

Chapter 5

Sitting in the Los Angeles Conference Center, Arnie stifled a sigh. Glancing at his watch, he noticed it was just after 4:30. Almost time for this less-than-intriguing session on cellular changes - found in the bloodstream of test rats, of all things – to end.

He neither knew, nor cared to learn, that these little hairy, disgusting creatures could mimic the same diseases that humans did. His expertise focused on actual human cells and how a variety of diseases they were subjected to caused the cells to mutate and develop immunity to certain damaging viruses. He was especially interested in finding out why the same mutations did not occur with other types of diseases, like HIV, cancers and certain brain dysfunctions, like Alzheimer's and other types of dementias. Scientists were still trying to isolate the genes that contributed to many of these illnesses, all too many of them currently considered incurable. It was Arnie's belief, as well as some of his colleagues, that if they could genetically alter certain cells, they might be able to bypass some of these life-threatening changes before they could develop. He had been hoping to learn some new techniques to take back to his research lab in Seattle, since he'd been all but forced to come here. But, he was getting nothing from this session, except a sore back from sitting all day in their hard folding chairs.

Initially disappointed, he had spent the last forty-five minutes tuning out the speakers' monotone drone and thinking back on his wife's changing behavior over the past several months.

He recalled her outburst over dinner the other night. True, jealousy probably had a lot to do with it, and he was man enough to feel bad that he was the cause of it. But no matter what he said to reassure Sondra that he and Judy were only friends, which was nothing but the truth, she wouldn't believe him. He admitted that he would probably feel the same way if he found out his wife had a close male friend she was spending a lot of time with.

He thought back on their twelve years of marriage together. Although they married because there was a baby on the way, they had truly loved each other by the time the baby arrived. Maybe it would have been only a matter of time before they got married anyway, Arnie thought. He refused to remember that he had been planning on going to Seattle without Sondra after his semester ended. *The pregnancy only pushed things up a few months at most*, Arnie convinced himself.

Arnie loved having a wife to come home to as he struggled to finish college and, finally, after months of applying to hospitals and labs everywhere in Washington State, he landed this job with the University. He liked his job, *except for that pompous ass, Evans!* he amended. *Now there's a guy that thinks he's God's gift to women!*

He pictured Dr. Murray Evans, his supervisor. About six-foot, medium build, handsome according to the women that were always drooling over him whenever he came into the room. At 34 years of age, he was two years Arnie's junior. And, with his self-proclaimed sex appeal, the men who had to work closely with him, like Arnie, found him to be almost unbearably narcissistic. *I'm surprised we don't have mirrors on all the walls!* Arnie scoffed. But, to give the guy credit, he was very intelligent and knew his stuff, he admitted.

His thoughts reverting back to Sondra, Arnie acknowledged that she had the toughest adjustments to make once they got married. Having plans to continue college herself, get out of her menial waitress job and get a degree in pharmaceuticals, she had put her own career on hold to raise a baby – then two. She seemed happy to be a housewife, and never once vocalized regrets of not going back to school and getting her degree.

But, Arnie reflected, *maybe she wasn't happy after all. Maybe she was just a good actor all that time. I know she hasn't been acting very happy lately. And I haven't bothered to ask what was going on,* he admitted guiltily. *It's always easier to avoid conflict than face it,* he sighed. *I guess it's time we stopped pretending everything is all right, sit down, and get this all out in the open, once and for all!*

With that, he decided to call the convention a loss and head home. *Screw Evans,* Arnie declared to himself. *Let him whine and complain all he wants. My marriage is more important than this crap!*

He was about to gather all his papers and leave, thinking to give a quick call to his home to see how his daughters were doing, and maybe have a few words with Sondra, when a woman, hair up in a neat bun, stepped out onto the stage. She walked over to where the guest speaker was pointing to slides on the overhead projector, and whispered to him. He backed away from the mike, looking serious, as she took his place at the podium.

"May I have your attention, please," she said. "Is Dr. Arnold Martin in the room?" She looked around to see if anybody would respond.

Startled, his name being the last thing he expected to hear, Arnie stood up.

"That would be me," he said, self-consciously, partially raising his hand. He felt like a schoolboy who got called on and didn't know the answer.

"I need to speak to you, Dr. Martin. Would you meet me out in the hall, please." She nodded at the presenter, then turned and left the stage. The man returned to the podium to resume his lecture.

Arnie started to walk towards the door, listening to the buzz of speculations from around the room. He could feel his ears turning red in embarrassment at being the subject of their interest. He met the woman outside the room, where she then told him that the police needed to see him right away about family concerns. His heart hammering, thinking it could only be one of the kids, he followed the woman down the hall to another room, where two police officers waited to speak with him.

After the woman left, closing the door behind her, the officers introduced themselves, then instructed him to sit down. After listening to what they had to say, Arnie could only look back on the whole situation and wish it *had* been something as mundane as one of his daughters getting injured on the playground.

They assured him that his children were with his sister-in-law, and that they were here to get him onto a plane to return to Seattle.

"The King County police will meet you at the airport, sir," one of the officers instructed him, "Where they will then take you to the detectives that have been assigned to the case." Arnie cringed, hearing his wife referred to as a "case".

After retrieving his belongings from the hotel, the policemen led him to their squad car, where they were soon on the road to the airport. Arnie, not believing this could possibly be happening, felt like he was in a dream world, hoping he would soon wake up. But, all too soon, he was on the flight to Seattle, with altogether too much time to think.

*   *   *

Listening to the drone of the plane, Arnie couldn't help but remember Sondra as he had last seen her, hurt and teary-eyed. He wished he could have had happier memories to recall for their last conversation. He could still hear the angry slamming of the bedroom door in his mind. He recalled her as she was when they first met – young, bright, excited about their budding relationship, her classes, her future...it was his fault her plans were all destroyed, he told himself. If I hadn't been so ...horny! None of this would've happened. Sondra would be happy as a pharmacist today, she'd be alive!

He wondered if they would have still married if she hadn't gotten pregnant. Would they still have the girls...the girls! He rubbed his face and groaned, causing the lady in the isle seat across from him to glance over. What was he going to do about his two poor little girls? How could he raise two females by himself? All those things only women know, things he didn't quite understand, himself. He stared out at the fluffy white clouds outside his window. The sun was beginning to dip lower, causing the clouds to be tinged a pale pink in the center, surrounded by a deepening blue as evening lengthened. It was proving to be the longest two-and-a-half hours in his life.

Chapter 6

Upon landing at SeaTac Airport later that evening, Arnie found two blue uniformed Seattle police officers waiting for him. Despite his worry and fatigue, he was still able to find it a bit amusing that policemen always seemed to come in pairs.

The officers escorted him down to the luggage carousel to get his suitcase. He felt very self-conscious having two cops accompany him around the airport like a felon. He could see everybody stop and stare as they passed by, and felt the color rise in his face. He hoped he wouldn't run into anybody that knew him. He especially didn't want to be asked what was going on – since he wasn't exactly sure himself. But, he was sure the cops' presence would discourage any one from approaching.

Two detectives, in simple, single-breasted suits, were outside waiting for him by the luggage carousel. As he grabbed his large suitcase from the rotating track, Arnie thought to himself that he wouldn't have been able to picked them out of a line-up as being with the Department if it hadn't been for the ID badges they each held in their hands on his approach. The two Seattle policemen handed him over to them and made their departure.

John Wade introduced himself and his partner, Neil Cawston, extending his hand. John's first impression of the man was a feeling of power. But, on second glance, he could see that Dr. Martin, although appearing to have a large frame, was actually only of medium build and height, the broad shoulders giving the illusion of strength. Arnie, feeling like he was still in that bad dream, reached out and shook their hands in turn, wondering what was coming next. His handshake was firm, with only a trace of dampness in the palms.

The detectives invited him into the back of the Buick, explaining that they would now take him to their office at the Police Department and explain everything there, where it would be much more private.

Once the car started on its route into town, Arnie leaned forward to ask how his kids ended up with Libby in Portland.

"She's your sister-in-law, right?" replied Neil. "According to Mrs. Steel, your wife took them down yesterday. They had made plans to stay there a couple days, but Mrs. Steel says something came up and she left the kids with her to return home the next morning. We plan on interviewing her this afternoon, as soon as we had spoken to you about the matter."

Looking puzzled, Arnie said, "I don't remember Sondra saying anything about taking the kids to Portland. Maybe she decided to go at the last minute, since I'd be gone for a few days." *Maybe she was leaving me.* "The kids couldn't go back to school until they fixed the leaking water pipes in the older section of the building. I was wondering why nobody answered the phone this morning, and again later when I tried."

The two detectives nodded at one another, having received that same information from the school superintendent earlier. "What time did you call the second time, Dr. Martin?" asked John, pulling into the parking garage of the police station.

"Let's see...must've been about eleven? We got out for a quick break, and it wasn't lunch time yet, so...yeah, about eleven, I'd say."

Once they were parked in the gloomy basement garage, they took the elevator up to the first floor and ushered Arnie into their office. Looking around as he entered the room, Arnie thought it resembled a cross between a library and his daughter, Ashley's, side of the girls' bedroom. There were books and candy wrappers scattered all over the ancient pine desk, stacked onto the two torn, leather, wheeled office chairs, and merging into small mountains of files trying to take over the rest of the room.

Seeing the mess, John swooped some of the books off the chairs and invited Arnie to have a seat. Neil went over to the other office chair, leaving John to perch on the side of the desk, where he preferred to sit, arms crossed over his chest, one ankle over the other, depicting a very relaxed pose.

John flipped a hand at the clutter, "We were looking up some information, haven't had a chance to clean up," he explained off-handedly, not in the least embarrassed by the mess. He pulled out his notepad and studied the first few pages silently. His partner, Neil, was busy looking at his trouser cuffs, bending over to pick invisible lint from the dark gray material.

Arnie was sure this was just part of the BS, cop posturing they always did on TV. Done to intimidate their suspects with uncomfortable stretches of silence, while pretending to read something important from those little notebooks they all seemed to carry. *Funny how that really works,* Arnie reflected, crossing and re-crossing his legs restlessly.

John finally looked up, flipping his book closed with a snap, startling Arnie, as well as the younger detective, who flinched and sat up.

"When did you leave Seattle, Dr. Martin?"

"On Tuesday." Getting an eyebrow raised at him by the detective, he finished with, "That would be the...uh, the seventeenth, ...of October," he stammered.

"Did your wife seem alright to you when you left? Any unusual behavior?"

Arnie thought about the argument they had the night before and wondered if he should mention it. Deciding not to, at least not yet, he shook his head and said "No."

"Have you been back to Seattle between the time you left Tuesday morning and right now? Did you make contact with your wife between that time, aside from the failed phone calls?"

Surprised, Arnie cocked his head at the detective and asked if they thought he had killed his own wife! He began to get angry and stood up, looking the detective in the eye. "There are a lot of people who can testify that I was at the Conference Center, taking some boring classes, mind you, if you feel the need to doubt my innocence!"

Before he could react further, John waved him down into his chair again and told him that these were routine questions, that they weren't accusing him of anything.

Arnie slowly sat back down, now wondering if he should ask for an attorney before things got any further. And would that make him look guiltier if he did?

"Okay, Dr. Martin, let's start over. Keeping in mind that *everybody* is a suspect until proven otherwise, can you tell me what your relationship with your wife was like? Were you having any problems, was she acting out of character, anything you can think of that can help us with this?"

Arnie, knowing he would be better off telling them about the argument in case it came back at him later and bit him in the proverbial ass, chose to keep it to himself for now. "I guess we got along like any other couple. We had our disagreements, like every one does, but not over anything major. I'd say we were doing as well as the next couple." *Except for that last fight that made her decide to go to Oregon, Officer!* he thought. He shifted uncomfortably in his chair once again.

"Any enemies either of you might have had? Anyone ever threaten you or your wife, Dr. Martin."

"No!" exclaimed Arnie. "Why would anybody threaten us?"

John shrugged, "There's a lot of sick people out there, Dr. Martin. People who are willing to beat you to death just because you took their parking spot. Or looked at them wrong. Or just happened to be in the wrong place at the wrong time." He twirled his pencil around in his fingers before asking if Arnie could think of any person who disliked either he or his wife.

Arnie couldn't think of any one who might have a grudge, let alone hate any of them enough to kill Sondra. He told the detective this.

Just then a soft knock was heard, and a policeman poked his

head inside the door, beckoning John over. He whispered something into his ear, then turned and left, shutting the door.

John came back over to Arnie, once again assuming his favored, if sub-conscious, pose at the edge of the worn desk. "Your sister-in-law and your kids are on their way to Seattle. The officers will meet them when they get here." He paused. " It's not a good idea for you to try to stay at your house tonight, Dr. Martin. They won't let you enter the premises anyway, right now, since the place is cordoned off until the investigation is over. If you have nowhere else to go, I'll have an officer take you to a local hotel for the night, care of Uncle Sam, of course. But you're going to have to find some place for you and the kids to stay until this is all taken care of and you can go back home. Maybe a friend would be willing to take you in."

Arnie briefly thought of asking Judy, but just as quickly dismissed the idea. "How do I get my kids when they arrive? Will I be allowed to go get my car tonight?"

John shrugged apologetically. "They may want to take a closer look at your car, but you can probably pick it up in a day or two."

"What could they possibly want with my car," Arnie fumed, standing up once again to face the detective. "Does everybody think I've killed my wife and hidden the murder weapon in it?" Realizing what he just said, Arnie blanched and sat back in his chair, the fire gone out of him as quickly as it came.

"I'm sorry, it's procedure. They like to search for any particle or hair that might not belong to you or your family. Once they rule that out, you'll be free to take it home."

John looked down at the grieving husband, slumped sadly in the chair. "I have another question for you, if you can handle it, Dr. Martin."

"Your neighbor, Mrs. Chapman, told us she saw a slender, dark-haired young woman arrive at your place in a taxi this afternoon around two o'clock. Do you know who that might be?"

"My wife had many friends, I'm not sure right now who would fit that description," Arnie admitted. Arnie's head hurt, and his eyes burned like he hadn't slept in a month.

"Do you own any hunting knives, Dr. Martin?"

Arnie looked up in surprise. "No! I don't keep anything like guns or other dangerous weapons in the house – I have two small children! Besides, I don't hunt." He scowled at the detective, still pissed off that he was considered a suspect.

"Does your wife or anyone close to her own any unusually large knives, besides regular kitchen utensils? Anyone in *your* family? Friends, perhaps?"

Arnie looked at the detective reproachfully, ready to give him a piece of his mind again.

Seeing that Arnie was on a short wire, ready to explode at a seconds notice, he backed down. "Calm down. Sometimes people collect things, not thinking they could later be used to do damage to other people. Lots of people have gun collections, swords, knives, you name it."

"Yeah, well I don't."

"Any heirloom knife tucked away in the attic or someplace you might have forgotten about? You know, that ugly rusty Confederate knife your Uncle Tom might've passed on to you and you tossed it into a box somewhere years ago?" Seeing Arnie's expression, he quickly added, "I know, I know. I'm stretching it here, but we have a knife, of unknown origin, that was used to kill your wife."

Arnie didn't say anything. He felt sick to his stomach, a fleeting picture of Sondra, dead, having just passed through his mind.

John, seeing the color drain from Arnie's face, had Neil pour Arnie a glass of water, which Arnie accepted gratefully.

Knowing there were other items he should be addressing, John instead decided to let Arnie go to the hotel room where he could try to get some rest. He took him out to the main room, which was bustling with activity, and located an officer that could drive Arnie out to the Best Western Inn, which they occasionally used through the Department.

Once Arnie was settled into the hotel room, his only scenery the dingy gold carpet that clashed with the ochre bedspreads covering the two double beds, he thought back over his dismal day. He wished, once again, that it was just a nightmare, and soon he would hear the bedside alarm and wake up. He paced the small, dimly lit room restlessly, too anxious to sit down, afraid he'd miss the kids arriving if he went for a short walk.

He wondered when the kids would get into town, and if they had been told yet that they had no mother. He truly hoped the authorities weren't leaving that up to him! He wouldn't know where to begin, or how to say it. How could he explain that their mother had been murdered?

Lying down on the bed closest to the door, the mattress turned out to be far more comfortable than he expected it to be – *So many surprises today, Arnie!* He thought over the detective's statement about the dark-haired woman that came to visit his wife. Could it have been Judy? But why would she have gone to his house? Was she looking for him – *No, I had told her where I'd be and when I expected to get back. She had the number for the hotel if she needed something.*

Arnie sat up. He just didn't get it. If it *was* Judy, he couldn't think of a reason for her to go there. And what did Sondra think? The woman she didn't like in the first place, showing up at her house looking for her husband? He didn't think Judy was capable of such a horrible thing. She was secretive about some things, sure, but murder? Could this be just another mystery he didn't know about her?

*   *   *

While Arnie was being taken to the hotel, the two detectives got down to the business of locating the taxi driver that delivered the woman to the Martins. After about half an hour of chasing phone calls and being passed around, they finally had the name of the driver. Before they could pursue it further, however, Libby

Steel showed up at the station.

She was ushered into the detectives' small office, while the two girls, looking pale and frightened, were taken under the wing of Lieutenant Hobbly, who had five children of his own and had a good idea how to deal with two such sad little beings.

While Libby spoke to the detectives, Hobbly entertained the girls with his disappearing-penny trick. Although he got a tiny smile out of the younger one, he could see that the older girl would need more than parlor tricks to lighten her heavy heart. It always hurt him when children were effected, being very devoted to his own brood. It was part of the reason he decided to become a cop, hoping to help stop kids having to suffer through things like this, losing a parent through murder.

Twenty minutes later the trio came out of the office, a grim expression on Libby's face. Grabbing the kids, Libby followed John and Neil down to the parking garage to get the Buick. Ashley, feeling very confused about the whole thing, held the Lieutenant's penny tightly in her damp fist. She wanted to curl up on her bed and cry, but her sister wasn't crying, so she wouldn't either. Heather, walking stiffly beside her, held her lips together tightly, resembling her father more than ever. She wasn't sure just how to respond to the news that her mother had been killed. She felt numb, like her emotions were no longer there.

They drove to the hotel where Arnie was staying. He was overjoyed to see his girls, and hugged them both long and hard. Seeing their father again, both kids let their resolve go and began sobbing. Arnie held them while they cried, wondering why things happen in life to cause so much grief to such little angels. Looking up, he met Libby's angry glare. Taken aback, he pulled away from the girls, leading them over to one of the beds to sit down with them.

Moments later, asking Libby to stay with the girls, John told Arnie that he needed to talk to him privately, outside, for a few minutes. Telling the girls he'd be right back, Arnie followed both detectives down the stairs to the lobby, wondering what was going on now. He was sure it had something to do with the look on Libby's face.

They asked him to have a seat in one of the chairs clustered around a scratched coffee table in a quiet corner away from the desk clerk, pulling their own chairs closer. Like the room Arnie was in upstairs, the lobby was poorly lit. The arms of the well-worn chairs were covered with green upholstery dating back to the 70's, threadbare and stained. The straggly gold shag carpeting also dated itself around the same era. There was a cracked oval mirror hanging crooked on one wall, while two antique looking, oil-painted prints of unknown beaches decorated the section of wall behind them. Their gold-leaf frames, without the protective glass, were peeling and lopsided. The whole effect was one of depression and neglect.

Except for the clerk, who was currently in the back out of sight, they had the room to themselves.

"Your sister-in-law", said John, "told us that your friend, Judy, was supposed to be visiting your wife at two o'clock." Arnie shook his head in denial, but John put his hand up to stop him and continued. "According to your neighbor, Mrs. Chapman, a young lady fitting the same description your wife gave Mrs. Steel, visited your wife around this same time. Your wife was found dead fifteen minutes after this person came running out of your house." Both detectives watched for any reaction to this statement.

Arnie rubbed his face, not believing what he was hearing. It couldn't be true! Why would Judy go to his house?

"Nobody in the surrounding area recalls seeing anyone else visit your house after this young lady left." Arnie looked up and realized that both detectives were watching him very closely. This made him uneasy, and he had a hard time maintaining eye contact with them.

"We need to know who Judy is, and what your relationship is with her."

Arnie didn't know what to say. "Her name is Judy Larson. We're friends," he said lamely.

"Friends," mused John. "Like 'lovers' kind of friends? Business friends? Let's-go-to-the- movies kind of friends?"

Arnie shrugged. "We went to dinner a few times, like friends do, to talk. We are just friends," he insisted.

John stared at the man across from him, not saying anything for a while. He watched how uncomfortable Dr. Martin became, how he rarely made eye contact, watching, as his face was slowly infused with a red blush.

"It's time for you to come clean with us, Dr. Martin," he finally broke the silence. "We can't solve this murder if you aren't willing to tell us everything you know." He said it gently, yet Arnie felt like he had just been yelled at. Like he had just been accused of something unpleasant.

He told them he had known her for about three months. That nothing serious had gone on between them. "We met at a restaurant once in a while. She was very easy to talk to. I admit I was attracted to her, but I didn't have an affair with her!" he said defensively. He wondered why he felt guilty if he didn't do anything wrong.

"Do you know where she lives?"

"Yes." He admitted he had been there several times. "I don't know the exact address, but I can tell you the street, the name of her building, and her apartment number."

Neil handed him a pad and pencil and instructed him to write it all down. When he handed it back, Neil glanced at what he had written, then whispered to John that, according to the information they got from the taxi driver, he had picked the lady up from a different location than what was on the pad.

John asked Arnie if Judy had a car. He said he had never seen her driving one, but he couldn't say for sure if she did or not. "Although, if she had a car, why would she have bothered to take a taxi to my house today?" Arnie pointed out.

John, not bothering to reply, told Arnie he could go back upstairs to his kids. They would go and check out Ms. Larson's residence and try to speak with her. He was told to stay in the area, within city limits, if possible, and be available for any further questioning, as needed. He was also instructed not to contact Ms. Larson until they had given him clearance to do so.

"Make sure you notify the police immediately where you end up staying after tonight, and give them a number where we can reach you."

Before he turned to go, Arnie asked what had been done with Sondra's body.

John, sounding very distant, told him that the body was currently with the Medical Examiner. After the autopsy and all the tests had been completed, he would be informed when the body was ready to be released. Arnie winced every time he heard the word "body," and wondered why the detective was suddenly acting so callous.

Hearing the change in Detective Ward's tone once his relationship with Judy was mentioned, he knew he had lost some kind of important connection that had been established between himself and the older detective. As he walked slowly up the two flights of stairs to his room, Arnie realized that it bothered him that he may have lost the man's respect. He also wondered if he should be concerned about that.

As soon as he opened the door, Libby bluntly informed him that she had put the girls to bed. "I'll be staying with a friend tonight, but I'll come back in the morning to help with the girls." Arnie said "Thank you" and walked her to the door. But then, with the door barely inches open, she stopped and turned back.

Looking her brother-in-law squarely in the eye, she bluntly asked, "Who's Judy?"

Surprised by the question, as well as the anger in her voice, Arnie instead asked what was on his own mind. "Did Sondra tell you she would be meeting Judy today?"

Libby nodded. "When Sondra told me Judy was your girlfriend, I didn't believe her! I stuck up for you! Now, I'm beginning to think I should have believed her. Look what you've done to my dear sister!" she sobbed. "You may not have killed her yourself, but you will go to hell for this just the same!"

She looked over at the two sleeping bundles on the far side of the room. "I feel sorry for Ashley and Heather. Because of your stupidity, they have to grow up without their mother!"

"She was just a friend," Arnie said softly, instinctively backing away from her ire.

"Friend! Right!" said Libby, and slammed the door behind her.

*   *   *

Late night

The sky was dark and weeping– *Just like me*, Arnie thought to himself. His tears had dried up some time ago, but he had remained where he was, staring out at the night traffic and bright neon signs on the front of a nearby tavern.

He turned from the grimy hotel window, glancing at his watch, and was amazed to see it was only 11:30. Only seven hours since his life had been torn apart.

He walked the short distance to his bed and sat down. Propping the two pathetic excuses for pillows behind his back, he swung his feet up onto the bedspread and watched his daughters sleep. Despite the turmoil they had just recently undergone, both seemed to be sleeping peacefully.

Heather was lying on her right side facing the wall, her slight body occasionally twitching in what, Arnie hoped, were good dream memories. Of the two girls, he was the most worried about his oldest daughter. It was tough enough to go through all the pre-teen confusion and physical changes puberty brought about, without having to go through this, losing the one person who could help her through it all. *What do I know about teen-age girls? Maybe they have some videos on all of this. Or, as the kids nowadays would probably say, I could surf the Internet!*

Ashley, snoring lightly, was curled into a ball, hands tucked

70

under her chin, knees drawn up closely to her chest. She was facing his side of the room, and he was gratified to see a brief smile occasionally flash onto her little pixie face. Prone to talking in her sleep, he could hear her murmur disjointed sentences about puppies (being famous in their family for periodically bringing up the subject of how much she desperately needed one), "you dipwad!"(her word of choice this month), and of course, imaginary conversations with "J.C.", one of the young performers in the popular singing group, N'Sync, and currently her all-time favorite crush. Until the next one came along.

Not feeling like he could fall asleep himself, despite sandpaper eyes, and a feeling of heaviness throughout his body, Arnie started to think back on his times spent with Judy. He still couldn't imagine her as a killer, let alone murdering his wife.

He let his thoughts drift where they might, and found himself remembering when they had first met, on the return trip home from LA in early August.

Chapter 7

"United Airlines, flight 607 to Seattle, will be boarding in five minutes", he heard on the tinny overhead speaker. He was sitting in the terminal at the Los Angeles Airport, waiting to go back home after a lengthy absence. He looked at the gold faux-Rolex on his wrist, it was four forty-five. The face of the watch was scratched, and he had the band changed twice over the years since his mother gave it to him on the day he graduated from college. But he was reluctant to exchange it for a newer one, as it was a pleasant memory of his mother, who passed away several years ago.

He had been killing time by going through the abundant notes he took at the conference, trying to decipher his own scribbles, when the announcement was made. He gathered up the papers and stuffed them haphazardly back into his briefcase. *I'll have plenty of time to straighten it all out on the plane,* he figured, *since I have over two hours to entertain myself.* When it was time to board, he joined the line of passengers streaming into the tunnel that led into the plane.

Finding seat #14b, the isle seat, Arnie stowed his bulky coat in the overhead bin and sat down, not fastening his seatbelt until the flight attendant was ready to give her pitch later. He pulled out his laptop and began translating some of his notes into a legible report.

The Captain announced that take-off would be in about five minutes, and to please shut off all phones, electronic equipment, fasten seat belts and please remain seated until the seatbelt sign went out. Arnie glanced over to the seat beside him, still empty. He was in a row with only double seats, as opposed to triple seats in the other section. Deciding that he'd rather sit in the window seat, as long as nobody else had it, he picked up his laptop and moved over to the other seat. Thinking he now had plenty of space to sprawl out in, he put his stack of papers and computer on the isle seat.

He just got comfortable when, looking up, he noticed a very pretty woman standing in the isle next to his row, watching him. The first thing he noticed was her dark hair piled up in a bun of some sort, with a few curls hanging tantalizingly down from her temples. Next, he saw that she was fairly tall for a woman, although, glancing at her feet, it could be an illusion, made by the two-inch heels she wore. He was admiring her lovely figure, in a black skirt and silky cream blouse, when he realized he had been staring for far too long, and turned a nice shade of red.

Seeing his embarrassment, she merely smiled and asked if it was okay if she sat down, indicating the clutter on the other seat. Arnie hastily grabbed his papers and tucked them back into the briefcase down at his feet, mumbling an apology. Then, realizing she was the occupant of the window seat, he stood up and began to move out into the isle.

"Oh, it's okay, you don't have to move!" she exclaimed, as he tried to juggle his belongings. "It's my fault that I'm late."

"No, it's fine," Arnie said, as he moved out into the isle, allowing the woman to step in and take the window seat. It was, after all, really her seat. She was toting a large suede bag, and Arnie offered to stow it up in the carry bin, which he did before taking his own assigned seat on the isle.

Once the plane took off, he was very conscious of the attractive woman beside him and tried to look nonchalant, flipping through his notes, but not seeing them. Out of the corner of his eye, he could see his seat mate searching through her handbag, looking for something. Being rather shy and quiet, Arnie was never the one to start a conversation with a stranger, let alone a beautiful one. When the seat belt sign blinked out, Arnie gave a quiet sigh of relief and opened his computer, planning on keeping his nose buried in his work. Soon after, he was deeply involved in typing up his research notes.

The woman, sitting comfortably beside him, took the opportunity to study the man. Of medium build and height, she figured him to be in his mid-thirties. His buzz cut showed no signs of gray amongst the short, dark brown hair. She wondered what he did for a living. A teacher? No, not correcting schoolwork, she noticed. He was dressed casually, in tan khaki slacks, light blue dress shirt, no tie. She saw a plain gold wedding band on his left hand, so he was married. She felt a twinge of disappointment.

She turned towards the object of her curiosity. "You must be a very hard worker to be doing it so diligently on the plane!" she commented with a smile in her voice.

Startled, Arnie looked up. "Um...Yes. Well..." he stumbled. "I just attended a conference, so before I forget everything, I need to jot it all down. Plus," he added, with a little grin. "I can never read my handwriting twenty-four hours after I get home!" He held up a pile of notes, indicating the chicken-scratches that covered the pages. "As soon as I can, I type out as much of the presentations and discussions as I can recall. That way, I can e-mail it to my supervisor, so he can see how hard I'm working at earning my pay!" Arnie jested.

Suitably amused, the woman told him that was a very clever idea, and Arnie grinned.

He was surprising himself by feeling comfortable enough to joke with her. He had a good sense of humor, but people didn't really see it until they got to know Arnie better, once he felt more relaxed around them. Some people, after first meeting him, thought he was a bit of a snob. But most, later, realized it was just because he was not very out-going. He was well liked by his co-workers, if you didn't include his supervisor, who didn't seem to like anything without breasts.

After sharing another smile, the woman turned to look out the plane window. Arnie, assuming the conversation was over, returned to his notes.

Just then, the flight attendant pulled up with her beverage cart and asked them if they would like something to drink - a soft drink, juice, water, or alcohol. The young woman said she would like a scotch and soda, and handed her the money. The hostess handed her a glass of ice, a can of Canadian Mist soda water, and a little bottle of scotch whiskey.

Asking Arnie what he would like next, he asked for the same thing, then asked her if she could please wait a moment until he got his money out of his wallet, which he just realized he had left in his jacket pocket up in the luggage bin overhead.

Beginning to rise, the lady placed her hand on Arnie's arm to stop him, telling him that she would be glad to pay for his drink. "You can give me the money later, Okay?" she said, with a bright smile. He nodded and thanked her. She offered to share the can of soda, since there was more than she could use with just the tiny bottle they were given, saying it would just go to waste. They made their drinks, and then the woman raised her glass up and proposed a toast to "a good flight." Feeling silly, but liking the sensation, he clicked his plastic glass to hers, then took a sip.

"Do you live in Los Angeles or Seattle?" he asked. She set her glass down on the tray in front of her before answering. "I live in Seattle. How about you?"

"I'm in Seattle, too."

"So, why did you go to L.A., if you don't mind me asking. What do you do?" She nodded her head at the computer, still lying in his lap, although the lid was now closed.

"I'm a research scientist," he answered, hoping that didn't sound too boring. "I've been at a conference there the past two days."

"Oh?" she said, tilting her head in interest. "Research in what?"

"I study the brain. How things affect the memory. We're trying to find out how to stop a lot of the diseases out there."

"Wow! That's pretty heavy stuff. But very interesting."

Arnie was pleased at her interest. He realized he didn't even know her name, and they would be sharing close quarters for a couple of hours. He leaned in closer. "By the way, I'm Arnold Martin. Folks call me Arnie."

"I'm Judy Larson. Nice meeting you!" They shared a smile.

Arnie noticed she had sharp, blue eyes. He imagined her hair would be quite long if not in that bun. It was held on top of her head by a gold clasp. She seemed to be fairly young, maybe in her early twenties, but Arnie thought he could be wrong, not being the best person to ask to guess ages. He enjoyed talking to her, thinking, whatever her age, she seemed to be very mature and personable.

"So," Arnie hesitantly asked. "What is it you do? For a living, I mean."

"I'm in sales." She took a sip of her drink, and Arnie watched how her lips fit around the rim of her glass.

"What kind of sales? Cars?" he joked.

"No!" she laughed. "I work for Life Style Designers. I'm in clothing sales."

"Well, I guessed wrong on that one!" said Arnie with a shrug.

Judy turned towards him, so she was sitting almost sideways in her seat. "What did you guess I do for a living?" she asked, curious.

"Modeling!" he replied sheepishly, knowing he was probably typecasting this attractive woman.

Judy told him that was a very nice compliment, but that it was far from what her job involved. "No runways in my daily grind" she commented.

There was a comfortable lull in their conversation. Arnie briefly wondered if he should get started on those notes, but he was enjoying talking to Judy too much. He put his notes back into the briefcase at his feet, and set his laptop down beside it. Effectively telling his seatmate that he was open to continue their conversation.

"So," Judy began. "Were you born in Seattle?"

"No, I was born in Portland, Oregon. I moved here about

76

twelve years ago to take the job I have now." He studied Judy's pleasant face, how the curls at her temples accented her heart-shaped bone structure. "How about you?"

"Seattle born and bred!" she confessed with a smile.

Watching the flight attendant serving drinks to the other passengers, Judy suddenly laughed, covering her mouth with her hand.

Arnie looked around, saw nothing happening, and asked Judy what was so funny.

"Did you ever watch that one movie with Steve Martin, a long time ago? He meets this big guy that makes a pest of himself and they get into all kinds of trouble?"

"Oh, you mean 'Planes, Trains, and Automobiles'?" Judy shook her head yes. "I thought most of that took place in a car?"

"Maybe you're right, it just struck me funny just now. I love comedies. And action flicks! How about 'Passenger 57'?" she asked. "The one where a special officer is undercover to stop a bunch of hi-jackers? Hope that doesn't happen on this flight!"

"I take it you're a movie buff?" Arnie didn't think she looked like she spent her time in movie theaters. *But then*, he reminded himself, You *know virtually nothing about the girl.*

"Sometimes," she explained, "when I'm home by myself, I like to rent a video and just veg out. It feels good to do nothing sometimes, you know?"

They started talking about movies they'd seen and liked, books they'd read, and other casual small talk. Then Judy surprised him by asking, "So, do you have a family you're going home to, Arnie?" She looked pointedly at his ring finger, where the gold band was gleaming in the overhead cabin light. "I know you must have a wife."

Feeling a little uncomfortable to be switching to a more personal topic, although he couldn't have said why, he shifted in his chair before answering.

"Yes, I am married. And I have two really sweet daughters."

Judy said that was nice, and asked the ages of the girls.

"My oldest is Heather, she's twelve. The youngest is ten. She's Ashley." He pulled his computer back onto his lap and turned it on, producing a fairly recent picture of the girls from his files. He pointed out each girl and named them once again.

Judy studied the photo, then told him he had very lovely daughters. "They'll break a few hearts when they grow up." she commented.

Arnie laughed, "Yeah, maybe. But I think Ashley will scare all the boys away, she's too much of a Tomboy!"

They were both quiet for awhile after Arnie returned his computer to the floor by his feet.

"You must be very happy to be going back home to your little family."

"Yes, my kids are always glad when I get back. It's nice."

They continued to talk about many things, and Arnie noticed that, although she had a couple of tastefully be-jeweled rings on her hands, Judy was not wearing any type of ring on the wedding finger of her left hand. But he did not ask Judy if she was married in return, thinking it was a little too forward, and she didn't volunteer the information.

In no time at all, the Captain was announcing that SeaTac Airport was just ahead and they would be landing in a few minutes. Looking out the tiny window, they could see that the clouds had cleared, and appearing was a broad expanse of colored lights stretching out below. Seattle, and the many smaller cities surrounding it.

"Before I forget, I'd better get the money I owe you," he started to get up.

"I have a better idea," said Judy. "Why don't you buy me a drink in Seattle instead?"

"At the airport?"

Judy laughed and said, "No, some other day."

Arnie smiled and agreed. He reached down and got one of his business cards from a side pocket of his briefcase. Handing it to her, he told her to give him a call when she was ready for that drink. She put the card in her purse without glancing at it, and told him she would.

After the plane landed, they stood awkwardly in the terminal, saying how nice it was to have met the other, then both turned to go their separate ways with a light good-bye. Arnie didn't offer to give her a lift to her destination, and Judy didn't request it. Even though they had enjoyed each other's company the past couple of hours, neither really expected to see the other again as they made their way back into their own worlds.

*   *   *

While Judy caught a taxi to her apartment in downtown Seattle, Arnie walked through the multi-level parking garage until he located his car; recognizable by the sizable dent in the back passenger door where Ashley had learned how to "stop" with her new two-wheeled bicycle when she was eight.

Driving home along the brightly-lit back streets of his neighborhood to avoid any remaining traffic - always found on the main highways nowadays, no matter what the time of day - Arnie found himself humming to an old song that used to be popular on the radio. He reached out and switched his radio on, punching the buttons to find 92.5, a local channel that played a variety of older, as well as the new, music. He was in a pretty good mood.

When Arnie turned onto Dickson Road, he noted how nice his neighborhood was, lined with green, manicured lawns, and well-kept homes. He was proud to be living in such a safe and quiet community. He drove up to his own house, a modern, one-story, ranch-style he had proudly bought many years ago. He knew there were other houses on the street that were much bigger than his own, but his had plenty of growing room for two kids, and he considered it to be very comfortable – homey. He enjoyed giving his family the best, and he believed that he was doing just that.

When he pulled up into the driveway next to Sondra's brand new silver Volvo wagon, the girls, who had heard him drive in, came running out to greet him.

"Daddy! You're home!" they shouted, giving him lots of hugs and kisses. This is what Arnie loved about traveling the most - coming home to his girls. They walked into the house with him, each taking some of his luggage. Sondra stood just inside the doorway. He couldn't tell what kind of mood she was in by her expression, but she wasn't smiling.

"Have the kids eaten dinner yet?" He tossed his coat at Ashley, who squealed and caught it, carrying it towards the back hallway to his bedroom.

"Yes," she replied, "I fed them over an hour ago." She turned towards the bedrooms and told the girls to get ready for bed.

"In a minute, Mom!" they chorused, from somewhere down the hall.

"No!" she said, raising her voice. "Now! It's nine o'clock, past your bedtime!" Arnie could hear the tense tone in her voice and wondered what had happened while he was gone.

"Why don't you let them stay up a little while longer and visit with me? I've been gone." he wheedled. "It's not going to hurt them to miss a little sleep."

Sondra threw him a less-than-understanding look. "You go away on trips all the time. Then you come back and spoil them. They don't listen to me anymore!" Her voice had started to get louder. Her hands on her hips, she continued. "If they don't listen to me *now*, they certainly aren't going to listen to me when they're older! Girls! You'd better be in bed by the time I come in there!" She turned and stomped off to the kitchen. Soon, he could hear her slamming dishes around on the counters, the sound of running water as she did dishes. The kids got very quiet, having slipped into their beds before their mother decided to come back and check on them.

Arnie quietly made his way down the hall to their bedroom, where he changed into his pajamas and his favorite robe, a raggedy plaid thing he's had for too many years. Although he usually slept in the smaller guest bedroom, more-so nowadays, he still kept all his clothes in the one he used to share with Sondra. *In happier times-the good old days,* he mocked. Picking out his clothes for the next day, he went next door and laid them neatly across a chair in "his" bedroom.

His stomach growled noisily, and he made his way to the kitchen, wondering if he could talk Sondra into heating something up for him, while he found out what had happened to make her so irritable. Sondra was no longer in the kitchen, having made her escape into the bedroom as soon as Arnie had entered his own. He quietly searched through the leftovers in the fridge before settling on some cold macaroni and cheese, and making a piece of toast as a chaser. He ate his poor dinner as quickly as he could in the cold, lonely kitchen, then placed his dirty dishes in the sink with the many others he found there.

Wondering if the girls were still awake, he silently entered their room. Finding them asleep, he contented himself with leaning over to brush a light kiss on each of their foreheads, first having to dig through a pile of blankets to find Ashley. He watched them for a few precious moments, thinking himself a very lucky man, indeed, to have two such wonderful kids.

Crawling into bed, for once not interested in staying up late, reading, Arnie found his thoughts looping back to the flight, and Judy. Remembering how polite, how humorous she was, Arnie found himself wondering why Sondra couldn't still be like that. He remembered Sondra's laugh, how pretty he used to find her. She still took good care of herself, dressed in nice clothes, but there was a difference in her lately that he couldn't put his finger on. His sleepy mind conjured up pictures of Sondra and himself at their hasty wedding, the birth of their two babies, other pleasant memories.

But, soon, those pictures were over-shadowed by his more-recent memory of the woman from the plane. Wondering what it would be like to be married to a woman like that, he slowly drifted off to sleep.

Chapter 8

A week after meeting Judy on the plane, Arnie and his supervisor, Murray Evans, decided to go to lunch at a restaurant near the hospital, the Place Cafe. Being close to the hospital, as well as the college, the Place was usually filled with an interesting mix of lab coats, suits, and casual wear, with the occasional dark Goth dress and makeup thrown in. Arnie and Murray often went to lunch there when they could spare the time out of their busy schedules. Murray made no secret of the fact that he went there to check out the women, hoping to score a new love-interest. Although Arnie had yet to see this happen while the two of them were there together, he had heard through the clinic grapevine that Murray had a high success rate of "catches" taken from inside it's walls. Being only thirty-four, and good-looking, Arnie supposed that wasn't too hard to believe. He knew Murray could pour on the charm when he felt he could benefit from it. Whether a bank rep to extend a grant, or a pretty lady to get into bed – *I reckon they aren't too different, if you think about it.*

Arnie, on the other hand, liked to come to this restaurant for the down-home food it offered, and it was a great place for people watching, a relaxing pastime *he* enjoyed. Arnie, having already ordered, looked around the crowded room. The tables by the large front window, facing the street, were filled with laughing college students, books piled under some of the chairs, post-test relief apparent in their postures and the few words Arnie could make out in the muted roar of the room.

"Man! I thought ... sure I ... failing this one!"

"Did...question...nerves!"

Arnie remembered what it used to be like back in his own college days, at the University of Oregon, and felt himself missing those carefree days. No family responsibilities, no bills (if you didn't count his ever-growing tuition costs), being able to party all night and still get through the lab exams the next day. He realized it had probably been glamorized over time in his memories; all the stress of studying, getting assignments done on time, getting lost on the campus when you only had a half minute until your next class, wondering if he'd ever meet somebody that he had more than molecular biology in common with.

His attention wandered to the left of the students, where there were a few tables set up for only two occupants. He was pulled out of his reverie when his glance landed on a familiar face. Judy. Then, realizing Murray was speaking to him, he tore himself away and tried to pay attention to what Murray was saying.

"Hm?" Arnie blinked.

"I asked how your pretty wife was doing." Murray was watching two college girls - too young in Arnie's opinion- at a nearby table, their heads close together to better hear each other in the noisy din of the room.

"Oh, she's fine." He looked back over to the window, wanting to verify who he'd seen. There was Judy, talking to an older man in a very nice suit. *An Armani? Yeah, like you'd know what one looks like!* He didn't care about brand name clothing, anyway. He knew what looked good on him and what didn't, no matter what the cost. He was also well aware, though, that it bothered Sondra, as she attempted to keep up with what she thought society expected of a doctor's wife. *Even though I'm buried in a lab 90% of the time, and not performing some brilliant piece of surgery. I wonder if she's disappointed that I'll never get my name on the cover of the Times or appear on a talk show so all her friends could be envious of her.* He mentally shrugged, nothing he could do about that part of Sondra's dreams. Seeing Judy with this well-dressed fellow, however, made him wonder if maybe he should be putting more effort into his appearance. *Maybe Sondra's got a point, a nice suit does wonders for this hoary old guy!*

Arnie knew he was being spiteful. He put a stop to where his thoughts were taking him, and studied the twosome. Judy was dressed simply in a navy blue shift, long-sleeved matching cardigan covering her bare arms. Her hair, once again up in a stylish bun, was gleaming in the bright, although overcast, light streaming down through the lacy curtain on the window. On sunny days, these wispy pieces of material kept the bright sun from reflecting off the nearby Green Lake and blinding the customers trying to enjoy the view. He could see no jewelry sparkling at her neck or wrists. Leaning slightly forward, arms folded across the tabletop, she appeared to be listening intently to what her gentleman friend had to say.

Her companion was fairly large at the girth, but more from inherited build than from fat. He threw back his large, balding head to roar at Judy's reply, tipping his chair dangerously in the process. Thinking the man's laugh seemed a bit overdone, Arnie still felt a twinge of jealousy. He shook it off, telling himself, "He's got to be at least fifty-five, maybe it's her father." Just then the man reached out and engulfed Judy's much more petite hand in his own large, meaty one. After only a few seconds, Judy casually withdrew it, reaching out to pick up the wineglass beside her partially empty plate. This didn't seem to phase her friend, who once again barked in laughter at whatever Judy chose to tell him. As for himself, Arnie was feeling irked!

He was jerked back into the real world when Murray again spoke to him. He turned back to his supervisor to see a frown twisting his eyebrows into a vee-shape, and realized that he had probably missed something important. Murray did not like to be ignored. Glancing over at the next table, Arnie noticed that the two objects of Murray's attention had left.

"Wha...What?" he choked out. "I'm sorry, what were you saying?" He picked up his cold coffee to cover his blunder. Even cold, a good double-shot vanilla latte', with a hit of caramel, Arnie's favorite espresso drink, was a treat - unfortunately, this was not one. Arnie grimaced and waved for the waitress to replace it with a hot cup.

"Just what is so amazing over there that you're not listening to a word I'm saying," Murray exclaimed. He raised his eyebrow when he spotted the lovely woman sitting in the direction in which Arnie had been staring. "Well, now!" He laughed, a sound that made Arnie's skin crawl. "Who would've guessed, you old scoundrel!" *If he slaps me on the back, I'm going to deck the guy,* Arnie said to himself. *And I'm* not *old, only two years older than you are!* "Maybe you're human after all, Martin!" He tried not to see how his supervisor studied Judy with interest.

Thankfully, Arnie was saved from further ribbing by the arrival of their food, and Murray was too busy stuffing his mouth to make idle conversation. *I hope he doesn't eat like that on his dates!* But he knew Murray liked to get eating over with so he could get down to the reason they were really there, to try to resolve work problems outside of the pressure of the office.

Despite himself, Arnie couldn't help but take occasional quick peeks at Judy and her companion. He wanted to approach her, but knew that wouldn't be the right thing to do, since he'd only met her on the plane, and she hadn't bothered to contact him for that drink. *Probably just being polite.*

Forty minutes later, after discussing some of the problems they were encountering with the latest experiment at the lab, Arnie and Murray were ready to go. They each picked up their own checks and rose to go to the cash register, Arnie leaving the tip, since Murray didn't bother. Murray was of the belief that his money was only good for the pretty waitresses, despite the quality of service, and this one had been on the homely side. Arnie was used to his boss' pettiness, and made a point to tip the less-than-pretty girl with a few extra dollars, earning a token scoff from Murray, and a pleased smile from the waitress.

After settling their bill with the cashier, Arnie and Murray headed towards the door, still talking quietly about what they could do to get the test results they needed. Discreetly keeping an eye on the pair, Arnie now noticed Judy and the big man coming towards the door, too, and hung back. Catching her eye, he smiled at her, opening the cafe door for her.

"Hello, Dr. Martin," she said, smiling back. The big man, standing protectively beside her, glared at both men in turn, not at all happy with the attention they were giving his lady friend. Without a word, he pushed ahead of the two doctors and ushered Judy out the door, giving her no time to say anything else, and earning a rude comment from Murray.

As they were walking back to the hospital, Murray asked with a smirk, "So, was that your girlfriend, Martin? Got something going on the side you need to tell Uncle Murray?" Inside, he held the lab door open for Arnie, gallantly waving his arm for the other man to precede him, as if Arnie had done something worth recognizing. "Just when I thought you were an old fuddy-duddy, you surprise me, Doctor." He gave him a big smile and wanted details of the sordid affair. Arnie almost hated the man when he tried to be "one of the guys." He preferred him to stay cold and calculating, up on the top of the chain of command. Where he didn't have to deal with him more than necessary. Or pretend to like him.

"There's nothing going on between us. She's just a woman I met on the plane the other week, coming back from Los Angeles." Arnie didn't know why he was bothering to explain, he knew Murray would believe whatever he chose to. "Like that young, beautiful woman would want *my* body?" He patted a non-existent beer belly and tried to joke about it, wishing she *did* want his body! *Do I?*

Murray was kind enough to point out that she was with an ugly, old man who could've been her grandfather. Then mused that maybe he *should have* gone to that conference after all so he could have met her himself, since Arnie was letting the encounter go to waste. "Are you planning on seeing her again? Maybe you can introduce us sometime," he added hopefully.

Arnie wondered how much he should be talking to his

supervisor about Judy, seeing what great pleasure Murray took in teasing him.

"She paid for my drink on the plane when I couldn't get to my wallet, and I told her I would buy her one in return sometime. Hasn't happened so far, so I guess that's that. I doubt I'll be running into her again, even though she lives in Seattle. Besides," he felt the need to add, "I've heard about your reputation with the ladies. I don't think she's the type that would go for that," he said with a lame laugh.

Disappointed, Murray turned away, and Arnie was glad to go back to the familiar business of running lab tests.

*   *   *

Getting ready to call it quits for the day, Arnie was cleaning up the papers that had somehow gravitated to his desk when his phone rang, startling him, a cascade of papers floating to the floor. Closing his eyes and taking a deep breath, he bent over to begin picking them up, lifting the receiver at the same time. The voice at the other end stopped him in mid-stoop, and he stood up again quickly, changing the receiver to his other ear.

"Hi! This is Judy, the girl from the plane." Arnie swallowed, then said he knew who she was and how was she doing?

"I'm fine. I just wanted to apologize for not talking to you at the restaurant this afternoon. I was with a client." She paused, and Arnie said she didn't need to apologize, since they hadn't seen each other since the plane trip. He wondered if that sounded as forward as he felt it did.

"About that," she said. "I was going to call you a few days ago, but I've been so busy, I haven't had time." Arnie felt his heart soar at this. *She was going to call!* "Since I saw you today, I thought I'd better make the effort to call so you wouldn't think I was putting you on the other day —about the drink, and everything."

Trying to think of what to say, Arnie said the first thing that popped into his head, "So, that guy with you, you said he was just a client? *"Oh, no! That sounded like a jealous boyfriend!* "I mean, he didn't seem too happy that you said hello to me." Arnie wiped his sweaty palm down the thigh of his black slacks, then traded hands on the receiver, and wiped that palm dry, too. He couldn't remember being this tense since his high school dating days! And puberty had a lot to blame for that, besides! He didn't have that excuse now, as he sat down and anxiously tried to think of something to say to keep her on the phone. He liked the sound of her voice, soft and sweet.

"Well, you know, sometimes you get a client from hell! And he was a big one! Client, I mean. A big client..." She gave a little laugh, and he realized she sounded just as nervous as he felt. He found that very endearing, it made him feel slightly less nervous, himself. "So," she continued, "When are you going to buy me that drink?"

Hearing only silence on the other end, she quickly added, "Unless I just made a fool of myself! I'm sorry, I presumed you were serious about that offer on the plane. If this is a bad idea, just tell me!" She sounded upset with herself.

"No! No!" Arnie quickly protested, afraid she was going to hang up. "I was looking at my desk calendar to see when I was free!" he lied to cover his blunder. "I'm sorry you got the wrong impression just then!" He felt like a dope. "Looks like I can do it anytime in the evening, just name the place and time!" *They ought to commit you, Arnie! What are you doing? You're married, you have no business taking this beautiful woman out for a drink*! he chastised himself. "How about tonight?" He slapped his hand to his forehead, not believing that snuck out of his mouth.

After a lengthy silence, while Judy looked through her daily planner, she said, "I'm free about five o'clock tomorrow, if you'd like." Arnie glanced at the clock on the wall above his file cabinet, and estimated that would give him at least half an hour to get there after work. He agreed.

"Where would you like to go?" Arnie tried to think of a nice place they could meet, one where he wouldn't run into his co-workers, if he could help it. "There's a place off of Green Lake Way, the Emerald Wok. Do you like Chinese food? They have a lot of different kinds of dishes besides that, too, if Chinese doesn't do it for you," he was quick to add.

Judy said she happened to be fond of Chinese food, and that was fine by her. So Arnie gave her directions from the I-5 freeway, and they agreed to meet in the bar at five o'clock the next day. Dripping with nervous perspiration, Arnie hung up, feeling exuberant and guilty at the same time.

Chapter 9

After a particularly slow day, so it seemed, four o'clock finally came around. Arnie tried to distract himself by cleaning up the day's clutter. Papers, empty test tubes, wrappers from lunch (but not his own, having kept too busy to stop and grab something) – *How does all this stuff end up in* my *office!*

He then sat down at his desk to plan what he would say to Sondra. He couldn't recall a time he had ever had to lie to his wife about where he was. And, not feeling good about doing it now, yet still going through with it, he picked up the phone and dialed home. He usually left his office between five and six, but occasionally, and more often lately, he had to stay later to see a test through to its critical end, or to meet a deadline.

Using the former excuse, he told Sondra he might be late, and not to wait dinner for him, he'd grab a bite from the downstairs cafeteria when he had a chance. Hanging up the phone, after first listening to her gripes about his job interfering in his family life, he finished cleaning up, and was out the door by four twenty-five.

Arnie ended up leaving his car two blocks away, parking spaces being scarce in this popular neighborhood. He could see why many people chose to commute on bicycles, despite all the steep hills Seattle was famous for. But here the streets were mostly level, and, even at the peak of the dinner hour, many people were out taking advantage of the mild, dry evening.

Walking along the tree-lined streets, Arnie had plenty of time to think about what he was doing. Dodging a man on yellow rollerblades and a lady jogging, pushing one of those fancy strollers with over-large wheels, he wondered if he was starting something he shouldn't be. *It's just a drink. This doesn't mean anything. It's not wrong to repay a favor. I owe her one drink, then it'll never happen again. We'll go our separate ways, and I'll never see her again.* So bolstered, he took a deep breath of fresh air, and was instantly hit with the tantalizing smells of the approaching restaurant. His stomach growled noisily.

Standing at the entrance, Arnie rolled his tight shoulders a few times to loosen them up, then stepped into the warm atmosphere of the eatery. Not seeing Judy amongst the crowd, he asked the hostess to reserve a table for two, then took a seat in the lounge. Ordering a scotch with soda water, he sat on the end of the bar where he could see whoever entered. It was five-o-five.

At five-ten, Arnie hardly having touched his drink, the waitress came over and told him they had his table ready in the dining area. Telling the girl that his dinner partner had not shown up yet, he told her he would take the next available table instead. Looking at his watch, he told himself that he would give Judy another five minutes, then go home. He took a long drink of his watery scotch and grimaced.

At five-fifteen, Arnie couldn't help but feel like he'd been stood up. He told himself he shouldn't feel that way, that he *should* be glad that nothing had a chance to happen. He knew he was getting fond of this woman, and he didn't even know her very well. He just felt like this was somebody he could truly fall in love with – if he wasn't already married, he reminded himself reluctantly.

At five-twenty Arnie, not sure whether to be relieved or angry, decided he'd given it enough time. Before he could talk himself into giving her even more time to show, Arnie stood up, ready to go home. He laid a dollar on the bar for a tip, then began to put on his overcoat, preparing to leave. Checking the time on his watch one more time, he saw it was almost five-thirty. If he heard from her again, he could tell Judy he waited an appropriate length of time for her.

As he started to stand up from his bar stool, he realized that

Judy was standing there, only a foot or so away, an apprehensive expression on her face. He sat back down again, not sure what to do, waiting for Judy to make the first move. She did, approaching him slowly, laying her hand on his sleeve as if to prevent him from walking away. She stood there, looking down at him. He could almost feel the heat of her hand through his jacket.

Clearing his throat, afraid to speak, Arnie finally broke the building silence. "You came. I was about to look through the restaurant to see if you were here, maybe we misunderstood where to meet," he lied. He realized he never used to lie like this before, to save a woman's feelings.

Judy said, "I am so sorry! This is the second time I came late." She looked contrite. "You're going to start thinking bad thoughts of me."

"Never," he assured her with a smile. He told her it was all right, that she was there now. He invited her to have a seat and they both sat on the barstools, Arnie once again removing his coat and placing it across his lap. He told her he hoped she wouldn't mind, but he had signed them up for a table, not having eaten since breakfast. She murmured that it was fine, she could stand to eat a bite, also. They fumbled awkwardly for something to say, waiting for the bartender to come down their way so they could order. But, before that happened, the hostess was back, their table was ready, so they adjourned to the dining room, where just the presence of more people put them at ease.

When their waitress arrived and asked if they would like something to drink before they ordered, Arnie looked at Judy to go first. She was trying to remove her black leather coat while she ordered. The coat was floor-length, and to avoid getting it stepped on, the waitress offered to take it out to the front station and hang it on a hook behind the desk once their orders were placed. Judy ordered a scotch on the rocks. When asked if there was a special brand she preferred, Judy replied, "Yes, make that a Chivas, please."

"And you, sir?"

Arnie asked for the same thing, only with soda water instead of ice. The waitress took Judy's long coat and disappeared into the reception area. Judy silently hoped her coat would not be stolen, since the busy staff had better things to do than watch her coat.

Once their drinks were placed in front of them, Judy commented, "Looks like we have something in common," At Arnie's questioning glance, she lifted up her glass, and replied, "We both like scotch!"

"Oh, yes. I noticed that on the plane, too." He nervously took a sip, thinking that this drink was far better than the one he had earlier let turn to water at the bar. *Because of the company.*

"How is your family?" she asked, to get things started.

"My daughters are happy to have Daddy home again," he said with a fond smile, thinking of his little girls and how they always welcomed him home with their affectionate hugs.

"Did you get your notes translated before you forgot them?"

"Yes, I did, in fact. I got it all done the next morning. Thankfully, things were a little slow that day."

After ordering, they made small talk until their meals arrived.

"And how was your day today?" Judy asked, wrapping a piece of pasta around her fork before popping it into her mouth. Neither of them thought it sounded strange to hear such a "wifely" inquiry. Arnie was too distracted watching her delicately licking the creamy white sauce from her lips to notice.

"Nothing special happened. Meetings to attend, reports to make, cells to colonate," he joked.

She laughed and told him he was quite the witty guy. Arnie beamed. He asked how her day had been in return.

"I had an early breakfast meeting with a client at eight. Then spent the rest of the morning at the clothing store. After lunch I went to a fashion show to see if there was anything the store would be interested in purchasing for the spring sales. Such atrocities this year! Won't catch *me* wearing any of those selections, but you have to cater to the fads." She stopped eating and looked into his eyes. "And now I'm here."

Trying not to read anything into her look, he commented, "Sounds like you had a busy day." He took a cold sip of his scotch, giving a little groan of pleasure down in his throat.

"Not really. But sometimes I have to deal with difficult clients, and that can be tiring. I'm sure you know how that feels." Thinking of Murray, Arnie agreed.

Judy asked him why he'd chosen this restaurant. "Do you come here often?" She picked through her fettuccini, trying to find all the shrimp. Arnie found it interesting to see that she ate her seafood pasta one "species" at a time, next going after all the scallops. "This is wonderful, would you like to try a bite," she offered, pushing her plate closer to his.

Arnie declined, preferring his more traditional steak and baked potato. He cut off a portion, and dipped it into the rich, brown gravy, chewing it with his eyes partially closed in pleasure. He had ordered it rare, liking the soft, meaty taste. Watching him bite into the bloody meat, Judy had wrinkled her nose in distaste, but to her credit, had said nothing about it.

Swallowing, Arnie returned to her earlier question, explaining that he had come here once when his parents were up visiting from Oregon. "My daughter, Ashley-I think she was around five at the time-insisted on having the General Tao's Chicken. We tried to tell her it would be spicy, but she has a way of brow-beating us all into submission, so we let her order it." He grinned. "Oh, my God! You'd think she just got poisoned! She was crawling around under the table, choking and coughing, I really thought she'd bring up a hairball! If it wasn't so embarrassing, it would've been very funny! My mother and my wife were not amused!" He wiped at a tear at the corner of his eye from laughing so hard. "In fact, they never went to another restaurant with us until Ashley was older.

"I love my folks, but they still tend to think of me as a little boy." he confessed. "Always trying to put my life into order, that kind of thing. So, brief visits are plenty! I guess I have to thank Ashley for her theatrics. Something always happens to cut their visits short!" He held his glass up and they toasted his daughter. "I guess I needed to come back here to redeem my reputation!"

They laughed, feeling much more comfortable by now. Arnie was amazed at how much he was enjoying her company, all thoughts of doing something wrong were long gone. He hoped it would never end.

"You talk about your kids, but never your wife." Judy brought up later. "You haven't even told me her name."

"Oh," he said, not realizing this. "Her name is Sondra. We've been married about twelve years now. How about you?" He was eager to get off the subject of his marriage. "Are you married? Any prospects lined up?"

"No, not married," she wiggled her left ring finger at him. "And not planning on it, either."

"Why not?" Arnie was curious. A woman as beautiful as this one, she should have been scooped up by now. He could see her happily married, a bunch of children at her side. *I could picture a life with this woman.* He quickly ducked his head and grabbed his cold drink, appalled that he'd allowed himself to have a thought like that. He hoped Judy couldn't tell by his expression that he'd been thinking very unmarried thoughts!

"For one thing, marriage requires a very large commitment. For another, I'm too busy to put in the time needed to make a relationship work. Maybe later, when I meet the right man, I'll be willing to give all my time and energy to a serious relationship, but not now."

Arnie found himself asking her what qualities her Mr. Right would possess.

"Let's see," she thought. "He'd have to share many of the same interests, have a good sense of humor, be sexually appealing, sensitive, tall, reasonably good-looking, and rich!" They laughed. "Is that asking too much?"

"No. Well, maybe the "rich" part." he amended. "But how are you going to find him if you're not looking? There's probably only a handful on the planet Earth that fit your description, and, like myself," he teased, "The good ones are already married!"

"Well, then," she said matter-of-factly, "I guess I'll have to wait for one of them to get divorced!"

Arnie, not sure if she was joking or not, decided to change the subject, somewhat.

"Do you like kids? Do you want to have any some day?"

"Yes, and no." He threw her a puzzled look and asked what she meant.

"I like kids, sure. But they are a lot of responsibility. I'm not sure I'll ever be ready for kids." She looked glum. When she didn't volunteer to explain further, Arnie dropped it and went in a different direction, telling her a little about the small lake they could see from their window if it hadn't been dark.

"There's a path around the lake," he told her. "Actually, it's more like a wide, paved road. I suppose that's where they got the name of the restaurant. Emerald *Wok – walk.* Get it?" Judy just rolled her eyes. "Have you ever walked it? The trail, I mean."

"No, I never had the chance. I've always thought it would be nice to take a stroll some day, but..." She shrugged. "I guess it's easy to use work as a cop out."

"My wife and I used to walk on it, before we had both kids, that is. Once you have a baby and a preschooler, there's no more long, romantic walks! You tend to find things to do that you can get over with in a short time – before the kids start howling!" he joked. "It's a beautiful path, the sun sparkles on the water, there's duck poop to avoid, bikers to get in the way of! You're supposed to stay on the side of the trail marked for bikers or walkers, to avoid hitting each other, but when you're too busy staring at the scenery, sometimes you stray onto each other's side. I've nearly demolished a bike or two in my days!" he bragged with a laugh. "It's not much of a lake, but it's two point nine miles if you walk all the way around it."

"Aren't you pretty much committed to finishing once you start?" Judy pointed out. "Unless there's a bridge or something to take as a short cut?"

Arnie thought about that. "No, I guess you could drop off anywhere along the way and take a taxi back to your starting point! Now that's *my* kind of exercise!"

The mood greatly lightened. They were soon involved in talking about a variety of subjects: the growing traffic, the unceasing rain, and, soon, the earlier unpleasant episode was forgotten.

*   *   *

"Oh, my God!" Arnie looked at his watch and couldn't believe it was eight-forty. "Time flies when ..."

...you're having fun," Judy finished for him. They shared another laugh.

"I really should get home, it's late. My kids will be waiting and worrying about where I am." He waved at the waitress for the check, digging his wallet out of his back pocket.

"There you go again," she admonished playfully. "You didn't mention your wife, just your kids!"

He just smiled. "Thanks for coming. It was a good idea." He was starting to feel a little awkward again. "I had fun. How about you?"

"Yes, I had a good time, too. I'm glad I met you on the plane."

They picked Judy's coat up from the front desk and exited the restaurant. *This is where the girl says she had a wonderful time, you walk her to her apartment, and you give her such a romantic, heart-stopping kiss that she invites you up for a night cap.* Arnie gave himself a little smirk when Judy wasn't watching. "Can I give you a lift? My car's not far from here, it's an easy walk. And," he turned the palm of his hand up towards the sky. "It's not raining!" Referring to an earlier part of their conversation.

"No, that's okay. I live about ten blocks from here, I'll just catch a cab."

"Are you sure?" He wasn't sure if he wanted to continue the evening, or quit while he was ahead. It was still early enough to make a fool of himself.

"Yes, on this I'm very sure." She softened it with one of her delightful smiles. "Besides, you have some kids waiting for their Daddy to come home!" She turned to go, then stopped. "See," she pointed a few hundred feet ahead. "There's a taxi now, and it has my name on it if I hurry!"

They said good-bye and went in opposite directions. After only walking about thirty yards, Arnie had the urge to turn and look back, so he did. Judy, standing beside the open door of the taxi, was looking back in his direction. She smiled and waved, like she'd been waiting for just that moment before she could go.

He returned the wave, then stood there until the red taillights were mere dots amongst many in the city, before returning to his chilly car, and home.

*   *   *

Arnie walked through the door at nine-fifteen. Not sure what to expect from Sondra after coming home so late, although not the first time, he treaded carefully when he saw her. Hearing the key in the lock, she got up from the couch and went into the entryway to greet him. Arnie was surprised when she gave him a warm hug and took his briefcase from him. *Just like she used to.* He couldn't read the expression on her face, but she didn't look angry.

"I wasn't sure what time you'd make it home, so I fed the girls earlier." He hung his coat up in the hall closet, and followed her into the living room. "Have you eaten? I can warm the pot roast up, if you're hungry." He felt a twinge of guilt at her comment. And at her pleasant attitude.

"I managed to grab something earlier, I'm okay." He listened for the girls, all was quiet. "Are the girls still up?"

"You know their bedtime is at nine. It's after that now," she pointed out, showing the first signs of displeasure.

"Yes, you're right. I'm sorry." His sincere apology seemed to diffuse the tension before it escalated into an argument, and Arnie

98

breathed a sigh of relief as Sondra returned to the couch to watch the rest of her TV program. Ironically, Arnie could tell by the sound that it was "ER", a weekly show about doctors handling emergencies in a hospital somewhere. *New York? Chicago?* He could never keep them straight. There was always at least one medical show on every year.

Leaving her to enjoy her show, Arnie went down the hall to his daughters' room. He softly opened the door – and found both girls sitting up in bed waiting for him.

"Daddy!" He opened the door all the way and went in. The girls got up and scrambled over to him, wrapping their soft, little arms around his middle.

"You're late!" Heather accused, her pretty blue eyes reproving.

"Yeah, Daddy!" complained Ashley. "How come you're so late? You missed dinner and everything. I had a story I wrote in class I wanted to read to you!" Ashley sniffed, although no tears were to be seen. "I gotta A on it, too," she pouted.

Arnie, feeling extremely guilty now, Ashley's melodramatics notwithstanding, gave them both a big hug and helped them back into their beds, tucking them in snugly. "I'm real sorry, babies. I needed to stay late and finish a very important job." His lie felt hot in his throat.

"More important than us," Ashley asked, her concern genuine this time.

"No, not more important," he reassured, picking up a strand of her light brown, baby fine hair, straightening it off her face. "Just something I needed to do." He looked over at his other daughter, who was watching him intently. It gave him a start, and caused him to wonder if she suspected where he had really been. *Of course not! She's only twelve, why would she suspect I was doing anything except working?* He knew kids learned a lot on TV nowadays, maybe too much.

"I promise I'll try not to be so late again, okay?" Looking at their dear little faces, Arnie found himself meaning that. Nobody was worth hurting his little girls for. Not even Judy. Feeling better with that declaration, he told Ashley to go get her story, and spent the next fifteen minutes enjoying the delightful company of his own family. Oddly, Sondra never came in to tell him he was keeping the girls up, that they would be too tired at school the next morning. And Arnie was having too much fun to notice.

Later, in bed, Arnie thought about the girls. How much he enjoyed spending time with them. He couldn't imagine them not being in his life. Nor could he fathom how some fathers didn't want to be involved with their children, and were content to send money every month instead. He knew plenty of men like that at the hospital. No family pictures on their desks like he had. No family outings, spilled mustard, or torn clothing for them. They were content to let their wives, or strangers, raise their offspring, resuming their lives as if they had no children – and no wives, in some cases, thinking of his earlier behavior with Judy.

He thought of his increasingly stressful marriage, how moody Sondra had been becoming lately. He could think back to just a few months and see a difference in her behavior. That was before he had even met Judy, and he was coming home on a fairly regular basis. What had changed? True, they hadn't been in love when they got married, but he thought they had formed a pretty close relationship over the years. *Had she met somebody else? Was she in love with another man? So now she resented being trapped in this marriage?* Arnie didn't know what to think. A while back he wouldn't even have considered such a thing could happen. But now that he had met Judy...

Had he been staying in this marriage just for the kids all these years? Or did he harbor some genuine feelings for Sondra. Arnie rubbed his face with both hands, confused with all these thoughts racing around in his head. *Going nowhere fast, either,* he admitted, closing his eyes and trying to wipe his mind clean of all conflict. He rolled over and buried his head under the covers, trying to hide from the tumultuous feelings he was being bombarded with. He eventually fell into a restless sleep, broken up by dreams of the kids, Sondra and Judy.

Chapter 10

Several mornings later, Arnie was sitting at his desk in his office, trying to focus on making the mathematical equations needed to change the results of his recent project in cell manipulation. Getting frustrated after multiple configurations, and still not getting what he wanted, it was almost a relief when the phone rang just before eleven. He had spent the past few days wondering if each ring of the phone was Judy, and what he would say if she asked him to meet her somewhere again. His mind preoccupied with neural stem cells and nerve fibers, he picked up the receiver and absently said "Hello" into it, continuing to scribble on the paper before him.

"Hi! This is Judy!" said a cheery voice on the other end.

Arnie, taken aback, was quiet.

Less assured now, she added, "You know, the airplane girl? Green Lake?"

"Oh, yeah, sure." Arnie wasn't sure he was glad to hear from her. "How are you, Judy?"

"Fine." She hesitated, not sure her idea would be accepted now. "What are you doing for lunch?" she plunged in with both feet. Silence. "I'm going to be close to the restaurant we were at the other night, the Emerald Wok. I was wondering if you would consider joining me there."

Arnie thought about her offer. *It won't make me late tonight, since it's for lunch, and I do have to eat.* "Okay, I guess that would be all right. I'll be able to get out of here in about half an hour, is that okay?"

Judy, relieved that he hadn't passed her off, said that was

perfect. "I'll meet you there at noon. Only this time I'll get there before you do!" she declared.

"We'll see," Arnie replied.

Arnie walked into the restaurant at almost exactly twelve. He was surprised to see Judy already seated at a table, a big grin on her face. "See, I told you I'd be first!" She told him to sit down, patting the chair beside her. Without being outwardly rude, Arnie had no choice but to take it, although he would rather have sat across from her so it would lessen the feeling of intimacy. To add to this feeling, he was aware that they were seated at the same window seats they had been at the last time. *Coincidence?* But today, with patches of blue sky peeking out of the gray clouds, there was a fine view of the sparkling water Arnie had been describing on their last visit.

As if reading his mind, Judy said, looking slightly guilty, "I hope you don't mind, I asked the waitress to give us this table, since the sun is so pretty today. I wanted to see this famous lake you were talking about! And it was the only one left by the window," she felt she needed to add.

Okay, that sounds probable.

"This is fine." He sat down, discreetly admiring the woman sitting next to him. In a tan bulky knit sweater, dark brown skirt ending at mid-calf, and her hair in a French braid, Arnie wondered if she could look bad in anything she wore.

"So, how did you do it?" he asked, picking up the lunch menu from the table.

"Do what?" She squinted her eyes in puzzlement.

"How did you get here so early? Did you run here right after you called me?"

Realizing he was giving her a bad time, she haughtily opened her own menu and pretended to be offended. "Are you insinuating that I'm always late, mister?" Then she laughed. "Don't tease me, I'm not usually a late person."

"Only for me, huh?"

"Only when the circumstances are out of my control, smarty."

It felt good to be able to relax and joke around with Judy again. Now that he was there, he was glad he accepted her invitation. Yet found himself scanning the room to make sure there were no familiar faces in the restaurant.

"It's nice to be able to go out to a meal with a friend, instead of always a customer. And I consider you one of my friends, Arnie."

Feeling uncomfortable, Arnie quipped, "Well, as long as you don't think of me as your enemy, that's good enough for me!" Then he felt stupid, and opened his menu to hide his embarrassment. Judy didn't seem to notice, and chatted about her latest client until the waitress came to take their orders.

"So, tell me," Judy asked, tipping her head to one side. "Did my phone call surprise you?"

Arnie felt out his answer carefully. "Surprised me, no. But I must admit I'm quite curious about what you want from me, Miss Judy Larson." He arched an eyebrow at her, waiting for her reply.

Judy put a hand just below her throat. "What do you mean?" she exclaimed.

"I'm a married man, I'm not young anymore. I'm not rich, or handsome. But you," he lightly touched the arm she had brought down to rest on her lap. "You are a young, single, very beautiful," which brought a blush to her cheeks, "not to forget to mention intelligent, woman. I can't help but wonder what it is you want from an old goat like me."

"I know you love your children, Arnie. And I'd like to believe you're happily married, although I have my doubts. You probably aren't rich, judging by those antique loafers you're wearing!"

"Hey," Arnie protested, holding a foot out from under the table. "These are genuine collector's items! And they're comfortable!"

"Yeah, yeah," Judy laughed. "Just like those holey boxers you probably wear at home, huh?" She continued, "But I find you nice to talk to." She ignored Arnie, as he rolled his eyes up at the word "nice". "You're funny, interesting, and I feel very comfortable sitting here with you. You're polite, well-educated, and I feel like

I can learn a few things from you, share ideas with you."

Arnie, feeling like she'd break out into the Boy Scout oath any minute, remained silent.

"I don't feel like you're just humoring me so you can get me into bed. When I've tried to be friends with younger men, they always think I have an ulterior motive. That I'm interested in them sexually, when I just want their friendship." Arnie felt bad about questioning her motives now.

"With you, a married man, I don't have to expect any commitment greater than friendship. I can be myself, say anything, enjoy the moment without trouble coming up at the end of the evening."

"I can understand that, it makes sense. Does that happen a lot?" Arnie was thinking about how beautiful she was, that any man in his right mind would want to take her home after spending time with her.

"Yes, with my clients." She didn't expand on that.

"I'd like to keep seeing you once in a while, Arnie. As friends," she clarified, seeing the worried look that crossed his face.

Thinking it wasn't such a good idea, that now was the perfect opportunity to call it quits, Arnie agreed that he'd like to continue meeting with her for an occasional meal or drink.

"As long as there is no misunderstanding that if I have something else going on, or it's taking me away from my family, that I'm not expected to go. There won't be any hurt feelings if I don't always say okay to a lunch invitation, right?"

"Oh, absolutely." she agreed. "It will just be two friends meeting once in a while when the other one calls."

Arnie noticed it was one o'clock and said he needed to get back to the office.

"I don't have to be at my appointment until two," said Judy, "so you go ahead and go. I'm going to stay here a while longer until I have to leave. I'll catch the tab this time." She pulled a shiny brown leather wallet out of her matching purse.

"No way," insisted Arnie. "No more 'I buy now, you pay me back later,' okay?" He laughed, taking some bills from his wallet and tossed ten dollars down onto the table. "Let's start this friendship up right," he said. "Here's my half, no commitments." She agreed, laying her money down on top of his.

"I'll be away for a few days," she told him before he left. "I have to go visit a client in Las Vegas tomorrow. Then I go to Los Angeles from there for three more days. I'll be back in town about Wednesday."

"Well, traveling girl, you have a safe flight. Try not to meet any rich, handsome men on your way back!" Then he left, feeling younger than he had for a long time.

*   *   *

Coming home from work, a few days after his lunch with Judy, Arnie found several new dresses draped over a chair in the living room. Thinking Sondra must have been out shopping earlier, he casually picked up one of the price tags. Frowning, he reached out and checked the tags on each dress. None of them were less than four hundred dollars! He located the receipt, from a downtown clothing store, and nearly choked at the total cost, $1,589.00! For three dresses? Arnie thought he had to be wrong, but saw nothing else, *no new Mercedes*, on the receipt. Finding Sondra in the kitchen with the girls, he questioned her about the expensive dresses.

Sondra, very defensively, told him she'd needed to get new clothes. When he challenged the prices, she angrily replied, "Would you like me to go naked? I needed some nicer clothes, so I went out and bought them. What, do I have to ask for your permission to spend your money now?"

"No, I just don't think you needed to spend this much on just a few dresses, is all!"

"I bought what I thought I'd look good in. You make enough money, you should be glad you have a wife that cares what other people think of this family. Do you want your wife to go around dressed in rags? That would make a good impression on your colleagues!" About to give his own angry retort, Arnie noticed the distressed look on the girls' faces and decided to drop the subject. Walking out, he noticed Sondra got a smug expression on her face, believing to have won the argument. Growling to himself, he stayed in the guest room until dinner was ready, knowing he'd restart the argument if he went back into the kitchen.

Worried about him, Ashley came in to snuggle up to him on the bed. About the time her head was beginning to droop onto Arnie's lap, she was startled awake by her mother calling her back into the kitchen to help set the table and fix the salad.

Arnie reassured her that everything was all right, and she trudged reluctantly out of the room, turning back to give him one of her sweet smiles.

After a very quiet dinner, Arnie checked the girls' homework, then read them a fairy tale. Going to bed early, he refused to think about the ugly episode with the dresses. He fell asleep with only agreeable thoughts on his consciousness, and was rewarded with pleasurable, if occasionally erotic, dreams.

By morning, he wasn't quite as upset about it, blaming it on the pressure Sondra was probably getting from her doctors-wife friends. Tentatively broaching the subject over coffee and cereal, he told her not to worry about spending money on clothing, but would she try not to spend his life-savings before he earned it! His attempt to lighten things up was met with a dark look. He went to work, wondering where Sondra had pawned her sense of humor, and if it was too late to buy it back.

Chapter 11

Four days after his last meeting with Judy, Arnie was already feeling lonely for her company. It was cultivated by the silent treatment he seemed to be getting from Sondra. *Or maybe we just don't have anything to say to each other anymore.* Kissing the tops of the girls' heads, he left for work as usual, telling Sondra he'd see her later. She nodded her head in response, not bothering to look up. A*t least she hears me, even if she won't talk to me,* he mollified himself.

He made a point of keeping busy the rest of the day, helping his co-workers with their projects while he waited for test results to come back on his own. It seemed to work, and the day was quickly coming to an end before he knew it.

Just before he was ready to leave for the day, he got a call from Judy. "Guess what? I got back from Los Angeles early!" Arnie found himself smiling. "I thought maybe we could meet somewhere for a quick drink."

About to turn her offer down, Arnie remembered that Heather had choir practice tonight. Since they usually made it a big treat for the girls by taking them out for a bite to eat afterwards, he knew Sondra and the girls wouldn't be home until later. It bothered him that Sondra hadn't reminded him of the practice this morning.

"Sure, why not," he finally agreed. "I feel like talking tonight, let's meet somewhere."

"How about our 'usual' place, say in about fifteen minutes?" Judy suggested.

After agreeing and hanging up the phone, Arnie checked his

voice mail, hoping to find a message from Sondra about Heather's choir practice, but there was no word. He left a short message of his own, just in case they made it home before he did, telling them he was hung up at work and would be home as soon as he could. He didn't feel nearly as bad about lying this time, and wondered if that was a terrible thing.

They arrived at the restaurant about the same time, Arnie in his car, Judy in a local taxi. They walked in together, and Arnie caught himself automatically checking out the place for familiar faces again. They saw that "their" window seat was again available and Arnie asked the waitress if they could take it. It wasn't a busy time of day, so she picked up two menus and led them to the table they wanted.

Judy, quiet up to this point, had been studying Arnie as they ordered their drinks, plus a light appetizer to go with it. Once the waitress returned with their scotches, hers on ice, his with soda, she put her concern into words.

"You don't look very happy, Arnie. What's wrong?" she asked gently, her concern apparent in her lovely indigo eyes.

Not planning on discussing his family problems, Arnie soon found himself spilling his personal problems right out onto the table. "I had an argument with my wife last night."

"Oh, I'm sorry. I hope it wasn't about me!" She didn't want to cause him any problems just because she selfishly enjoyed his company.

"No, don't worry. She doesn't even know about you." *That sounded suspiciously like I'm covering up an affair, didn't it.*

"You didn't tell her you had dinner with me?" She cocked her head, looking at him in that way she had that made her look like one of his daughters. "Why not?"

"Let's just say the opportunity never came up. She's been so moody, I don't think it would be a good idea to tell her right now, anyway." He sighed and leaned his chin on his hand, looking out into the growing dusk.

Seeing how depressed and sad he seemed, Judy asked him if

he'd tell her how he and Sondra met. "I'm always interested in love stories," she encouraged.

"Ours isn't exactly a love story," he said, but the corner of his mouth turned up, just the same.

"All marriages have a little love story in them somewhere," she told him. "Sometimes you just have to look real hard to find it."

"I'm not sure where to start. It might be a long one." He didn't know if he should share his private life with another woman. What the repercussions might be if she got to know him too much. Got too close.

"It doesn't matter. Just start where your heart tells you to."

It started to pour outside, hitting the street with a muted sound that could still be heard inside the restaurant. Watching the downpour, he thought of how soothing the sight and sound of rain could be. Then, with a little more encouragement from Judy, he started to tell his tale.

*   *   *

Taking a sip of scotch to steady himself, Arnie began telling Judy about the time when he had first met Sondra. Hesitant and clumsy at first, he soon got into it and found it easier to tell her this more personal side of his life as he progressed.

"Twelve years ago I was still a med student down at the Oregon Health and Science University, in Portland. I decided to go to this college because they focus on biomedical research, as well as regular clinical medicine. I was pretty sure I wanted to go into research from the start. It sounded so note-worthy, like I could make a difference with my research someday.

It was a seven year program, pretty expensive, but I was willing to put in the time and cost to do what I wanted most of all. I thought maybe I'd be the next Jonas-Salk, and create a vaccine to wipe out polio. Except that I was fascinated with the brain and how it worked, how it controlled so much of our basic progression through our life - and its decline. I was full of questions that needed to be answered, and college was a way to get them."

He stopped, "Sorry, I got off the track there!" He took another small drink and set it down.

"I'm finding it very interesting. It's good to hear somebody have so much passion in what they want to do. Please, go on," Judy encouraged.

"Well, I was living in a small apartment near the campus at the time. My folks helped me pay my tuition, but it was too much for them to afford to pay for a campus room. So I found this little place, rather run down, but cheap. Half the time the heat didn't work, and I had to use a plunger on the toilet every other day- but, hey! It was home." He chuckled, remembering the challenges of living there. "I was able to tutor a few other students on my study break to bring in a little spending money, too. So it wasn't too bad of a set up, actually. For a college student, anyway," he was quick to add.

"I never was one for cooking much, and I wasn't about to try it on the temperamental stove in the apartment, fearing that I'd burn the place down! So I usually ate cold foods, like sandwiches and chips or found something easy to heat in the beat up old microwave that I bought at a second hand store.

Whenever I felt in the mood to splurge, I liked to go to a little restaurant near the university. It was called "Betty's" or "Barnie's" or something along those lines! I'd almost forgotten about it. I'll have to ask Sondra about the name.

It was one of those little places stuck off the beaten path. It had the traditional plastic table cloths, faded, tacky curtains, that lovely stale cooking grease smell in the air!" This made Judy laugh, just as he'd intended. "It had pretty good food for a reasonable cost, so it got the business of a lot of us poor, starving college students. I usually sat in one certain section because there was a real pretty girl working there, and that was her area. She had the prettiest blue eyes, dark blonde hair cut in one of those short hair cuts," he waved his hand below his ear level.

"A page boy cut?"

"Maybe.   Anyway, it's a lot longer now, down to her shoulders, and I like it that way better. Longer hair is prettier, sexier..." He stopped, realizing the woman across from him had long hair. "She was in her early twenties then, just a little more slender than she is now, before having two kids.   I wasn't especially attracted to her, but I know a beautiful woman when I see one! And the apron they had to wear, with the bib up over the chest, accented her...hmm...accented her bosom!" Judy again laughed with him. He went on to describe a little more about the restaurant and the young waitress. Then he fell silent.

He was lost in thought for a while, and Judy didn't interrupt, thinking it was healthy for him to be remembering some of the things he'd blocked out from his past.

Suddenly back to the present, Arnie smiled shyly, looking down at his hand around his glass. Noticing it was leaving a wet trail down the side, he wiped the condensation off with a napkin, then blotted the table where it sat. He knew he was stalling.

Judy reached out and placed her warm hand over his colder one. "It's okay. You don't have to continue if you don't want to."

"No, I'm all right. I'd like to tell you - if I'm not boring you to death!" She gave him a warm smile and told him to go on when he felt ready.

Taking a deep breath, he said, "Not having any real close friends I could talk to-if you didn't count the med students I'd go out with once in a while for a quick beer or a game of pool. I quickly became friendly with the girl, and made a point of coming to the restaurant as much as I could. After a while, she got to know what my favorite dishes were, to hold the mushrooms without me asking, and sometimes she would sneak me a dessert!" He paused for effect. "Do you know who that young girl was?"

"Sondra."

"Yes, it was Sondra."

Judy found the tale romantic, and told him so.

"I don't know about romantic, but it was nice. I enjoyed spending time with her at the restaurant, but I never asked her out or anything."

"Why not?"

"On my poor salary? I was a pauper! I wouldn't have been able to take her out to the movies very often, or buy her nice dinners somewhere. I could afford it once in a while, but girls expect more. And, to be honest, I'm not sure I even thought about dating her. I had a good time talking and joking with her whenever I came in, but I can't say that I missed her company when I was at class, or at home studying." He was trying to be as straightforward as he could with Judy. He wanted to paint a real picture of how it was, without glamorizing it, so she'd know how he truly felt at the time. Something he hadn't let himself think about for years.

"About a year after meeting Sondra, I went there to get breakfast one morning and found her sitting in a booth in a corner, crying. When I asked her what was wrong, she wouldn't say. She was quiet, and wouldn't talk to me, no matter how much I tried to get her to open up.

Finally, the manager, who had known me from coming in all the time, called me over. He told me that Sondra had a huge fight with her stepmother, who she'd been living with, and her stepmother kicked her out!

I found out from Sondra later on that her real mother died of some kind of cancer when Sondra was eight, and her father had later re-married a younger woman who resented having to raise somebody else's kids. So, once Sondra's Dad passed away a few years back, and wasn't there to buffer things between his wife and daughter anymore, they had a lot of arguments. Sondra's younger sister, Libby, had it a little better, because she didn't look like their real mother, like Sondra did. But their stepmother was always finding things to complain about with Sondra. Nothing she did was good enough."

Arnie's throat was getting dry from so much talking, so he had to stop and take a cold drink before he could go on with his story. He was amazed that he had so much to tell, but even more so that

Judy chose to stick with it and listen.

"I felt sorry for her after I heard she had no place to stay, so I went over and sat next to her. I told her I knew why she was upset and that I would help her pay for a motel for a few days, maybe a week, until she could find someplace else to live. She was embarrassed and wouldn't think of accepting my help. But when I asked her if she had another place to go, she shook her head no and started to cry again."

Judy interrupted to ask what the fight had been about with the stepmother.

"I don't know now. I think it was just something she started as an excuse to kick Sondra out. She was a bitch, according to Sondra and Libby. They were both glad to leave her household, and I don't think either of them have ever seen her since."

Judy murmured something to the affect that it was a shame, then waved her hand for him to keep going.

Picking up where he left off, Arnie said, "I felt sorry for her, but I felt close to her, too. I wanted to help her out, so I insisted she let me help her with a motel. She finally agreed, on the condition that she would pay me back every cent. I told her I'd come and pick her up after her shift was over and take her to a motel where she could stay. Then I took off for class, feeling pretty good about the good deed I was doing.

So, about six that evening, after a quick dinner at her restaurant while she finished up her shift, I drove her to a little motel not far from there that I had heard was cheap but fairly decent. There was a 'No Vacancy' sign outside. So I drove down the road to another one, same thing. The manager inside told me there was a big convention in town, and we wouldn't be able to find a room anywhere in town all week.

I could see that Sondra was feeling pretty desperate, so I told her she was welcome to stay at my apartment if she felt she could trust me. She knew I hadn't contrived the whole thing just to get her into my apartment, so she told me she did trust me and that she would accept my offer until she could find another place to stay.

When I gave her a tour of her new digs she was nice enough not to comment on how shabby the place looked. I was embarrassed to bring her in there, but..."

"She wouldn't have said anything, she was probably too happy to have a place to sleep." Judy pointed out.

"Yeah, I know. But I still remember how mortified I felt to see it through her eyes that day. I gave her the little bedroom, and I took the sofa in the living room. The way my feet hung off the end, it would've been funny if it hadn't been so sad.

I finally fell asleep, but woke up again around midnight. I heard someone crying. You could hear all kinds of stuff through those thin walls, so I wasn't sure, at first, where it was coming from. Then I realized it was coming from my bedroom, that it was Sondra crying.

I knocked on the door and went in when she didn't answer. I knew she was probably too ashamed that I'd heard her crying. I found her curled up on the bed, sobbing into her hands. She looked so lost and scared. So I went right over and sat down on the bed beside her, putting my arms around her to try to comfort her and get her to stop crying. I don't recall what I said to her, probably something about 'it'll be all right,'- the usual crap."

Arnie stopped and sat back in his chair, letting his breath out with a whooshing sound. He looked around the restaurant, suddenly self-conscious about the topic, worried that the people around him might have heard. He didn't feel so bad when he saw that the tables around them were empty. That there was, in fact, hardly anyone else there.

He avoided looking at Judy as he broached the next part of his tale.

"Sondra wrapped her arms around me when I sat down. It felt good. I felt like we were as close as we had ever been in the last year. And then we were kissing. I don't remember who started it, or if it was mutual, but there we were. Then things just kept heating up, and, well..." He cleared his throat. "We slept together for the first time that night. I'm sure I don't need to go into details." Judy shook her head.

"Next morning when I got up, she'd made me breakfast. We didn't talk about what had happened the night before, but I'm sure we were both thinking about it. I dropped her off at the diner and went to my classes at the "U". We started sleeping together every night after that. She'd make my breakfast, kept the apartment clean, and washed my clothes. It was a comfortable feeling, I liked it. So I didn't push her into finding her own apartment. It sounds kind of cold now, but I figured we were both content with the arrangement. I only had about four months of school left and I wasn't planning on staying in Portland once the semester ended. I suppose I thought it would just end all by itself once I was ready to pack up and head for Seattle, where I wanted to work. We weren't in love, but we liked the routine we'd established, so we both let it go on as it was.

Then almost three months into the relationship, I came home and Sondra hadn't started dinner like she always did before. She took the bus home, so it was natural for her to get dinner going. When I got home about a half-hour later, I'd help with whatever I could. I found her lying on the bed. She didn't say anything when I asked her what was wrong, was she sick. I went over to the bed and sat down, and I could see in the dim light that she'd been crying. Her eyes were puffy, her hair was all tangled up like she'd been tossing and turning in bed. When I asked her again to tell me what was wrong, she sat up slowly and blurted that she was pregnant!

I was shocked! It was the last thing I'd expected to hear her say. I couldn't believe it and didn't know what to say. I asked her if she was sure, and she said she'd left work early to go to the doctors two days prior and had just received the news on the phone.

She got all teary-eyed and asked what were we going to do. Now, I may not always act like it, but I'm from a very Christian family. So I didn't believe in getting an abortion, although I decided not to mention that possibility to her and get her upset.

We considered the options – marriage, raising an illegitimate child. In those days it still turned heads and got tongues wagging if a woman had a baby without a husband. Sondra insisted I didn't have to marry her just because she was carrying a baby. I, myself, didn't know what to do.

"I ended up going to the university library to think. I couldn't figure out how this had happened, we had been careful to use birth control. I started to wonder if maybe she got pregnant on purpose. But I knew Sondra had looked into taking night classes at the "U" this coming quarter. She had been pretty excited when her application for a grant had gone through to help pay for her tuition. When we first started talking at the restaurant, she had often mentioned wanting to become a pharmacist someday. She had already taken a few classes the previous semester. I couldn't see her sabotaging her career plans to get married to somebody she wasn't passionately in love with.

The more I sat there thinking about it, though, the more I started to see what probably had happened. That first night, when Sondra was so upset, we made love without any protection. You never think anything can happen after once, and we were very careful from then on, but apparently, it was too late.

We didn't talk anymore when I got back home, but I slept on the couch that night. I didn't get very much sleep, and by the way Sondra looked in the morning, neither did she. For the first time I was aware that she was in the bathroom throwing up. I'm not sure if I just didn't hear her before or if she was able to wait until after I left each morning. I felt very bad that she was going through that. I decided that I couldn't live with my conscious if I left her or allowed her to have an abortion if she wanted to have one. After all, I was partly responsible, and should be man enough to accept that responsibility. I couldn't imagine going through my life knowing I had a son or daughter out there, being raised with another man. I always wanted kids, although not like this!

So, I told her I wanted to marry her and raise our baby. Sondra got tearful again, but with relief and happiness this time that the problem would be taken care of. We got married in front of a Justice of the Peace a couple weeks later. Boy! Were my parents pissed at me for not letting them know! My mom was pretty hurt that she hadn't been invited to go witness the ceremony, but we let her throw us a big reception with all the relatives and all, so it soothed her. And she was too excited about her coming grandchild to hold a grudge! My Dad warmed up to Sondra over time, but they never got close. But my Dad doesn't get close to anybody, so it was no big deal.

"Anyway, to make a long story even longer! I finished up my doctorate program, got a nice impressive Ph.D. degree to hang on my future office wall, and we moved to Seattle. I worked at a few piddly jobs until I landed this University job. We bought a nice house, had another baby, and here I am. One big, happily married family man!" He raised his nearly empty glass of scotch in a mock toast, then drank it down.

Judy frowned. "You don't regret any of it, do you? I know you married her out of a sense of obligation, but surely you must have felt something for her after all those years together?"

"Things seemed to be fine after the baby - Heather - was born. Sondra seemed very happy to be a new mother, even though she didn't really know what to do with a newborn when the baby first came! But it seemed to bring us closer. Trying to figure out how to change a twisting, kicking infant is quite an ordeal! But we persevered! And it was fun. We felt like a regular family."

Arnie gave one of those heavy sighs, the kind that seems to come from deep within.

"Then Ashley came along and things were different. I'm sure Sondra loved both girls, but it was like something snapped inside of her after she had a second baby. Her attitude changed, she didn't have any patience with the girls. She'd yell at them over the least little thing. I knew she had a rough childhood. By then she had told me how her stepmother had treated her and Libby. I guess their stepmother yelled at them all the time, so under stress, that's what Sondra would revert to. They say the cycle of abused and abusers continues like that."

"Did you try to talk to her about it?"

"Many times. She just wouldn't admit she had a problem, and if I even hinted that she was turning into her stepmother, things got *real* ugly!"

"So how did you handle it? What about the girls?"

"I tried to be home as soon after work as I could. The girls were in preschool, then regular school most of the day. I encouraged Sondra to look into classes again, but she said she had too much to do taking care of her family right now to take on more work. I didn't seriously consider getting a divorce, but I did run it through my head more than once.

But then, as the girls got older, Sondra seemed to handle it better. She wasn't quite as impatient as she was. In fact, things started getting so much better that we started taking short vacations again, having fun. We even started having sex again, something we had been avoiding for some time. It's hard to make love to somebody when you're ticked off at them all the time!" He grimaced.

"Anyway, these past few months it seems like she's angry at us all over again. There doesn't seem to be a reason, she comes down on the girls all the time, she yells at me or gives me a cold shoulder. It's been getting tough to go home at night. I have thought about how much easier it would be to get a divorce and be done with it. But I think about the girls. I know Sondra will fight for the kids, and I can't live with myself if I lose them. They mean everything to me." Arnie wiped a tear from the corner of his eye. "I just don't know what to do anymore." He sounded so defeated.

Looking up, he saw a tear run down Judy's wet cheek and fall to her lap. She didn't bother wiping the wetness from her face. Arnie was grateful that she was able to commiserate with his sorrow and not make light of it.

"Well, I guess you got more than you bargained for!" he tried to laugh, but failed.

"I'm very glad you told me all that, Arnie. It helps me to

understand you better. Thank you for sharing your sad story." She reached out and took his hand as she said this, giving him a small amount of comfort.

Arnie noticed how bare of patrons the place was. Looking at his watch, he gasped. "It's almost ten o'clock! I can't believe how late it's gotten and I didn't even notice! I've really gotta get out of here!" He stood up quickly, grabbing the check from the table. He hadn't even noticed when the waitress had brought it.

Judy said she hoped her question hadn't ended up getting him into big trouble.

He replied that he'd soon find out! Then he asked her if she'd like a ride home, since taxis would be scarce this time of night on a weekday without calling and waiting for one. She accepted the ride this time.

Arnie drove while Judy gave directions. It wasn't far from the restaurant, less than ten blocks, like she'd said before. He pulled over at the corner where she pointed, and she started to get out after saying the appropriate parting phrases. Arnie stopped her by putting his hand on her sleeve.

"What if I feel like talking to you, assuming you still want to be friends after hearing my pathetic life story! How can I call you?"

Judy put her hand into her pocket and brought out a small white business card. She handed it to Arnie and told him she would be pleased if they could still talk and be friends. "I think there's a lot more I need to find out about you, Arnie," she said, briefly caressing his bristly cheek with a soft, warm hand. Then she was gone.

Arnie, wondering at the sign of affection, then passing it off as a reaction to his sob story, placed the card in his wallet and began to worry about his reception on the way home. He didn't have to worry – *not tonight anyway.* The house was dark and quiet when he got there after ten-thirty. Everybody was in bed, if not asleep. He walked directly to the guest bedroom, not even stopping to look in on the girls this time. His thoughts were filled with Judy, her tear-laden face, her expressions, her caress at the end of the night.

He was very glad he met Judy, a friend he could talk to at such a deeply emotional level. But he wondered if he was fooling himself into thinking there would be no ramifications to his relationship. How long could he kid himself into believing they could remain just friends? And how long before he fell in love with her?

He fell asleep slowly, and dreamed deeply. Of a woman with long, dark hair and two laughing little girls.

Chapter 12

The next time Arnie went to lunch with Murray at The Place restaurant a few days later, the memories of seeing Judy there came rushing unexpectedly in. He looked around, but didn't see her at any of the tables. *I should look for that business card she gave me and give her a call,* he thought. *I wonder where I left it? I really hope Sondra hasn't run across it, but then, she'd just think it was business-related anyway.*

Arnie found himself watching the door, disappointed every time the person entering wasn't Judy. He had a hard time concentrating on what his supervisor was discussing, and finally, picking up on Arnie's lack of attention, Murray cut it short and suggested they get back to the lab and get some work done. For once, Arnie was glad for Murray's lack of interest in why he was so distracted and that he didn't care enough to inquire into it.

Searching through his desk after lunch for the card, he breathed a sigh of relief when he found it beneath a small stack of papers in a side drawer. He remembered putting it there when he was reading over Judy's phone number and one of his co-workers popped in to talk about something with him.

The card was elegantly simple, with gold embossed letters on a white background.

Judy Larson, Consultant

Life Style Designers

There was no address on the card, but Judy's phone number was in black beneath the name of her business. Arnie fingered the card, feeling the raised surface of the gold letters. Picking up the phone, he dialed the number before he could talk himself out of it.

He was thrown off guard when her voice-mail clicked on and instructed him to leave a message. He had expected a secretary, if not Judy herself, to answer. Unprepared, he stammered a brief message. "Hi, this is Arnie. I...uh...I was...uh... just calling to see if you're in town. Nothing important." He quickly replaced the handset, feeling stupid, and immediately wanted to call back and exchange his inane message for something a little more intelligent.

He stared at the phone a while, wondering if he had made a big mistake by calling her. Would she call back today? What would he say? He wasn't even sure why he had called her. Then, pulling some papers closer to him, he tried to get to work and ignore his churning stomach. The phone didn't ring all afternoon.

*   *   *

Three days after Arnie had left his message, Judy returned his call. "Hello. I heard you called?" her smooth voice questioning over his office phone.

Pleased beyond belief that she had called him back, he set his work aside, knowing he wouldn't be able to concentrate and talk to her at the same time. "Do you know any other Arnie?"

"Yes, but only in name." He could hear the smile in her voice.

Before he could lose his nerve, Arnie jumped in. "How about dinner tomorrow night? I feel like talking." He waited for her answer, not realizing he was holding his breath.

"More marriage problems?"

"What, you're also a marriage counselor on the side?" he teased.

She responded with a little laugh, "All women are marriage counselors, haven't you heard! If you need a counselor, Arnie, I'm your woman! And I'll only charge half my usual rate, just for you!"

"Yeah, and what is your rate?"

"Dinner with a most-handsome doctor."

Feeling a little out of his league with the direction the banter was going, Arnie nonetheless responded in kind. "Well, I'll have to see if my supervisor is free! Women seem to think he's quite the catch!"

Judy laughed at his teasing. "No, no, no! I will only accept dinner with my *favorite* doctor, one Mister Arnold Martin, scientist extraordinaire!"

Glad that Judy couldn't see the blush creep up his neck, he asked her if that meant "Yes" to dinner.

She said she'd be happy to have dinner with him tomorrow night, that she had no plans, and they agreed to meet at "their" restaurant by Green Lake at 5:30. Arnie found himself toying with her, telling her that they were really meeting at 6:00, but he told her 5:30 so she would make it there on time. She laughed and, with a cheery "See ya at 5:30, wise guy!" she hung up.

Danny, one of the lab technicians coming down the hall, wondered why Arnie came out of his office with a big grin pasted on his face, looking like he'd just gotten lucky! He made a point of peeking into Arnie's office as he walked past to see if there was any sign of a daytime liaison. No short-skirted bimbo in sight, he quickly went on his way.

*   *   *

When Arnie walked into the restaurant the next evening, he was pleasantly surprised to find Judy already there. Walking up to where she was seated, only a table away from where they sat last time, he commented that she was early. Judy smiled and said, "No, you're late!"

"What!" Arnie looked at his watch. It was 5:32. "Very funny! I'm only two minutes late!"

"Doesn't matter. Late is late!" Laughing, Arnie sat down across from her. He ordered their usual Chivas drinks, admiring how pretty Judy was in her casual slacks and turtle neck sweater, both in shades of green.

"So, what is so important that you wanted to talk to me about?"

She asked, seconds after the waiter left.

"Well, nothing like beating around the bush!" Judy smiled but didn't say anything, waiting. "Nothing really," he confessed. "For some reason I always have a good time just being around you, talking to you. I just needed an excuse, I guess."

"You don't need an excuse to talk to me, Arnie. Remember, we're friends, you can talk to me whenever you want to."

"Just no commitments allowed!"

"Hey, no fair using my words against me!" Judy said in mock offense.

"But it *is* the truth, just the same. This works because there *is* no commitment between us." He felt slightly disappointed to be saying that.

"I suppose you're right." Changing the subject, she asked Arnie how his week had been going.

"Nothing out of the ordinary. No mutant virus went on the rampage, so I guess everything's been going okay!" He got a raised eyebrow, then Judy snickered, before turning serious once more.

"I'd like to find out more about your profession, Arnie. It sounds fascinating. I'm interested in how the brain works, how people get mentally ill, brain disorders, you know?" She leaned forward in anticipation. "Tell me about the brain, Doctor."

"Good God! I don't have the time to go into all that! It took *me* years to learn it, I wouldn't even know where to start!" Arnie was afraid he'd offended her, but Judy just smiled and told him to start anywhere, that she just wanted to know *more.*

"Just give it to me in a nutshell."

"You don't ask for much, do you lady? Let's see if I can simplify it a little for you." He thought about how he could explain the functions of the brain without getting too technical.

"You probably know that a virus or bacteria can affect brain function, just as certain chemicals and drugs can cause cancer or tumors." Judy nodded her understanding. "Likewise, physical and mental abuse can affect how a person functions. You see it all the time with abused children, battered women..."

"Unfortunately, I do see what you're talking about. If somebody is badly treated while they're growing up, it alters how they perceive their world around them, how they interact with other people."

Arnie was impressed with Judy's intelligence. "Exactly. Birth defects and hereditary diseases can also mess with a person's mind. You've heard of the 'self-fulfilling prophecy'?"

"No, what is that?"

"It means, if you think something is going to happen, you tend to do things to make sure it *will* happen. On a sub-conscious level. If you find out you have a high chance of inheriting a bad disease that will cripple you, you might start to get less attracted to outdoor sports, do a lot of things sitting on your butt, thus maybe bringing on the debility faster."

"Yes, I see. But, I would think a lot of people would go out and do a lot of things they think they might not be able to do later, get *more* active, try to *fight* the disease."

"Sure. But it depends on your *mental* condition how you will react. If you've had lots of encouragement and love from your family and friends, you'll probably have a good attitude about not letting it get the best of you without a fight. But if you were mistreated or put down a lot as you grew up, you'll no doubt have a self-defeating attitude instead. It's not just the functions of the brain that's involved, it's the whole *environment* around you."

"Yeah, that makes sense. I never thought of it like that. Tell me more," she said eagerly.

She was leaning against the table, her arms outstretched across it. Her hands were almost touching his own, folded together and resting on top of the tablecloth. He could have easily taken hold of them, had this been a simple case of two people on a date. He restrained the urge, keeping his hands as they were, tightly intertwined.

"First," Arnie bargained. "You tell *me* why a design consultant wants to know about brain disorders?" He was very curious about why she was so interested in something so unrelated to her profession.

Judy leaned back in her chair, drawing her hands back to her side of the table. "Okay, but first, let me explain to you what *I* know about the brain, okay?" Arnie nodded. "The brain is where you hold all your memories. Memories are created by feelings. Feelings from what you see, hear, smell, touch and taste. You use all those senses when you make love, play with your child, enjoy a movie, etc. Those feelings create biochemical reactions, which in turn, make an imprint on the brain and become memories. Memories can be good or bad. To give you an example - I remember my 12th birthday very clearly. Not because it was the best one I'd ever had, it was the worst - my dad had left us. Not scientific, but are you still with me?"

Arnie nodded again. He felt she had a good layman's grasp on the whole idea.

"Well, I believe your memory is what makes you – you. It is a collection of events that make up who you are. Who each of us becomes. If your memories are of bad things, then you act bad because that may be all you know. Kind of like what you said earlier. Am I correct so far?"

"I'm impressed! You have a lot of knowledge about the subject. How did you learn all this?" Their drinks arrived, but neither of them paid attention. The waiter scooped up the money Arnie had left on the table, made change, and left silently.

"I've been interested in the functions of the brain, and how things can affect it. So I've done a lot of reading on the subject. The rest I just assumed or made up!" She grinned at him, taking her first sip of scotch.

"Very good! Now I'm going to be afraid of talking to you about my research – you might know more than me and find errors in my work!" Noticing his own drink for the first time, he picked it up and proposed a toast, "To our brilliance!" They clinked their glasses together, feeling very companionable at that moment.

A few minutes later Judy looked at her watch and told Arnie

she needed to make a phone call. Getting up, she walked towards the entryway, pulling a cell phone out of her purse. Arnie couldn't help but watch how her narrow hips swayed in rhythm with her walk. Then, telling himself he was a dog for doing so, he pulled his eyes away. Glancing down at the floor, he noticed a small gold case. Picking it up, he saw it was a business card holder, plain, with no engraving on the cover. *Judy must have dropped it when she took her phone out of her bag.*

Opening it up, he saw it contained several business cards. Flipping casually through them to see if he recognized any of the names, he realized that the first name on each of the cards was "Judy", followed by a different last name and company title.

Studying the cards more closely, Arnie was puzzled by this. *Who is she? Is she some secret government agent? CIA? KGB?* He scoffed at his paranoia as soon as he thought that. But it got him thinking.

Does this have anything to do with her interest in the brain? Is that why she's been so interested in me? Arnie briefly felt hurt at that thought.

Looking over his shoulder to where Judy had headed, he saw her standing by a potted palm, still talking on her phone. He turned back around and continued to try to figure out why Judy would be in possession of several different identities. He wondered if she was trying to find out more about his research. He'd heard of corporate spies that stole information for other companies. But they weren't nearing any breakthroughs yet. Most of the research was still in the experimental stages, not ready for testing on humans, or publishing. He worked for one of the best research and teaching hospitals, but other labs were working on some of the same projects, it was no secret. *Maybe I should contact one of the other labs and see if they've had snoops around.*

He turned to see if she was on her way back yet – N*ope, still on the phone. I wonder why she had to leave the table to make her call? Does she have a secret code name, like Foxy Lady?* He turned away, a trace of smile on his lips.

He could only wait until she returned. Not knowing why, he stuck the cardholder into the pocket of his jacket.

She was gone for ten minutes, apologizing profusely when she got back to the table. Having lost the mood, Arnie told her it was all right, and asked her if she was ready to go. They both walked out to his car, parked nearby this time. Arnie offered her a lift, which she gladly accepted, pulling her coat closed tightly against the damp night air.

Arnie, deep in thought, didn't talk very much on the drive to her apartment. Judy was puzzled about his silence, but didn't ask him about it, thinking that maybe he was ticked off that she had spent so long on the phone.

When they arrived in front of her building, Arnie surprised her by asking if he could come up and use her washroom, that his stomach was a little upset. Relieved, assuming that that was the cause of his change in mood, she invited him up.

Arnie, his stomach just fine, had decided to do a little investigating. He pulled the car into a space and they both got out. She led him through the front lobby door, where an elderly, blue uniformed security guard was sitting at a small desk, reading.

"Good evening, Miss."

"Good evening, Sam. How are you?"

The security guard looked Arnie over, saying he was fine as they passed through the lobby to the elevator. Seeing that all was well, he returned to his book.

Going up the elevator to the twelfth floor, Judy asked Arnie what was wrong.

"I don't know, maybe it was something I had for lunch." He watched the numbers climb. "This is a very nice building. Must cost a fortune!" There was a gentle ping, and the elevator doors swooshed open.

She returned his smile as they stepped off the elevator and turned towards her apartment down the hall. "Maybe."

They stopped at her door. She turned towards him, her expression cautious. "This is the first time I have invited a man into my apartment."

"You didn't invite me. Technically, I invited myself. Does that mean you trust me?" He looked into her dark eyes.

She seemed to think about that before answering, not letting go of the contact between them. "Yes, I think it does. Besides," she reminded him lightly, turning back to her door, "it's not the *trust* that's an issue, it's the *commitment!*"

Smiling, she unlocked the door and flipped on a light just inside the entry. Arnie whistled in awe as he followed her in. It was decorated like a small palace. Beautifully upholstered furniture, sculptures positioned at various corners in the large living room, what looked like original paintings on the walls, and heavy, shimmering gold curtains hanging practically from ceiling to floor. Arnie was amazed, and speechless.

He had forgotten why he had come up here until Judy gently nudged him towards a door leading out from one side of the room. "It's that way."

"Hm? What is that way?"

She smiled in amusement, "The bathroom is that way. Through that door."

"Oh, I forgot! Your decor blinded me!" Even the bathroom was impressive. It had a double-headed shower behind the cream-colored shower curtain, as well as a cream outer curtain accented by splashes of pink, peach and light blue and green. It was very neat, and organized. A ceramic cup, soap dish and toothbrush holder sitting on a marbled gray counter matched the peach rugs and tank covers. It boasted a floor so clean you probably *could* eat off of it, Arnie thought.

Feeling like a sneak, he opened the medicine cabinet a few inches, hoping it wouldn't squeak. Only the usual aspirin, box of Band-Aids, and other basic medicines were inside. He figured she must keep her more personal items in another bathroom in her bedroom. Running water and pretending to clean up, he came back out to join Judy, again amazed at the expense and care that had gone into creating such a beautiful apartment.

"Can I offer you something to drink? Or maybe coffee, if you'd rather?" Judy was standing in front of a glass-encased oak cabinet. There were many bottles of liquor in the cabinet, of various size and color. Judy was holding a decanter of Chivas Regal Whiskey in her hand, ready to pour it into a small crystal glass. At Arnie's assent, she poured out a measure of the amber liquor, reaching into a black ice bucket to drop a few small ice cubes into the glass. She had gone out to the kitchen to get the ice during his absence.

"You're not joining me?" he asked when she came towards him with only the one glass of whiskey

"No, not this late. I can't sleep if I have too much alcohol, and I already had my quota at the restaurant. But I will have a little Kahlua to help me digest all that food I ate earlier." They each had one glass, sipping it between idle conversation.

She invited him to sit down on the gold and cream couch, sitting on the opposite end, her body turned to face him, her legs curled up under her. The picture of relaxation.

Arnie took a full sip of his drink. Looking her directly in the face, he asked, "Judy, who are you? Are you with the FBI? CIA?

*   *   *

Her mouth dropping open in initial surprise, she quickly recovered. "Oh, my!" she laughed. "Why on earth would you think that?"

Embarrassed now, Arnie pulled the gold cardholder out of his pocket and handed it to her. Judy took it from him, fingering it absently.

"You dropped this at the restaurant. Why the different names? What's your *real* name? I can't help wondering if all this has to do with why you're interested in the brain. In my work." He waved a hand around at their surroundings, "How can you afford this apartment as a design consultant? They can't be getting paid *that* much, or I'm in the wrong business!"

Judy had turned a little red at his tirade. "You've gotten yourself worked up over nothing, I assure you."

"I've asked myself many times why somebody like you would be interested in me. A married man, with a boring job. No real money to speak of. Now I know you want something from me, definitely not my body, right? What? Information? You cheated me!"

"Oh, how do you figure that?" She was getting just as angry as he was now. She stood up, looking down at him. Making him wonder if he had gone too far. "How was I cheating you?" she asked loudly. "I never offered you anything but friendship! I enjoyed talking to you, no commitment, nothing but companionship! Just like I told you from the start. You want to know who I am and what I do? I don't think you can handle the truth!" She was standing very closely to Arnie now, her legs almost touching up against his own, fists on her hips, her face contorted in anger.

"I can handle anything you tell me, as long as it's the truth this time!" he yelled back.

Not stopping to think about what she was saying, Judy shook her finger at him. "My name *is* Judy Larson, just like I told you. I *am* a design consultant. But I'm also a companion with an escort service. I am a high-class companion for rich, high-profile people. *That's* where my money comes from, if you need to know! I get paid to escort rich people around, keep them company, show them around town if that's what they want, attend parties to make them look good...." Judy stopped, seeing the color had fled from Arnie's face at this unexpected confession.

"You get paid to have sex with these people? You're a hooker?" The disgust was obvious in his voice, which made Judy angry all over again.

"I am *not* a hooker!" she said emphatically. "Yes, sometimes I choose to make love to one of the men or women I escort. Just as anybody would on a date. I get paid to keep them *company*, I have *sex* with some of them for my own pleasure!" she clarified.

132

Confused, Arnie was having a hard time absorbing all this information. "Wait, you make love to women, too? Are you gay?"

Tiredly, Judy started to walk away. "I don't owe you any explanations. Just go! I thought I had found an understanding friend, I was wrong." She stopped at a doorway, probably leading into her bedroom, he supposed.

"Why didn't you tell me all this in the first place?"

"You give yourself too much credit, Arnie. Would you have given me the time of day if I had told you, 'Hi, I'm in the escort business. Would you have dinner with me?' Of course not! You're all alike. You choose to believe the worst in people."

Recovering from her shocking news, that served to make Arnie angry all over again. He stood up, "That's not true!"

"Just go. Go back to your comfortable little family and your dull little life. And it would be to your own benefit not to spread this all over the world, since it'll be *your* reputation that suffers, too, from being seen with a 'hooker'!" She turned away so Arnie couldn't see the tears that had started to run down her face.

Arnie stalked to the door. "Fine!" he exclaimed, slamming the door behind him.

On the elevator ride back down to the lobby, Arnie started to feel lousy. About losing her as a friend, how awful he treated her. He was glad the security guard was dozing at his desk when he reached the main floor.

Picturing Judy's distraught face, he felt empty inside as he walked towards his car. His mind far away, he didn't hear the car speeding towards him from behind as he opened his door and prepared to climb in.

Although just a glancing blow, he was hit hard, thrown into the air along with the car door, which took the brunt of the blow, and cushioned his landing several feet away. Luckily, he was unconscious when his body hit the hard unyielding pavement, the mangled car door beneath his shoulders and head. If not for this, he would have surely been killed by the impact.

Hearing the noise, and seeing the taillights of the hit-and-run driver fishtailing out of sight, a witness called 911. Soon the night was lit up with the red and blue flashing lights of the police and ambulance vehicles.

Upstairs, unaware of the commotion, Judy did not see the ambulance take Arnie to the nearest hospital, stanching the blood from a slight head wound. Trying to get the incident out of her mind, she settled into her deep bathtub, brimming with bubbles, not seeing the grisly scene below her, or the wallet a cop picked up near the battered door. Nor was she aware of the cop going through the wallet to locate the victim's address to notify the nearest relative of the tragedy. Sighing deeply and taking a large swallow of her scotch, Judy closed her eyes, slid down in the tub as far as she could, leaving her mouth and nose above water, and tried to forget that Arnie Martin had ever come in to her life.

Chapter 13

Just before 1:00 a.m., a police cruiser pulled up to the Martin house and two police officers, a man and a woman, walked up to the door and rang the bell. No response, the house remained dark. They tried it again, accompanied by a loud knock. After the third try, lights began coming on in the house, and eventually, a woman peeked out of one of the living room curtains to see who was making all the noise this late at night.

With an expression of trepidation, Sondra asked the cops what they wanted.

"Is this the Martin house?" the policewoman asked her.

"Yes, it is. Is there a problem, Officers?"

"Is Arnold Martin your husband, ma'am?"

Sondra gasped, clutching her robe tighter around her throat. "Is something wrong?" Her heart was beating rapidly. "Where is he? Is he all right?"

"Your husband," said the female cop, "was in a car accident near the Green Lake District. He's alive" she quickly inserted, not wanting the woman to think she'd lost her husband. "He's been taken to Providence Hospital with several injuries. We don't know how severe the injuries are, but he was alive as of several minutes ago. Do you have somebody who can take you to the hospital, ma'am? Would you like us to drive you there?"

Sondra, upset with the news, couldn't think straight at first. "I have two little girls sleeping, I can't leave them. Why would Arnie be out this late? I don't know what to do!"

The woman cop came in and put her arm across Sondra's shoulders, leading her over to a chair to sit down. She told her to calm down, then asked her if she had relatives or a neighbor that could come and stay with the kids until she got back from the hospital.

Sondra thought of Laveen. A call was placed to her neighbor, who came rushing over without changing out of her nightclothes. Laveen tried to assure her that Arnie would be all right, and after several hugs between the good friends, Sondra got into the police car and they drove to Providence.

On the way to the hospital, Sondra asked the officers where the accident had taken place. Given the information, Sondra couldn't think of anybody they knew in the Green Lake area, particularly not the apartment where they said the accident had occurred. She wondered whom Arnie had been visiting this late. Her mind conjured up all sorts of visions, from drug dealing to a hot, sweaty sexual encounter. She'd soon find out!

Escorted into the emergency entrance and handed over to a helpful intern, Sondra was soon talking with the doctor that had treated Arnie. A broken collarbone, several fractured ribs, and a mild concussion, her husband had been very lucky indeed to come through it alive, the doctor told her. No surgery was required, so he had been moved up to the orthopedic floor, where he was currently under the affects of a strong painkiller and would undoubtedly sleep through the rest of the night. The doctor recommended that she return home and get some sleep, and come back in the morning to see her husband.

Reluctantly agreeing, she approached the two cops, who had been hanging around talking with two employees they knew on the nursing staff. Their shift was ending, and they were willing to take her back home before they returned to the station to make their reports.

Sondra, her worry only partially resolved, would have to wait until morning to get the rest of her questions answered.

The next morning Judy was rebuking herself for how she'd treated Arnie the night before. She told herself it was her own fault that the argument had occurred, and that if she'd been straight with him from the beginning, it may not have happened. She had no inkling that he'd been in an accident when she decided to give Arnie a call and apologize, providing he would even speak to her. Judy picked up the phone and dialed his office number, hoping he wouldn't slam it down again when he heard her voice.

When a woman answered, she asked to speak to Dr. Martin, thinking he must be away from his office, working in his lab. She'd just been lucky to have caught him at his desk the previous times she had called.

"I'm sorry, Doctor Martin isn't available at this time. May I take a message?"

"No, that's all right, I'll call him again in a little while. Do you know when he'll be in his office?"

She caught a hesitancy in the woman's voice before she was told that Doctor Martin wouldn't be available for quite some time.

"Oh, no! Something happened, didn't it!" She pictured him getting mugged on the way to his car, beaten senseless. "You have to tell me! I'm Judy Larson, a good friend of Arnie's. He's okay, isn't he?"

"Well..." The woman had to think it over, then decided it couldn't hurt anything if she told her the truth. "Arnie was hit by a car last night, downtown. He's in Providence Hospital. I haven't heard anything further."

Judy thanked the lady and hung up, praying for the best. She hurriedly got dressed and jumped into a taxi, rushing to the hospital. Stopping at the admissions desk, she inquired as to which floor Arnie was on. Taking the elevator to the Critical Care Unit on the fifth floor, she worried all the way up, knowing her temper had contributed to his accident.

Arriving at the floor, she asked the first nurse she saw for Arnie's room number. She also asked her what condition he was in, and would he be all right. The nurse told her that he was still unconscious from the trauma and the painkillers, but would probably be fine with time. She directed her to a room down the hall and left to answer a call light that was quietly beeping at the nurses station nearby.

In the CCU, the rooms were enclosed by wire re-enforced glass from waist level to about a foot from the ceiling, allowing the nurses a quick view of anything happening in each of the surrounding rooms as they passed by. From her position in the hall, Judy could see Arnie lying on a sterile white bed, tubes leading from his arms to two IV poles nearby. She could also see a lady in the room with him, slender, with shoulder-length dark-blonde hair, seated between the bed and the window. She was holding his still hand, a concerned expression on her face. Judy assumed this pretty woman was probably his wife.

Hearing children's voices behind her, she turned, noticing for the first time a row of chairs along one side of the hall. Two young girls occupied the chairs closest to Arnie's room, quietly talking to themselves. They looked up at her as she turned, and she realized with a start that they were the faces from the photo Arnie had shown her on the plane.

She felt sad for them, knowing how close they were to their father. She was about to say something comforting to the girls when movement caught her eye. The woman had risen and was coming out of the room. Judy moved away from the window and took a seat two chairs down from the girls, pretending to be waiting for one of the other patients.

Seeing their Mom coming out, the girls jumped out and excitedly approached her.

"Mom! Is Dad talking yet? Can we see him?" They crowded up to her, seeking reassurance that all was right with their world.

Now Judy knew for sure this was Arnie's wife, and she carefully studied her, trying not to be obvious. She was even prettier up close, and she could see a resemblance between her and the older daughter. She felt a stab of jealousy.

"Yes, he'll be all right, and no, you can't see him just yet. He's still sleeping. They gave him some pretty strong drugs to keep him from feeling the pain when they set his collarbone. He'll probably sleep for a while longer." Squatting down to their level, she put her arms around both the girls when they gave a mutual groan of disappointment. They laid their heads on each of her shoulders, needing her comfort. Sondra noticed the dark-haired woman seated down the hall and looked over at her, wondering if she, too, had a loved one in one of the beds nearby.

Noticing her attention, Judy smiled at her and told her she had a couple of beautiful daughters. Sondra, self-conscious about her emotions around strangers, stood up, thanked her briefly and herded the girls down the hall, telling them they'd go get lunch down in the cafeteria and give their father time to sleep off the effects of the drugs.

After they left, Judy got up and stood in the doorway, afraid to enter. She noticed how still he was. There was a large bandage poking out from behind his head, and some smaller ones covering abrasions on his chin and left cheek. A nurse came in and checked out the clear bags of liquid hanging on the poles, replacing one that was empty with quick, practiced efficiency, then injecting something into one of the IV leads. Probably some type of antibiotic, Judy presumed.

"Is he in a coma?" Judy asked, not taking her eyes off Arnie.

"No, he's just had a rough time. The doctor had to set his collarbone so it would heal properly, so he's got a healthy dose of codeine going through his system right now. He'll be waking up soon. Are you his sister?" she asked curiously, noticing she had dark hair like the patient. She jotted something down on a clipboard and stuck it back into a bin on the wall of the room.

"No. Just a good friend." She wondered if the nurse would tell his wife that a strange woman had been visiting with her husband. Then she decided she didn't care, and stepped further into the room. "Can I stay with him a while?"

"Only family is supposed to be allowed in here, but...sure, just don't mess with any of the equipment. If an alarm goes off, don't panic. It just means the IV probably ran dry!" she warned with a friendly smile, and left the room.

She told herself she would only stay a few minutes, leaving

plenty of time in case his wife and girls came back. Looking up at the large-faced clock on the wall, she gave herself a fifteen-minute time limit. "No use making more trouble for Arnie." she cautioned herself.

Sitting down in the chair recently vacated by Sondra, she reached out and picked up his right hand, lying limp and pale on the bed covers. The other arm was encased in a blue immobilizer, with a wide strap wrapping around his chest to keep the arm, shoulder and clavicle from moving, and another going up and around his undamaged shoulder and attaching to the wrist of the sling. It was meant to keep the extremity from moving while the delicate bone, located to one side of, and between, the neck and sternum, had a chance to heal properly.

She stroked his hand while she studied his face, realizing how much he meant to her, how close she had come to losing him for good. She hoped that, after his recovery, they could talk about everything, maybe resume their previously comfortable relationship. And, for the first time, she found herself wanting more from this strong, kind man.

Before she could examine those feelings more closely, her thoughts were interrupted by a weak movement from Arnie's hand in her own. She sat up straighter and waited for further signs that he was coming around. His eyes fluttered and he groaned, moving his arm and causing the IV to pull tightly, which activated an alarm.

A different, older nurse hustled into the room in response to the alarm, chasing Judy out of the way so she could silence the alarm and reactivate it. That done, she asked Judy if she was the wife, and getting a negative response, told Judy she would need to leave so the patient could get his rest. "Only family is allowed in here, you can visit him once his strength improves," she admonished. Judy decided she did not like this nurse, but silently obeyed and left the room.

After one more glance at Arnie through the window, she headed for the elevator. She realized it was probably for the best not to be the first face that Arnie saw when he regained consciousness. The elevator pinged, and the doors slid open. Deep in her thoughts, she was startled when Sondra and the girls stepped out. The smallest girl, Ashley, looked up at her as they passed and said "Hello." Judy returned the greeting with a smile, including the whole family. Sondra watched her but said nothing, pulling Ashley closer with a tug on her thin little arm. Judy, feeling like 'the other woman' and not liking it, saw that Sondra was still watching her until the elevator doors closed and blocked her vision.

Leaving the hospital, Judy wondered if she should attempt to see Arnie again. She kept seeing his wife's suspicious stare. She didn't want to make trouble for him. She would wait until tomorrow and see how she felt about it then, she decided.

Chapter 14

After a sleepless night, Judy waited as long as she could, then caught a taxi to the hospital around eleven the next morning. Hoping Sondra wasn't with him, Judy kept looking around as she made her way into the hospital, keeping her eyes out for Arnie's family. Not liking the air of subterfuge, she still was not going to let it stop her from seeing Arnie, if even for just this one time.

She entered the hospital just in time to see Sondra and the two girls coming out of the elevator onto the main floor, and was relieved when they turned in the opposite direction to go out another door leading to the side parking lot.

Standing there pretending to read a bulletin, Judy waited several minutes to make sure they weren't coming back in, then went upstairs, her heart beating quickly with anticipation.

She could see Arnie, propped up in bed, watching TV. The IV's were gone from his arms, his immobilized left arm supported on a pillow. He looked a lot better than he did the last time she'd seen him. She hesitated outside his room, unsure if she should go in. She wondered if he would still be angry at her, blame her for the accident. Maybe he wouldn't want to see her face ever again. Unsure of what to do, her decision was made for her when Arnie looked over at her just then, a big smile on his face, and waved for her to come in. Relieved, she did.

"Hello. What are you doing here?"

She stopped at the foot of the bed. "You're not mad at me?"

"No! Why would I be..." Then remembering, "Oh, forget it. I had no excuse judging you like that. I want to apologize for my behavior." Arnie pointed to the molded plastic chair against the far wall and invited her to sit down.

Judy, happy that he wasn't going to chase her out, pulled the chair up beside his bed and took a seat. "I came to see you as soon as I heard about your accident." When Arnie asked her how she heard about it, she told him about calling his office. "How are you feeling now?"

"Like I fell down twenty flights of stairs! I hurt everywhere, so I try not to move, but I'm feeling slightly better than I did when I first came-to yesterday. It hurts to breath, but I guess I'll live!" He gave her a weak smile. She thought he looked very tired, and said so.

"I've been sleeping off and on all day. I think it's the drugs. Good stuff!"

Gesturing to the arm in the sling, Judy asked him if he'd broken any bones.

"Nothing important," he chuckled, then clutched his left side in pain. He looked over at her, seeing the concern on her face. "Ow!" he whined, trying to get a smile out of her. It didn't work.

"The Doc tells me I broke my collarbone and a few ribs and banged the hell out of my head, but nothing that won't heal good as new," he reassured her. "Scraped the skin off my face and arms in a dozen places, and tore my brand new Docker jeans to shreds, too! Hope they nail the idiot, he owes me some new clothes!" He was trying to lighten up the situation, for both of them. He knew how closely he'd come to being killed.

To Arnie's dismay, Judy burst into tears. "I knew I shouldn't have been so mean to you yesterday! If I hadn't chased you out, you wouldn't have been hit! It's all my fault!" She buried her head in her hands and cried, her relief coming out through her tears. Arnie reached out to brush the top of her dark head with his hand, but a sharp pain caused him to stop and pull it back. Wincing, trying not to make a noise, he told her it was *not* her fault. That if he'd been paying attention, he could have avoided being hit.

When her tears dried up, she dug in her purse for a handkerchief to wipe her face, not concerned whether her makeup had survived, and asked him how the accident had happened.

"I was upset with how I had acted up in your apartment. So I wasn't paying attention to anything. I didn't hear the car cruising at me, so when I opened my car door to get in, I guess it hit the door, and sent me - and the door - flying down the road. Witnesses said the guy kept going, didn't even flash his brake lights! That SOB! Sorry," he added, forgetting to watch his language like he usually did around women and kids. "The cops haven't caught him yet, last I heard, so they don't know if he'd been high, drunk, or just a really bad driver. I'm just glad somebody saw what happened and called the cops! They say if I hadn't landed on the car door, I'd probably be dead - Hey! No more crying!"

Sniffing, Judy gave him a watery smile and told him she wasn't. "Allergies!"

"I don't remember anything after that until I woke up in the hospital yesterday with a gigantic headache. I have no memory of the actual accident, either, which is probably a good thing."

"There's that memory thing again," she said with a little laugh.

"Hey, I'd join you, but it hurts to laugh," he teased, glad she was feeling better about the whole thing.

"I'm really sorry about causing the accident," she apologized again, taking his hand, rubbing it gently where the skin was discolored and purple from the placement of the IV needle.

Squeezing her hand, he again told her it *wasn't* her fault. "Not unless you were driving the car that hit me! Now, I don't want to hear that again, okay?"

"Okay," she agreed. Although, inside, she still considered herself to be at fault.

After the nurse had been in to check his vitals - taking his temperature, blood pressure, and listened to his heart, all part of the routine – Judy told Arnie that she had seen his wife and kids the other day.

Alarmed, Arnie wondered why Sondra hadn't said anything. "You came yesterday?"

"Yes. As soon as I heard the news. But you were still unconscious. Your wife was sitting here," she patted the chair beneath her, "the girls were sitting outside the room. They're very pretty."

"Did you talk to my wife?" Arnie wasn't happy that Sondra had seen Judy. The mention of his wife caused him to pull his hand out from Judy's grasp. Even though nothing had actually gone on, he didn't think he was up to defending himself just yet.

"Yes. And no."

"What's that supposed to mean!" Arnie tried to sit up higher, groaning despite himself. He accepted Judy's help, allowing her to adjust the pillows behind him once he was situated. Her hair, left loose today, brushed against the side of his face as she leaned over to move the pillows, her breast was pushing against his shoulder as she struggled to pull the pillow from behind his back. He couldn't help the thrill of intimacy that it gave him. Realizing where her breast was resting, she backed up and quickly sat back down on the chair, smoothing her short skirt over her legs to cover her embarrassment.

Arnie tried not to enjoy her discomfort. Even injured, he was able to appreciate a soft breast and a very nice pair of legs. Instead, he asked her to clarify her previous statement.

"How can you talk to Sondra, yet not talk to her?"

"Well, she was coming out of the room, and I told her she had two beautiful girls. And she didn't say anything back, just hustled the girls to the elevator to have lunch. So, I guess you could say I talked to her, but didn't really talk to her. See?"

"Did she ask you if you were there to see me?"

"No, that was the extent of our 'conversation'." Arnie was relieved.

"I was sitting further down the hall, she probably thought I was there for some other patient. Why, did she say anything to you?"

"No," Arnie shook his head, careful not to move it too quickly and cause the room to spin. "But then, we don't talk much nowadays. It's just that she's been so quiet lately – except for when we fight. I don't know if I'd recognize if there *was* something specific bothering her. Something's wrong, I know. But, I don't think it's because she knows I'm friends with you. Yet." He took a sip of water, wrinkling his nose at the flat, tepid taste. Seeing this, Judy got up and filled his glass with fresh tap water, letting it run until it was cold. Arnie took a deep, appreciative drink. "Ahh. That's good! This warm room makes my mouth dry all the time."

"It might be the medicine, too. Should I crack a window open?" At his "Please do", she walked over to the window and pulled it open a couple of inches, letting in a small cool draft of air. The sun, earlier peeking out through an occasional patch of blue sky, had now disappeared. It looked like it would rain again, gray clouds moving in from the north.

"That's better. Thanks." While Judy got the water and fixed the window, Arnie had mulled it over and decided to tell her his concerns, since it involved her. "I think Sondra might suspect I'm seeing somebody. I mean, I think she probably suspects I'm having an affair. Boy," he said glumly. "Any way I say it, it sounds bad, doesn't it?" He rubbed his sore neck, taking care not to get too close to the contusion on the back of his head where he'd hit the car door as he landed. It was still covered by a large gauze pad, the edges of which came around and were taped to his neck and just below his ears. It itched.

"She knows the accident took place downtown - where I had no business being - at an hour that I should've been in bed! My own, preferably! I'm sure it's only a matter of time before she asks me what I was doing at that apartment, at midnight. What am I supposed to tell her!"

"But you *weren't* having an affair! You were having a fight with a friend! Tell her that, maybe it'll go better." She tilted her head towards him, giving him a saucy look.

"Thanks bunches, you're a lot of help!" Getting sleepy, he lay back against the pillows. "What do you recommend I tell her?"

"I think you should just tell her the truth. She needs to know you have a female friend. She has to be told before she finds out from somebody else – like a nurse."

"You think it's wise for me to tell my wife I go out for drinks with another woman?"

"If you tell her we're only friends, *just* friends. And that you had dropped me off at my apartment and only came up to use my bathroom. You don't have to mention anything else."

"Do you honestly think she'll believe that nothing is going on between us?"

Through the side window, Judy could see a nurse heading their way. "You have to try. She needs to know. Soon. It's better that *you* tell her." She stopped talking as the nurse entered the room with a covered tray.

"I'm afraid visiting hours are over for awhile. This young man needs to eat some lunch, then have a nice, long nap."

Arnie thought the nap sounded heavenly. The food he could live without.

"I'm happy you are doing better. Get well soon." She started to leave.

Arnie stopped her. "Does that mean you aren't coming back? Won't you come back and visit me later this afternoon?"

Judy thought about the risks. "Maybe," was all she said, as she turned and left.

Chapter 15

Later that afternoon, Judy's phone started ringing while she was going through some of her mail. She absently picked it up and tucked it under her chin, leaving both hands free to slit open the envelopes and pull out the contents. The important items she set aside to look at further, the advertisements and junk mail she tossed into the small garbage can beside her desk. As she said "Hello" into the receiver, she dropped another credit card ad into the growing pile at her feet.

"Hello, Judy. This is Arnie!"

"Well, Hi! I didn't expect to hear from you. You're not home already are you?"

"No, not yet. I thought I'd invite you over to my place, I'm bored out of my mind!"

She laughed, "Your 'place', huh? How can you be bored so quickly, I just left you a few hours ago! Haven't you gotten addicted to the Soaps yet on TV?"

"Not my cup of tea, sorry. Would you consider coming over and entertaining this poor, wounded soldier?"

"What about your wife? I certainly don't want to run into her while I'm there!"

"She just called. She has to take the girls to the PTA open house tonight, so she said she probably wouldn't be able to make it until after dinner tonight. If I don't get a little company before then I'll go mad!" he pleaded.

She laughed again, glad that he hadn't lost his sense of humor in the accident. "Okay, I'll see what I can do. But I have to leave before four o'clock. I have an appointment I don't want to miss."

She waited for him to ask if it was for the escort service, but he remained quiet. She looked at the mess of papers and torn envelopes on her desk.

"Can you give me about half and hour? I'm in the middle of something. Let me finish this up and I'll be on my way, okay?"

He agreed, telling her not to forget about him.

Arriving at the hospital, Judy couldn't stop herself from scanning the lobby for signs of Arnie's family, doing it again when she got to the fifth floor CCU. The young nurse who had let her visit with Arnie that first time stopped her as she passed the nurses station.

"If you're on your way to see Dr. Martin, he was just moved up to the orthopedic floor." Seeing her alarm, she quickly added, "That's a *good* thing! It means he's out of critical status and into general care. It's up on the seventh floor, the nurses at the station can tell you what room he's in."

Judy thanked her and got back onto the elevator. The seventh floor was more active than the previous floor. There were a few visitors standing outside the rooms talking to each other. An elderly patient, in a standard hospital gown, robe, and non-skid bootie socks was strolling slowly down the hallway, getting a little exercise, pushing her IV pole along with her. A few noisy call bells were ringing incessantly at the nurses' station, waiting for the busy nurses and aides to attend to them.

Trying to locate a nurse that could help her, Judy soon gave up and started walking down the hall, looking at the names on each door until she found the right one. Taking a deep, calming breath, she walked into the room, tapping lightly on the door as she did so.

Arnie was very happy to see her and automatically tried to get up. Grimacing, he laid back against the pillows and had to be content to wait for her to come to him.

"You came! I was getting worried. They moved me and just now switched my phone line so I could call out. I'm already starting to get bored!"

"Glad I can keep you company for a while. Nice digs!" She

commented on the lovely white bedspread that so perfectly matched the white sheets and window blinds. Arnie snorted, making sure he held his elbow up against his ribs while he laughed.

Judy sat on the edge of the bed. "So, what would you like to talk about?"

"I don't care, anything." He looked thoughtful, and Judy was almost afraid of what he would say next. "I told you all about myself, how I met my wife, my pathetic little life. I think it's your turn. Let's pick *your* brain for a while." He adjusted his back against the hard pillows and waited, an expectant look on his face.

"You trying to study my brain or me?" She looked around for a chair. This smaller room boasted a tiny sink and a door that supposedly led to a bathroom, but no chair to encourage visitors. Shrugging, she got comfortable on the edge of the bed, pulling her jeans-clad knee up onto the mattress, her other leg dangling down to the floor.

"Okay, I guess that's fair. Let's see..."

"I was born in Seattle, and I went through all my school years here, too. We had a very nice house – I can still see it in my mind. I was an only child, so I got a lot of things many kids didn't get to have because they had to share everything with their siblings. Like clothes, new shoes, special toys – my own bedroom. I think some of the kids were only my friends so they could play with my cool stuff!" She laughed, not at all upset with that memory.

"My mother and father met when they were in high school, but they didn't get married for several years after that, so they knew each other a long time before they got married.

"Mom was working in a bakery part-time and would bring home all kinds of sweet smelling goodies! I love donuts to this day! My Dad worked in construction as a supervisor and was making pretty good money for those times. He went wherever the company sent him to work, so he was out of town a great deal. Often for months at a time until a project was completed. Then he would be home for a few days or weeks, until the next job was bid on and he had to go handle it. Most of the time the jobs were local, but once in a while they accepted special projects that took them out of state.

"One day my Dad was sent to Dallas, Texas. I don't remember what they were building, but my father was excited about going because it would be bringing in a lot of money for the company. He spent a lot of time on the job sites, but he was also in the offices and job shacks, dealing with contractors, making sure every detail was completed on time so they could get a bonus for finishing ahead of schedule – or fined for missing the deadline. You could always tell when that happened! He was not a fun person to be with until the next project took him away from home again and put him back into a good mood.

"Anyway, when he went to the job in Dallas, he was gone for over two months. He called my mother only once in a while, but he was never one to like talking on the phone, so my mother had learned to just accept this over the years. My father came home after the job was done and told us he was moving out. He had fallen in love with the assistant in the office, and had been having a "relationship" with her for the past two months. My Mom never suspected. I was twelve years old. I couldn't understand what had happened.

"It made a huge impact on me, losing him like that. I rarely saw him after that; he was too involved with his new life. My Mom was in shock. She quit going to work, and soon we couldn't afford to keep living in the house – plus it was too hard on my mother to live where all those memories of my father were. So we sold it and moved into a small apartment further downtown.

"My mom started to work again, but she was barely functioning. I heard her crying a lot at night. She would tell me that it was only because of me that she's still living, that she loved my father so much and couldn't believe he'd do this to her. I was worried about her, and scared. I blamed my father for what was happening to my mother, but, because I was only twelve, I also started blaming *all* men for our troubles. I started hating men, telling myself I would *never* get married and allow a man to hurt me like that. I decided I would never have kids, so they wouldn't have to hurt like I was hurting."

Judy stopped to collect herself. Arnie didn't say anything to break the mood.

"My mother's behavior started to change. She stopped taking care of herself; she wasn't bathing, she would forget to eat. Her hair, the same color of my own, so soft and long, was now stringy and unwashed. Her memory even started to fail.

"I was planning on going to law school after graduation. I got an A+ on most of my subjects, and I was considered one of the top students in my entire school. But my mother's condition was getting worse. She wasn't working anymore, her memory was starting to cause problems with bill collectors and the landlord - money was getting very tight. With my excellent grades, I could have applied for a scholarship, but I had to start rethinking my career plans. Did I want to go to law school, or find a way to support and take care of my ailing mother? I ended up dropping out of school before graduation and looking for work. I got a job as a receptionist with an insurance company by dressing up in one of my mother's nice dresses and putting my hair up in a bun to make myself look more mature and hide my real age.

"My mother was pretty sick by then. "I had to rush home, bathe her, force her to eat. She stayed in bed all day, so at least I didn't have to worry about her wondering away and getting hurt. My wages managed to cover our basic expenses. Once in a while my father would send us a little money, but he had several other kids to support by then. He refused to get involved any further in our lives. I didn't even know where he was living, since the checks he sent us always came through his job.

"I was eighteen years old, taking care of a sick parent. After a while it got to be too much and I let the doctors check her into a mental hospital. She's still there. I visit her once in a while, but she doesn't even know who I am anymore." Judy realized that at some point in her story Arnie must have taken hold of her hand,

and she was currently clasping his tightly. She released his hand and stood up, letting the blood flow through her tingling legs.

"So, now you know why I'm interested in how the brain works."

"Yes, I guess I do understand now. I'm very sorry you had such a traumatic childhood."

"Thanks. Well, it's getting late, I have to go. Once more my reputation has been sullied!" she joked, referring to the fact that it was past four o'clock.

"Sondra will be here soon. I'll come back tomorrow, and we can talk some more, if you'd like." Judy felt like a load had been lifted off her shoulders. Maybe confession *was* good for the soul, she thought.

"I'd like that. Same time, if you can make it? Sondra's coming in the morning after she drops the girls off to school. She said she had a lot of things to do later, so doesn't expect to make it back at all in the afternoon. Guess the honeymoon's over!" he said wryly.

"I'll do my best," she said with a little salute, then turned and waved as she left.

Arnie started to feel lonely as soon as she rounded the corner. He pulled the extra pillow out from behind his back and tried to get some rest, Judy's sad story tumbling around inside his head.

He admired her courage, a young girl, a teen-ager, really, dropping out of school to support an ailing mother. Yet she was always pleasant, smiling easily. He found himself comparing her childhood to Sondra's. *A lot of similarities. Why couldn't Sondra have remained as cheerful and pleasant?* He immediately felt terrible about thinking that.

He was still going over the story when Sondra arrived with the girls in tow. Ashley, seeing her father awake and up, scurried over to the bed and hopped up on it. She would have given him an exuberant hug if her mother hadn't reached in and pulled her back at the last moment. She wasn't happy about it, but she settled for hugging his right side, and placed a gentle little kiss on a bare patch on his cheek. "Ooh," she complained, rubbing her lips. "You're porky piney! You need a shave!"

"Yeah, well, I'm glad to see you, too, pizza breath!" Ashley giggled and settled in against his uninjured side, pulling the covers protectively up to her Daddy's chin.

After Arnie was greeted by the other two with semi-hugs and kisses, he asked the girls how school had been, how the open house had gone.

"I don't want to go to school, Daddy. I want to stay here and take care of you." Ashley announced.

"Sorry, kiddo, no can do. You need to get a good education so you can support your old man!" He loved hearing Ashley laugh and squeezed her tightly against him until she squealed "I can't breath!" before letting her go.

Sondra put a pack of cookies on his nightstand. "How are you feeling?"

"A lot better. The doctor said I might get to go home in another day or so – if I'm able to get out of bed to pee, that is!"

Heather, standing on his left side, rolled her eyes.

"Hey, that's important!" he joked. "Having my girls around me makes me feel better already!" He noticed Sondra was not smiling and asked her what was wrong.

"What were you doing downtown so late, Arnie, the night of the accident. Are you having an affair?" she asked quietly.

He couldn't believe she would ask this in front of the girls, and told her this was not the time or place to be discussing something like that.

"I need to know," she persisted. "Are you seeing someone else?"

"No, I'm not having an affair, Sondra! You know me, why would you even think that?"

"How would I know that? You're behavior has said otherwise."

"Because I'm telling you right now, I'm *not* having an affair. That's the end of this conversation, I refuse to talk about anything like that with the girls present," he said firmly. Both girls were sullen, watching their parents. Arnie gave them a smile and told them that everything was going to be all right.

He got them to talk about the open house, what they've been doing with their friends, and soon they were excited to be with their Dad again.

"What do you do here all day, Dad, watch television?" Heather had noticed the small TV up by the ceiling.

"I wish I could stay in bed and watch TV all day," added Ashley.

"No, I mostly sleep. Sometimes my friends drop by to visit for awhile, I read the newspaper, flirt with the nurses," he said with a wink. The girls laughed, Sondra cracked just a tiny glimmer of a smile.

"Can we stay here with you tonight?" This from his youngest.

"And where would the two of you sleep?" He waved a hand at the small room.

"With you!" Ashley exclaimed, snuggling up even closer.

Arnie laughed and said he'd be home soon and then they could sleep with him if they wanted to. He ignored Sondra's displeased expression. She had always believed that it was detrimental to a child's welfare to sleep with a parent. They needed their own bed, their own room to feel secure, she insisted.

The rest of the visit went well, but soon Arnie, feeling the effects of his long day, let out a giant yawn.

"We'd better let Daddy sleep so he can get well and come home. Say good-bye, let's go!" Sondra leaned over and gave him a light kiss, automatically moving a wisp of hair that was hanging down close to his eye. He missed her affections, he thought.

Was it too late for them? Thinking of Judy, he wondered if he *wanted* to pursue repairing their relationship at this point in his life. He was still struggling with it when he fell into a deep, dreamless sleep.

Chapter 16

It was late the next morning when Judy walked into hospital room 714. Arnie was propped up in bed, the local newspaper spread out across his lap. He was trying to turn the page with one hand but it kept buckling in the middle. Seeing movement out of the corner of his eye, he raised his head and saw her as she stepped through the door. He thought she looked gorgeous, and was inordinately pleased that she had come.

"I was wondering if you were going to show up or not!" He tried to fold up the newspaper, but it had a mind of it's own, so he gave up and let it slide to the floor. Judy picked it up, folded it neatly and placed it on his nightstand, "tsk, tsk"-ing at him as she did so.

"Thanks."

"I had to think about it, but here I am." Arnie pointed her to a chair that had appeared since her last visit, and she sat down. Arnie didn't need to ask what she had to think about. He knew it was a risk for her to come to visit him, chancing a run-in with his wife and the scene it would ultimately cause.

"Have Sondra and the kids been here this morning to see you?"

"Yes, they came right after breakfast. Poor things, they didn't want to go to school, they wanted to stay with me instead." He recounted the events of the previous evening, when Ashley wanted to spend the night with him. "They miss me." He knew exactly how they felt.

"How much longer do you think you'll have to stay in the hospital? When does the doctor say you'll get to go home?"

"Maybe another day or two. They want to make sure my ribs

heal a little more before I get too mobile so I don't puncture a lung or something. And I can barely get out of bed yet. So guess I'm stuck here a while longer." Arnie shifted in bed, using his right arm to try to scoot up a little. Unable to get anywhere, limited by the sharp pain in his side and the inability to use his left arm at all, he ended up putting the electric bed down flat, then pushing with his legs until he was higher. Being naked under the flimsy facility gown, he tried to keep the blankets covering his lap while he did so, not willing to show his bare legs – or anything else- to his visitor. He was then able to raise the head of the bed and sit more comfortably. He heaved a big sigh when it was all over.

Hearing clapping, he turned towards Judy and found her smirking at his acrobatics. "Bravo!" she teased. "I see you have mastered the art of bed mobility."

"Yup! I'm a pro now. If it wasn't for this," he slapped the bulky blue immobilizer over his left arm, "I could do a lot more," he grumbled.

"How long do you have to wear it?"

"Four to six weeks! Over a month, can you believe that?" He shook his head at himself. "That's what I get for being stupid! I was thinking of taking a few days off, but I never thought I'd be spending them like this!" He had to laugh though, finding it amusing despite himself. But that caused his chest to heave, which resulted in a stab of pain, and the humor quickly fled. Judy jumped up to see if there was anything she could do. He waved her away, keeping his eyes closed until the pain in his side subsided.

"They lied, laughter is *not* good for the soul," he groused.

Eyes twinkling, Judy pointed out, "I guess now we know why you're not ready to go home." He breathed shallowly, afraid to take a deeper breath. But he returned her smile.

"At least they took off the bandage on the back of my head this morning, see?" He turned his head, careful not to twist his trunk, and showed her the back of his head, hair matted and discolored with blood. Judy wrinkled her nose and turned away from the sight. "They can't give me a shower yet, but the nurse said the aid will be in later to sponge me off. They have to let my noggin heal a bit more before I can get my hair washed."

Then, feeling like paying her back for making fun of him earlier, he watched her face as he described his wound. "You should've seen the bandage when they took it off. Completely gross! Hair sticking to the blood and goo that oozed out of my skull, you could hear it crackling as they pulled it away from my head – ouch!" He grimaced in not-so-imaginary pain.

Judy squinted her eyes, her lips thin and drawn to one side. He saw her swallow like it went down hard. "Okay," he took pity on her. "It wasn't too bad. I didn't even see the bandage; they tossed it before I could ask to see it. And it hurt like a son-of-a-gun!" He rubbed the tender spot very carefully where the dried blood was causing his scalp to itch.

"So, what did you do yesterday after you left here?" He continued to gently explore the wound on the back of his head.

Judy smiled. "Do I hear a question behind the question?"

"Why do you say that?" He started rubbing the scraped spot on his chin, wondering if he'd have a scar. They had removed that bandage earlier, also. The cut on his cheek was deeper, requiring several stitches. He must have cut it on a sharp piece of metal on the torn car door. They told him he'd need to keep that one covered for a few days yet to prevent infection from setting in.

"Never mind, not important. I went to my apartment, got dressed, and went to a big party downtown with a client." She avoided looking him directly in the face.

"Did you have fun?" Arnie fought off that jealous twinge again, knowing he had no right to feel it.

"Yes and no." She wondered if Arnie was ready to hear more about her "other" life. "Yes, I had fun because there was good food, some great music playing, I got to speak with a few people I don't see very often. And no, because it was rather a stuffy function. The Seattle Mayor, the state Governor, and some other

VIP's were there. Not," she clarified, as Arnie tilted his head in interest at the titles, "as impressive as it sounds. I've never been into listening to politics as entertainment!"

"We never finished our conversation from last night." Arnie abruptly interjected.

Judy blinked, not expecting such a dramatic change in topic. "Which was...?"

"You were telling me about your mother ending up in a mental hospital when you couldn't handle it anymore." He held her gaze.

"Oh. Are you sure you want to hear more? It's not that interesting." She looked away, not able to maintain eye contact. Knowing uncomfortable subjects were not far away.

"Not true. I think everything you said the other night was *very* interesting. I'd like to hear more about how you survived being a teen-ager in the cruel world, all by yourself." He gave her a smile of encouragement. "Please."

Judy looked like she might refuse, and Arnie got ready to bargain and plead.

"All right," she conceded. "I guess I'll tell you more, but only on the condition that you let me know when you get tired, okay?"

Arnie brought his knees up to get more comfortable, refusing to admit that his left shoulder, which had taken the brunt of the fall, was beginning to ache. Had Judy seen it, she would have been amazed at the color spectrum that was covered. From yellow, to plum, to deep purple, it looked painful and swollen. Starting at the base of his neck and working its way down to mid-bicep, it spread out across his chest around the clavicle, which showed more deep purple, and ended near the nipple. If he was able to use his left arm, he would have found it intensely painful. But the sling, as irritating to Arnie as it was, served its purpose in supporting the arm and preventing him from trying to use it.

"Well, let's see." She thought about where she'd left off. "I told you I was almost nineteen, I think, when my mother went into the psychiatric ward. I tried to visit her every other day, when I could around my job and everything. Sometimes she'd ask me who I was. It hurt that she didn't know me, I was pretty upset when that happened. I knew she was getting worse. But I still went to see her, hoping she'd get better.

"A few months after she was admitted, my office manager told me he'd been invited to an important party, but his wife was unable to attend. He asked me if I'd like to join him, see how the other half lived. I didn't really want to, but, at the same time, I needed the job and didn't want to upset him. So I ended up agreeing to go with him.

"He picked me up at my apartment and drove to a grand hotel, where the party was taking place. Every body was dressed very nice, in expensive clothes and jewelry, drinking champagne and eating caviar. I'd never seen anything like it. And here I was in a dress I had *thought* was my best one, until I saw all the gowns at this affair! I felt positively shabby. My office manager didn't seem to think anything was wrong, but I was too ashamed to go up to anyone and speak to them. Once in a while my boss would come over and talk to me, otherwise I kept to myself.

"About halfway through the evening, I was standing to one side of the throng, sipping on my champagne when a tall, good-looking man, about thirty- five years old, came up and asked me to dance. I had noticed him earlier, watching me, but I thought it was because I stuck out in the crowd in my dowdy clothes. I looked over at my manager, who was standing nearby, and he nodded his head that it was okay. So, I let him take my hand and lead me out onto the floor. It was a slow one, and he danced very smooth and had a nice rhythm. He asked me my name, which I told him. Then he asked me something that took me totally by surprise." She stopped.

Arnie, left hanging, had to prompt her to keep going. "What did he ask, for Pete's sake!"

"He asked me, 'How much is he paying you tonight?'"

"What? He asked you what?" Arnie's mouth was open in disbelief.

"He wanted to know how much my office manager was paying

me to be with him at the party! I was shocked. I didn't know what he was talking about at first, and then I could feel my face turning red and hot. He thought I was some kind of hooker! Then it got worse. He told me he could pay me ten times more than what my friend was paying me. I told him he was mistaken. That I was just his secretary, taking his wife's place tonight. He said, 'I know, I checked and found out he is your boss'. He handed me a card and told me that if I ever wanted to make good money and live in style, to give him a call. I put it in my pocket and we finished the dance.

"When the song was over, he escorted me back to where my manager was talking to some other gentlemen. He whispered, 'Call me,' then let go of my arm and walked away.

"Sometime later, at the end of the party, I was getting into my manager's car, when I saw the handsome man that had danced with me heading towards a shiny black luxury sedan. It looked brand new – and very expensive. I watched as he traded places with the valet and drove away, thinking about what he had told me.

"On the way back to my apartment, my manager tried to get funny with me. He'd had too much to drink, and shouldn't even have been driving. He kept trying to put his hands all over me, swerving all over the road, I was getting scared and told him to stop the car. He wanted to know if I wanted to get naked here in the car or go to my apartment for a little fun! Trying to fend off his hands, I told him 'let's pull over and do it in the car'. Then, as soon as he pulled the car to a stop, I jumped out and ran away before he could stop me. I caught the first taxi I saw and went home. It was so scary, I lay there for hours, waiting for a knock on my door, but he never tried to come over."

Judy had to stop and force herself to relax, reminding herself that it had happened years ago. She was tempted to stop, but she also wanted Arnie to know what had happened in her life. She needed him to understand.

Before she could continue a nurse entered the room. Seeing Arnie's tight expression, she mistook it for signs of pain and asked him if he needed his pain medication now. He gladly accepted the pills when she brought them in a few moments later.

Judy slipped away to freshen up after that stressful tale. Laying his head back for a short rest until she returned, Arnie thought about what Judy had been through. He felt sorry and very angry for her. He wanted nothing more than to hunt down that cowardly womanizer and beat the crap out of him! He closed his eyes, his head throbbing. Still weak from his injuries, Arnie fell asleep.

Chapter 17

Waking up disoriented, Arnie looked around at the stark white walls and remembered he was at the hospital. Then it all came back to him in a rush. *Judy!*

He located Judy sitting over by the window, reading a magazine she must have found out in the lobby. When she heard him stir, she stood up and came over to his bedside.

"You're awake."

"Yeah, sorry about that. How long was I asleep?"

Judy looked at the slim, gold watch on her wrist, "Almost forty minutes."

"Forty minutes! Must've been the pain killer." Then realizing she had stayed all that time, he mentioned it. "Aren't you afraid my wife will walk in on this cozy scene?"

"Funny you should mention your wife – she called."

"What? Called here?" He glanced over at the telephone on the nightstand. "Tell me you didn't answer the phone?" His heart started to flutter in his chest.

"I did, as a matter of fact. I didn't want the phone waking you up when you needed the rest, so I took the chance. I make a good impression of a nurse, apparently. She didn't even ask who I was." She shrugged.

"What did she say?"

Judy came closer to the bed and looked down at his tussled hair, the fatigue still apparent by the dark bags under his eyes. "She said to tell you that she wouldn't be able to make it until later today. She had things she needed to do."

Arnie didn't look too pleased with the news. He scowled.

Judy, unable to resist, reached out and smoothed his hair back into place, her hand gentle and warm against his skin. Telling himself it was a comforting caress rather than a sexual one, he closed his eyes as she continued to softly caress his forehead, enjoying the unexpected affection.

He opened his eyes and found himself staring into Judy's. Dark, sharp, unreadable.

The sharp ring of the phone caused them both to jump, Arnie let out a little groan of pain at the sudden movement.

Judy picked up the receiver and stated "Arnold Martin's room, may I say who's calling, please?" She gave a little smile and handed the phone to Arnie. "Okay, hold on. It's your daughter, Ashley."

"Thank you, Nurse Judy," he intoned. She shook her head at him and rolled her eyes to the ceiling, reminding him of his daughter, Heather.

"Hey, Baby. What's going on, shouldn't you be in school?" He listened for several minutes, made a few appropriate sounds of agreement, then told her he'd see her soon before handing the phone back to Judy.

In answer to her silent question, asked with a raised eyebrow, he told her Ashley had called at lunch time, from the school nurses office, just to see if he'd gone home yet. "She's pretty disappointed, because their mom told them they probably wouldn't be coming with her this afternoon to see me, they'll have to wait 'til tomorrow."

When Judy asked him why, he started to shrug his shoulders, then, remembering his injury, settled for a flip of his hand. "Who knows. Sondra has her own agenda nowadays."

He squirmed around until he was able to find a fairly comfortable spot. Then he asked Judy if she would finish her story if he promised not to fall asleep on her this time. She pretended to think long and hard about it, then, after making him ask again, she continued.

"The next morning I didn't feel like going to work. I didn't know how I was going to face my manager after he'd groped me like that! I just couldn't go in and act like nothing happened. So I stayed home. I thought about what other type of job I could get, with no high school diploma, I didn't know much about the job world and what was out there. Then I remembered the good-looking guy from the party.

"I went to my bedroom to look for my clothes, wadded up in a pile on the floor where I'd thrown them when I had undressed. The card was still in the pocket of my dress and I dug it out and looked at it.

"It wasn't a fancy card or anything. Simple black lettering that said Life Style Designer, Paul Malcolm, President. It sounded very intriguing, so I took a chance and called. A lady's voice answered, 'Life Style Designers, where can I direct your call?' I almost hung up, but then I asked for Mr. Paul Malcolm. She asked for my name and I gave it to her, thinking Mr. Malcolm wouldn't waste his time talking to me when he didn't recognize the name. I really didn't think he'd bother to remember a plain-Jane from a big party filled with such beautifully dressed people.

"So it took me by surprise when his low voice answered and said, 'Hello, Judy. Have you recovered from the party? Are you ready to try an interview?' He had remembered me!

"I murmured a 'Yes, I think I am,' and he told me he'd pass me back to his secretary, who would make the arrangements with me. Then he told me 'Good luck,' and I was suddenly speaking to the lady again. She asked if the next afternoon at one o'clock would work for me, and I said it was fine. She said it would take approximately four hours to complete, bring my resume and credentials, and to make sure I arrived on time. I said 'I will,' she said 'I look forward to meeting you,' we hung up, and the deal was on!

"Then I was very nervous! I had no idea what I was in for. What kind of interview lasted four hours! But I'd been too overwhelmed to ask the lady, so I'd just have to find out when I got there. So," Judy asked with a gleam in her eye. "Are you bored enough now?"

"No, I think it's getting more exciting by the minute! Go on, go on!" Arnie encouraged. "You're quite the story teller."

Before she could make a reply to that, the door of the hospital room, which Judy had closed before beginning her tale, opened. A white-bearded man, maybe around fifty-five, strode in, a stethoscope swinging around his neck. Seeing Judy, he stopped in mid-stride.

"Well, well. And who is this lovely lady?"

"This is my friend." said Arnie, not too pleased at his interrupting their special time together. He didn't want to share a minute of her with anybody, he realized, and hoped the doctor didn't have anything major on his mind.

The doctor made a little bow to Judy. "Can I be your friend, too?" His bushy white eyebrows bobbed up and down when he spoke, causing Judy to laugh.

"Of course you can."

"This," explained Arnie needlessly, "is my doctor. Dr. Clark, I'd like you to meet Ms. Judy Larson."

The doctor gave Judy a tiny nod of his head, and told her it was a pleasure to meet her.

"I guess that's my cue to leave," said Judy, beginning to gather up her belongings.

"No, that's all right. Stay. I'm just going to look over this fine fellow of yours for a minute or two and catch up on his chart. Stay." Back to business, the doctor pulled Arnie's chart out of the bin near the bed and flipped it open as he turned towards his patient. He spent a few moments reading through the chart, while the other two remained silent.

"Well, looks like you're definitely getting better, young man! Maybe she's the reason, huh?" he said with a jerk of his head towards Judy. He patted Arnie's arm, his smile big and toothy. "Let's take a listen, shall we?"

The doctor peeled his stethoscope from around his neck and placed the ends into his ears. The doctor lifted the hospital gown to one side, and Arnie winced as the cold metal of the 'scope touched his chest. Listening at various spots, the doctor appeared satisfied and stood up, looping the 'scope back into its original position at his nape. Removing the immobilizer briefly, he checked to see if the swelling had gone down before replacing it.

"You're going to be quite colorful for a while yet, but you seem to be doing well." The doctor asked him several questions about his elimination patterns, and Arnie found himself getting embarrassed as he explained how many times he had urinated and had a bowel movement since he was admitted. He totally avoided looking to see Judy's reaction to such personal information. "I'll check on you again sometime tomorrow, maybe you can leave in a day or two, hm?" Returning the chart, he started to leave the room.

Arnie told him that it sounded good and tried to thank him, but Dr. Clark just continued out the door with a wave of his hand.

"It's good to know you're regular!" Judy laughed, knowing Arnie had been mortified.

"Ha, ha!" Arnie responded. "Now, back to you. How about finishing your story?"

Looking at her watch, she agreed to continue, but had to leave in thirty minutes. "I'll tell you as much as I can within that time." She pulled the chair closer, having moved it out of the doctor's way earlier.

"Well, I showed up for the interview the next day, promptly at one o'clock, like the lady told me. It was in one of the tallest buildings in Seattle, and had a security guard at an information desk in a huge, marble lobby. I asked him which floor Life Style Designers was on and he told me the "twenty-third floor, the suite." He pointed the way to the elevators, so I didn't feel like I could ditch the interview and run with him watching me– like I really wanted to!

"Riding up to the twenty-third floor, I had all kinds of second thoughts going through my head. I was scared and wondering if I was making a very bad choice. On the other hand, I was very curious. I had no idea what kind of business this was, what I would have to do, nothing! I was shaking by the time I arrived at the suite. I didn't think my legs would hold me up as I stepped out of the elevator. But then I saw the decor! I was stunned, and I forgot all about being scared to death!

"Everything was decorated to perfection. The furniture was gleaming oak, every surface shone, even the plants scattered about the reception area were green and robust.

"I approached the lady sitting behind a huge curving desk. She was middle-aged, slim, well dressed in a simple suit and skirt. Her makeup was so well applied as to be unnoticeable. She smiled and welcomed me to Life Style Designers, then asked me what she could do for me, so I told her about my one o'clock appointment. She looked at a delicate gold watch on her wrist, then, after taking my drivers license and resume, directed me to have a seat. I had only been sitting for maybe a minute before a tall, attractive brunette with gold highlights came towards me from down the hall.

"Welcome, Ms. Larson, I'm Dianne Templeton. If you'd please come with me, we can get started." She led me down the hall, her heels clacking against the inlaid wood flooring. Directing me into a room filled with hues of blue, she told me to take a seat. I later learned this was called, obviously, the Blue Room, where most of their interviews took place. There were other rooms, too, in various other color themes. I haven't been in most of them, however.

"I sat down on one of the elegant Victorian-style chairs. Sitting on a chair at a diagonal from mine, Ms. Templeton looked me over. Ignoring her, I looked around the room. I tried not to gawk, but the furnishings were so lovely. I wanted to walk around and look at all the paintings and vases placed all over the room. I decided that I wanted a place of my own that was equally as impressive and artistic.

"Well," began Ms. Templeton. "You have already passed the first test - your looks. Mr. Malcolm approved of that himself when he recommended you to this company."

"I didn't know whether I should thank her for that or not, but before I could say anything, she continued.

"The rest of the interview will be testing your skills in intelligence, communication, manners, poise, dressing style and fashion sense, as well as your physical shape. Do you have any questions before we begin?"

I was having a hard time figuring out just exactly what I was interviewing for! So I asked her what type of job this was for.

"We have many different areas and positions. After you complete the interview process, I'll sit down with you and we'll see which area is suitable for you. You can decide from there if this is something you want or not. Does that sound feasible?" Her voice was pleasant and refined.

"I told her yes, but I was still full of doubts. But I figured it might be worth a few hours of my time to get a better career - and avoid people like my old office manager. So I decided I'd go through with this strange interview."

Judy glanced at her watch and told Arnie that she'd used up all her time and needed to get going.

"Will you come back tomorrow? You can't just leave me hanging!"

She told him, "I'm not going to promise, but I will try, okay?"

As she was leaving, Arnie thought back at all she'd told him. *She's a great storyteller. I wonder if she's just telling me another story or if this all really happened like she says?* Then he recalled how splendid the furnishings were in her apartment, and decided she probably *was* telling the truth. *With maybe a little embellishing?* No, he was beginning to think there was a lot more to Ms. Larson than met the eye, and he couldn't wait to hear the rest of her story.

Chapter 18

About the time Arnie was getting bored counting the acoustical tiles that made up the ceiling of his hospital room, he could hear children's voices coming from the hallway. He could recognize Ashley's voice, rising in pitch with excitement, as well as Heather's more mellow tone. And soon they came rushing through the door, giving him careful hugs. Sondra followed at a slower pace, giving the girls time to have their dad to themselves.

They chattered about their day, then wanted to know when he was coming home.

"In a day or two, the doctor says."

"Yeah! Daddy's coming home!" cried Ashley, excitedly.

Sondra, just coming into the room, heard only the last sentence. "You get to come home today?" Was it his imagination, or did she sound disappointed? She didn't look exactly as he pictured a loving wife would look upon hearing that her absentee husband was finally able to come home.

"No. In a day or two. Don't you *want* me to come home?" he accused.

"It's not that. I just need a little warning to get the house straightened up, that's all. Don't give me that look, Arnold Martin!" she exclaimed when he threw her a disbelieving glance. "Do I need to pick you up? I mean, will they take you home in an ambulance, or can you ride in a car?"

"Yeah!" squealed Ashley, bouncing on the side of Arnie's bed until he had to reach out and stop her, his head starting to ache with the jostling. "Let's go in the ambulance! With the siren on and everything!"

"Oh, yes," her mother replied with a smile. "Might as well come home with a bang!"

She turned her attention back to her husband. "Should I talk to the nurses and see if we need to arrange something?"

Arnie wasn't sure himself, but he told her he didn't see why he couldn't ride in a regular vehicle, since it was his arm that was hurt, not his legs or back. He told her he'd let her know for sure when he could go home, but perhaps she should get the house ready for him *now*.

Sondra seemed puzzled by his abrupt manner, and he felt guilty about treating her that way, so he softened his approach and asked her how her day had been. Despite the truce he and Sondra apparently had slipped into, he still occasionally caught a questioning expression on her face when she thought he wasn't looking. For the girls' sake, she wasn't going to bring up his midnight escapade. And *he* sure wasn't about to bring it up, knowing it wouldn't be pleasant, but he knew he couldn't avoid her questions forever. He thought about inviting her to come by herself tomorrow so they could talk things over, but quickly changed his mind. *Why do today what you can put off indefinitely,* he told himself. *Maybe she'll just forget all about it and never ask me why I was at Judy's in the middle of the night.* He sighed, knowing the storm would break soon.

While the girls entertained themselves by exploring all the drawers and closet, he and Sondra were able to discuss more mundane topics, like the girls schoolwork, bills, and things that needed done around the house when he was well enough to get to them. *It's almost like it used to be between us,* Arnie realized. *Maybe we needed something to shake our marriage up to get us back on track.*

All too soon it was time for the girls to go home to bed. They didn't want to leave, but Arnie reminded them that he would heal faster and be home that much quicker if he got lots of rest.

He gave the girls extra long hugs good-bye, then exchanged a small peck on the lips with Sondra before she herded her little

171

brood out the door. Thoroughly enjoying this visit with his family, the room seemed extraordinarily quiet and lonely after they left.

*   *   *

Dr. Clark placed the cold stethoscope on Arnie's chest and directed him to take a deep breath several times as he moved it around, listening. "Well, no sign of congestion – that means no pneumonia setting in from sitting on your butt for days! Your collarbone and ribs look like they are healing pretty good. But I'm a little concerned with the drainage at the head wound site. I think I'll have them take a culture and check it out, just to make sure no infection is starting up."

Arnie rubbed the bandage that had once again been placed on the back of his head. At least it was smaller than the original. "Does that mean I can't go home today?"

"Fraid not. Not unless the culture comes back negative and I haven't already left for the Community Clinic to be able to sign you out. I volunteer a few days a month of my time helping out there. It's a free clinic on the less fortunate side of town, and this is my afternoon to work there."

The doctor scribbled some notes in the chart and handed it to the nurse, who was just walking into the room. "Send a specimen over to the lab, will you? Let's see if our boy is cooking something up in that wound of his. Change the bandage each shift and continue the Tylenol 3 for pain if he needs it." The doctor bid Arnie good-bye and left. The nurse went to get the items she would need to take a culture of his head wound. And Arnie lay there wondering if he'd ever get out of there and be able to go home. After the nurse was finished getting a sample for the lab, Arnie tried to keep busy reading the newspaper, watching TV, and waiting for Judy to show up to finish her story. She never came.

Arnie looked up at the clock for the hundredth time that afternoon. Almost four o'clock. *Where is she? She said she'd come around eleven. Maybe she got busy and plans to come later,*

172

but Sondra and the kids are coming after school. If she sees them, she might go home again.

As he predicted, Sondra and the two girls soon showed up, school having let out at 3:30.

"Daddy," asked rambunctious Ashley. "Can we take you home with us now?" She was again on the side of his bed, bouncing merrily, one leg up under her bottom, the other on the floor providing the momentum against the shiny gray linoleum. Arnie reached out to still her.

"Sorry, Baby. Daddy might have an infection in his head, and they want to check it out and make sure it's all right before they send me home."

Ashley started to look at his face closely, her eyes squinting with concentration.

"What are you doing, you silly goose?" Arnie asked, gently putting his hand to her chest to push her out of his face.

"I'm looking for the 'fection."

Arnie explained where the infection was and showed her the bandage. He had to laugh when she insisted on seeing the 'fection' for herself and wanted him to take it off. He soon got her redirected to other things by asking her questions about her friends, and what she did today at school. Chattering away, the infection was quickly forgotten.

"Daddy," Heather interrupted when she could get a word in. "We have to write a short story in English class. Can I write about your accident, and staying in the hospital?"

Surprised, Arnie said he didn't see why not. "If you're willing to put your whole class to sleep! That'll probably get you a big fat F!"

"Daddy!" Heather protested. They spent the next half-hour going over the details, at least the ones Arnie felt were appropriate for twelve-year-olds to hear. Sondra, who was hearing some of this for the first time, was as attentive as Heather was. Ashley lost interest soon after the subject came up, and was sitting on a corner of her dad's bed, leaning against his pillow, busy making her father a bead bracelet. Arnie hoped the staff wouldn't be too upset finding little multi-colored beads everywhere.

Even though he loved his family dearly, he was relieved when it was time for them to pack up their stuff and give him back his peace and quiet. The girls had quickly adjusted to seeing him in his hospital bed and the sterile environment, but Sondra still remained very quiet and somber on these visits. He couldn't help but wonder if it was the setting - or him. Before they left, he told Sondra he would call her when he found out the results of the culture and when he could go home for sure.

After a short, reviving nap and a fairly edible dinner, Arnie noticed it was almost seven and Judy had yet to show up. He refused to get disappointed, giving her the benefit of the doubt that she would show. Having made that determined choice, Judy walked in. Arnie could feel his face light up, but did nothing to hide the fact that he was happy to see her.

"I'm sorry, I couldn't make it this morning. How are you feeling? I expected you to be gone by now!" She sat down on the edge of his bed.

He told her about the suspected infection. "I should be able to go home in the morning if the lab says I'm okay."

"Are you planning on going back to work right away?"

"No, I think I'll be needing a week or two to recover. I hurt everywhere. I still get tired so easily. Plus, I don't think my boss, Murray, would let me in the lab with this sore on my head! He'd be afraid I'll contaminate all the experiments!" He gave her a wink and a grin. I'll start thinking about work once I can move and walk without this pain."

"That's a very nice bracelet you're sporting there". Judy picked his arm up to look more closely at the jumble of colored beads strung on a piece of orange twine. Arnie told her his daughter had made it for him. "It's quite lovely, matches the yellow in your bruises!" She fiddled with the bracelet, then let his arm drop to the bed. "I saw your wife and girls on my way in. Actually, I was waiting until they left before I dared to come in at all!" She laughed at her own cowardice.

"You're not afraid of her, are you?" Arnie hadn't thought of that.

"No, it's not that. I just don't want to cause any problems for you, that's all. If she knew I was visiting you everyday, she might think something is going on between us. I don't think you need any more trouble right now. She needs to know we're friends, but not until you're stronger."

Arnie thought about it. "Yes, I think you're right. So, what were you doing after they left, you didn't come up right away."

"I was up on the baby floor! I may not want one, but I love to see them! There are five tiny little bundles in the nursery – they are so cute! I guess I spent longer up there than I thought I did." Her face was shining and happy as she recounted how the nurse had lifted up one of the babies so she could see it better. Arnie couldn't help but think that, subconsciously, maybe she really *did* want a baby. But he wouldn't say anything. He just enjoyed her happy expression and listened to her talk about the newborn's tiny fist and scrunched up face as it wailed in the nurse's arms.

When the subject of the baby grew dry, Arnie asked her if she'd continue her story for him, "Seeing as you won't have your captive audience much longer!"

"I suppose. Where did I leave off – oh, yes." She stood up from the bed, much to Arnie's disappointment. Pulling the chair over to the bedside, she made herself comfortable before starting. "The interview."

"I was impressed by the company's professionalism, their punctuality, the office decor, everything that I saw there. They had told me that there were many types of positions available, and looking around, I decided I would take *any* position they offered, even if it was as a janitor! Just to be able to work in such a magnificent building.

"The interview was long, just as the lady had warned me. It was well prepared, and organized. By the time it was over, they knew everything about me, from my past, to what size underwear I

175

had on! No kidding! They tested my math skills, how I walk across the room, what ensemble I would pick out from a closet full of various clothing for different occasions they named, and even had me wash all my makeup off and had a professional redo it.

"Hours later Ms. Templeton sat me down and told me that I had done well in most areas. But they would now look over all the results and call me if they have a suitable position open for me. I thanked her, and just like that, it was over and I was shown the door.

"I didn't expect to actually hear from them, and had started to feel sorry for myself and wonder what to do next for income, when I got a call from Life Styles two days later. They wanted me to come in that afternoon to talk about the interview results and my qualifications. Having nothing better lined up, I agreed to meet with them.

"I was taken to another beautiful room, this time done in shades of rose and pink."

"Let me guess," interjected Arnie. "The Rose Room, right?"

Judy laughed and told him he was correct. "Ms. Templeton laid a file on the table between us with my name on it. It's kind of scary knowing somebody has a file on your life. I felt like I was on the FBI Ten Most Wanted list or something.

"A woman brought in a silver tea tray and delicate ceramic cups. After we were served, she left, closing the door behind her. I wondered if that was the kind of position they had for me. I could do that, I thought to myself.

"Looking through the file briefly, Ms. Templeton put it down and looked me over. I felt drab in the skirt and blouse I had chosen to wear, but I had put extra pains into copying the makeup technique the beautician had used on me for the interview. I knew I looked good.

"We have decided you would be a benefit in the Escort field. There is a position open if you're interested. Let me tell you about it before you decide. It involves accompanying interested parties to different functions. It will pay two thousand dollars per day, three days minimum a week. Are you interested?"

My jaw must have dropped a foot! 'But I still don't really know what the job is. How can I take a job that I don't know much about.' I had to admit."

"If you agree to except, I will have you sign confidentiality papers, then I will be able to tell you more. I can tell you that you won't be put into a position where you will have to do anything you don't want to physically. Does that reassure your mind?"

"Somewhat" I replied. I thought it over, then went ahead and signed the papers. I didn't really think I had much to lose by then anyway.

"Your job will be to escort wealthy clients to parties, business trips, other functions where they need a companion or need to look good for whatever reasons."

"If they're rich, why do they need to buy somebody to take with them to parties?" A natural question.

"We don't ask, we just take their money!" It was the first time I had seen her smile since she greeted me that very first time. "And, you are never to ask a client that question. You have signed a privacy contract, nothing is to leave this room, no information a client tells you will ever be used against that client, sold to a newspaper, spread to your friends, etc. You will read in your contract that if anything is ever leaked out about a client you were with, there will be very serious repercussions. Is that understood?"

"I was flabbergasted at her change in manner. I agreed, again wondering what I'd gotten myself into. She went on to tell me more about my new job.

"So, you are telling me that I am not obligated to have sex with any of these clients?"

"That's correct. If you should decide you would like to take the date further, that is at your discretion. As long as it does not reflect badly on Life Styles, and no money is exchanged for sexual favors. The clients can tip you to show their appreciation, but do not accept money for sex. That is not what this company is offering. We have managed to keep a good reputation over the years, and we expect you to keep that in the highest regards."

"Why do they pay so much just for somebody to keep them company?"

"Most of our clients are very careful who they take to functions. They can't afford to make a bad choice, and end up having to pay millions of dollars in a law suit when the woman claims they were raped or are pregnant with their baby – just to get hold of some of their money. It happens all the time. So, we offer them a safer option. We can provide them attractive companions, no fear of marriage or law suits, no commitments of any kind. Just a pretty face to impress society with. That's basically all they want from our company. You fit all the requirements. You're unattached, beautiful, have a good dress sense, you're personable, the list goes on. Now are you interested?" She gave me another rare smile and sat back to await my answer.

"And you guarantee no sex is involved?"

"Not unless *you* want it to go there. The clients also have to sign a contract to take our girls out, so we know a lot about them before we hand one of our girls over to them. If any client tries to force himself on you, we are to be notified immediately. We have only had one incident, but that was a case of the client getting mixed signals, so it wasn't entirely the client's fault. It was straightened out, and we are pleased to say that, except for minor events, we haven't had any further problems. You will get some training on how to act to avoid sending signals you don't intend to send before we assign you to a job."

"And I just go out with them, be nice to them?"

"Yes. You will be witty, you will listen to them, you will look your best for them, sometimes all they want to do is have a quiet drink somewhere, sometimes you'll attend a grand party in Europe. You never know. It can be quite exciting!" Her body language was telling me she had personally experienced what she was telling me. So I had to ask.

"Did you used to be an escort, too, Ms. Templeton?"

"As a matter of fact, I was. I often miss those days, but I chose to have a family instead and settle down, so they offered me this position, and ...the rest is inconsequential. Perhaps some day you will be sitting here in this chair, interviewing prospective clients and escorts."

"I ended up taking the job. She made it sound safe, and the money was just unbelievable."

Judy stopped to see how Arnie was taking all this. He seemed interested. No disgust written on his face, so far.

"How are you holding up? Too many details?"

"So far, so good," he replied. "Carry on."

"I have a reason for telling you so many details about it, later you'll see why. Well, I had to attend a sort of training session after that. That was where I learned how to eat and talk around rich people."

That's where she got her mannerisms from, why she talks so refined, dresses so nicely.

"They taught us ten things we had to swear by before we were allowed to be with a client. You ready," she asked Arnie. "Here goes -

1) Use only your first name, or use a different family name with each client.
2) Never talk politics, religion, or other personal beliefs with a client.
3) Never argue with a client.
4) Since the client is paying for your time, you must get permission from the client before you leave his side.
5) Never tell anyone that you are a paid companion.
6) Never take a client to your place of residence.
7) Dress according to code. Life Styles will inform you each time of what to expect so you will know how to dress.
8) Never give your personal phone number to a client.
9) Change your hairstyle periodically. You should not be recognized by wearing the same hairdo constantly. Variety can make the "dates" more fun for the client. Changing hair color is at your own discretion.

10) Never discuss your fee with a client. Tips are acceptable."

Judy laughed at Arnie's expression.

"You have a good memory! That's a lot of rules!"

"I remember all of those because we are required to. It keeps things going smoothly for Life Styles, as well as the clients. I was given a cell phone that I was instructed to keep with me at all times. I had to get a private phone line separate from my regular phone and give them the new number as soon as possible. This was how they would contact me when a client was lined up for me. Life Styles would then give me the pertinent information, like pick up time and place. No client names were divulged until I arrived at Life Styles to choose my clothing, just in case somebody had equipment that allowed them to listen in on my cell phone or private line."

"Very secret-agent-y!" Arnie supposed he should be upset about Judy's profession, but so far he couldn't see that there was anything wrong in the career she chose. He was impressed by the money they could take in for one day! "Do they need any male escorts?" he joked.

Judy ignored this jibe and continued her tale. "My new phone was silent for three days before I got a call asking if I was ready to get my feet wet. The person calling didn't give her name, she just said there was a job for me the next day, did I want it. My stomach fell to the floor, I realized I was scared. But I said I would take it. She briefly told me this client had recently separated from his wife and wanted somebody to take to a wedding party. Probably to make his wife jealous or angry, or maybe he was just lonely. I accepted the job and was told to go to Life Styles, where I got more information, like the clients' name. I would need to dress very elegantly for the wedding, and would be picked up by my clients' limo at ten o'clock sharp in the SeaTac Hilton lobby.

"Life Styles has a huge show room of all kinds of clothing we were allowed to choose from until we could afford our own. It was fun picking through all the beautiful dresses and shoes – most of us were close to the same sizes to make buying the clothes easier, I suppose. I spent at least two hours in there, trying on all sorts of dresses before settling on the perfect one. I felt like a princess in a lacy pale peach affair, with matching shoes, purse and shawl.

"The next day, in my fancy duds, I nervously waited in the lobby of the hotel, very self-conscious at that time of the morning in such rich clothing. I got a lot of stares and comments, but for the most part, people chose to ignore me.

At ten, a man wearing a black chauffeur's uniform and hat, came up to me and asked me if I was Ms. Judy. He asked me to come with him, that Mr. Buckley was waiting for me in the car. I walked out with him, and there was a new-looking black Mercedes Benz, dark tinted windows shining in the sunlight, parked out on the curb. The chauffeur opened the rear door for me and I got in and sat next to the gentleman already inside. He closed the door and got into the driver's side, pushing a button to lock all the doors. That made me nervous, but I knew it was to protect the man sitting beside me, not to keep me in the car.

"Hi, I'm Greg Buckley." He appeared to be around fifty years old, in fairly good shape, with a charming smile and attractive deep-set eyes that were emphasized by the laugh-lines at the corners. "And you are Judy--?"

"I hadn't thought about a last name in all the excitement, so I said the first thing that came to mind. "Manson. Judy Manson."

"Any relation to Charles Manson?" he laughed.

"No!" I laughed nervously.

"That's good. One less thing to worry about," he joked. He seemed nervous, too, which helped me to relax a little. "You can call me Greg, and I'll call you Judy, okay?"

I told him that was fine. While we drove to the party, somewhere in east Bellevue, I studied the man next to me. He was a large-boned man, maybe a football player at one time? He was nice looking, polite, courteous to me, had a nice sense of humor, although I could see a sadness underneath his cheery attitude. He smoked a pleasant smelling cigar at the party, along with several other male party-goers.

"The wedding was an awesome affair, too elaborate for my taste. But the reception that followed was quite the event. Foods you wouldn't believe, wines that probably cost more for one bottle than I had earned for a month at the insurance company!

"I spent the whole day with Greg. Met his whiney wife, and couldn't figure out why he seemed to be still in love with her and missing her. Thankfully, we were able to avoid her most of the day. The women came up and commented on my lovely dress, my complexion, and other trivial things. The men would tell me how lucky Greg was to have found such a beautiful date. Many were curious about how Greg and I had met. We had decided in the car earlier that we would tell them that we were introduced by a mutual friend. If they wanted to know who the friend was, we would just tell them that they wouldn't know him and let it go at that. One thing about the wealthy, they know not to pry in other's affairs. At least to your face!

"At the end of the evening, I was dropped back off at the same hotel, where Greg paid me a large tip and I took a taxi home from there. I had enjoyed my time with Greg. My first job had been a success. The next day I got a call on my cell phone that money had been deposited by Life Styles into the bank account I had been instructed to get. Also, as instructed, I withdrew half of it that day and put it into an account in a different bank. This was to make sure I had access to money if Life Styles was ever investigated and they located, and put a freeze on all of our accounts. It made me nervous to think about it, but in all the time I've been with them, it hasn't happened yet.

"So, with a little money now, I could pay my rent, and I was starting to feel a little brightness coming into my life again, something I hadn't really felt since my father left us years ago. My confidence level had risen a bit, too. Nothing like a big wedding with a bunch of drunk men to make a girl feel attractive!" Judy laughed, and Arnie couldn't help but laugh, too. "I felt like I would soon be in a position to take care of my mother again, maybe hire private nursing to come in and help out so she could be at home instead of the hospital. But that wouldn't happen for a while. I had only had one "date," I would have to go on quite a few more to get that kind of money."

A nurse, carrying a loaded tray, interrupted them at that time. Placing the tray on the bedside table, the nurse told Judy she was sorry, but she'd have to chase her out now. It was almost nine o'clock, visiting hours had ended an hour ago, and she needed to change Arnie's dressing.

Judy said she understood and was sorry she stayed so late. To which the nurse replied, "Oh, it's all right. You seemed to be having a good time in here, so we didn't want to say anything. It's good for healing when a patient has their loved-ones around them."

Arnie and Judy exchanged a glance at her words, but neither commented on it.

Wanting to dilute the discomfort of that last comment, Arnie told Judy, "I might be going home tomorrow morning, if all is well. How will I get to hear some more of your story?"

"Once you're able to go back to work, maybe you can give me a call. We can meet for a drink again. I'll see you soon, take care of yourself, Arnie." And she was out the door with a little wave.

Arnie had no time to miss her because the nurse pulled his gown out of the way and starting poking and prodding, adding to the humility by bringing in one of the aids to help him clean up with a wet cloth before changing his gown to a fresh one. It did feel good when they were finished with all the cleaning and re-bandaging, Arnie had to admit. He had no difficulty falling to sleep, dreaming of being a wealthy client, the beautiful Judy Larson on his arm.

Chapter 19

After a breakfast of scrambled eggs, Cream of Wheat, and orange juice, Arnie relaxed in the chair by the window, where he had eaten his meal this morning, and read his daily newspaper, which the nurses were kind enough to let him read before the other patients got hold of it. He used the bedside table to support the paper, which left his right arm free to manage the pages. He would no longer take for granted the ease in which a person could manipulate a newspaper with two good arms!

With a minimum of discomfort and effort, he had been able to get himself out of bed and over to the window without the nurses' help. A bit weak from lack of exercise, he was still proud of his regained independence. It felt good to be able to sit in a chair after all that time in bed. He stretched his back and right arm, still feeling a tightness in his shoulder and ribs with the movement, but not the sharp pain he had previously experienced.

He was impatiently awaiting the doctor this morning and could only hope he would tell him that he could go home today. His scalp, under the bandage, had been itching unmercifully all morning, and he absently rubbed it. *That better not be a sign of infection! My mother always said that itching is a sign of healing. Let's just hope she was right. Where is that doctor?*

Dr. Clark, like the other physicians in the hospital, usually made his rounds after breakfast. It was only a matter of time before he reached Arnie's room, but he was eager to go home.

The sun was at its best this morning. Looking at how the bright rays lit up the cars in the parking lot below, you would never guess the temperature was in the forties. Only the turning leaves and the breath clouds coming from passersby gave away the fall nip in the air. He had opened the window earlier, using the crank to roll it open to its maximum of two inches. *Can't have people jumping out the window because they were told they couldn't go home because a little bug decided to infest their head!* But now, feeling the chill of the air after sitting still for awhile, he reached out and closed it again.

"Aw, Dr. Martin!" boomed Dr. Clark's voice from behind him, causing him to jump. "How are we doing this beautiful sunny morning?" His doctor, in full whites, strode towards him, chart in hand. "Good news, no infection!"

Relieved, Arnie put the paper aside and turned awkwardly towards the doctor, pushing the table off to one side. After checking him out, the doctor cautioned him against trying to use his left arm until after his appointment in two weeks. "We'll send you home in a basic sling to give it a little support for a while yet, but it won't get better if you over do it. Use the techniques your therapists showed you and you'll do fine. Everything will heal in good time if you take it easy for a while." So saying, he signed the chart and was off to the next patient.

During his stay, Arnie had been seen by both Occupational and Physical Therapy. The former had shown him how to dress and perform his daily rituals using one arm, had recommended a raised toilet seat be placed in the bathroom to make it easier to stand and various other ways that would make his life easier while he recuperated.

The latter had worked at getting him to be able to get out of bed and take the few wobbly steps he needed to start being able to walk again without collapsing, which included exercises and practicing techniques until they found one that worked for him. Sondra had been provided a list of different things to pick up, like the toilet riser with attached arms to help him stand, and had been shown his exercise program so she could assist him once he was at home.

Arnie liked to call it his 'New Adventure.' He'd gone through medical training himself, but his focus had been on the research aspect side of it and he was surprised by how much he didn't know about the field. He had learned a lot during his stay.

Arnie picked up the phone and called his wife with the news. She would pick him up about eleven, which gave them an hour to get his medications arranged with a nearby pharmacy, and get all the paperwork ready for his discharge. Looking around, he would almost miss the place, especially all the friendly nursing staff that had helped him. *I'll have to send them flowers or something.*

Sondra arrived before eleven, and with a sense of unexplained trepidation, Arnie returned home.

*　　*　　*

"I want to know whose apartment you were at, Arnie. The night of your accident."

He had been home two days now. Arnie, fooled into believing the subject was not going to come up, felt his stomach knot up in dread now that it was brought out in the open. He knew he would have to tell his wife about Judy. The sooner, the better.

He had spent the past two days getting used to his house again. He was surprised to find himself tiring easily, not unexpected, he supposed, in this larger territory. It was good to be in the comfort of his own home, surrounded by his giggling children and familiar surroundings. But, all of a sudden he wished himself back in the safety of his sterile hospital room.

Seated at the kitchen table, the girls having just rushed out the door to catch their bus, Arnie looked up from his pancakes, pushing his plate aside at his sudden loss of appetite.

"I want to know who she is, Arnie." Sondra's voice was firm, but he could hear the barely contained anger in it, too. Watching her now, he also saw a deep sadness in her eyes. He felt ashamed that he was the cause of so much hurt in her life lately.

"All right," he said, resigned. "Will you sit down while I talk?" He pointed to the chair next to his. "Please." Looking as if she might refuse, Sondra stood away from the counter, where she'd been leaning, and pulled out the chair across from his instead.

Arnie wasn't quite sure where to begin and how much he needed to divulge to pacify his wife. Reluctant to give all the details, he settled with the bare bones. If she wanted to know more, he was sure she'd ask.

"Remember the last flight I took to Los Angeles?" Sondra nodded, her arms folded tightly over her chest. Her back, ramrod stiff, was in close competition with the set of her mouth.

"Well, my seatmate on the way home was a woman named Judy. We got to talking and, well, she's a nice lady." Seeing Sondra's expression, he hurried on. "Well, she ended up buying my drink when I couldn't get to my wallet. So, to return the favor, I bought her one later when we were back in Seattle. I know how that sounds, Sondra! Don't jump to conclusions!"

Sondra looked like she was about to say something very nasty, so Arnie hastily continued. "Nothing happened between us, I swear!" he insisted. "We just started meeting once in a while for a drink, talked about our jobs, just trivial things. I'm not having an affair with her, I promise you." He was worried that Sondra wasn't saying anything. He'd expected her to explode by now. "The night of the accident, I just ran up to her apartment to use her bathroom. Nothing else, really. Just her bathroom," he finished lamely.

They sat, unspeaking, for several minutes. Arnie waited for further questions, but none were forth coming. The silence stretched uncomfortably. Arnie was afraid to add anything further, afraid he'd only make things worse. So he waited for a sign from his wife, for her to say something, but she sat unmoving, mute, her expression grim.

Arnie knew she was thinking it all through, deciding how to deal with the news. He expected an angry tirade, sobbing, accusations. What he got was a watery, heart-broken look. Sondra's shoulders slumped and she pushed herself away from the table, walking quietly out of the room.

Arnie swallowed hard, feeling the tears beginning to roll down his cheeks, realizing just now, the depth of the hurt he had caused her.

*   *   *

Over the next few days, Arnie would have welcomed that stony silence. After her first shocked reaction, she had spent the time since causing Arnie grief. They had argued daily over the same things. Sondra constantly accused him of having an affair. Arnie repeatedly told her nothing had gone on between them except friendship. After a while even the girls could feel that something wasn't right between their parents and started to avoid being around them when they were together in the same room.

This, more than anything, saddened and bothered Arnie. His behavior had not only affected their marriage, but the lives and well being of their children. This had to stop, but how? He wasn't seeing Judy anymore, hadn't even called, despite wanting to. Every day he fought the urge to pick up the phone and hear her voice, talk about the troubles he was facing. And every day he told himself it would be disastrous if he did. With divorce rearing it's ugly head already, he didn't want to do anything to bring it on more rapidly.

He was puzzled by his ambivalence about this. Surely he should be feeling something other than confusion about which direction to go. Did he want a divorce, to be free of all the mixed emotions and withdrawal he'd been facing with Sondra for the past few years? Or did he want to start over, seek outside help to try to save their crumbling marriage? Did he even think it was possible to pursue a relationship with Judy? Who had such a mysterious career? Who didn't want any commitments at this time? Was he sugarcoating his feelings about Judy because she represented everything he was missing in his marriage?

He rubbed his left shoulder, the sling on top of a file cabinet nearby, where he'd tossed it the day he got home from the hospital. He was sitting at his desk, a large, handmade, scratched-up pine monster he'd picked up shortly after they bought the house. It occupied the place of honor in the back corner of the large living room. Sondra, finding it to be the ugliest piece of furniture she had ever seen, had made it her hobby to try to talk him into replacing it with something more attractive. He often found an advertisement with an oak-finished desk, circled with black marker, lying on top of the usual clutter. But he was attached to this hulking monstrosity, and had no plans to switch to a manufactured one with no personality.

He'd been sitting there for some time, trying to write up an article for the University paper. This was his "office." When his thoughts needed reviving, he could watch the huge weeping willow sway in the gentle breeze outside the window in front of him. In the spring he had the pleasure of watching the birds build their nests and flit back and forth feeding their ever-hungry hatchlings. In winter, he occasionally got mesmerized by the falling flakes of snow, a rare, but very pleasurable sight.

Three bookcases, crowded with all his college medical books, research manuals, and information gathered (and collecting dust) over his career, occupied the greatest space against the wall to his left. He drew comfort at the sight of them on days when he couldn't seem to get it together, like today, when his creative juices seemed to have dried up.

Murray had been asked to provide a short article about what the lab was currently working on, which they did once or twice a year. So he had passed it on, directing Arnie to put his recovery time to good use and produce something. So far, looking at his computer screen, he had ...nothing.

Arnie was bored. The kids spent the day at school. As soon as she'd sent the girls off in the morning, Sondra usually disappeared, going shopping, spending the day with her friends, anything to keep her away from the house until time to get dinner ready. Arnie knew she was avoiding him. It beat arguing all the time, but he was getting desperate for the company of another adult. He looked at the phone, an old-fashioned white and gold absurdity put there by Sondra in an attempt to "de-uglitize" his corner of the room – unsuccessfully. The sleek body of the phone, looking out of place amongst the dusty books and timeworn surface of the desk, only accented its ungainliness.

He picked up the receiver and listened to the dial tone for several seconds before replacing it. He desperately wanted to call Judy. But once he did, he knew he would want to *keep* calling her, talk to her. Every day. Was he addicted to her? He laughed, but then, sobering up, he considered the impact of that. It would be so easy to rely on Judy for comfort. Every time he felt sad, lonely, or troubled, he wanted to call her and talk about it. *Am I in love with her? No matter what you call it, she's a high-priced call girl, for God's sake! Can I risk having my children around something like that?*

He gave it some serious thought. If he did decide to leave Sondra, if he and Judy *did* develop a closer relationship, a romantic one, would she want to continue her career as an escort? Would she be willing to settle down, like that Ms. Templeton did? He would have to insist that she have nothing to do with Life Style Designers if that were the case. He got a crawling feeling inside his stomach at the thought of her sleeping with other men, her clients.

On the other hand, without me here, what would happen to the girls? He pictured Sondra yelling at them, how miserable she would make their lives out of petty revenge for her husband's unfaithfulness. If he *did* ever leave her, he would fight fiercely to get custody of the girls. *But, once a judge found out he was keeping company with a prost...a call girl,* he amended, *would they give custody to Sondra?* His greatest fear was losing his girls, who meant more than any thing to him. *I can't let myself fall in love with Judy, that's all. That's the way it has to be. For all our sakes.*

Feeling depressed, and lonelier than he was before, he stared at his blank computer screen and tried to focus on writing the article.

Chapter 20

Arnie was more than ready to go back to work after his two-week check up with the doctor. He'd been cleared to resume his regular duties, with the exception that he had to avoid lifting anything heavy with his left arm until the clavicle bone was fully healed.

Walking into the lab the Monday following his doctor appointment, Arnie felt like he'd been gone for months instead of three weeks. Everybody went out of their way to be helpful, telling him they were glad to see him back, getting him coffee without him asking, volunteering to do tasks that would have required begging on his part to get them to do before his accident. It was starting to feel a little creepy and he finally had to tell them to stop babying him before he started to think they'd been taken over by the pod people!

Arnie was grateful that nobody questioned where the accident had taken place, or mentioned anything about Judy, providing they knew about her. Except Murray, who took great pleasure in telling Arnie that apparently, seeing from who's apartment he'd been coming out of, his little friend *did* want his body after all, eh? Giving him a hearty slap on the back, Murray left, leaving Arnie to feel like a worm.

He wondered if this rumor had circulated around the office, and started to watch the expressions on his co-workers faces whenever he encountered one of them. But all he saw was good will and genuine friendship, so his fears were soon put to rest. If Murray had his suspicions, he was selfish enough to keep them to himself.

Things quickly got back to normal after that, and Arnie was able to resume his usual routine around the office and lab.

*   *   *

Feeling tired, but satisfied with his accomplishments, Arnie took a breather at the end of that first day. Almost before he could talk himself out of it, he found himself picking up the phone and dialing Judy's number, which, by now, he knew by heart.

No answer. Hanging up without leaving a message, he told himself she must be out of town or with a client. He refused to feel anything at that thought. Gathering his papers up, he quickly left the office and headed home, deciding he'd take the family out for dinner if Sondra didn't have anything planned yet.

The next day he did the same, still no answer, still no message left. He set his mind, and wouldn't call her after that, thinking it was for the best to let it drop and cease all contact. Having decided this, the phone seemed to draw his attention more fiercely than ever, and he found himself seeking things to do in the lab to avoid being in the same room with it.

So it was, at a rare time that he happened to be in his office several days later, that his phone rang. Arnie stared at the phone, his heart pounding. He let it ring five times before slowly reaching out to pick up the receiver.

"You *are* there!" a sunny voice exclaimed. "I was beginning to think I'd missed you," said Judy. "How's it feel to be back at work?"

Arnie hesitated before replying, trying to sound normal. "It's been tiring, but things are going well." He sounded stiff and formal even to himself. Picking up on this, Judy lost a bit of her cheerfulness.

"Is something wrong, Arnie? Is this a bad time to call?"

"No," he said. "Not really. I've just had a lot to think about lately, that's all." Hearing her familiar, soft voice touched Arnie. It would be so easy to tell her all about his loneliness, Sondra's

193

hurt and anger at him. But he couldn't.

"I called the hospital first, just to make sure you weren't still there for some unexpected reason. I've been out of town for the past week and just got back into town. I'm glad you're doing better."

"Thanks," he said awkwardly.

"I miss talking to you, Arnie," she said gently. He didn't say anything, not trusting himself to open his mouth and say the wrong thing. "Will you come to dinner with me tonight? Tomorrow night? Ever?" She sounded dismal.

Without thinking it through, knowing it was probably a big mistake to start it all over again, Arnie found himself agreeing to have dinner with her the next evening after work, at the Emerald Wok, five-thirty. Like old times. Like his marriage wasn't already falling apart without this extra help. His heart was doing a little waltz inside his chest at seeing her again as he hung up the phone.

*   *   *

Ten minutes after six the next night, Arnie was still waiting for Judy. He had already downed one scotch and was nursing a second. Twenty minutes later his mood had changed from thinking he'd have to tease her about being late, to one of worry and dejection. *She's not coming this time.*

Getting up, he tossed back the last of his drink and left the restaurant, leaving word at the reception desk that if a lady fitting the description he gave showed up, he had gone home.

On the drive home Arnie wondered what had happened. He was positive he didn't get the day wrong. She'd never missed one of their "dates" before. Maybe she had gotten sick, and with no way of contacting him, she'd had no choice but to let him sit there until he figured out she wasn't coming. *No*, he told himself, *she could have looked up the number in the phone book. Maybe she ran into a mean client that got rough with her, or she got into an accident. Why am I worrying about her, anyway,* he thought angrily. *She probably just chose to go out with a client instead. I'll just wait and see if she calls. Let's see what excuse she gives me then!*

Annoyed, it was Arnie's good fortune that there were no cops on duty along the route he took home, as, fueled by the two drinks he'd consumed on an empty stomach, he didn't care how reckless he drove.

*   *   *

Despite his resolution to wait until she contacted *him* the next day, when he still hadn't heard from Judy after lunch, he found himself calling her at the first opportunity. When there was no answer at her home, he didn't leave a message. Instead, he called the restaurant and asked to speak to the lady who had manned the courtesy desk the night before. She happened to answer the phone, so he was able to speak with her directly. He described Judy and asked if she ever showed up after he left, and started to worry when he was told that nobody bearing that name or description had approached her. He thanked her and hung up, the worry etched into his forehead.

He thought about calling the police, but knew he was over-reacting. When his imagination kicked in, and he found himself wondering if his wife, Sondra, might have done something to her, he knew it was time to stop thinking about it and find something to occupy his mind. Yet he still called her periodically throughout the rest of the afternoon, hoping the next call would be answered. To save a little of his pride, he left no messages before hanging up each time.

It was close to quitting time that afternoon when he received a call from Judy. She apologized immediately for standing him up at the restaurant. Arnie told her it was okay now, that he had been very worried that something had happened to her.

She explained that she had received a call yesterday from her mother's hospital, telling her that her mom was very ill and had asked for her. Without thinking about it, she had dropped everything and gone to her mother.

"I wanted to call you last night from the hospital, but it was getting too late, and I didn't think I should call you at your home. Today I was helping take care of my mother and just now got a chance to give you a call. I'm sorry I couldn't talk to you sooner."

"How is your mother now? Is she better?"

"She's very sick. She's running a temperature, and she's been hallucinating. Sometimes she recognizes me, but most of the time she doesn't. I'm going to stay up here for a week or so to stay near her. Maybe that will help. I feel like I need to do this for my mom, you know? Even if she doesn't remember me anymore. I'll give you a call when I get back, okay?"

Arnie told her he hoped her mother got better soon, and Judy thanked him and broke the connection without saying good-bye.

*   *   *

Three weeks crawled by without word from Judy. Arnie and Sondra's relationship was not improving. In fact, it was slowly unraveling. Arnie, avoiding the constant battles he had to fight at home, found himself spending more and more time at the office. If any of his co-workers noticed, they were tactful enough not to say anything. The rest of his time he spent with the girls, reading them stories, taking them to the mall to see a movie, buying them little gifts, and just trying to make up for the rift between him and their mother.

One afternoon, Arnie got a surprise call from Sondra, telling him that she was in town with his daughters. "The girls would like to come and see where you work, would it be all right if we drop by?"

Pleased, he told her to come right on over, he wasn't in the middle of anything that couldn't wait.

Shortly after, the two girls came hesitantly into his office. He stood up from behind his desk and they hurried over to his side.

He hugged the girls, then let them see what he had been typing up on his computer. Declaring it boring, Ashley wanted to go see his lab. Arnie warned her that she wouldn't be seeing any monkeys with electrodes on their heads or anything like the movies always show. Shrugging, Ashley said "That's okay. I just want to see where you do all your 'speriments." She took her father's hand and led him out the office door.

Sondra declined to accompany them, saying she would keep herself occupied in his office with a magazine or something until they got back. "Take your time."

He left Sondra sitting behind his desk, casually looking at the contents of the drawers. Warning Ashley, who was more apt to get into things, not to touch anything once they got there, he asked the secretary to bring some coffee to his wife, then led the girls to the laboratory.

They met Murray Evans on the way, who, seeing Ashley and Heather, stopped to talk for a minute or two, asking them how they liked their Daddy's place of business. Not having seen much of it yet, they didn't have much to say except "Fine."

"Where is your mother? She didn't come with you?" They told him she was still in their Daddy's office, and Murray cut the visit short and hurried away, saying he would just pop in and say "Hello."

"He's weird," piped Ashley. Heather giggled, and Arnie, hoping his supervisor hadn't heard, ushered them off to safer quarters in his lab, where his youngest's unsolicited comments couldn't get him into hot water.

Twenty minutes later, an empty beaker in her hand, Ashley was more than ready to leave the lab. Disappointed at seeing the shelves of the refrigerator filled with rows of labeled test tubes instead of body parts, she quickly attached herself to one of the lab assistants and had helped him carry files and books back and forth to the small library nearby. Heather, on the other hand, had seemed genuinely interested as he explained what they were trying to do, and had even been asking some intelligent questions. He wondered if she would follow his path some day, and thought it would be wonderful to be working side by side with his daughter. Hearing the crash of something unbreakable, he hoped, hit the floor, he decided it was time to return the girls to their mother before something disastrous occurred.

Returning to his office, he found Sondra, still sitting behind his desk, chatting with Murray. They were acting very friendly in Arnies' opinion. Arnie paused in the doorway, hearing first hand how debonair Murray could be with the ladies, and didn't like it one bit! Not with his own wife!

As soon as Sondra noticed they had returned, she jumped up, absently smoothing her skirt back into place. Murray unabashedly watched, not bothering to turn his head while she adjusted her clothing. Arnie seethed.

"Did you have a good time?" Not waiting for a reply, she told them it was time to go.

Ashley, not happy with another man giving her mother attention, glared at her and told her she wanted to go home with her dad. Heather agreed, looking up at her father with a silent plea. He nodded and said that would be all right, he would be leaving soon anyway.

"Okay, I'll see all of you at home then." She shook Murray's hand on the way out, a pleased look on her face when he told her it had been a delight to speak with her.

Arnie agreed with Ashley's "Hmph!"

Chapter 21

Arnie was preparing samples in the lab Monday morning, when one of the assistants took a call that came through to the lab. After a moment or two of listening, she told Arnie that a woman was on line two for him, assuming it was probably Arnie's wife. Not wanting to take it in the lab, he asked her to tell the caller to hold while he cleaned up and took it in his office.

It was Judy, just as he'd hoped, but had been afraid to ask. "Are you back in town?"

"Yes, I got in late yesterday."

"Is your mother doing better now?" There was a moment of silence, and then Judy started weeping. Thinking the worse, he asked her if she was all right.

"Yes. I'm all right-now. It's just been a very emotional time for me lately."

"So, your mother. She's okay?"

"Yes. I feel bad about leaving her alone, but I have to get on with my life. I have too many commitments to stay away for long."

"I'm sure the nurses take good care of your mother," he assured her, remembering the care he, himself, had received during his own hospital stay.

"Yes, they are wonderful with her. But I feel - I don't know, happier, I guess, when I'm near her. It's hard to explain, considering she doesn't know who I am the majority of the time."

Arnie told her he understood. It was, after all, her mother.

"Would you like to get together and talk about it?" he ventured. "I'm free for lunch if you'd like."

"Yes, sure. I'd like that, Arnie." They decided the crowd would be minimal this early in the week, so they agreed to meet in an hour at the Emerald Wok. She told him she would definitely show up this time.

*   *   *

Judy was waiting for him at eleven-thirty. When she saw him entering the restaurant, she got up and walked towards him. Without conscious thought, Arnie let his jacket drop to the floor and wrapped his arms around her, holding her tightly against his chest for a long while. Then, beginning to realize the scene they were probably causing, he broke away and picked up his coat.

As they headed towards the table, Arnie felt that he needed to apologize for his breach in behavior, referring to the unexpected, and somewhat lengthy, hug.

"Don't be silly! I liked it!" They sat down. "We're good friends who haven't seen each other in a long time, there's nothing wrong with hugging each other, Arnie."

He smiled but didn't say anything. The hug had felt like a lot more than just good friends, to him. And worse, he wanted to hold her even more.

"How are the kids doing?"

"Not as happy now that their Daddy had to go back to work and they don't get to spend as much time with him. But, I don't go in on the weekends anymore, so I can spend more time with them. I'm on Murray's hit list now, but the girls put me at the top of theirs, so who gives a hoot!" He found himself grinning like a fool. Judy's presence was making him giddy. *Can't be the alcohol, I haven't had any yet!*

His mood suddenly switched when Judy asked about Sondra.

"How is she doing now? Is your marriage better after spending more time at home?"

"No. If anything, it's gotten worse. We've come to the point where we feel better avoiding each other - not healthy, for sure.

200

But we can't seem to agree on anything. She knows about you now." Judy flinched. "I told her about our meeting for drinks when she wanted to know who I was with the night of the accident. She thinks we've been sleeping together, especially that night." He folded and unfolded a napkin, not wanting to meet her eyes when he told her that. "I can't change her mind. She hasn't been a happy person for a long time, and this was just another reason for her to be rude and angry at me."

"I'm real sorry, Arnie. I was hoping you could patch things up, for the girls' sake, if nothing else." She sounded sad, but he still wouldn't look at her.

"Yeah, me, too. So," he said, putting the mutilated napkin down and changing the subject. "Tell me about your mother." Sitting back and crossing his legs, he now looked over at her. "What happened?"

Respecting his desire to drop the subject, Judy told him about getting the phone call from the hospital. "My mom was remembering the time when dad left us. She was shouting and calling my father's name. The staff couldn't control her and they were afraid they'd have to sedate her before she hurt herself. So they called me to see what I wanted them to do.

"By the time I got to the hospital, about thirty-five minutes away, she had calmed down somewhat. But she was very hot and teary, and was running about a hundred and three temperature. She seemed to recognize my voice, my face, and wanted to hold onto my hand all night until she fell asleep. So I stayed with her all night. Whenever I left her side she got restless, so the doctors let me sleep on a cot in her room the first couple of days until her fever was gone. Then I rented a hotel room and spent much of the time with her, helping her get dressed in the morning, going to her activity classes, just spending time with her. I hadn't been with her for any length of time since she'd been admitted. It was nice." Just talking about it seemed to lift a weight from Judy's shoulders. Arnie could almost see it happening as she spoke.

They paused to take a sip of their drinks that Arnie had ordered while Judy was talking, an iced tea and a Diet Coke, respectively, since it was the middle of a workday. It seemed unreal to Arnie, sitting here as if nothing had happened. Like they had stepped back in time, before the accident, before Sondra had been told about their special friendship. That reminded him...

"Hey! You still owe me the end of your story! You weren't quite finished with it, if I recall."

Judy, flashing him an impish smile, said, "Is that right?"

"You're quite the story-teller, and I've waited with baited breath all this time just to hear how it ends. Come on, cough it up!" It felt good to return to their light-hearted bantering.

"Okay, where did I leave off?"

"I believe you had just returned from a night of partying with your first client."

"Ah, yes. Well, after actually seeing how easy it was, not to mention how much money I could make, I decided to keep working for Life Style Designers. The plan was to someday be able to hire nurses to care for my mother so I could have her at home with me.

"All communication was by phone, although I did go to the office building to get clothes to wear, but only at first. I was quickly able to afford my own gowns and nice accessories, and soon I stopped going there at all. Having built up trust in me, I no longer had to go to Life Styles to get the name of my client, either. Everything was passed onto me by a nameless voice over my private line. And, of course, as I mentioned before, all money transactions took place through automatic deposits.

"After that first "date" with Mr. Buckley, I assumed all the clients would all be about the same. I was so wrong! Some wanted a pretty face hanging on their arm to make a lover, male or female, jealous. Some were just very lonely people who didn't have any true friends and just wanted to go out with a nice girl. Those were my favorites. They treated me pleasantly, and, once the initial awkwardness passed, we usually had a good time. They weren't copping a phony attitude to impress other people. It was almost like we were on a real date.

"The worst ones had such chauvinistic attitudes! They seemed to think that, because they paid for my time, they could boss me around. I had a hard time not punching a few of those kind in the face and calling it quits!" She chuckled in remembrance. "But the money was too good, and I knew that the next client was bound to be better, so I stuck it out."

"I was surprised how many rich people there are out there, afraid to share their lives with somebody for fear they'll have to share their wealth, too. Sad, really."

Arnie couldn't help himself. "And what about sex?"

Judy gave him a small smile. "I knew that would come up sooner or later." She took a sip of her Coke, stalling. "Yes, occasionally I have met a special person that I was interested in sharing a bed with. I often run into clients, men, as well as women, who ask me to have sex with them." She stopped, trying to think how to word it delicately, so as not to come across as being loose.

Not sure he really wanted to hear anymore, Arnie still prodded her on. "So, how did you handle them asking you for sex? How did you determine who you wanted to sleep with?" Then he had to know. "Did you sleep with women, too?" He felt mortified that he'd actually asked that. He turned a deep shade of red and hid behind his glass as he took a long, refreshing drink. Thankfully, Judy didn't appear to notice.

"Sometimes you meet a person, and right away you know you're sexually attracted. I think we all feel that way, we *know* there's something there. It didn't happen very often, but when it did, I just went with the flow. We can't be *forced* into having a physical relationship with a client, but there's nothing in the rules saying they can't *ask*. I've had more than my share of passes made at me, but only a few sexual encounters. And only with men!" Judy pointedly remarked. Arnie, embarrassed, was still relieved to hear this.

"I had several repeat clients that would ask for me, but I only slept with a couple of them. It suited both of our purposes - great sex, no commitment."

Arnie blushed. He'd never heard so much talk about sex since he was a teenager, speculating about it with his buddies. "I understand the no-commitment part," he finally said. "So tell me. Do you actually like your job?"

"I've been asking myself that same question since I started five years ago. I don't know. It makes me happy that I can take care of my mother, even though I decided she's getting the best care she can right where she is. I can afford a very comfortable life. But I can't have a normal one, a normal life. It's been better since I've recently taken on the job of purchasing all the gowns and shoes for the girls. I get to go to suave fashion shows, travel to Paris and the like, and the company trusts me to buy the best out there..." She fell silent for a moment. "But I'm always working to please other people. My clients, the staff at Life Styles. I've learned a lot about people working in this kind of job, though."

"Like what? Explain it to me."

"Well, I'm always around wealthy people. But I can see that being rich doesn't necessarily make you happy. Many of them have married into a high society family just for the prestige and money. For show, or status. They stay together, not for love, but because dissolving the marriage would mean losing a big chunk of their money or property, sometimes their reputation. They don't even consider the children, how putting their wealth before their happiness might be affecting them. This is important to me because of how my own father left me. Never considering how I was feeling, never involving me in his new life. He took away his love when something else came along. And it affected me for the rest of my life."

Judy leaned forward across the table, as if to get closer to Arnie. "That was one of the things I admired in you, Arnie. From the first day I met you, you've been devoted to your children. Even with Sondra's behavior, and your marriage falling apart, you still stay with her for your daughters' sake. Because you love them. People choose to stay together for many wrong reasons. Money, the house, because of the rumors that would go around...only a few people stay together for the sake of their kids."

"Yes. Some of us make a commitment and stick by it." Arnie replied. "Sometimes we have to make sacrifices for our principles." He paused, thinking that over. "You do what you have to do to get through it. I don't think it's necessarily good for two people to keep slugging it out just so the kids will have two parents, though. There comes a time when, after you've tried everything, and it's still not working, perhaps it's in the best interest of those same kids to call it quits. Give them two calm, loving homes instead of one stressful one." He studied Judy's face. She seemed paler than he remembered. Possibly from the strain of taking care of her mother the past few weeks.

"Answer me this," Arnie said, curious. "What is your idea of a perfect marriage?"

Judy thought about it for a while. "Well, first you *must* marry for love. You need to be able to trust each other and enjoy life together. And you are committed to each other forever."

Arnie gave her a little smile. She made it sound so simple. "Okay, give me an example of a perfect couple."

"That's the problem, I can't. I'm sure there are some out there, but I don't know anyone right now."

"Ah, the grass is greener on the other side!"

"All right. Turn about is fair play. What's *your* idea of a perfect marriage?" She rested her chin on her hand, waiting to see what he would say.

Arnie grinned. "I guess I asked for that! I shouldn't have asked you that question, because there's no simple answer, but let me give it a try." Arnie thought about his words before answering.

"Well, first off, let's ask ourselves, what is a perfect marriage? Are we genuinely happy with each other, or is it only perfect in perception, satisfying the society we live in?" Arnie stopped to take a drink of his iced tea, the ice cubes rattling against the glass as he tipped it up.

"People," he resumed, "are different in nature. That's why the world is so interesting. It takes two to make a marriage, so marriage is a two-person issue, not just one. You have to learn to give and take, a balancing act, so to speak. And it takes commitment and understanding by both parties."

Arnie studied Judy's face to see if he was getting over her head, or if she was following what he was trying to say. Judy, reading his concern, smiled and nodded at him to continue.

"Okay, so let's start with the understanding that marriage, like most other things, goes through stages. The first test, I suppose," Arnie stated, holding up one finger, "is Falling in Love." Judy could almost hear the capital letters in this phrase as he said them and dabbed her mouth with her napkin to keep from smiling.

"People fall in love for many reasons. It can be a physical attraction, or maybe the sense of power they would achieve, money, or simply a feeling of being comfortable with each other. Something pulls two people towards each other and causes them to want to spend time together. They don't even have to be attracted to the same thing. Maybe he's in it for the physical side of the relationship, and she's enjoying spending his money. It happens all the time. Right?"

Without waiting for her to reply, Arnie continued.

"Second test: To get to know each other, they need to learn each other's likes and dislikes, and change their own habits to comfort each other – Give and take. Sometimes people learn these things before they get married, while dating, sometimes after. This helps them develop their comfort zone with each other, where they prove they care for each other's happiness. With me so far?" Arnie asked with a raised eyebrow. At her nod, he went on.

"Third: Build trust. I suppose how much and how quickly you learn to trust your partner depends, in part, on how you were raised, the environment you grew up in, as well as how your partner is interacting. Intelligence also plays a part. For some couples this takes longer than with others. And some blindly trust their partner when they shouldn't! But that's an entirely different story that we shall debate at another time, miss." Judy had to shake her head at his snooty tone. Throwing her a quick grin, he continued in a normal tone of voice.

"Fourth: There's the Physical Needs side of a relationship. What some of us like to call "sex." I don't think I have to go into great detail on the subject, I'm sure you know enough already." Judy laughed.

"Sexual compatibility plays a major part in what I think can make, or break, a marriage. Now, hear me out." He raised his hand to stop Judy's protest. "If you get along in bed, chances are you can carry that through into other areas of your life together, too, isn't that true? How many couples do you know of who hate each other, yet have a wonderful sex life? Hm, let me count...none! Case closed!" Again, Judy had to laugh at his playful tone. She was enjoying this immensely.

"Fifth: Responsibility. Taking responsibility and doing your part. In keeping a job, running a household, providing for each other's needs. Again, not just taking and taking, but giving of yourself, as well.

"And, finally, sixth: Children. If you haven't mastered the first five stages of your marriage, you are in a world of hurt if you decide to bring children into it. They are like the *hugest* responsibility you could ever imagine!"

"Do you think it's imperative that people be sure of the first five stages?" Judy asked thoughtfully.

"Yes, very much so. If one of the partners doesn't want children, because of the responsibility or any other reason, they shouldn't have any. Did you know that 42% of the US women executives or professionals don't have kids? They put their careers before babies. Having children is a big commitment and they understand this."

Arnie paused to give Judy time to let all this sink in, and to ask any questions she might have. After a couple of minutes in comfortable silence, Arnie jumped back in.

"A 'perfect marriage' might have a different meaning in different cultures. I think a person's culture and their parent's influence play a big role, too. In India, for example, the parents arrange all the marriages. Astrological charts are studied to check compatibility before marriage. If the charts don't agree, no marriage. It's their belief. If you're a girl, and you had sex out of wedlock, then nobody will marry you. You are soiled. The Indian culture has many rules and regulations, and if the couple follows them, they can achieve a perfect marriage-according to the Indian culture. India has the lowest divorce rate in the world. But, that doesn't mean all the marriages are happy.

"Here in the west, we don't have all those stringent rules. We do what our heart and head tell us to do. So, the bottom line is trust. Couples have to trust and care for each other to make a successful marriage. They have to try to succeed at all the stages I mentioned.

Arnie was feeling like the conversation had become a little too serious. "And so, to wrap up. The ones who have been able to achieve all these stages can become the so-called perfect couple! They can have a 'perfect marriage,' according to *me*. Now, I know, you're asking yourself - Has Arnie Martin achieved a perfect marriage? Well, let me put it this way. I have gotten *very* good at stage number four, but I need a *lot* of work on the other stages!" They both laughed.

"Well," Arnie sighed and pushed his chair back. " I better get going, it's getting late, and I still have some work to get done. My supervisor, Murray, was scheduled to attend a conference, but he informed me that he's sick, so has requested that I go in his place. I have to leave for the conference in LA tomorrow, and I should be back in four days. I have an early morning flight, so maybe we can get together for dinner or something when I get back."

Judy looked disappointed that their time was up. "That's what, the twentieth? When you get back?"

"Yes," Arnie replied, laying a tip down on the table.

"Sure, I think that's do-able." They both stood up. "Just give me a call." They parted company, each going in opposite directions.

Arnie was unaware that he had just had his last conversation with Judy before disaster struck.

Chapter 22

Late evening

Detectives John Ward and Neil Cawston arrived at Judy Larson's apartment building close to ten-thirty. Looking up at the immense ceiling of the lobby, with its intricately carved oak wainscoting, Neil gave a low whistle.

"Now this is the type of place I want to live in someday!"

John laughed. "You're dreaming! If you work for another thirty years and don't spend any money, you still wouldn't be able to afford their smallest apartment on your detectives' salary!"

They walked over to the security desk, where they introduced themselves and showed the security guard, Sam, their ID badges. Sam, caught dozing, was now all business, making a point of studying the badges closely before handing them back.

"What can I do for you, gentlemen? You're out kinda late, aren't ya?"

"We need to speak with Ms. Judy Larson, do you know if she's in?"

On the defensive, very protective of his tenants, Sam squinted at the detectives and asked if there was any trouble.

"No, not yet, anyway. We're here to get some information from her. Can you tell us what floor and room she is in, please?"

Sam looked like he was about to challenge their right to know, so John casually tapped his ID badge against the top of the counter to remind him who was in charge. He raised a questioning eyebrow and waited him out.

"All right. She lives on the twelfth floor, suite 1204. Elevator's over there," he said gruffly, tossing his head in the general direction.

John thanked him and pocketed his badge. They turned and headed in the direction the guard had shown them.

"I'm ringin' her up and warnin' her you guys are on your way up!" the security guard yelled out, determined on regaining control of the situation. John, not bothering to turn back around, just gave him a wave over his shoulder in acknowledgment.

Both detectives were stunned by all the lavish decorations, the original piece of artwork hanging on one wall, and elaborate wallpaper they encountered just inside the huge elevator. Neil jokingly wondered out loud where the manservant was to operate the elevator controls, like you see in the movies.

Arriving on the twelfth floor, the door pinged and opened with a gentle whoosh.

"Holy crap!" Neil exclaimed. "What do you suppose it costs to rent a place like this?" His mouth hung open in awe. The lobby couldn't compare with the elegance that met them on this floor.

"I don't know, but I'm pretty sure it's more than the whole police division makes combined!" John noticed that there were only two doors on this floor, separated by a small lobby. The one they wanted was to the left of the elevator, "Suite 1204" placed in gold letters on the golden oak-stained door. He headed that way.

Having received the security guards warning call, Judy was expecting them and opened the door before they could knock.

Once again showing badges and introducing themselves, John apologized for the late hour, and asked if they could come in to talk to her about a serious matter.

"I was getting ready to go to bed, can't this wait until morning, Detective?" Judy was dressed in a silk, turquoise robe, which she was holding together tightly in front with one hand. Her other hand kept the door closed, allowing a five-inch gap to speak through.

Neil couldn't help but look her over. Her feet, or what he could see of them through the crack of the door, were bare. A thin, gold toe ring was placed below the knuckle of her left middle toe; he could see it gleaming in the dim light of the hall. With her hair down, long and shining, as if she'd just brushed it out, Neil thought she had to be the most gorgeous creature he'd ever met.

John coughed discreetly to get Neil's attention, hoping their interviewee hadn't noticed him staring so blatantly at her - or they'd never get in the front door!

Neil, looking up from Judy's very sexy feet, in his opinion, caught John's eye and had the grace to look guilty at being caught ogling the suspect. He cleared his throat and looked down at his own black-leather clad feet.

"I'm afraid this can't wait. Can we come in, please, then I'll tell you what it's all about."

Glancing at the closed door at the opposite end of the hallway, Judy seemed to make up her mind and moved aside to invite them in. It didn't go unnoticed by either detective that she left the door open several inches.

"I hope this isn't going to take long. I have to get up for a very early appointment in the morning." She ushered them into her living room, light and inviting, even at this time of night.

The detectives each took a seat on the sofa, while Judy, wrapping her robe around her legs, curled up in one of the matching chairs. Trying not to feel overwhelmed by their elegant surroundings, the detectives sat at the very edge of their seats.

Unable to stop himself, Neil told her he felt like he was sitting in a palace. Smiling for the first time since they showed up, Judy thanked him, then directed her full attention to John and asked him what this was all about.

"Do you know Arnold Martin?"

Not expecting this, Judy was caught off guard, "Yes! Yes, I do." She sat up in her chair, placing her feet onto the carpet. "Has something happened to him again?" She was thinking of the night he'd been hit by a car, right outside her building. John was surprised at the distress that immediately took over her previously annoyed visage. He wondered just how close she and Dr. Martin had actually been.

"Are you familiar with his wife, Sondra Martin?"

Puzzled, Judy told them that she knew *of* Sondra, but did not know her personally, and had never really met her. When John wanted her to explain her last statement, she told them of seeing Sondra in the hospital when she'd visited Arnie after his accident. "Arnie used to talk about her and the girls all the time, but that was the first time I had seen her. And we didn't talk or anything. Why?"

"Mrs. Martin was killed this morning. We suspect foul play." John watched her reactions closely. Her response seemed natural, not acted.

"Oh, my God!" She put a hand over her mouth. "Poor Arnie! And those little girls!" Tears started to run down her face. Discomfited with women's emotions, he turned to Neil, silently asking him to do something.

Neil reached over to the lamp table and plucked a couple of tissues out of an ornate white and gold tissue box. Taking a few steps to her chair, he handed them to her, then returned to his seat. Judy sniffled, and tearfully thanked the young man.

"How did it happen?" She dabbed at her eyes and seemed to get herself under control.

"She was stabbed. What is your relationship with Arnold Martin?"

She looked up, tears still sparkling on her lashes. Even with a tear-streaked face, Neil thought she couldn't be any more beautiful. Smitten, he sighed quietly. She was way out of his league and he knew it.

"I don't have a relationship with him. Well, we're good friends," she added.

Taking his notepad from his jacket breast pocket, John sat back and crossed his legs.

"Where were you from two this afternoon, to about, say, five o'clock?"

It took several moments for this question to sink in. Then,

astounded, Judy's immediate response was to stand up. "I'm afraid I'm not willing to answer any more questions unless my lawyer is present. You'll have to leave now."

John leaned over and whispered something to Neil. Then they both stood up, John closing his notebook and replacing it in his pocket, shaking his head at the turn of events.

"If that's how you want to handle this, fine. Call your lawyer, but you'll have to come down to the station with us for questioning there."

"What! This is outrageous! I'm not even dressed! And I'm expected in Vegas in the morning, I can't just not show up!" Her cheeks had taken on a ruddy hue as her anger built up. "You'll have to get a court order, or whatever they do in these cases." Spine stiff, arms crossed, she was determined not to back down.

John hated riling up the suspects, it was always better if they came willingly. He kept his tone low and expressionless, not letting her see that he was getting a bit ticked off at how he had mishandled the questioning – not to mention *her* lack of cooperation on top of it.

"I'm afraid there's nothing we can do about your trip to Vegas, ma'am. But if you'll go get dressed and give your lawyer a call, maybe we can get this all straightened up in time for you to catch your flight. We *are* taking you to the station," he added firmly, crossing his own arms across his chest, equally determined on getting his way.

At his no-nonsense tone, Judy flung her hair off her shoulder and stalked into her bedroom, slamming the door.

"Do you suppose she'll go out the window or something?" asked Neil, slightly amused.

"No, although it wouldn't surprise me if she had a little private elevator in there." He rolled his eyes in exasperation. "She's a feisty one, I have to give her credit for that."

Dressed in designer jeans and a well-worn Mariners sweatshirt, Judy came out of her bedroom and glared at the detectives. Neil had the urge to defend himself and tell her it wasn't *him*, it was his *partner* causing all the trouble here! But he wisely kept his thoughts to himself.

"My lawyer says he's on his way and will meet us at the station." She grabbed her purse and stomped to the front door. "Let's get this over with, shall we?" She pulled the door open the rest of the way and waited for the two men to proceed through so she could lock the dead bolt.

As they went down the elevator and out into the night, John asked her if she owned a car, and what make.

Judy stopped and thrust her chin up in the air. "Yes, I do. It's a BMW. I keep it in the garage. Why? Do you want to take it for a spin?" Judy knew her sarcasm would undoubtedly come back to haunt her, but she couldn't seem to help it. This man rubbed her the wrong way!

Grinding his teeth, John mentally counted to ten. "Do you mind riding with us? We'll bring you back after all the questions are asked."

"Do I have a choice?" she asked flippantly.

John shrugged. "Not really." Neil tried not to laugh. He was getting a big kick out of the sparks flying between this admirable lady and his partner.

John threw him a hard glance that told him to shape up. Then he directed Judy to climb into the back seat of their sedan. Seeing her wrinkle her nose at the plain, unadorned vehicle, John couldn't help but retort. "Sorry, we forgot to bring the Rolls Royce." He slammed the door as soon as she pulled her legs into the car.

Hearing Neil snicker, he told him to shut up and drive, and they both got into the car. Neil, not at all cowed by his older partner's admonishment, grinned as he slid behind the wheel.

Neil, glancing frequently at Judy in the rear view mirror, was thinking to himself that this lady was too stunning, too refined, to have committed murder. He wasn't naive enough to think that beautiful people couldn't kill, it happened all the time. It was her personality, and his gut instinct about her. Killing somebody in cold blood? It just didn't feel right. No way. Not this lady.

John, slouched in the passenger seat, thinking almost those same thoughts, reached out and adjusted the mirror, preventing any further spying on their back seat passenger.

*   *   *

Their arrival at the station caused quite a stir. Used to dealing with junkies, drunken spouses, and other riffraff at that time of night, the station came to a standstill when Judy entered the building with the two detectives. They were all wondering what such a beautiful woman was doing there. She didn't look like a criminal as she walked between the two men, head held high.

John led her to a room in the back, and told her to have a seat. Leaving her there to steep in her own ire, John signaled for Neil to come with him and they left the room. On his way through the station, he stopped at the desk and had one of the men take a trip out to talk to the taxi driver. "See if he can make an ID on the lady."

"What am I supposed to show him for the ID? You got a photo or something?"

John went to his office and retrieved a copy of Judy's high school junior year photo they'd obtained earlier. The officer being sent to talk to the driver reached out and took the photocopy.

"You're kidding, right? I'm supposed to show a photo of a kid?" He waved the paper in disbelief.

"She hasn't changed much since then. Just go. Now."

"All right! I'm going." The officer turned on his heels and left, still of the belief that a year book picture wasn't going to cut it. He'd seen the lady in question when she had come in. He shrugged and left on his mission.

Returning ten minutes later, John and Neil were accompanied by a slim, serious-looking man. At fifty-three, Walter Rodenberg spoke in a firm, no-backing-down tone of voice. All of the officers at the police station knew Rodenberg. He was the best criminal lawyer in town and had the reputation of having never lost a case yet. This could have been an exaggeration, but he was tough, and the cops knew, if he was on the case, you'd better watch out. He was very expensive, and very good. Some of the judges were even afraid of him, and dreaded seeing his name on the docket.

Watching him stride aggressively through the station house, several of the officers murmured to themselves. "This is going to be big." "She must be very important to be able to afford that shark!" "John got himself into a mess this time!"

Ignoring the hushed comments, John escorted the lawyer to the interrogation room, closing the door behind them. He was also wondering just who this woman was to know Rodenberg. And what kind of connections she had to be able to get him to come to the station on such short notice. Just who was Judy Larson, he wondered silently.

The lawyer quietly greeted Judy and told her everything would be all right, that he'd have her out of there as soon as possible. "Okay," said Rodenberg, turning his forceful attention to the detectives. "What's going on here!"

John, counter-acting the lawyers booming voice with his own softer tone, explained that Sondra Martin, wife of one Arnold Martin, who was also a friend of Ms. Larson's, had been killed in her home earlier that afternoon. "A witness has placed Ms. Larson at the scene of the crime and had seen her rushing from the house approximately fifteen or twenty minutes before the death was discovered."

Hearing this for the first time, Judy's face blanched.

"Is there any other evidence against my client?" Barked Rodenberg.

"No, sir. Not at this time. It's still being investigated. We need to ask her a few questions now that you're here."

"All right. Leave us alone for a few minutes," he ordered. "You can ask your questions after I speak with my client."

Summarily dismissing the detectives, who had no choice but to leave, Rodenberg sat down next to Judy, who looked very shaken and pale.

"You, my dear, are a very lucky girl. I had just arrived home from New York two hours ago when your people at Life Style Designers called me." The very tall lawyer lifted his wrist and squinted at his watch. "Almost twelve. I'm getting too old for this!" he stated, but with a kind smile.

"Okay," he said, switching to a more serious tact. "I need to get to bed and get some rest, so let's get right down to it. I'm only going to ask you once, so don't waste my time. If I find out you lied to me, I will no longer represent you, is that clear?"

"Yes, Mr. Rodenberg. I won't lie to you." Her voice was shaking, she was scared.

"Did you kill Sondra Martin?"

"No, sir!"

"Did you have anything to do with her death?"

"You mean like hire somebody to do it? No!"

"So how did you get involved in all this? How do you know the victim's husband?"

"I met Arnie - Dr. Martin - on a flight coming from Los Angeles a few months ago. We talked and hit it off, we've been friends ever since."

"Were you sleeping together?"

"No. We just met for a drink once in a while, to talk. That's all." She weaved her fingers together; they were as cold as ice.

Nodding, Rodenberg wrote some notes on a yellow pad he'd pulled from the worn briefcase he'd carried in with him. Then he told her to describe what had brought her to the Martin home that afternoon.

"Well, Mrs. Martin believed her husband and I were having an affair. She called me two days ago and invited me to her home for a chat. I told her that Arnie and I weren't having an affair! She wouldn't believe that we were just friends, and said that it was causing a lot of arguments between the two of them. She said if we got together to talk about it, I could help clear things up. So I agreed to meet with her. I thought maybe then all the fighting between them would stop. I was only trying to help," she said miserably.

"I believe you. But the courts might not. What happened after you got to the house?"

"Sondra was decent for a while, but then she started shouting at me and getting angry. Her sudden change like that scared me and I got out of there!"

"Did you touch her, maybe shove her out of your way when you were trying to leave?"

"No! I never laid a hand on her. I'm positive. I backed away from her and ran out the door!"

"Okay. I'm thinking we won't have that much to worry about, then. We'll go over the details with a fine toothed comb later, after we both get some sleep." He turned towards the door and called John back in.

"I'll give you fifteen minutes to ask your questions, then my client and I are both leaving to get some sleep. Agreed?"

Feeling like he hadn't actually been given a choice in the matter at all, John took out his own notes and began the questioning.

He asked her to tell him how she knew Arnie and Sondra, and what led up to Judy going to Sondra's house. She repeated what she had told her lawyer, including how Sondra's personality had suddenly changed to anger.

"Was she trying to hit you, so you felt you had to defend yourself?"

"No, not at all. She was just screaming at me that I'd stolen her husband."

A tap on the glass window of the door interrupted them, and Neil walked in. Approaching John, he told him they had spoken to the taxi driver.

"And?"

"We showed him the photo we got from her high school yearbook and he has positively identified her." He gave Judy an apologetic look. "The time matches his sign-in sheet, too."

John stood up, and asking Rodenberg to come with him, he

walked out into the hallway without waiting for a response.

"I'm sorry, Sir, but we have enough evidence to keep Ms. Larson here, at least overnight."

"What evidence! That she rode in a taxi?" Rodenberg blustered.

"With a witness placing her at the scene of the crime before and after the victim's death, and another witness, the taxi driver, confirming that she was picked up shortly before the death was reported, we have enough evidence to book her."

"With a school picture? You must be joking! That won't hold up in court!"

"The lady herself is saying she was at the house until shortly before the victim was killed." John reminded the attorney.

Rodenberg rubbed his chin thoughtfully. "Who is the witness that saw her go into the house?"

"The lady who lives across the street, Laveen Chapman. She's somewhat of a nosy-body, but she seems reliable, according to the neighbors. She also saw Ms. Larson leave the scene of the crime and was the one who discovered the body."

"Bit of a rough go for the woman, hm?" He just didn't think Judy was guilty. He usually had a keen sense about people, and his senses were screaming that she was innocent. "Did the neighbor see her kill the woman?"

"No, of course, not. But she can place her as the last person to see the victim alive."

"Let me go talk to her again. Alone." And he closed the door before John could follow him into the room. A moment later, Neil, who had stayed with Judy while they talked, came out with a disgruntled look on his face.

"He's sure a bossy one!" John could only agree. Not sure if he should wait or let the lawyer find him, John chose to remain in the hall. They might get it over with faster if he hung around.

Judy could tell by looking at the attorney that something was wrong.

"They don't believe me?" She rubbed her arms; a chill had

passed over her.

"It isn't a matter of believing you or not. Even though they have no proof that you actually killed Mrs. Martin, they have just enough circumstantial evidence on you being at the crime scene at a crucial time that they can keep you here tonight. They're going to have to book you. I'm sorry."

Judy put her hand to her face. "You mean I'm being arrested?" A tear started tracking down her face. "This can't be happening. I didn't do anything!" She started to sob into her hands.

Rodenberg didn't think she'd had a hand in the murder and it broke his heart to see this young lady in such distress. "Aw, don't cry! I can't stand seeing a woman cry," he exclaimed, handing her a napkin from the table. "I'll get bail posted tomorrow after the arraignment, and you'll be home in no time. You have to have patience, these things don't happen overnight. You need to trust me. We'll find the real killer, and you'll be free and clear of this whole mess. You'll see. Now, come on, buck up! You have to be strong."

Judy gave him a watery smile. "You're sure I only have to be here one night?" At Rodenberg's nod, she took a deep breath. "Well, looks like I have no choice, then. I'll have to trust you."

"That's my girl!" The attorney went to the door and told John he could come in.

John had an officer read Judy her Rights, and then a female officer led her to a detention area. They had her remove everything from her pockets, took her fingerprints, and finished up by taking photos of her facing forward, then in profile. Judy was having a hard time keeping her tears from flowing again, and sniffed frequently in an attempt to maintain control. She kept thinking that all this would end as soon as she woke up. It was the only way she could get through it. Especially after she was placed in a holding cell, and the metal bars of the door clanged shut with such finality. She shivered, as much from fear as from the chill air, and let her pent-up tears fall.

John, walking back to his office after finalizing things with

Rodenberg, had just gotten his way with the best lawyer in the state of Washington. He was feeling ten feet tall – as long as he didn't allow himself to picture Judy Larson's sorrowful face, or the stark fear he saw in her blue eyes when they had led her away.

Chapter 23

John walked up to the Chapman door and knocked. Laveen, dressed casually in jeans and a red, Henley T-shirt, answered, looking surprised, and worried, to see the detective again.

Standing below the stoop, one foot on the top step, he cut straight to the chase, telling Laveen that he needed her help.

"My help? How?" She looked like she wanted to shut the door on him.

"I need you to come down to the station with me and identify the woman you saw going to and from the Martin house yesterday."

Laveen glanced over her shoulder, but John couldn't see past her to see what she was looking at. "I need to discuss it with my husband first."

"I understand your reluctance, but it's important. I'm running out of time. It won't take very long, and you'll be back in no time. Please." He tried not to let his exasperation show.

John could almost see the wheels turn in her head as she thought it over, then made her decision.

"All right. But only if I don't have to talk to the woman, and you bring me right back!"

John, relieved, nodded and told her that he promised to have her back before the next hour. Laveen told him she needed about five minutes to get ready and ushered John into the living room to wait. A well-worn man in his early sixties - Mr. Chapman, John surmised - was sitting in a chair nearby, his balding head reflecting the light from the lamp. He was reading the morning paper, a cup of steaming coffee on the lamp table beside him. The rich smell it was exuding started to make John's stomach growl. Laveen went over and quietly spoke to him before going to get ready.

Jake Chapman nodded at the detective, then continued reading the news. A few minutes later he got up to poke his head into their bedroom to tell his wife good-bye, once again nodded at John and was out the door, heading for City Hall where he worked in accounting.

A man of few words, John thought.

Less than fifteen minutes later, John and Laveen were at the police station. John wasn't too happy to hear that Walter Rodenberg and his client were already there. He was hoping to have a few minutes to regroup before he had to face the powerful lawyer again.

John escorted Laveen to a small room with a window overlooking a second room. Laveen was nervous until John explained that it was a one-way mirror, and the people inside the other room could not see them standing there. "Just like the movies!" exclaimed Laveen. "This is rather exciting, isn't it?" John couldn't help but smile at her infectious attitude, the weather lines at the corner of his eyes crinkling up in response.

He directed her to look into the room and see if she recognized the woman from the taxi. In the room on the other side of the glass was a narrow stage. Several minutes later, eight women were led out and told to stand against the wall, facing the window, then to turn in either direction for a side view.

Laveen recognized the woman that had visited Sondra right away. "That's her! She's the one I saw with Sondra the day she died!" She stabbed a finger at the glass in her excitement.

John let out the breath he didn't know he had been holding in anticipation. Things were finally going somewhere. "Please state the number, Mrs. Chapman."

Laveen counted and said, "The fourth girl from the right." She thought the woman was very lovely, and looked distraught. She had time to feel brief pity for the woman before she was ushered out of the room and back into the detective's office.

After having Mrs. Chapman fill out and sign a witness report, John had one of the officers run her back home, telling Laveen they'd be in touch with her if they needed her to testify. Feeling very important, Laveen couldn't wait until she could get to the phone and tell her friends what she'd been up to today.

Changing the order of the line-up, John repeated the process with the taxi driver, who had been brought in by his partner. The driver walked in with a big smile on his face, glad to be doing something different from his ordinary day of driving. After looking them over carefully, the driver pointed to one of the girls. "The pretty one with the red and blue dress."

"Which number would that be, sir?"

"The second one from the left." John thanked him, and directed him to his office, switching on the intercom and telling the guard inside the room that he was finished with the line-up and they could take Ms. Larson back to the room where her lawyer, Rodenberg was waiting for her.

That done, John called up the lab to see how the testing was going on the evidence found in the victim's home. He got the chief lab technician, Milo Potter.

"We were able to get two partials and one good print off the small bottle found beside the victim. And we found a fairly decent thumb print on the leather knife handle. We ran them through the computer, but no matches were found. That just means that whoever left the fingerprints didn't have a criminal record.

"The good news is that the prints on the bottle match your prime suspect. The bad news is that the lab techs were able to get a close match of the knife print to the victim herself, which means she probably grabbed hold of the knife after it was inserted, smearing the killer's prints, which would have been over-laid by her own. Sorry, man."

"What about the cloth itself?" John switched the phone to his other ear to better take notes.

"Just your standard fifty percent cotton/fifty percent polyester hankie. No prints were distinguishable, probably because the chemical used eradicated them. We're still running tests on it, as well as on the body, but it's looking good that she had a healthy dose of Chloroform or Ethyl Alcohol in her before she died."

John knew that both were easily obtained. Previously used in products such as fire extinguishers and spot removers for dry cleaners, the incidence of fatalities and possible link to cancer had made manufacturers take a second look. It was mostly used nowadays as a reagent in laboratories, meaning it was used in chemical processes to detect other substances. He wasn't sure how that worked, just that it made the substance obtainable to anybody with connections to research or lab work. *Like Arnold Martin,* mused John.

"She's also tested positive on the drug screen, but we're still trying to pinpoint specifics, so I can't give you that info just yet. I'll buzz you when I have more."

"Thanks, Milo." He hung up, wishing he had more to work with, but it was a start. He hitched up his trousers, hypothetically donning his armor, and went to speak to Rodenberg. "Let's see what he has to say about *this*!"

John knocked on the door, interrupting whatever conversation was taking place between Rodenberg and Judy. "Rodenberg, I'd like to see you for a moment."

Judy looked up. John had to look away from the stark fear in her pretty eyes. She had a 'Now what has happened?' expression on her face.

Closing the door behind him, Walter Rodenberg joined John out in the hallway.

With a confident voice, John informed him that they had ample evidence against Ms. Larson to take the case to trial.

"What evidence?" Rodenberg stood at least a head taller than John, who was over six feet himself. But because of his thin build, it gave the lawyer the illusion of extra height. John subconsciously drew himself up straighter, trying not to be intimidated by the attorney's curt manner.

"The neighbor lady, Mrs. Chapman, and the taxi driver

positively identified your client as the lady she'd seen leaving the Martin house just before she found the body. Plus we have fingerprints on the bottle found at the scene that matches the ones taken from your client. I'm sorry," John felt the need to say. "But we have enough to go to court."

Looking stormy, Rodenberg glared at John, then turned sharply and went back in to talk to Judy, slamming the door in his wake. John flinched and turned to leave, wondering what he'd said that had pushed the lawyer's button so hard. He didn't feel too badly about it, either!

Rodenberg stood by the door, looking angrily at Judy, making her wonder what the detective had told him that had made him so mad. And what she was about to hear.

"You," the attorney exclaimed loudly, pointing a finger at her. "You lied to me!"

He stalked over to her and pulled a chair out roughly from the table, dropping heavily onto it despite his slight build. Judy, scared, rose from her own chair, watching the lawyer carefully.

"Why do you say that? I never lied to you!" Her hand drifted to her mouth, lingering there before going down to clasp the other at waist level. "I didn't lie to you!" she insisted again. "Tell me what happened out there! What did he say?"

"They found your fingerprints on some of the evidence. Can you tell me how your fingerprints got all over everything if you weren't part of the murder?" He had calmed down somewhat but his anger was still simmering below the surface.

Judy was shocked, and sat down again. "I don't know."

Rodenberg sighed. "This is going to be a tricky case. Are you absolutely sure you had nothing to do with the murder? Not even an inkling of what was going to take place?"

"I swear, I had nothing to do with it! I didn't know it was going to happen. How could I have known something like that!" Judy rested her head on her palms, her fingers covering her eyes for a moment. She couldn't even cry anymore at this latest news.

"Okay." Rodenberg apologized for yelling at her and losing

his temper. "Every minute this case seems to get worse. I'm going to get a hearing to set bail and get you out of here. Then, I want you to tell me everything you did from the second you entered the Martin house to the instant you walked out their door. If I'm going to get you cleared of this murder, I need to know every little detail, okay?"

Judy agreed. "Do I have to stay another night in here," knowing what the answer would be before she asked it.

"I'm afraid so. With this latest evidence against you, we'll need to go in front of a judge, plead 'not guilty', and have bail set. With any luck, we'll get the arraignment in the morning, and get a sympathetic judge."

*　　　　*　　　　*

"I have to stay here two more days!" Judy cried. Her depression had just gotten worse. Everything had felt so hopeless, and now this latest blow.

"I'm sorry," her lawyer informed her. "It's the best I could do. Things are pretty booked up, with all the crime going on everywhere. We're lucky State law requires the arraignment to be held within forty-eight hours, or you might be here longer! It's unfortunate that the weekend adds time to that - no cases on Sunday, you know."

He was sitting with Judy in a little room set aside for client-attorney meetings. They spent the next hour going over all the details of her visit, what led up to it, what was said in the Martin home, even what she was wearing that fateful day.

Leaving the holding wing of the jail, Rodenberg went straight to his office. He stopped at his assistant's desk and asked her to look up everything she could find on Arnold and Sondra Martin. "Anything on their marriage - like counseling they attended, doctors visits, anybody having any affairs on the side, you name it! I don't care how you get the information, just get it!"

His assistant, Rebecca Simms, was a twenty-six year old

recently graduated intern from Stanford University. Petite, with her hair cut in a short, pixie style, she looked as if Rodenberg could have eaten her for breakfast. But looks were deceiving, and the tiny assistant had quickly learned to hold her own with the gangly lawyer, and had become invaluable to him. She was used to his gruff personality, and let it slide over her whenever she dealt with him.

"Got it," she replied now, getting up to return to her own desk. She hated to admit it, but she actually liked this part of her job, digging up dirt on the victims and their families. Not that she liked slamming other people, but because it made her normally repetitive job a lot more interesting. And she was good at it, too. People took one look at this cute, harmless looking young lady, and just started opening up with all their deep, dark secrets. In the short time she'd worked here, she had proven over and over again that people, especially men, thought that blondes were empty headed creatures, and often bragged about things they wouldn't otherwise have revealed. She milked it for all it was worth. And keeping up with her regular peroxide treatments didn't hurt any, either!

*   *   *

Midnight

Judy had been sitting in her cell thinking. There was little else to do *but* think. At first she had occupied her time by trying to make out the graffiti, barely discernible on the slate gray concrete walls. It looked as if somebody had recklessly slapped a few coats of paint on at some point in the past, but which now had begun to fall off in great thin flakes. Parts of old drawings and words intermingled with the latest verses and obscene illustrations that had been added on the top layers, making it difficult to figure out the messages. It was probably just as well, Judy thought. She didn't think she really wanted to know what was on the minds of the former occupants.

She stared at a tiny moth that had been keeping her company. It's minuscule wings beat futilely against the metal screen surrounding the dim bulb over her head. She felt like that moth. Trapped.

The difference between her apartment and this shoebox-sized prison cell was like comparing a refuse heap to Mount Everest. "And it smells like a garbage dump, too!" she murmured to herself. She was sure that the people who had resided in the cell before her must have preferred to use a dark corner rather than the primitive-looking, rust-stained contraption barely passing as a toilet.

She was huddled up against the wall, seated on the hard cot they provided. She could feel the cold, metal frame under the thin mattress pad. She thought about everything that had led up to her being imprisoned, her depression deepening.

"I have been able to solve so many other people's problems. Why can't I solve my own?" She thought about Arnie. If she hadn't met him, she wouldn't be in this situation.

"No, that's wrong," she told herself. "If I hadn't thought I could help with his marriage problems, I wouldn't be here." She had always been so careful in the past, tried not to do anything foolish, didn't get herself into any predicament that could endanger her life or her way of living. Yet, here she was. Had it been a mistake to get so close to Arnie? A married man with a family? It hadn't felt like that. Like a mistake in judgment.

She wondered if he would come to see her after he found out that she was the prime suspect in his wife's murder. And would he think she had done it. That, more than anything, disturbed her. She didn't want Arnie to go through the rest of his life thinking she was the cause of his wife's death. Arnie deserved so much better in life than what he was getting.

She watched the moth, scenes of how she'd met Arnie on the plane, talking with him in the restaurant and hospital going through her mind like a movie. She pictured the two girls as she'd seen them last, sitting in the uncomfortable hospital chairs, walking with their mother from the elevator. The oldest looking like a miniature Sondra, the youngest like her father. What would happen to Heather and Ashley now, without their mother? How was Arnie handling his grief? He had always doted on the girls, had been so patient with Sondra through it all. And as for herself, well, he had always treated her so nice. She admired his good looks, his faithfulness to his family, his intelligence and sharp sense of humor.

"Everything I wanted in a man, and didn't even know it." She continued to follow the little moth, on its useless mission, unaware of the warm tears sliding down her face.

Chapter 24

8:45 a.m. - The arraignment

Two female officers came to Judy's cell that morning to take her through the jail tunnel that led to the courthouse across the street. Rodenberg had prepared her for the bail hearing, but she was still overwhelmed by the whole process. Trembling, she was led to a hard wooden bench to wait her turn, set for nine o'clock. One of the officers stayed with her, taking her place beside the bench, but remained standing. *At least I don't have to wear handcuffs. Or one of those gaudy orange jump suits,* she thought, unsuccessfully attempting to make herself feel better. She looked straight ahead, refusing to see who might be in the courtroom. Very afraid that she would see TV crews, or worse yet, Arnie.

Shortly before nine o'clock, Judy was led to the front of the courtroom, and instructed to sit at a table and chairs facing the judge's bench, where she was soon joined by Walter Rodenberg. He squeezed her hand and told her it would be okay.

Detective John Ward, accompanied by the prosecuting attorney, Fred Moore, and a very pregnant woman, entered the room and sat at the table on the opposite side of the room. Rodenberg was apparently familiar with them, as he nodded and greeted them solemnly.

"Morning, Detective. Fred. Miss...?"

"Good morning, Walter," replied Fred, putting his statements onto the table in preparation for the hearing. "This is my assistant, Irene Hill."

"Mrs. Hill," he said, with a tip of his head. She replied with a slight smile, concentrating on sitting down gracefully, a feat in itself since her belly protruded to the point where nothing could be done without a contortion act. She sighed in relief when, with Fred's helpful arm, she was safely seated on the sturdy, wooden chair.

Arnie came early and found a chair in the back, where he could watch the proceedings without being obvious.

While Rodenberg got his own notes ready, he explained to Judy who they were, but was soon interrupted by the Bailiff calling, "All rise!"

Judy, standing up as the rest of the people in the room rose, happened to glance behind her. In the back, almost hidden behind a tall, heavy-set woman, was Arnie. Her eyes were drawn immediately to his familiar form, a questioning look on his face. She quickly dropped her glance and turned to the front, her worst fears acknowledged. She wondered why Arnie had to come and witness her humiliation.

Arnie caught Judy looking over at him and squirmed on the hard bench seat. He wasn't at all sure how to react, and was relieved when she turned away.

Judge Anne French was in her early fifties, short brown hair infused with gray, her brown eyes kind. She had become a friend of Walter's over the years, and, not always liking his stern, unforgiving approach, still respected his style and knowledge.

Judge French, squinting through her reading glasses, briefly re-familiarized herself with the charges before asking the prosecuting attorney to state those charges to the court.

Fred Moore stood up. "The State of Washington charges Ms. Judy Larson with the murder of Sondra Martin, your Honor."

Judge French looked at Judy. "Do you understand the charges against you, Ms. Larson?"

Looking nervously at Walter, she said, "Yes, I do, your Honor."

"And how does the defendant plead?"

Walter stood up, patting Judy's shoulder as he did so. "Not

guilty, your Honor," he replied, his voice confident and firm.

"A 'not guilty' plea is entered." The judge nodded to the court secretary. "Bail to be set at five hundred thousand." Judy blanched.

"Your Honor", Fred Moore rose. "The State requests bail be withheld until the trial. We feel the suspect is a high risk for fleeing, your Honor, given the high amount of funds available to her, and the nature of the crime."

"Is there evidence that can prove this young lady committed the murder?" She scanned the courtroom.

John stood up. "Yes, your Honor. I am Detective John Ward, assigned to this case. We have obtained fingerprints on some of the evidence found near the body, there are two reliable eyewitnesses placing Ms. Larson at the scene and the suspect herself has confirmed being at the residence only shortly before the murder took place. We also ask at this time for a search warrant to enter the suspect's apartment."

Arnie, hearing all of this, felt the dread build up inside.

"Counselor?" Judge French looked over at Walter, who once again stood up.

"Your Honor, I would like to point out that my client has never been arrested for, or convicted of any previous crime. Yes, Ms. Larson admits to being present with the victim around the allotted time the crime took place. But she did not kill Mrs. Martin!" he stressed. "Just because my client was visiting with the victim, and handled a few items in the house, does not prove that she committed the murder. I also see no need to violate Ms. Larson's home, seeing as there is no justification for searching it. I would ask that, taking into consideration, that my client does not have a criminal record of any kind, the search warrant be withheld, and she be released without bail, your Honor." He sat down.

After a few tense moments of looking over her notes, Judge French made her decision.

"Based on the information I have heard today, bail will be denied. The trial date will be set for..." The judge looked over at the Bailiff, who glanced at his calendar before answering.

"Wednesday, November 15, nine o'clock a.m., your Honor."

"Gentlemen, please see the bailiff for your schedules," the Judge continued. "Your application for the search warrant is granted, Counselor," she said with a slight incline of her head in Fred's direction. Judge French stood up, effectively ending the hearing.

"All rise!" said the Bailiff.

Judy, stunned by the judge's decision, stood up only when her lawyer pulled on her arm. She dropped back onto her chair the second the judge left for her quarters and the people were allowed to relax.

This meant she had to stay in jail until the trial date – over two weeks! She hung her head and cried. Arnie, leaving the courthouse, couldn't believe it. Hearing the evidence against his friend, Arnie found himself, for the first time, doubting her innocence. Could she really have killed his wife? He started to wish that he had never met her.

*   *   *

With search warrant in hand, John and Neil took a handful of officers and headed out to Judy's apartment. The apartment was clean and, as they were able to explore it in depth, very luxurious. They carefully searched every inch of every closet and cabinet, and eventually turned up a light yellow dress, broken up by one inch-wide diagonal stripes of navy blue, tossed in the bedroom hamper, bearing bloodstains on the front. Also found was a business card case holding several different cards bearing various names, but always with Judy as the first name. This puzzled the investigators. A thorough search of the rest of the apartment turned up nothing further.

Chapter 25

Sondra's funeral, accompanied by the oppressive rain, was held two weeks after the Medical Examiner finally agreed to release the body for burial. McDaniels had determined that they got all the information and samples they could possibly need, and saw no further need to keep the family waiting.

Under a sea of umbrellas stood her many family and friends, trying to offer solace to the two black-clad little girls, weeping and holding tightly to their father's large, comforting hand, as well as to the tall, somber man sitting stiffly beside them.

Arnie, feeling numb, was having a hard time hearing the words the pastor was saying, meant to reassure them all that Sondra had gone to a better place. Listening to the gentle patter of the rain on the canopy overhead and pinging onto the umbrellas ringing the gravesite, he was disturbed by his thoughts. Thoughts of Judy, his wife, his kids. He was thinking of selling the house, which the girls had practically grown up in.

Move to a new city, a new job, a new house – one that doesn't have blood stains all over the living room carpet! He shuddered and placed an arm around his daughters shoulders, seated on each side of him, drawing them tightly against his chest. *Make a new start for the girls and me. Maybe we can make it if we go somewhere far away from here.*

He wanted to go see Judy, talk to her, see why she did this horrible thing. But, to be honest, he didn't think she *did* do it. He seemed to be the minority holding that opinion, and was tired of seeing it on TV, hearing it on the news. Everybody was saying

Judy Larson was the murderer. The *alleged* murderer. He wanted to go and find out her side of it, but he knew it wouldn't look right if he went to visit the person accused of killing his wife.

Kill. What a horrible word. He just couldn't fit it to the sweet person he knew Judy was. He had heard that her trial date had been set for the fifteenth. The public was allowed to attend, so he had decided he would go. He wanted to hear what would happen next, and, if he was honest with himself, he wanted to see Judy again. Maybe for the last time?

*   *   *

Nobody came to visit Judy except her lawyer, Walter Rodenberg, making the next three weeks seem extremely long and boring. Because of the nature of her supposed crime, she had been kept in a private cell, no bigger than a bathroom, but at least she didn't have to deal with an assortment of roommates. She had seen some of the questionable characters she was lucky enough not to have to spend time with, and had to tolerate listening to their non-stop chatter echoing throughout the halls as it was. There was nothing they weren't willing to share with their neighbors, from abusive boyfriends to the latest sexual techniques. Some of the topics she actually found quite interesting, but didn't have the urge to join in, thinking it would feel too permanent to make "friends" in the jail.

So, she whiled away her time reading the books Walter Rodenberg, whom she was now on first name basis with, was kind enough to bring her. Much time was also spent on talking about her relationship with Arnie and the visit to see Sondra, going over and over every step with a fine-toothed comb.

After spending so much time with Judy, Walter felt that his client was a very intelligent, sensitive young lady who would not purposefully hurt another human being. He had the distinct feeling - that gut feeling we often get - that somebody else had committed the murder between 2:45, when Judy left, and 3:00, when Mrs. Chapman had found the body. Something had happened in those fifteen minutes. But what? Could it have been Laveen Chapman, herself? But, unless she was a great actress, which he highly doubted upon meeting her himself, the woman came across as too genuinely upset and innocent of the crime. So who did it? That was the piece of the puzzle that they just couldn't find.

Having spent time talking to the two Detectives, Ward and Cawston, he got the impression that neither of them truly believed she was guilty, either. Although he figured the younger one, Neil Cawston, was so smitten with his client that he'd believe she was innocent even if she chopped somebody up in front of him! They hadn't said it in so many words, but he felt that the detectives were also hoping to find evidence to prove somebody else killed Mrs. Martin.

They had thoroughly checked out the few names they had been able to dig up of prospective characters that may have held a grudge against Sondra Martin, as well as Judy. None of them fit the profile, and most had good alibis for being elsewhere on the day of Sondra's death. They weren't able to turn up any body with even a distant desire to harm Arnie or his wife.

Even the file on Arnold Martin had hit a dead end. No criminal record or misdemeanor, except a speeding ticket or two over the past eight years. He had been in Los Angeles surrounded by witnesses at the time of his wife's demise, and nothing any of his friends and co-workers had to say about him pointed to the possibility that he had hired someone to do the job. He was too clean to go after. Even Walter liked him.

Sondra Martin also had no record of criminal activity, although two previous cases of teenage shoplifting had been mentioned by the sister, Libby Steel, all sealed up in her Juvenile Offender file. Libby told him they had been done out of spite towards their stepmother, not out of intention to steal. Nothing there, anyway, that would help this case.

Walter did find it interesting, however, that Sondra's hairdresser, who had been cutting the victim's hair for almost six years, had mentioned that Sondra had been picked up twice by a man other than her husband after her hair appointment. When questioned regarding a description, the hair dresser could only give vague details - short, dark hair, driving a dark sedan- since the man in question had not come into the shop, but had waited outside for Sondra, remaining inside his car. That, unfortunately, fit at least half the residents of Seattle. And, since Sondra was a frequent visitor to the salon, no months and dates could be specified either, except that they had taken place within the past six months.

But she was positive it had not been Arnie, whom she had met on many occasions over the years when he either dropped off, or picked up, his wife. The silhouette, as well as the car itself, had not been the same, and Arnie almost always came in with his wife to say hello.

So, Walter mused. Was Sondra having an affair? Had it gone sour and the disgruntled boyfriend decided to call it off – by killing her? But, with so little information to go by, Walter would have to wait and see what evidence the prosecution turned up before he would lay this small bit of knowledge on the table.

Meanwhile, Arnie had returned to work to try to get back his life. He and the girls had moved temporarily into a large apartment until he could decide what to do with the house. He would not be going back there to live after what had happened there.

Murray Evans, his supervisor, had, surprisingly, turned out to be extremely helpful to them. He was the one who had told him about the apartment available not too far from the hospital, and had made the arrangements for some of their important belongings to be packed up and brought over to their new living quarters. Murray had even provided Arnie with a number he could call to get nanny service for the girls. Arnie was grateful to his boss, beholden to this before-unseen side of his supervisor. He would figure out what to do with the house and the rest of their stuff when things settled down. With less to worry about, Arnie could concentrate on helping his girls recover from the death of their mother. And getting through the trial.

Chapter 26

"The court is now in session. All rise!"

Judge Ann French, who happened to draw the case, entered the room, her black robes swirling around her legs. She sat down behind the large podium desk, shifted her reading glasses from the top of her head to her nose, and read the case in front of her.

"We are here for the case of the 'State of Washington versus Judith Lynn Larson,' case number KC539-72. This is a criminal case brought by the State of Washington charging the defendant, Judy Larson with intent to cause the death of Sondra Jean Martin. In support, the State claims that on October 19th, Judy Larson visited the victim with premeditated intent, then attacked and killed Sondra Martin. In defense, Ms. Larson admits she was present shortly before the time of death, but did not commit the murder and had no intent to injure Mrs. Martin."

Judge French put her glasses back on her head and turned towards the man standing to her left. "The bailiff will now swear in the jury."

Turning to the men and women in the jury box, the bailiff announced, "Will the jury please rise and raise your right hands? Please indicate your agreement by saying 'I do.' Do you swear or affirm that you will base your decision solely on the evidence presented before you in this case, not allowing any prior knowledge or judgments to influence your final decision?" There was a chorus of 'I do's', and they were directed to resume their seats.

In the defense box, Judy studied the jury, trying to decide if they would vote sympathetically or see her as guilty. It was split almost evenly between men and women, there being five of the former and seven of the latter. Looking over the men, an older Asian man caught her eye. Dressed in a dark gray, light wool suit, he sat very straight in his hard wooden chair. His wrinkled face put him somewhere between fifty and seventy, she couldn't tell. His expression gave nothing away as to how he was feeling, and Judy, unable to read him, moved to the next man.

An African-American in his early twenties looked very eager to be there, sitting at the edge of his seat, rocking almost imperceptibly, as if waiting for something to happen. It was obviously his first time on jury duty. Another black man resembled Cuba Gooding, with the same handsome baby face, and dimpled cheeks. Judy hoped both of them were as compassionate as their appearance led you to believe.

The other two men were white, ages maybe mid-twenty and later forties. The older one with arms crossed over his chest, had a scowl on his rough-cut face when their eyes made contact, letting Judy know exactly how he felt about her in this case. He reminded her of a pit bull- once they got something in their teeth, it was hard to get them to let go. She quickly looked away, over to the final man in the jury box.

Dressed in a pale blue dress shirt, he was sitting with his elbows on his knees, chin on top of his folded hands. Fair in looks, with short, reddish-blond hair, he was what Judy would have referred to as a 'computer geek' before he became so important to her. Seeing her looking at him, the "geek" smiled at her. Not expecting that, Judy started to return his smile, but instead, looked down at her hands.

After a moment or two, Judy looked back over, wanting to assess the women who would play such a valuable part in her life over the next hours, possibly days. With all the makeup, hair dye, and even cosmetic surgery to help nowadays, it was difficult to tell their true ages. Judy guessed they ranged somewhere between mid-twenty to late fifty. Two were definitely black, a very pretty woman in her late thirties wearing a business suit and an older woman with dusty gray hair under a Forest Green turban. Another younger woman appeared to be of mixed descent, possibly Hispanic. She looked scared and didn't hold eye contact throughout the entire trial. The other four were of Caucasian mix, various ages and hair color. Nothing notable about any of them, except one in her forties, who, pencil flying, seemed to be busy taking notes. Judy later found out she had been drawing illustrations of some of the characters in the courtroom, not expert quality to be sure, but entertaining. From then on Judy thought of her as The Artist.

Arnie was sitting towards the back again. Not sure of his feelings at this point, he was not quite willing to insert himself into the fray of things just yet.

Judy scanned the benches until she located Arnie. He wouldn't meet her glance, and she turned away, wondering what Arnie believed. *Does he think I did this, or does he think I'm innocent?* Her thoughts were interrupted by the judge opening the proceedings.

"Mr. Moore, is the prosecution ready to make their opening statement?"

"We are, your Honor." Fred Moore stood up as he said this, leaving his notes on the table. He pulled the lapels of his neatly pressed, gray suit jacket together, and walked straight up to the jury box. Fred scanned the men and women for a moment or two to build up effect before launching his statement. He introduced himself, then began.

"Ladies and gentlemen of the jury. What we have here is a cold-blooded murder of an innocent woman by her husband's clandestine lover! One Judy Larson, seated right over there." He pointed a well-manicured finger directly at Judy. All the jurors followed his gaze to the woman seated at the front of the courtroom.

Judy gasped and pulled back as if to keep the attorney's finger from reaching all the way across the room and touching her. She couldn't believe he'd say such a thing. Walter patted her arm, telling her that he'd warned her to expect the prosecuting attorney to get ugly from the get go. "It's just a ploy to get the jurors sympathy, ignore it."

That was fine for *him* to say, they weren't besmirching *his* character! Judy thought, shaking her head. Defiantly, she returned the juror's stares until most of them looked away. Except the pit bull, who continued staring stonily at her, his pale blue eyes squinting in the bright court light. He looked like retired army service to her, causing her to wonder if she was in for a bad time with him on the jury. Unable to stare him down, she broke contact first, and he switched his attention once more to the attorney.

"We have a taxi cab driver of reputable character, stating that he dropped the defendant off at the Martin home at two o'clock, and again picked the defendant up at two-forty-five, shortly before the victim's body was found by a friend and neighbor of the victim at three o'clock. Another witness, the friend who found poor Mrs. Martin, saw Ms. Larson run out of the Martin house, in seeming distress, at the same time as verified by the taxi driver. And last, but not least, we have the defendant herself claiming to have been with Mrs. Martin, and that she had run out of the house as she did because the victim had been yelling at her for sleeping with her husband! Now," Fred turned to look over at Judy again, before turning back to his audience. "Despite all the eyewitness accounts placing Ms. Larson at the scene when the death occurred, let me assure you that we have even more evidence against her. A search of the defendant's apartment turned up a dress, worn by Ms. Larson on her visit to the victim's home – smeared with blood that has been tested positive as the victim's own!" he finished dramatically.

"We don't need further proof that this young woman committed this heinous crime against an innocent, betrayed wife and mother. What we need is justice," he emphasized with a fist on the railing, causing many of the jury, as well as the on-lookers in the room, to jump. "Justice for that poor woman, justice for her two daughters who will go through their lives without their mother." He turned his back to the jury, and slowly began to walk towards his table, wrapping up his statement. He pointed a finger at Judy once more.

"We have no doubt in our minds that this young, seemingly innocent woman sitting here today is guilty of this crime. We need you," the attorney swung around to face them, holding an arm out beseechingly, " the jurors, to look at the evidence, listen to what the witnesses have to say, and find her guilty, so that she may get the punishment she deserves, and the family can get closure. However, the State is willing to rescind our pursuance of the death penalty in return for her confession to this murder. Thank you, your Honor, jurors." He returned to his seat, sparing only a quick glance at his opposition to see what kind of impact his speech had made on them.

Judy felt breathless. Her face had lost all color when the lawyer had mentioned the death penalty. Walter encouraged her to take a deep, steadying breath and to remember it was like acting. She recalled the words he'd told her earlier, "We have to put on a show for the jury so it will make a big impact on them and affect their thoughts later when they deliberate on all the information they collect throughout the trial."

"Counselor, you have an opening statement?" asked the judge, focusing on Walter.

"Yes, your Honor, I do." He stated his name for the record, then walked around the table and over to the jury, his stride very self-assured. He studied the men and women sitting before him, then the on-lookers sitting in the benches behind his client. Including all of them, he said, "That was a very nice speech. But in our country, you are innocent until proven guilty! Yes, there were witnesses to say Ms. Larson visited Sondra Martin on the night of her murder. And yes, she was seen leaving the house in apparent stress. But, my client, Ms. Larson, readily admits to all of this. There is a reasonable explanation for the blood ending up on Ms. Larson's dress that day. And we will explore this further, I promise you." Walter turned to Judy, making her cringe. He held his hand out towards her, palm up. "My client has never tried to hide the fact that she was in their house. She has never tried to lie about the time she was there. And not once has she tried to cover up the state of distress she was in when she left." He now turned his full attention on the jurors.

A few of them, who had been slouching down in their seats, now sat up. The 'geek' remained in his favorite position, elbows on knees, listening avidly. The Hispanic woman, eyes wide, would not look directly at the attorney, keeping her eyes focused on the wooden railing in front of her. Judy wondered how she had gotten picked to be in on a murder trial, and what possible help she could be when they went back to discuss the evidence and vote on her freedom – or imprisonment.

"Let us be careful about making conclusions that can affect an innocent person for the rest of her life. The court system is in place to protect the innocent, and to punish the guilty. We must listen, indiscriminately, to all the evidence and testimonies presented in this trial before we make our decisions."

Walter walked over to his table and perched on the end of it, still facing the jury. "Yes, it was a cold-blooded murder. Two young children lost their beautiful mother in one heartless act. A husband will forever miss the wife who tended to him, gave him his children, loved him..." He stopped and held eye contact with each juror in turn, with the exception of the Hispanic woman, who kept her eyes turned away.

"You must be one hundred percent sure, not a doubt in your mind, that this young lady is the killer," Walter said forcefully. "And that, ladies and gentlemen of the court, is why I am here. I will take you through that fateful day step by step, frame by frame, until you completely understand that my client, Judy Larson, is blameless! That, beyond the shadow of a doubt, she did *not* kill Sondra Martin! Thank you, your Honor, people of the court."

Walter returned to his seat, giving Judy a nod of satisfaction. Judy, bolstered by his confident air, couldn't help the little smile that escaped, lighting up her face. Most of the jury, following

Walter's progress back to his chair, caught this. Had she heard their thoughts, Judy would have taken heart, as most had already begun to believe she was too lovely and guileless to have committed such a nasty crime.

"I would like to look over this mornings findings. We will break for lunch at this time," announced the judge. "Mr. Moore, be prepared to call your first witness when we reconvene at one."

"Yes, your Honor."

Judy was glumly led off to the cafeteria, where she would be ensconced in a corner booth, escorted by two guards. Judy couldn't see Arnie anywhere as she exited out a side door of the courtroom.

Chapter 27

At precisely 1:00, the judge was back and the trial resumed.

"Please call your first witness, Prosecutor."

Fred Moore, after conferring with his assistant, Irene, called the taxi driver to the stand. A short, heavy man with a white beard and almost no hair on his head, got up from the back of the room and came forward. He was sworn in by the bailiff, then took a seat in the witness chair, wringing his large, meaty hands nervously.

"Please state your name and occupation for the court," instructed Fred.

"Uh, my name is Paul Smith. I drive a taxi in the Seattle area." He named a well-known cab company, then looked expectantly at Fred for further directions, not having testified before.

"How many years have you been a cab driver, Mr. Smith?"

"About fifteen years, give or take a couple months, Sir." He shifted uncomfortably in his seat.

"Can you tell the court how you keep track of all the rides you take on a given night, Mr. Smith?"

"Uh, well. When somebody jumps into my cab, I have to clock, uh, write down the destination and how many miles they go. Oh, and the time, too."

"Would you take a look over at the young lady seated at the table in front of you. Not," he added with a twinkle, "the pregnant one!" Several people laughed, Walter just rolled his eyes at the lame joke. "Can you tell the court if this is the same woman you delivered to the Martin home on October nineteenth?"

"Yes, sir. That's her."

"Where did you pick her up from? Before you took her to Dickson Street."

"I saw her trying to flag a taxi down by the Space Needle, on Broad Street, by Denny Way. I didn't have a fare, so I stopped and asked her where she wanted to go."

"What time was that, Mr. Smith?"

"Well, that was about one thirty or so. The lady said it was important for her to get to Dickson by two, and could I get her there on time. Traffic's usually pretty light right around then, so I told her 'No problem, hop in.'. And she did."

"Did you make it on time?"

"Yeah." The driver shrugged, as if to say 'Of course.' "We drove up at one fifty-eight. I know because it's a habit to look at the clock whenever I have a fare. 'Cause I have to write it all down, you know. Plus the lady wanted to get there before two and all."

"Was the lady happy, gave you a big tip?" He winked at the audience, and was rewarded by a few laughs.

"Quiet!" ordered Judge French, banging her gavel once on the block while giving Fred a warning look.

"The lady," he nodded in Judy's direction, "She gave me more than the fare was worth and told me to keep the change. Then she asked me if I could stay there and wait for her, or come back about two-thirty, two-forty-five to pick her up again."

"And what did you reply to that, Mr. Smith."

"Well, I told her I'd wait as long as I didn't get a call to pick up another customer. She seemed satisfied with that."

"Can you tell the court the house number where you dropped her off?"

"No, sorry. I had no reason to check it out," said with another shrug of his well-padded shoulders.

"So, she didn't give you the house number, just the name of the street?"

"Yup! Uh, I mean yes." He adjusted the tight collar of his white shirt. His face had started glistening with sweat. "Actually, she didn't tell me that, either." When Fred gave him a questioning look, he expanded on that without being asked. "She told me to drive down the main street in that area, and she'd tell me when to turn."

"Why would she do that? That's rather unusual for a...fare, to do it that way, isn't it?" Fred cocked his head, encouraging the cabbie to continue.

"Well, not really. Sometimes rides don't know where they want to go until they see something interesting. You see a lot of weird stuff in this business, ya know. The lady told me she'd forgotten the directions and would recognize the street when she saw the name. There wasn't no traffic to talk about, so I drove slow enough that she could read all the signs. Pretty soon she saw it and told me to turn, so I did."

"And which house did she want to be dropped off at, considering she didn't give you an address?"

"She told me to keep driving slowly and she'd let me know."

"And did she find the house she wanted?"

"Yes, sort of. I was creeping down the road, and she suddenly told me to stop, so I pulled over to the curb. She got out, then came back and that's when she asked me to wait for her."

"Did you wait?" Fred asked, curiosity in his voice.

"Yeah, sure." Another broad shrug. "I didn't get any calls, so I just stayed there. I keep a book in my cab for times like that, when it's slow. So I just kicked back and relaxed 'til she got back."

"Did you see which house the lady went to?"

"No. I stopped paying attention after she paid me." He flushed, realizing how brash that sounded.

"Did you think she was acting like she wanted to hide where she was going?"

"From me?" He gave one of his famous shrugs. "I don't see how she could do that, I was the one who had to take her there," he pointed out.

"Okay. Was she acting unusual, funny, or odd?"

"I didn't think so at the time, but now I understand it all."

"Understand what, Mr. Smith?"

"How nervous she was, not remembering the address, stuff like that. Thinking back on it, she was behaving kinda like she was going someplace she didn't really want to go."

Walter stood up, startling Judy beside him. "Objection!" he said loudly. "The taxi driver is not a psychologist! He cannot give expert testimony on my client's supposed behavior!"

Fred protested. "I can show a reason for this line of questioning, your Honor, and that it is relevant to this case."

"Objection overruled. Proceed."

"So, you waited for Ms. Larson to return. How did she act when she got back? Was she jumpy, crying, or did she act calm and cool?"

Walter again stood up. "Objection! Mr. Smith still hasn't become a psychologist in the past couple of minutes! And you are leading the witness."

"I'm just trying to get a feel for how Ms. Larson looked upon her return to his cab."

"Objection overruled. Watch how you ask your questions, Counselor."

Fred nodded his acknowledgment to the judge. "Tell me, Mr. Smith, in your own words, what state of emotion did she appear to be in?"

"She was in a hurry, I know that much! In fact, she jumped into my cab so suddenly, it scared me!" A snicker or two was heard around the courtroom. "She looked very upset, not crying or anything, but like something had gone wrong and she just wanted to get way.

Walter started to rise from his chair, then changed his mind and settled back down.

Raising an eyebrow at Walter, Fred asked the driver, "What time was that?"

"When she came back?" Fred nodded. "About two-forty-five when I started the engine to leave."

"Did you see any blood on her clothes?"

"No."

"Think real hard, Mr. Smith. Are you sure?"

"I think I'd remember something like that! No!" he exclaimed.

"The lady in question," he pointed loosely towards Judy. "Was she happy to see you had waited for her?"

"She seemed to be." He glanced over at Judy, feeling bad that he had to say all these things about her.

"Did she say anything to you when she came back?"

"Besides 'Thank you for waiting?' No."

Fred paced the short distance in front of the witness stand. "So, let's add all of this up. She gets into your cab at approximately one-thirty. Directs you to go to a street that she doesn't know the name of, and has you drop her off at a house with no known address- which happens to be almost a block from where she had the taxi stop- at two o'clock. Then, after about forty-five minutes, she runs out of the house and comes back to your cab, obviously upset. Is that right, so far, Mr. Smith?"

"Yeah, I guess so."

"Where did she have you take her after she got back into your cab?"

"She gave me an address over by Green Lake. I dropped her off in front of a big apartment building." He recited the address to the court when Fred directed him to do so.

"Did you see her go into the building?"

"Yeah, that time I was watching where she went 'cause it's a different neighborhood there.

"Hm," mused Fred, almost to himself. "So, we have the defendant acting in an abnormal manner." Seeing Walter about to object, he hurried on. "Asking the driver to drop her off down the street from the actual destination, then returning, acting emotionally distraught."

Walter stood up. Instead of protesting Fred's last statement, he asked, "Is there a definite plan behind all this rehashing of information, or have you finished questioning the taxi driver-psychologist?"

Several giggles were heard, and the court erupted into conversation amongst the rustling of many people trying to find a more comfortable spot on a hard surface. The judge banged her gavel a few times to settle everybody down.

"I am done with my witness, your Honor." He gave the jury a big smile and returned to his seat.

Arnie, listening to what the taxi driver had been saying, wondered why Judy had been trying to find his house. He hoped the answer would soon be clear.

"Any questions from the defense?" the judge asked, with an expectant look on her face.

Walter stood up slowly, perusing his notes one last time before approaching the witness stand.

"Hello, Mr. Smith. How are you holding up?"

"Fine, I guess." He wiped the increasing sweat off his face with one hand.

"Tell me, Mr. Smith. Did you see any blood on my client's dress when she got into your cab?"

"No, sir! I would've seen it. She didn't have her coat on when she came back. Guess she forgot it in all the hurry."

"Interesting. Have you ever seen anyone running to catch a taxi before?"

Thrown by the change in subject, Smith stumbled over his next answer. "Well, yes. Lots of times."

"So why did you tell the court that it was unusual for this lady?" Walter waved a hand towards his client. "For the defendant, to be running back to your cab?"

"I don't know," he said glumly. He already could see where this was going and wished he were back in his cab - or anywhere else but here, for that matter!

"Is it unusual for people to look upset when they get into your taxi?"

"No, I guess not. I see it quite a bit."

"And what made you think that the lady *was* upset?"

"Well," her face was sort of red, "It was mostly a gut feeling, I guess."

"When people run to your cab, don't they look flushed, maybe exhausted from all that running?"

"Some do. Yeah. When they run."

"This 'gut' feeling you had. Are you a psychologist? Had some training in this area?"

"No, sir. Just a g...Just a feeling I got about her, is all."

"Objection!" Fred rose from his chair. "He is harassing the witness."

"I have a purpose in mind, your Honor."

"Over ruled."

"Can you be more specific? What exactly made you think my client was upset besides her red face and possibly a bit of rapid heart rate from running?"

The taxi driver looked confused. "I don't know."

"And didn't you say that people often don't have an address to give you when they use your services?"

"Yes."

"So, based on your testimony, this young lady didn't display any more unusual behavior than a lot of other people you've encountered. Is that right, Mr. Smith?"

The driver thought about that for a moment. Then he shrugged one last time. "Yeah, I guess that's right."

"No further questions, your Honor." Walter didn't show any emotion, but Judy gave his arm a gentle squeeze when he sat down. She knew by the displeased look on Fred Moore's face that they had scored a point in their favor.

Arnie, though not happy about the whole thing, seemed to feel a little lighter with the outcome.

*   *   *

"Please call your next witness, Mr. Moore." the judge said, still scribbling her notes.

Judy watched the people in the jury box, knowing her life depended on them. The Artist was taking advantage of the time by making quick, efficient strokes with her pencil, to be filled in later when she was out of court. The lady in the turban was chatting quietly to a tired housewife, who looked as if she needed a vacation, not jury duty. The pit bull was minding his own business, but the geek was looking directly at her, trying to catch her eye, which she refused to acknowledge, even if it meant turning his vote against her. No sense in encouraging some kind of crush, if that's what it was.

Her perusal was interrupted by Fred, calling Officer Patton as his next witness. He was sworn in, and took his seat on the stand.

"Please state your name and occupation for the court."

"Officer David Patton, with the King County Police Department."

"Tell us what you found when you arrived at the house on Dickson Street the afternoon of October nineteenth, Officer."

"My partner and I, that's Officer Kent Lotze," he added for the benefit of the court secretary. "We had just been called to the scene. We arrived at the victim's house at three-o-five. The neighbor had found the body and made a call to 911. We were the first on the scene. The neighbor, Laveen Chapman, was waiting for us on the door step of the Martin's home."

"How long did it take you to respond to the emergency call?"

"We were up the road a peace, so it only took about four minutes."

"What happened when you approached Mrs. Chapman?"

"She told us she had found her friend's body in the house. That she'd been murdered. So we went in to check it out."

"What did you find?"

"We found the body of a woman lying in a pool of blood on the living room floor, a knife next to her. I felt for a pulse, but she was gone."

"Could you tell if it had happened recently or, say, the night before?"

"The blood was still very wet. When I felt her neck for a pulse, her skin was very warm to the touch, so it had to have happened fairly recently."

"What did you do after you checked the body for signs of life, Officer?"

"We called it in to the station, who then pulled the Investigation Team in to the scene. Detectives Ward and Cawston arrived about ten minutes after that and took over the crime scene."

"So, the blood was still wet, therefore, would you say she was murdered only a few minutes prior to being found by Mrs. Chapman? Maybe fifteen, twenty minutes before that?"

"Yes, sir. That would be my guess."

"That's all I have for Officer Patton."

"Any cross-examination, Counselor?"

Walter got up and approached the officer. "Officer Patton. May I ask where you acquired your expertise in determining how old a body is after you find it? Any special training, maybe a few classes?"

"No, sir. Just what I've learned on the job. It's mostly using common sense in this case."

"I see. That is interesting. You are using common sense to solve a murder, is that what you're saying, Officer?"

"No! I'm just ..."

Walter interrupted, not letting the officer complete his explanation. "I have no further questions, your Honor."

"You may step down."

Frustrated, Patton gritted his teeth and returned to his seat at the back of the courtroom.

"This court is now adjourned. The case will reconvene at nine o'clock tomorrow morning."

Everyone rose from their seats, a welcomed relief after the long morning parked on unforgiving wooden benches, as the judge left the room. The jury party was led through a side door to another room, to await the van that would deliver them to a nearby hotel. There they would stay until the hearing was completed.

Chapter 28

Having been exposed to the court atmosphere the day before, Judy was less scared the next day-but not much. She noticed the lady with the turban now wore a white one, matching her white jacket. Pit bull was still as stony-faced as ever, but she could swear the Asian gentleman was showing just a touch of a smile today as he talked to the lady next to him. The geek was in a shirt almost the same as the one on the previous day, but in a light shade of green. Once the trial started, he assumed his familiar elbows on knees pose.

Curiously, the Hispanic woman was holding her own in a conversation with the eager young black man, and was appearing less fearful today. They seemed to be having a very involved chat, ignoring all else around them. Judy wondered if they had all been able to stay together yesterday after the trial before they had to go to their rooms for the night. Having spent another lonely evening in her own company after her attorney left, she felt envious of their new friendships.

Looking around, Judy found that Arnie had moved in closer today, and was seated on the other side of the room, near the prosecution table. She hoped that didn't reflect his beliefs.

"I'm calling Laveen Chapman to the stand." Fred announced. The judge had entered the room several minutes before and the jury had been reminded that they were still under oath.

Laveen walked slowly up the isle, feeling as nervous as she had on her wedding day-except she had known most of the people there, so this was ten times worse. Fred had coached her on the questions he would be asking her, so she was semi-prepared. The one she was afraid of was Judy's attorney. She had heard through several sources, mostly friends, that Rodenberg was the one to watch out for. He was a tough lawyer, won most, if not all – nobody was really sure – of his cases, and she expected he would be putting her through the gristmill. After the oath was taken, Laveen sank slowly onto her chair, looking as if she was thinking of making a run for it. They weren't too far off.

As directed by Fred, she stated her name and occupation-house wife- for the court.

"What is your home address, Mrs. Chapman?"

"1102 Dickson Street, Seattle."

"How far from the victim's house is that?"

"It's across the street. Not directly opposite, but more kitty corner from the Martin's. If I walk from my house to theirs I just cut across diagonal..." Realizing she was blathering, she stopped, a light hint of a blush crawling up her throat.

"It's all right Mrs. Chapman. We can understand that you're probably nervous," Fred sympathized. "Now, I want you to think back to the day you found Sondra Martin, October nineteenth. I'd like you to tell the court, in your own words, what happened that day, starting with what led up to you going over there, and what you found."

"Well, I was going to go visit Sondra after her company left. She'd come over earlier that morning and had asked me to drop in. I walked in the door..."

"Excuse me Mrs. Chapman, but I'm going to ask you to back up even further. What were you doing after Sondra Martin returned from her sister's? If you could start there, please."

Slightly flustered, Laveen bit her lip, trying to get her thoughts together. "Well, let's see...I guess...Oh! I know!" Laveen beamed at the attorney. "I had just eaten my lunch, so I was sitting in the lounger, watching TV. I usually have a nap right about then, but I was pretty interested in the program, so it was keeping me awake.

I saw a taxi drive up across the street – hard to miss, it being yellow and all. We don't usually see taxis out this way, so I wanted to see who it was there for." Then, feeling like she needed to justify why, she added in her defense, "We try to keep an eye out for each other. I belong to our Crime Watch program!" She took a deep breath and blew it out. Fred nodded and gave her an encouraging smile.

"What time did the taxi drive up?"

"Had to be about two, my show had just ended."

"Did you know the person who got out of the taxi?"

"No, never saw her before."

"I'd like you to begin your story from when the taxi drove up and describe the driver, who got out and what happened next, if you would."

"Well, the taxi stopped. The driver was a fat man - I'm sorry! I didn't mean that! He was a big fella, I could make out a beard. Couldn't see much else, too dark in the cab. He was turned away from me, talking to somebody in the back. Then a young woman got out, seemed very pretty, with long, black hair, but I couldn't make out a whole lot. Except her coat. One of those long, leather ones. Very nice, too." Fred cleared his throat to get her back on track.

"Oh. Well, the lady started to walk down the sidewalk, then she turned back and bent over to talk to the driver, I guess. Anyway, then she walked down the sidewalk, looking at the house numbers."

"How did you know she was looking at the numbers?"

"I could tell she was looking for *something*. She was going slowly, and her head was turning all over like she was hunting for something on the house. Then, as soon as she found the number, it must have been the wrong one, because she moved quickly to the next house and did the same thing. She seemed to recognize the next one, the Martin's, because she went up the walkway. She rang the bell and Sondra answered, then they went inside."

"Did anything seem to be wrong? Did either of them act

unusual towards each other?"

"Come to think of it, yes. The strange lady held her hand out to shake, and I thought it was not like Sondra at all to ignore it like she did."

"Did Sondra appear to be angry or frightened of the visitor?"

"No, I don't think so. And I'd remembered by then that Sondra had told me she was expecting company around that time. So she knew she was coming."

"What did you do after the lady entered the Martin home?"

"I took my nap. In the recliner, like I always do after lunch. Have to recharge the batteries more often nowadays, if you know what I mean!" Fred returned her smile. A few laughs were heard from around the room.

"What happened after your nap? Did you see the strange lady again after that?"

"Yes, I did. I woke up when the garbage truck made a lot of racket."

"What time was that, do you recall?"

"It was almost exactly at two thirty-five. I was afraid I'd overslept, so I glanced at the clock soon as my mind cleared. Sondra had invited me over for tea at three, I didn't want to be late. I got to wonder if her guest had left yet or if I would get to meet her, so I looked out the window. I thought it was very odd that the taxi was still there. But maybe, I told myself, it had left and came back. But I thought even that was weird, 'cause then why would it stop down the road again if the lady had gone to a house further this way? I considered whether I should go over there early, but decided not to. I wish I had now! Sondra wouldn't be dead if I had!" Laveen hung her head, too choked up to continue.

"Nobody can say if that would have saved her life or not. It may already have been too late," Fred reminded her gently. Laveen sniffed.

"I need you to answer a few more questions if you can, Mrs. Chapman." When Laveen nodded, her head still tipped towards her lap, Fred continued.

"What time did you see the young lady come out of the house?"

"It was two forty-five, because I checked the clock. I wanted to get ready and change my clothes, so I looked out the window again, wondering if Sondra was ready for me or not. Just about then the door of the Martin house flew open and the girl came running out. I thought it was because she didn't want to get wet - it was raining a little - but maybe I was wrong. And she left her umbrella and her fancy coat behind! She must've been in a terrible hurry to get out of there!"

"What did the woman do when she came out of the house?" Fred re-directed her before the defense could object.

"She hopped into the cab and they took off."

"Laveen. Is the young lady you saw that day here in this courtroom?" Laveen nodded, trying not to stare at her. Would you point her out for the court, please."

Without hesitating, Laveen pointed her finger towards Judy. Judy felt the blood drain from her face.

"May the records show that the witness is pointing to Judy Larson. Thank you, Laveen. Now, I want you to take a close look at this item, and tell me if you recognize it." Fred walked over to his table and took the brown paper bag his assistant, Irene, handed him. He pulled out a large, zip-lock baggie. In it was a wrinkled, yellow dress with narrow bands of dark blue across the material. There were five markings on the bodice of the dress, resembling portions of a hand print, each in the reddish-brown color of dried blood.

Taking the bagged dress over to the witness stand, he first showed it to the judge. "I would like to present Exhibit Number One, your Honor." Then he stepped closer to Laveen and showed her the dress, not allowing her to touch it, but instructing her to take a close look and see if it looked familiar.

"Yes, it looks like the one the lady," she pointed to Judy, "was wearing when she came running out of the house."

Arnie realized it was the same dress she was wearing one day when she was having dinner with him, seeming like such a long time ago now.

Fred pointed to the front of the dress. "Did you see any blood stains on it when she came out of the house?"

"I don't really remember. I wasn't paying attention to what she was wearing at the time. Except for missing her coat."

"I would like the court to note that this dress was found in the apartment of the defendant, Judy Larson." Fred set the dress on a table near the jury box, where it could be clearly seen by all present there. He returned to the witness stand.

"What did you do after that? After the cab left with the woman?"

"I went over to Sondra's house and rang the bell. When she didn't answer the door after the second time, I went in, calling her name to let her know I was there." Laveen stopped. She didn't want to tell the rest and looked pleadingly at the attorney.

"You need to tell the court what you found there, Laveen."

Laveen lifted her chin up - she could do this. Full of nervous tension, she plucked idly at her beige dress, then resumed where she'd left off. "I started to look for Sondra, thinking maybe she was upset after her company left. I called her name again, but I found her lying down on the carpet, over by her husband's bookshelves. There was a lot of blood around her and a knife in her chest." Laveen closed her eyes, picturing the horror all over again. "It was awful!"

Fred retrieved a large knife, also protected within a plastic bag. "I present this knife as Exhibit Two. Mrs. Chapman, take a real good look at this object." He held it out close to her so she could see it better." Is this the knife you saw next to the body?"

Laveen didn't want to look at it, expecting to see blood on it. Her friend's blood. Therefore, she was immensely relieved to see only brown stains on the leather handle, nothing she couldn't pretend was just grease stain. She studied it a while, before shaking her head. "I really couldn't say. I didn't look at the body very closely - it was dead! I know the handle was big and brown, like that one, but I don't know anything else."

Fred nodded to himself, he'd suspected as much. "Do you recall Sondra owning a knife such as this one? Or saw one around the house at any time during your years as friends?"

"No. Both the Martin's hated guns and stuff. I don't think they would've kept anything as dangerous as that in the house because of the girls. They wouldn't even let them watch TV shows with that kind of stuff on it."

"Thank you, Mrs. Chapman." Fred placed the knife next to the dress.

"How long have you known the Martin's?"

"About twelve years this past summer."

"How would you describe the family?"

"Like an ordinary family, I suppose. They went places together, had friends - like me and Jake - over for meals occasionally. I know they loved their kids. Didn't abuse them or anything."

"And you had never seen this young woman," pointing to Judy, "before the day she drove up in the taxi, is that correct?"

"Yes."

"I have no further questions for Mrs. Chapman, your Honor." Fred returned to his chair and began making notes.

The judge finished a note or two herself, then looked up. "Defense? Any questions for the witness?"

Walter strolled over to Laveen and placed his arm on the rail in front of her, casually leaning on it.

"How is your eyesight, Mrs. Chapman?"

"My eyesight? Okay for an old lady!" This got everybody laughing and the judge banged for order, reminding them they were in a court of law.

"So you are able to see objects clearly without glasses?"

"Sure."

"How about if the object is, let's say, twenty-five feet away. Can you still see it?"

" I think so. My problem is with close range, not distant. If you were to hold out a magazine at twenty-five *inches,* now that might be a different story!" The court again erupted into mirth.

"Quiet!" The judge banged her gavel twice, throwing the room a warning glance, settling on Laveen. "Just answer the questions, Mrs. Chapman."

"So, you had no trouble seeing the taxi? What was the company name on the side of it?" Walter tested her.

"I couldn't say. In fact, I don't believe there was a name on the door. Just a bunch of lines saying the cost of the fare and the phone number," she replied smugly.

"You said earlier that you couldn't make out distinguishing features, is that right?" Laveen nodded. "Take a good look at this woman, are you sure this is the *same* person you saw coming out as was going in?"

"Objection!" cried Fred. "There is no doubt that the defendant is the same person, she has admitted to the fact. We are not questioning the time frame in which she arrived and left, your Honor. Just what happened in-between. Defense is badgering the witness!"

"I will rescind that, your Honor." He continued. "Have you had any memory problems, Mrs. Chapman?"

"Objection!" Fred demanded. "He is insulting the witness, and this has nothing to do with this case."

Walter defended his line of defense. "It has *everything* to so with it, your Honor. The witness couldn't recall if the dress had bloodstains on it, and wasn't sure if the knife was the same one she saw. I'd say that was very pertinent to our investigation into the murder, your Honor."

"Objection over-ruled. Answer the question."

Fred Moore sat down in a huff.

Walter asked Laveen if she needed the question repeated. "No, I don't!" she barked. "There is *nothing* wrong with my memory!" She glared at him.

Walter decided he'd better drop this line of questioning before he totally alienated the witness. "Do you recall seeing anybody else visiting the Martin house that day, possibly close to the time of Ms. Larson being there?"

Laveen didn't want to deal with this character any more, but she knew she was committed to answer until they were done with her. "No. As far as I know, she," pointing to the defendant, "was the only visitor that day."

"Let the record show that the witness is pointing to Ms. Judy Larson. So, you saw no one around the premises, say, a newspaper boy, someone walking their dog?"

"No, not that I..." Remembering his reference to her memory, Laveen firmly replied, "No. I have other things to do besides watch everybody come and go, you know!" Walter groaned. Once again he had insulted the witness.

"What did you do between 2:45 and 3:00 that day?"

"After I saw the girl leave, I went to get dressed before I went over to Sondra's house."

"So it is likely that someone could have walked into the Martin house without your knowledge between 2:45 and 3:00 and murdered Mrs. Martin after my client had left?"

"Objection!" shouted Fred. "Defense is surmising. The witness can't answer what she hasn't seen."

"Allowed. Continue."

Walter prompted Laveen to answer the question.

"Yes, I suppose it is possible. My bedroom is on the opposite side of the house, I wouldn't have seen anybody else going to the Martin's while I was getting ready."

"How about any service vehicles, such as a plumber's van, not usually in your neighborhood? Any strange cars cruising around that week?"

"No, sir. Nothing that I haven't seen around there many other times."

"Did *you* kill Sondra Martin, Mrs. Chapman?"

There were many shocked gasps heard, including Judy and Laveen.

"Objection, your Honor!" Fred nearly flew towards the

judge's bench to protest. "Defense is badgering the witness again!"

"I am not!" Walter stated calmly. "I am merely exploring the possibilities. It would not be the first time a witness committed a murder, then reported it to the police."

The audience was discussing this new idea, making it difficult for the attorneys to hear the judge. Looking displeased at the rowdy scene taking place in her otherwise placid courtroom, Judge French picked up her gavel and repeatedly hammered on the base until there was silence once more. "I will have quiet in here or you will all be escorted out! Now, Mr. Moore, please take your seat. Objection over-ruled, proceed with the question." She looked at Laveen expectantly.

Laveen, eyes wide open at this new assault, and knowing she could very well be in trouble, didn't know what to say. "I didn't do it! I didn't kill her! I found her, that's all. I didn't even touch the body!" She started to cry silently, tears running paths down her pleasantly wrinkled face.

"One more question. Was Ms. Larson carrying a purse or bag when she entered the Martin house?"

"Um...Yes, a purse. A black purse." Laveen wiped her eyes and damp cheeks.

Walter walked over to the evidence table. "Think back on that day, Mrs. Chapman. In your best estimation, how big would you guess the purse Ms. Larson was carrying to be?"

"Objection! Defense is asking the witness to guess. Guessing is not fact, your Honor!"

"I have a reason for asking the witness to 'guess,' your Honor. And, I might add, that no one could give a more reliable answer to that question than another woman."

"I will allow the question, Counselor. Proceed."

"Could you give us an idea of the purse size, Mrs. Chapman?"

"Well, it wasn't a very big one. One of those shoulder strap kind, barely big enough to carry your wallet in. It was almost hidden by her coat sleeve, too, except she had to pull it out to pay the taxi driver, so I got a good look at it."

Walter picked up the bag containing the knife. "Reading the label the lab sent with the knife," Walter said out loud, "This knife is fourteen and three quarter inches in length." He showed it to Laveen. "Would this knife have fit in the purse you saw the defendant, Ms. Larson, carrying that day?"

"Not a chance! Her purse was about half that long. I'd have seen the handle sticking out of it. I suppose she could have had it in her coat pocket."

"Let the record show that the lab measured the pockets of the leather coat found in the victim's house, left behind by my client, and found them to be much too small to have carried the knife inside one of them, your Honor." Giving Laveen a big smile, Walter said, "Thank you, Mrs. Chapman. No more questions, your Honor."

"You may step down, Mrs. Chapman." And feeling very pleased, like she had done something right, she returned to her seat.

Chapter 29

After a tense lunch recess, Libby Steel, Sondra's sister, was next on the witness stand. Already slender, Libby had taken on a gaunt appearance. Since the death of her only sibling she had lost interest in eating, causing her husband, Ken, much worry. He had tried everything he knew of to get her interested in food before she took ill. But, realistically, he knew nothing would change until her sister's death had been solved.

Libby walked up to the witness stand, took the oath, and perched on the edge of the chair. She was wearing an A-cut, floor-length dress in a flowered pattern with a sweater over it. Her face, pale and thin despite makeup, was framed by short, light-brown curls. She glanced anxiously at her husband, seated several pews from the back. She spotted Arnie, too, which surprised her. She hadn't realized he was there, although it made sense that he would be, since it was his wife that had been killed.

"What was your relationship to Sondra Martin?" Fred asked gently. He could see that Libby was on her last thread, nearing breaking point.

"She was my sister."

"When was the last time you saw your sister?"

"The day she was..." Libby dropped her head, gathering herself to do this. "The day she was killed."

"You were at her house?"

"No, she had driven down to Portland to visit me and the girls the day before."

"You told me that you and the victim had a long conversation that day." Libby nodded. "Would you tell the court what was said?"

268

"Sondra told me she had a meeting with her husband's girlfriend, Judy. She wanted to leave the girls with me because Arnie was out of town." She will pick them up in two days. Let them have a little fun here for two days.

"Did she tell you Judy's last name?"

"No, she just called her Judy."

"What else did she tell you about the 'girlfriend', Mrs. Steel?"

"Just that she had called Sondra to talk about something involving Arnie. Sondra didn't know what she wanted to tell her, other than she needed to tell her what Arnie was up to."

Arnie, in the back of the room, was puzzled. Why would Judy have called his wife? Had she been trying to cause trouble between him and his wife? Looking around, he happened to catch Ken, his brother-in-law's eye. As if reading Arnie's silent question, he gave Arnie a mystified shrug and turned back to the front of the court. So far, Ken seemed to be the only one who believed he wasn't having an affair, and Arnie appreciated that immensely.

"What do you think she meant by those words, Mrs. Steel? 'Up to?'"

"Objection!" Walter called. "Are we making psychologists out of ordinary people, Fred?" Laughter. "Interpretations are different between various people, your Honor."

"Counselor, if you will re-word the question."

"Mrs. Steel, do you have an idea of what Judy wanted to tell Sondra about her husband?"

"No, I don't."

"When and where was the meeting with Judy to take place?"

"The next day, about two o'clock. Judy was coming to Sondra's house to see her. So Sondra stayed overnight, then left early the next morning so she'd have plenty of time before she got there."

"So, your sister came over the day of October eighteenth and left for the meeting on the nineteenth, is that correct?"

"Uh," Libby had to sift through her foggy mind, "Yes, that's right."

"Did you give her any advice for meeting this other woman?"

"Objection! This is not 'Dear Abby.' Her advice to Sondra Martin is not pertinent to the case." Walter Rodenberg insisted.

"On the contrary," replied Fred. "Her sister's actions after one of the last times she was seen alive may have great bearing on this case, your Honor."

"Objection over-ruled."

"Thank you, your Honor. Now," Fred paced back and forth. "If you could tell the court what you advised your sister to do that day."

"I told her she shouldn't go through with it, that it might be a big mistake, since she didn't know this Judy person."

"I think that is all, your Honor."

Fred sat down while Walter took his place.

"Let's back up a little bit, shall we? Why did Sondra take the kids, on a weekday, and drive, what, four hours one way, just to tell you about meeting this woman? Why didn't she just pick up the phone and call you?"

"I think she wanted the girls out of the way during the meeting. The girls were out of school because of repairs, she said. And Arnie was out of town for a few days, maybe she didn't want to stay alone that night. Plus, she had a few other things she wanted to tell me."

"Would these 'other things' have anything to do with the affair she was having?" A chorus of responses was heard, Arnie's sharp intake of breathe amongst them.

"Objection!"

"On what grounds, Mr. Moore?" Judge French looked up at the clock, not much time remaining before lunch.

"The victim is not on trial here, your Honor."

"Over-ruled, Fred. You should know that this could be a key suspect in the case. Sit down. Let's get this finished, shall we?"

Smarting from her chastising, Fred sat down, smoldering.

"I must remind you, Mrs. Steel, that you are under oath and

must tell the truth. Was Sondra Martin having an affair?"

Libby, eyes welling up with hot tears, refused the urge to glance at Arnie. "Yes."

"Please speak up, Mrs. Steel."

"Yes, she was having an affair!" she blurted.

"Did she tell you the name of the man she was having an affair with?"

Unable to resist any longer, Libby scanned the audience, finding Arnie. He sat ramrod straight, a stricken look on his face. Her anger at him totally defused, she turned back to the attorney. "It was with her husband's supervisor, Murray Evans."

Arnie couldn't breath. Surely not! He almost stood up and left the room, not wanting to hear any more. Then he saw the sad, sympathetic look on Judy's face, and found the courage to remain and hear what else he didn't know about his wife.

"Did she tell you if she was planning on meeting with Dr. Evans the same day as the murder?"

"Yes. Well, at least she said she was hoping to see Murray before Arnie..." She paused, feeling like a low life, then finished, "Before her husband got home."

"When did this affair begin, did Sondra tell you?"

Fred looked as if he wanted to object, but decided he'd do better to hear it out and see where it was going. He rested his folded hands on the table in front of him and held his peace.

"She said it started after his accident, the night Sondra found out Arnie had been with this other woman late at night. About six months ago, I guess. She decided to have this fling out of spite, to get even with Arnie. I think she thought she would sleep with this guy a couple times and call it even, but it got stronger." Feeling like she owed Arnie a vote of confidence after the horrible news she'd just imparted, she added, "Murray's the one that told Sondra her husband was having an affair! I asked her if she knew it for sure, had she asked Arnie about it, but she didn't seem to care. She was taking Murray's word over her husband's. I'm sorry, Arnie!" she cried.

"Order!" the judge rapped, calming the sudden wave of commotion.

"I have no further questions, your Honor." Walter avoided looking over at Fred, who he knew probably had a dismayed expression on his face. He would have to dig further into the Murray Evans story and see what he could find.

The judge called a recess for the day. They would not reconvene until Monday, giving Walter a few days to explore some new options. He instructed his assistant, Rebecca Simms, to get started and see what she could find on Dr. Murray Evans.

Arnie, appalled at what he'd heard, left the courthouse in a trance. He could not have said how he'd gotten home, being on automatic pilot while he thought furiously over and over about what he had listened to. Was it true? Had Sondra and Murray been sleeping together all these months while she accused him of playing around? Should he confront Murray? Maybe he should talk to one of the attorneys, but which one? Obviously not the one trying to get Judy convicted of murder. He realized that he no longer considered her the killer. He *knew* it had to be somebody else. At least he could feel good about that.

Chapter 30

9:00 a.m. - Trial Day 3

Arnie was ashamed to show his face in court that day after hearing about Sondra's relationship with Murray. But later, after thinking about it all weekend, he decided he had to go, no matter how many people whispered behind his back. He needed to know what would happen. So, dropping the girls off at school, he drove to the courthouse again and walked the short distance from the parking lot to the entrance in the howling wind and beating rain. The smell of wet wool permeated the halls of the court, as people in dripping coats rushed into their warm offices.

Today he didn't see Libby or Ken seated anywhere in the room. He supposed Libby wasn't strong enough to listen to all the testimonies, especially when they painted her sister as a less-than-desirable role model.

He watched the Jury be seated, stood up when the judge entered the room, and listened to the witness be sworn in. All the while, though, he was deep in thought about when his wife could have possibly started the relationship with his supervisor. He was pretty sure it must have started before she had brought the girls in to see him that day at the lab. He could remember how chummy the two of them had seemed, and how quickly Sondra had terminated the conversation when he and the girls had walked into the room. He wasn't sure he wanted to know the answer, either.

"State your name and profession for the court, please." Fred intoned.

"My name is Robert McDaniels. I'm the King County Medical

Examiner Pathologist."

"Can you tell the court what your part is in this investigation?"

"I examined the body shortly after it was reported, gathered evidence, such as body fluids and tissue samples for the toxicological analysis. I also completed the photographic documentation at the scene, and performed the autopsy once it was delivered to the morgue."

"How long have you been practicing as a Medical Examiner, sir?"

"Over twenty years, I'd say." He flipped a strand of hair out of eye with a shake of his head. "Ever since they got rid of the title of Coroner in '68."

"So, it's safe to say you've done autopsies and investigated violent deaths a few times?"

"Hundreds of times, is more like it!" McDaniels guffawed.

"When you examined the body of Sondra Martin, where would you place the time of death?"

"It was fairly recent, approximately between one and three p.m. Closer to the latter, though, I'd say.

"And what was the weapon used to commit the murder?"

"A long knife. It was next to the victim's body when I arrived on the scene."

Fred picked up the knife and showed it to McDaniels. "Would you say this is the knife you found next to the victim's body, Mr. McDaniels?"

McDaniels leaned forward to get a closer look at what was in the bag. "I'd say that was the exact one. I recognize the handle, and the slightly curved tip at the end of the shaft."

"Let the court records show," Fred said as he replace the knife onto the table, "that the Medical Examiner has identified Exhibit Two as the same one found in the body. Can you describe to the court, in layman's terms, how the knife cut the body and the extent of the damage?"

"I'll try my best," McDaniels replied, brushing a few unruly strands of gray hair out of his face again. Demonstrating the action with his empty hands, he explained, "The knife cut the let hand and stomach area at an upward angle. There were two cuts on the left hand and one on the stomach. This caused a lot of external bleeding, and without medical care immediately available, the victim bled to death."

"Was there only three cut wounds found?"

"Yes. But because of the length of the knife, almost fifteen inches, if I recall, it was deep enough to have caused major tearing of the hand and stomach. It's unclear if her life could have been saved even if paramedics arrived at the scene after it occurred because of the three deep cuts".

Taking a shot in the dark, Fred pointed at Judy. "Could a person of *her* height and build have lethally cut the victim?"

"Objection, your Honor! He's leading the witness. My client is not guilty until proven so." Walter squinted his eyes at his opposition, daring him to try that again.

"I am not accusing Ms. Larson of the murder, your Honor. I am merely using her physical characteristics to identify the possibility of size needed to swing the knife and made the cuts."

"Use examples other than the accused, Counselor."

"Okay. Let's use my assistant, Irene. If she wasn't pregnant," Irene rubbed her extended abdomen in exaggerated circles, getting a few chuckles, "would she be capable of inflicting the wounds?"

McDaniels looked at Irene, who possessed approximately the same stature as Judy. "Yes."

"Thank you. Now, let's talk about the chemicals you found. The toxicology report you submitted shows traces of drugs in her system. Was there a reason you tested her for drugs? And can you expound on that, please?"

"Yes. We routinely test for drugs whenever a questionable death occurs in case they committed drug-induced suicide or poisoning has occurred. An empty glass container, about the size of a baby bottle, was found near the body, and a cloth was positioned over her face, leaving us to believe chemicals of some sort may have had a part in her death."

"And what did you find, Doctor?"

"We found a large amount of undigested alcohol in her stomach contents, and a toxic amount of the sleeping pill, Chloral hydrate. What's curious here, is that we also found trace amounts of Trichloroethane, or Methyl Chloroform in her system, as well as on the cloth. Apparently she breathed it in before her death."

"What are the symptoms of Trichloroethane...."

"Trichloroethane," McDaniels filled in. "It acts as a depressant to the central nervous system, like common anesthetics. It can cause a headache, nausea, dizziness, and unconsciousness. And we found small hemorrhages in her lungs, which is another side affect."

"And the other drug, the sleeping pill?"

"Chloral hydrate. There were several partially digested capsules of this in her stomach, more than she needed to fall asleep. Over-use can cause depression, mental confusion, behavior disturbances, and irritability. Alcohol intensifies its lethality. So, it may have been only a matter of time before she slipped into a coma anyway, followed by probable death in this case. You may have heard of this drug, they used to call it a Mickey Finn in the old mysteries." McDaniels added as a note of interest.

"Where would one obtain this drug, Doctor? Do you need a prescription?"

"Oh, definitely! This can be pretty powerful stuff. Only a doctor can prescribe it."

"Is it possible somebody forced the victim to swallow the pills?"

"Objection!" Walter stood up, shaking his head. "You're asking the witness to speculate."

"Re-word the question, Prosecutor."

Fred thought a minute. "If somebody forced the victim to ingest these pills, would the effects be immediate?"

"No. It takes about half an hour for the effects to start taking place. Coma, then death follows in a few hours."

"Could she have taken the pills without her knowledge, say

they were slipped into her food or drink?"

"Highly doubtful. She had five of these pills in her stomach. It's hard to believe she wouldn't see them. They weren't chewed up either, but swallowed whole."

Fred stuck his hand out to his assistant, and Irene placed a small clear bag on his palm. Inside was a glass bottle, approximately six inches in height, three inches in diameter. "Doctor, is this the bottle you found near the victim?" He placed it on the railing in front of him. "Look at it closely."

"Yes, it's the same one. No numbers stamped on the bottom, nothing to distinguish what it was originally used for."

"Thank you. I present the bottle as Exhibit Number Three, your Honor. I have no further questions for the good doctor." He placed the bottle in line with the other two exhibits.

"Questions from Defense?"

"Yes, your Honor. "Did you see any evidence that she was forced into taking the drugs - bruises, scratches, any physical marks to suggest she didn't willfully ingest the pills or allow the poisoned material to be used on her?"

"No, we didn't find any physical signs, except the knife cut wounds and a bump on the back of her head relative to her hitting the floor."

"Did you find more of the sleeping pills in her home?"

"No. The Detectives searched it thoroughly after we got all our evidence and removed the body. No medications, or the pill bottle to the ones she took, were found."

"Thank you, Doctor. I have no more questions."

Judge French called Fred Moore up to the stand and asked him if the next witness would be a lengthy session. When he replied that it might turn out to be that way, the judge decided to call an end to today's session, as she needed to make an appointment early this afternoon.

"Court will reconvene tomorrow at ten o'clock."

McDaniels was glad to get off the stand so he could go out and have a much-needed smoke. As soon as he was excused, he made a bee-line for the lobby, then the great outdoors, determined to enjoy it even though he could barely get his cigarette lit through the driving rain. Shivering, he turned his collar up against the onslaught, deciding that maybe it was time to quit his three-cigarettes-a-day habit for good. He wiped the rain out of his eyes and tossed the barely smoked butt into the street, heading for his comfortable, dry car.

*   *   *

Returning from court, Walter Rodenberg hunted down his assistant, Rebecca Simms. He found her in the office library, her head down, cold cup of coffee at her elbow, buried in a pile of loose notes. She looked up as he entered the room.

"Walter, you're back early. How's the case going?"

Looking as tired as he felt, Walter sat opposite from her and took a sip of her coffee, wrinkling his nose at the bitter taste. "That's horrible!" He wiped his mouth, trying to get rid of the nasty residue on his tongue.

"That'll teach you to help yourself without asking!" Rebecca's eyes were twinkling. "There's a hot pot right behind you," she suggested hopefully.

Walter got up, taking Rebecca's cup, and dumped it out in the partial bathroom, where there was a toilet and a small sink. Filling two cups with hot, steaming coffee, he set one down in front of his assistant, heaving a big sigh as he kicked back and relaxed for a few minutes.

"So? The case?" Rebecca prompted.

"I don't know. It doesn't seem to be heading in our favor. I need something to turn it around, something conclusive to prove Judy's innocence in all this. What did you find out about the supervisor, Murray Evans?"

Rebecca waded through a few pages, then pulled one out. "You'll be pleased to hear that our dear Dr. Evans has been sleeping with the wife of just about every person on his staff!"

Walter raised his bushy eyebrows. At last, some dirty scoop he could use?

"I have found at least three women willing to admit to sleeping with him recently, and a lot of gossip about several different women being dumped by the crud. He's a heart-breaker, that one," she said flippantly.

"Is he married?" Walter took a sip of his coffee, feeling it carry some of the tension away.

"Thankfully, no. But all the women say he is devastatingly handsome, plus very smart, and we weaker creatures are drawn to the likes of him, so he takes advantage of it. Apparently he's very valuable to the hospital, got millions of dollars in grants recently from various agencies to keep their research on brain disorders going for a couple of years. No easy feat, I guess. I was interviewing one of his cast-offs in the hospital cafeteria earlier and she pointed him out to me. He *is* a looker, I'll admit. Fits the classic 'tall, dark and handsome' theme. But," she added, "It appears Evans loses interest very quickly, and has left a string of very disgruntled females along the trail. I would say there might be a lot of motive in there somewhere for one of these rejected hearts to want to take revenge on the person who has usurped her place in Evans' attention." Rebecca, looking very pleased, slapped the paper down onto the table and helped herself to a rewarding sip from her cup.

"Excellent job, Becca! Now, we just need to find out which of his many paramours would feel strong enough to want to commit murder." He tapped the handle of his cup thoughtfully. "Any of your interviewees come across as someone with enough anger at Evans or Sondra Martin to do the job?"

"Actually, no." Becca admitted. "They all seem to be pretty ashamed of their behavior, only talking to me if I could *swear* that their husband's wouldn't hear about their fiasco with the boss. None of them came across as angry, at least only mildly, now that it was over between them and Evans. I think it hurt to be dumped, but they were relieved, too."

"Did you find out anything on Evans, himself?"

"A little." Becca found her page of notes on this and scanned the sheet. "One important thing I discovered was that Evans was supposed to attend the conference in Los Angeles, but sent Arnold Martin there at the last minute. He claimed he was ill or something. He admits to being fearful of flying, but other than that, he was pretty closed-mouthed when I tried to speak with him. Staff says he didn't show up at his office for three days, including the day of the murder, so maybe he *was* sick. But the general consensus was that he sent Martin to do the conference so he could play, possibly with one of his ladyloves.

"I'm not sure where that leaves us then." Walter's feeling of being let down was written on his face. "But I want you to continue to pursue these women, just in case another one turns up, okay? And let's dig a little deeper into our playboy, Murray Evans. Find out exactly what he was doing the day of the murder."

"Will do," Becca saluted playfully. "I'm going to get all this chicken scrawl typed up and it'll be on your desk before I go home." She stood up, refilled her cup, and left Walter to his thoughts.

Chapter 31

10:00 a.m. - Trial Day 4

Walter was hoping today's testimony from the fingerprint expert would help prove another party was responsible for the murder. On top of everything else, he was *counting* on this.

An abnormally thin woman entered the courtroom, unfortunately accented by her height, which had to be nearing six feet. She was of Hispanic background, seen in the color of her skin and the dark, almost black of her eyes, but obviously had some other ethnic blood to blame her tallness on. She folded her long-limbed frame into the witness chair.

"State your name."

"Manuella Nathan."

"How long have you been a fingerprint expert?"

"About ten years."

"Can you tell us the different techniques you use to detect fingerprints?"

"Certainly. First we give the area a visual exam. Since our skin secretes a normal grease-like chemical, we can often detect prints with the naked eye. Next we might use oblique lighting, shining a flashlight across the surface, or reflecting the light off the glare of the surface to detect prints. There's many other ways to detect prints, I'm sure you don't want me to list them all?"

"No, that's not necessary." Fred paced the narrow length of the witness stand. "I've heard of luminol to detect prints, do you use that?"

Ms. Nathan smiled. "They like to bring that up in murder

mysteries a lot. But it's actually only used to detect the blood pattern, so detectives can see how far the blood sprayed, if the suspect dragged his victim to another area, and if he wash the blood up. Even after blood is cleaned up, and you think you got all of it, luminol still shows it on surfaces. Unfortunately, it doesn't help with the fingerprints themselves, which is a much smaller area with a lot of intricate detail this method can't pick up.

"What if the object is covered in blood? Can you still find prints then?"

"In most cases, yes. If the print itself is made of blood, say from the suspect putting his hand on the wound, then touching a wall, we will need a chemical to bring out the print whorls. Ninhydrin can be applied-an amino acid reagent-which will turn the print dark purple. More commonly we use amido black, a protein dye stain after we 'fix' the print with a pre wash so it won't disintegrate. If the object is small we can dip it into the solution of amido black, if it's large, we gently wash it in the chemical."

"What do you do with the print once you make it visible?"

"We photograph it and send it to IAFIS, the FBI computer fingerprint program. If DNA or blood matching is required, though, we need to get this information first, because the chemicals used to get the prints destroy any valuable analysis materials."

"How does this program, IAFIS, work?"

"Integrated Automated Fingerprint Identification System," Ms. Nathan clarified for those who hadn't heard of it, "is the FBI program used nation-wide by law enforcement agencies. We send them our photos and they run them through their computer system, which has over seventy million prints in its database." A few surprised gasps were heard. Holding her hand up, palm out, she pointed to the pads of her fingers. "Each of us has different markings on our finger tips, called ridges and furrows. The computer matches these ridges and furrows with patterns it has stored in its system. Hopefully, it's able to find a match, but the suspect has to have been in the criminal system as an adult to be detected."

"What is the accuracy of this computer matching?"

"There's a 90 to 97 percent accuracy rate, depending on the condition of the print." Manuella looked around the courtroom. She could see the glazed expressions on most of the faces from too much information. She hoped the lawyer would get to a new topic before they put them all to sleep!

As if reading her mind, Fred grabbed the bottle and set it in front of Manuella. "Here is Exhibit 3, the bottle of Trichl..." Fred frowned, trying to recall the name without going to his table to look at his notes. Then he brightened. "The bottle containing the Methyl Chloroform found by the body. Did you find any fingerprints on it?

"Yes, we did."

"And did you find a match for the prints on the bottle?"

"Yes, the only clear prints detected belonged to the suspect, Judy Larson."

Walter had to physically restrain himself from turning towards his client and questioning this latest find by placing his chin on his hand, elbow propped on the table. He doodled on his legal pad and continued to listen, albeit more impatiently than before.

Fred brought forth a glass, also in a clear plastic bag like the other items. Here we have a glass found in the victim's home. For the records, it is just a plain drinking glass, often used for water or alcoholic drinks. No designs or etchings. We will call this Exhibit 4."

Judy could see The Artist drawing the glass, as she had the other items presented as evidence so far. She wondered if she'd be putting all of this into a book after it was all said and done.

"Ms. Nathan." Fred held the glass up by a corner of the bag. "Is the glass you obtained for printing?"

"It looks like the same one."

"Did you find the same prints on the glass as were on the bottle?"

"Yes."

"May the court note that there was alcohol traces in this glass at the time it was found on a table near the victim." He set it gently on the evidence table near the bottle and picked up the knife. "And, Ms. Nathan. This knife, Exhibit 2. Were you able to find prints on this also?"

"No. Because of the blood from the wound smearing the surface and the type of leather binding wrapped around the handle - long thin strips versus a wider single piece - it was almost impossible to lift any prints from it's surface. Nothing substantial, anyway, that we could use."

Arnie, listening in horrified fascination, was learning a new respect for the technical side of the law. Judy, trying not to squirm in her seat, was feeling the overwhelming dread build up as witness after witness pointed their finger at her.

"Did you find the suspects fingerprints on any other areas of the house?"

"Yes, on a small table in the living room, and on a kitchen counter and cabinet door."

Fred replaced the knife with the dress. "And the dress the suspect was wearing the day of the murder, any prints?"

"Yes."

"Was the blood the same as the victims?"

Walter, waiting for any opportunity to vent his growing dismay, jumped to his feet and objected. "The witness is a fingerprint expert, your Honor. Unless she has a degree in this area that I am unaware of, Ms. Nathan is not in a position to answer this question regarding blood type."

"Sustained. Stay within the witnesses field, Counselor."

"That is all, your Honor."

Walter got up next, not sure what he could ask to swing things into their favor.

"Ms. Nathan. You have testified that you have found my client's fingerprints on various items in the Martin house. Have you found other prints that belonged to people not living in the home?"

"Yes, we've found many other prints. Some we have yet to identify."

"Can you tell me how many other people may have handled some of these items, as well as the kitchen area?"

"At least four firm prints were found, that is, from four different people. Many others were too faint, smeared or partials with not enough detail to use."

"So, it is likely that somebody else may have handled some of these," Walter emphasized with a sweep of his arm to encompass the evidence table, "after my client had left the home?"

"I'd say it was possible, yes."

Wanting to leave the jury with a niggling doubt, Walter thought it best to terminate the interview right there. "I have no further questions, your Honor."

"Any other witness, Counselor?" asked Judge Ann French, pausing long enough to take a sip of tepid water.

"Yes, your Honor. I would like to call Seattle's criminal department chemical analyst and chief lab technician to the stand, Milo Potter."

Sworn in and seated, Milo Potter remained steady and calm, having been on the stand many times in his career. He pushed his spectacles up higher on his nose and waited.

"Mr. Potter, how long have you been a chemical analyst?"

"Six years since I obtained my Masters."

"And where did you get your Masters Degree from?"

"The University of Toledo, in Ohio."

"Very well." Fred took Exhibit 3, the glass bottle. "This bottle was found near the victim's body. Can you tell the court what was inside this bottle?"

"We found traces of a chemical with anesthetic properties. Unfortunately, this stuff evaporates quickly, so it was very difficult to ascertain that it was even there. But, after heating the bottle to bring out the vapors, we were able to identify it as Trichloroethane, as was mentioned earlier by Doc McDaniels."

"Can you explain to the court what this chemical is used for?"

It's a heavy-duty cleaner they use as a degreaser for machinery and airplane engines. It's also in paint remover. So, it's fairly easy to obtain. If you inhale too much, which is why it's important to have open ventilation with use, it can cause you to pass out, leaves some serious damage, possibly can even kill you over time."

"How long would it take for this chemical to take effect?"

"Maybe about five minutes if the fumes were strong."

"Did you find any other drugs or chemicals in the lab samples or on the evidence?

"The drug screen tested negative for any drugs other than the one mentioned by the doc, chloral hydrate." Fred started to show disappointment at his words. "But, once we found signs of Trichloroethane in the bottle, we knew what to look for and found the same chemical in the victim's lungs, on her fingertips, and on the piece of material.

Fred walked to the prosecutor's table, where he dug into a large paper bag, the same one he had accessed earlier in the trial, located underneath. His assistant, Irene, was noticeably absent this afternoon, having had a baby check-up appointment as her priority. He found what he was looking for and returned to the witness stand. "I would like to present Exhibit 5, the cloth found over the victim's mouth. Mr. Wade, you say you found traces of the anesthetic on this cloth? Is it safe to say that the killer must have soaked this cloth in the chemical, then held it over the victim's mouth until she passed out?"

"Objection! The witness is being asked to speculate on the mode of death."

"Sustained. Rephrase your question, Counselor."

"If the chemical-soaked cloth was held over her mouth, would the victim pass out?"

"I'd have to say yes, if it was held there long enough to do the job."

"Did you do any tests on the blood?"

"Yes."

"Who did the blood belong to?"

"We found only the victim's blood-on the dress, the carpet and the knife."

"So the blood on the dress could not have come from the suspect? From a cut or other accident after she left the victim's house?"

"No, sir."

"So, the blood stains on the front of Ms. Larson's dress probably got there when the victim pushed her out of her way when she was being attacked?"

Walter was right on that, yelling "Objection!" at the top of his voice.

"Sustained." Judge French turned her graying head in his Fred's direction. Smiling to himself, Fred said he had no further questions.

When the judge asked if Walter had any questions of his own, Walter slowly shook his head, "No, your Honor. No questions."

"This has been a long morning, ladies and gentlemen. We will recess for lunch and reconvene back here at one o'clock." Judge French smacked her well-worn maple gavel on the block and exited out the door behind her bench to freshen up and have some lunch. She also hoped to sneak in a short nap.

*   *   *

Walter was not a happy man. The case was not going as well as he'd hoped. He called Rebecca into his office for a discussion.

Becca barely got the door closed before Walter slammed his fist onto the table.

"Dammit! This case is going from bad to worse! I believe this girl didn't do it, but then, who did?" He stood by the window, looking out onto the parking lot, but not really seeing anything. Becca, pad and notes in hand, poured them both a cup of coffee, then perched on one of the dark, maple-stained chairs, waiting for Walter to lead the conversation. "Whoever did this must have some knowledge of the human anatomy, maybe some medical training," he mused to himself. "That would give the person access to the sleeping capsules, but the anesthetic?" He swung around. "Check with the local hospitals, see if any of them use...what ever the hell it's called, to clean any of their machinery, possibly amongst the janitor's supplies. And contact the lab suppliers in the city to see if it's used for any research purposes and, if yes, who's purchased some recently, maybe as early as a year ago, to be on the safe side. Let's see if it's in the area before we go any further with that."

Becca wrote down the name of the cleaner, starting a list of hospital names that she could recall. She would look up additional information in the phone book. Walter continued, more like thinking out loud than talking to his assistant.

"Both Arnold Martin and Murray Evans are doctors. Both would have access to every area of the hospital. Martin has an unshakable alibi, Evans pleads ill with no witnesses to the fact. Martin doesn't come across as the type to do something like this, even to go as far as hiring a hit man. Evans...?"

"Is a snake in the grass." Becca filled in helpfully, a smile playing on her lips.

"Yes, well. We can't hold the man's unsavory habits against him, no matter how much we'd like it to be him." He shrugged and turned back to the window, seeming to get ideas from the glistening black of the damp pavement.

"Motive. What could be the motive? Martin and his wife were having some hard times, arguments daily. He didn't know about the affair, or so he claims. He was seeing another woman, although nothing more than close friends according to both parties. Evans was seeing everyone with a pair of breasts." He heard

Becca snicker behind him. "Including the victim. Maybe she was getting too close and he wanted to end it, but she wouldn't let him, demanding he keep the relationship going. So, he decides to sneak in the back door and waste her. Might work. But, on the other hand, maybe the husband *did* find out about the affair, and in his anger, took matters in his own hands, paying some hoodlum to off her. Just doesn't fit what I've seen of Arnie."

Walter came over to the table where Becca sat, jotting down the ideas as Walter had been voicing them. Seeing the second cup of coffee, he helped himself, taking a long draw, then sighing in pleasure. He did like his coffee.

"I still say Murray Evans is our weakest link, our best bet. He has the most to lose, mainly his freedom to continue his dalliances, easy access to drugs, being a doctor, and he'd have the knowledge needed to find just the right one to use, too. Not to mention he would know where to place the knife to cause the most damage. Plus, he's the only real lead we have."

"What about Laveen Chapman? She had time to kill her neighbor before she called the cops."

"Mrs. Chapman appears to be exactly what she portrays. A snoopy old woman who loves people, loved Sondra Martin, and doesn't seem to possess the capabilities to hurt someone to that extent. Plus, there's no motive that we can find for her to kill Sondra. No, I think we need to pursue our suspicions about Dr. Evans. But, just to cover all our bases, go ahead and see if you can find anything on Laveen Chapman while you're at it. It wouldn't be the first time we found a few surprises in an ordinary person's background."

Walter yawned and glanced at his watch, not much time before they had to go back into court. "We need to come up with some answers, time is running out on us, Becca. Soon it'll be our turn to bring forth our witnesses. We need some to present!"

"I'll do my best," assured Becca.

*   *   *

In the meantime, Arnie had returned to his office, not too far from the court buildings. He was contacting other research hospitals in the state, as well as those nearby, like Oregon and Idaho. He had decided it might be best to leave Seattle permanently and go some place else to live. He had the house listed with a real estate company recommended by one of his co-workers. He was determined to leave as soon as he found a job potential and the case was over with.

Arnie hadn't been back to his office since he'd heard about Murray's affair with his wife. He didn't want to run into him, wouldn't be able to look him in the face, and definitely didn't want to hear anything Murray had to say, since he undoubtedly had heard he'd been found out by now. He was sure he would never return to work here, just as he was sure nobody would blame him. Maybe, if there really *was* justice, Murray would get fired for this stunt! But he seriously doubted it, since Murray almost single-handedly got the wealthy to reach deep into their pockets and shower millions of dollars onto the hospital.

With a growl of anger, Arnie reached for the phone to place another long distant call, to the hospital in Roseburg, Oregon, this time.

Chapter 32

Arnie was already seated in the courtroom, only four rows back this time. Judy saw him as she was escorted to her seat in the front and threw him a questioning glance, as if to ask, 'Do you believe me?' Arnie, already trying to bear the guilt and hurt he believed he had caused through his association with Judy, turned his head away, refusing to hold her stare.

Seeing the distress on Judy's face, and the direction her attention had been aimed, Walter patted her arm and gently told her she needed to focus on getting through this. He told her he would be calling on certain people to testify next week, some of which might upset her. So, she needed to remain strong. They couldn't afford for her to fall apart now. He suggested she avoid eye contact with anybody sitting out in the observer's area, especially Arnie. Judy resolved to do just that, but it would be hard. She really wanted to talk to him. But, she agreed to keep focused and not lose it. At least until she was once again in the comforting safety of her own apartment.

"Any other witnesses, Mr. Moore?" inquired the judge.

"No, your Honor."

"Mr. Rodenberg, are you ready to call your first witness?"

Walter didn't expect that, believing this would take place later in the week, and had a surprised expression on his face that he quickly hid. He hurried to reassure Judy, telling her that maybe their next witness had not been available, so things got bumped up ahead of schedule.

He stood up. "Your Honor. May I request a few minutes with my client, please?"

"Defense?"

Irene nodded and said that would be all right with them.

"You will have ten minutes to prepare your client, Counselor."

Walter took Judy to a small room just off the court where they could confer in private.

His pep talk completed, Walter led Judy back into the crowded courtroom. She approached the bailiff and was sworn in, her voice barely audible. The room was exceptionally quiet, Judy thought that they must be able to hear the pounding of her heart. She wanted to see what the jury was doing, but was too scared to move her head. Were they sympathizing with her? Was there hate on their faces?

"I will be cross-examining you, just like I have with some of the other witnesses. I will be asking you the same questions I've asked you before, and I expect to get the same answers in return. If there is *anything,* even the smallest detail you think is different, you need to tell me now, so I don't get up there and look like a blundering fool when I find out something isn't jiving with what you told me previously. Understand?"

"Yes. But I've told you the truth all along. There's nothing to change." Judy was looking haggard, losing more sleep as the trial dragged on. Walter, not looking much better, was worried that his client might follow in her mother's footsteps and have a breakdown from all the stress she was enduring. He hoped this would be the final day, but he knew it was just wishful thinking.

The judge walked in at precisely 9 a.m., just as eager to get this trial behind her as the attorneys were. The jury was also looking on the weary side, the excitement of being there long worn off. Some of them were fanning themselves, the airlessness of the courtroom already felt as the sun burst from behind its light cloud cover, warming up the brick exterior, promising a record-temperature day. It was a welcomed relief when, shortly into the trial, one of the guards was thoughtful enough to turn the fans on, if only to help himself stay awake at the door.

"Defense, would you care to cross-examine your witness,"

began the judge.

"Yes, your Honor, I would."

The judge instructed Judy to take the witness stand, reminding her that she was still under oath.

Arnie, sitting in the last row in hopes that he could stay out of the lime light this time, was wondering what else he would find out about Judy today. What surprises will today hold, he thought to himself. What else would he find out about his mysterious friend?

Walter began with a simple approach to help ease Judy's tension. "Where were you born?"

"Here. In Seattle."

"Do you still have both your parents?"

"They're both still alive, yes."

"Will you tell the court about your parents, please?"

"Well, my father left us, my mother and me, when I was twelve. I haven't seen him since. My mother couldn't handle losing him, and she got sick. She's now living in a special hospital under a doctor's care."

"All that medical attention must be expensive. Who's paying for her hospital stay?"

"I am." Judy felt proud to be able to say that, no matter what people thought of her profession.

"Why go to all that expense? Surely the state would pick up the tab?"

"She's my mother. I love her. Why should somebody else take care of her if I can do it myself?" Judy felt the need to defend her actions. Too many people dumped their ailing relatives onto the state in her opinion.

"I see. A loving daughter caring for her mother the best way she knew how." He looked pointedly at the jury while he said this. He knew this would make points with the parents in the group, and possibly make a few others feel guilty about not attending enough to their own mothers and sway their opinions their way.

Irene was about to stand up and say something, but Fred put a restraining hand on her arm and cautioned her to keep taking notes, that Judy was bound to contradict her previous statement along the way, then they could nail her.

"Tell me how you met Arnold Martin."

"It was on a plane coming home from Los Angeles. I'd just been at a Senate party with a client, and Arnie was coming back from a seminar. He was in the seat next to mine, and we started talking. We didn't plan it, we just became friends."

"Did you have a sexual relationship?"

"No, we didn't even kiss or hold hands. We just enjoyed being together, talking and laughing." Several ladies in the jury smiled at this, perhaps remembering their own young love.

"Did you know he was married?"

"Yes, I did. Arnie was very up front about having a wife and kids."

"Can you tell us what it was that kept you seeking the company of a married man?"

"Like I told the court earlier, my father left me when I was little. Arnie has two beautiful little girls and loves them very much. I admired this in him. It was what I would have liked from my own father and couldn't get. Then I found out he's a research scientist involved in finding out what makes certain illnesses occur in the brain. Because of my mother's breakdown and her mental condition, I hoped to get closer to him, to learn more about what he does."

"Why is that?"

"I've always hoped I could find something that could cure my mother. I've spent a lot of time reading about experiments on the brain, drugs used to heal brain lesions, hormone therapy, anything I could get my hands on that might lead to my mother becoming a normal person again. I wanted to see if any of the research he was working on might solve my mom's problems. I deal with all kinds of people in my profession as a consultant. I know people. It was easy to recognize Arnie as a decent person, a kind and loving husband and father. A man dedicated to his family, as well as to his research to help others." Judy stopped, realizing how passionate she had gotten about the subjects that mattered most to her. Walter waved for her to continue, knowing she held the court in the palm of her hand now.

"So I kept seeing him. First for self-centered reasons, then because I truly enjoyed his company. I told myself that I wasn't interfering in his family by meeting for a drink or a meal once in a while. We even agreed that nothing would come of it, that we would remain just friends. Sometimes weeks would go by without any contact between us, so it wasn't like we were obsessed with each other. Just two friends that liked to get together and talk. It was nice." she said, a wistful tone in her voice.

Arnie was mesmerized by all he was hearing. It made him wish that they could just go back to the way things were. He missed their times together, even if he did have to handle an unhappy wife. But he knew he would do things different, too. Tell Sondra outright that he had a woman friend to get it out in the open. Maybe even have the courage to leave Sondra before things got so bad. He would never know now.

The judge called a fifteen-minute break, and one of the police officers, a woman, came to escort Judy to the restroom, while the rest of the court stretched and talked quietly to themselves until the judge returned. Arnie sat by himself, deep in thought, reviewing all he'd heard about Judy in the trial. He wasn't sure he could process any more information after all he'd heard so far. But he wouldn't leave. His reflections were interrupted by Walter's assistant walking over to him and handing him an envelope.

Opening it up, he saw it was a subpoena. He immediately felt his heart start to hammer in his chest. "What's this for? Am I a suspect?"

Rebecca Simms smiled reassuringly at him. "No. We just need to get some information from you that nobody else can tell us. It might help us, and your friend Judy, beat this trial. You're one of our few witnesses, we need you." She held Arnie's gaze for several seconds, trying to get a feel of whose side he was on. The bailiff called for all to rise, and Becca had to return to her seat before she was satisfied with her impression of Arnie. Arnie, his hands shaking, rose unsteadily to his feet, dreading what was to come. If he'd known he might have to testify, he would have moved out of state instead of coming here every day!

*   *   *

Walter got up and crossed the room to stand before the witness stand, where Judy was once again seated. "Explain to us about your visit to the Martin residence the day of the murder, Thursday, October 19th, and what led up to it."

Judy turned her head to check out the jury and found them all watching her intently. Some with merely curious expressions, and others, like the pit bull, with hard, emotionless ones. Swallowing the bile that suddenly rose up and seemed to want to choke her, she tried to focus on what Walter was asking her.

"Ms. Larson, are you all right?" asked Walter, seeing the color blanch from his client's face. Without makeup, she looked very pale, almost sickly in the bright lights of the courtroom. He knew she wasn't handling being locked up for this length of time very well. He needed to get her out before she turned ill, physically, as well as mentally. He wondered what she was thinking of as she stared at the men and women who were responsible for determining her freedom or incarceration. He called her name again and repeated his request.

"Hm?" Judy slowly brought her attention back to Walter. Then she seemed to shake off whatever emotion had been controlling her thoughts and gave her attorney her full attention once more. "Oh. Yes, well, I got a call from Mrs. Martin one morning, about two months ago. She said she knew about Arnie and I and wanted it to stop. I tried to tell her there was nothing between us besides friendship, but she hung up on me."

Arnie sucked in a breath of air in surprise. He didn't know Sondra had called Judy, or that she'd even known about her until later. She'd never said anything, which surprised him even further, since she was persistent in rubbing his relationship with Judy in his face in all other ways.

"How do you suppose Mrs. Martin got your number?"

"I figured she must have found the business card I'd given to Arnie on the plane. It had my cell phone number on it."

"Why did you give Dr. Martin, a married man, your number?"

Judy recounted the incident on the plane, and about Arnie owing her a drink in return for her paying for his. "I don't think either of us actually thought it would happen, but we ran into each other at a restaurant one day when he was with his boss and I was with a client."

"Mrs. Martin's sister, Libby Steel, testified that Sondra told her *you* had contacted *her* for the meeting. Can you explain this?"

"Yes. After getting to know Arnie a lot more, I realized that he would never leave his wife and girls despite Sondra Martin's strange mood swings and making his life miserable, accusing him of having an affair with me. So I decided to talk to her, to let her know that she had nothing to worry about. That Arnie wasn't talking about leaving her, and that I wasn't interested in stealing her husband. So I called her to see if we could meet and discuss it, even if it meant she would tell me never to talk to Arnie again."

Judy scanned the room until she found Arnie, his eyes full of concern and puzzlement. She knew his wife hadn't told him about any of this.

"How did you get hold of her number, did Arnie give it to you?"

"No. I only had his office number. After Sondra called my cell phone, it was on the phone bill."

"When did you call and set up this meeting with Sondra Martin?"

Judy had to straighten things up in her mind, and took a minute or two to think back. "I guess that would have been about Tuesday, the 17th, I think."

"What was the conversation that transpired that day on the phone between the two of you?"

"I told her I'd like to get together with her and talk about it in a civilized manner. I wanted to meet face to face, thinking it would be less threatening if she got to see me in person, rather than a voice on the other end of the line. She surprised me by saying, yes, we should meet, maybe become friends. I..."

Walter interrupted. "She said that? That you should become friends?" Walter made his voice sound incredulous. Maybe, he thought, he could make Mrs. Martin come across as sounding insane and they could win this yet.

"Yes. I thought that was very weird, but I asked her when she wanted to meet and where. She told me to come over to her house Thursday of that same week, that we could have a drink and relax. I preferred meeting in a public place, thinking it would be less awkward and I could leave if things got too difficult. So I suggested a nearby coffee house, but she insisted we had to have it at her house because her girls didn't have school that week and she needed to be home for them. I reluctantly agreed. I had a lunch date with a friend earlier that same day, so we agreed on two o'clock. She gave me the address and the color of their house and hung up."

"Tell us what happened that day, the day of the murder."

"I was at the Space Needle, having lunch with my friend until about one thirty. Then I looked for a taxi to take me to the Martin house. When I went to give him the address, I realized I'd forgotten it at my apartment, and there was no time to go get it, so I just told the driver to head towards the general area and I'd hopefully recognize the street name. Which I did!" Judy said hastily. "As soon as I saw the name 'Dickson Street', I knew that it was the one Mrs. Martin had said, so I had the driver turn there. Then I wasn't sure about which house it was because there were two together of the same color – white. I didn't think the first number sounded right, so I went to the next one and knocked, thinking I could come back to the first one if it was the wrong house."

"Why did you ask the driver to wait for you? Did you think

you'd only be there a few minutes?"

"I wasn't sure how it was going to go, and I didn't want to be left stranded if she kicked me out of the house as soon as she met me! I seem to have a strange affect on women that way," Judy said dryly, referring to her looks, which many women felt threatened by. "That's why I asked the driver if he could wait. And once I realized the second house was the right one, I saw no point in asking the driver to move his cab closer to that one instead. It wasn't that far to walk."

"Why didn't you just take your own car?" Walter asked, curious.

"I rarely use my car because I hate driving in traffic. And every one knows how bad Seattle traffic's gotten lately! I choose to pay somebody else to take me where I need to go rather than get a headache crawling from place to place."

"Good point," Walter commented, seeing many of the jury nodding their heads in agreement. "So, you've arrived at the Martin house. What did you do next?"

"I rang the bell and Mrs. Martin opened the door. I introduced myself and held my hand out to shake hers, but she ignored it and told me to come in. So I did. She pointed to a chair and asked me to sit down. She started out friendly, we talked about Seattle, then Portland where she was born. She talked a little about her daughters, then her cell phone rang and she went into another room- I assumed it was the kitchen- to answer it. I couldn't hear any of her conversation, so I just sat there and waited. Two or three minutes later she came rushing out of the kitchen and went down the hall towards where the bedrooms probably were. I wasn't sure if I should stay or not, maybe she'd received bad news on the phone or something. But I decided to stay a few minutes longer just in case. She was in there maybe five minutes or so before she came out. She looked a little angry, and her eyes were red like she'd been crying. I told her I should go, but, in a loud voice, she told me 'No, just stay there.'

"She sat down and asked me to tell her how I'd met her

husband, where did we go to eat when we went out to talk, things like that. So I simply told her everything. Then she told me she remembered seeing me at the hospital, when Arnie had his accident. I admitted that, yes, I had gone several times to visit him there.

"Then she got a tight smile on her face and asked me what I thought of Arnie in bed. Was he a good lover to me." Judy's face turned scarlet with these words.

Arnie, in the audience, felt his own begin to turn red. He hadn't known the extent of his wife's involvement in this whole thing until now, and he wished he was sitting here listening to somebody else's life being displayed so openly. He refused to look around, keeping his eyes towards the front of the room.

"Go ahead," encouraged Walter. "What happened next?"

"I insisted that we were just friends. She laughed - a low, humorless sound that gave me goose bumps. Then she suddenly got angry and shouted at me, 'Friends? Oh, yeah, right, I'll bet you were just friends!' Something like that anyway. Then she calmed down, apologized and told me we needed to have a drink and talk about it like two adults. She told me to follow her to the kitchen and pointed a finger towards a cabinet and told me to get the bottle while she got a couple of glasses. All I saw was a short, fat bottle half full of a clear liquid, so I grabbed it and handed it to her. She told me it was the wrong bottle and had me set it on the counter while she went to a different cupboard and pulled out a large bottle and poured it into the glasses. I didn't see a label on it, so I asked her what it was before I would take a sip. She said it was vodka, a Russian friend had given it to her. I took a sip and it was very strong! She asked if I'd prefer mixing it with something and got some orange juice from the refrigerator, which I added to my glass."

"Was Mrs. Martin drinking, as well?"

"Yes, she had poured herself a lot more of it in her own glass, then drank it down pretty fast. I wondered if she planned on getting drunk so it would be easier to talk to me."

"And did she get drunk?"

"She didn't have time. She dropped her empty glass and it shattered on the floor. She started to pick up the pieces with her bare hands, so I asked her if there was anything I could do to help, thinking I should go get a broom or something. She stood up, and now she was looking mad again. I thought at first it was because she'd been clumsy and was furious at herself for breaking the glass. But then I realized it was directed at *me*. She stood there glaring at me. She must have cut herself because she was bleeding a little, on her hand, here." Judy touched the pad of her index finger to show where she had been bleeding. She came closer and started shouting angrily at me."

"What was she saying to you?"

"She said 'You're going to help me? You took my husband and now you want to help me?' Then she pushed me and told me not to talk to her husband anymore. I was scared of her hysterical behavior, so I grabbed my purse and ran out of there. She screamed at me as I left, telling me to stay away from her husband. I've never experienced that type of hatred before in my life. I was scared by her actions so I ran. I was very happy to see that the taxi was still there, so I jumped in and told the driver to take me home."

Judy's heart was hammering as she relived the terrible scene in her mind. She could still picture the enraged woman standing there, blood starting to drip down her palm. She'd looked insane, but Judy wouldn't say that in court, not with Arnie sitting there, listening. It was bad enough he had to hear such horrible things about his wife as it was without her adding to it.

"Walter walked to the evidence table and picked up the glass bottle. "Is this the first bottle you took out of the cupboard?" Judy responded that it was. "And," he showed her the drinking glass, "is this the glass you drank from?"

"It looks like the same one."

"Thank you." Walter turned towards the jury. "So, we now know why Ms. Larson didn't give an address to the taxi driver-because she'd forgotten it at home- and the reason she was seen running back to the taxi later- because she feared for her own safety."

Judy, feeling miserable and strung out from her ordeal, felt her eyes begin to water. She blinked rapidly, trying to maintain a semblance of calm for all the eyes watching her. She wondered if the jury- and more importantly, Arnie- even believed her.

Walter replaced the items and came back to the witness stand. "Did you see Mrs. Martin take any drugs, of any kind, while you were with her?"

"No, I didn't."

"Did you kill Mrs. Martin?"

Judy's eyes went wide. She didn't expect such a blatant question from her own attorney. "No! No, I did not!"

Walter smiled at Judy, as if to tell her she did a good job. "No further questions, your Honor."

The judge released Judy to return to her seat. Then, seeing that there wouldn't be enough time to call another witness before lunch, she dismissed the court until the afternoon session.

Chapter 33

With the few minutes they had left before the trial started, Walter coached Judy intently. "They are going to try to tear apart your character, and I want you to be prepared for the worst. Don't break down. Be confident that nothing you have done is wrong. I'll be ready to jump in and stop any funny business, okay?"

Judy nodded, too afraid to trust her voice just yet.

"If you're not sure about an answer, just tell them you don't know, or you can't remember. If you lie, they'll catch you on it and we'll be up shit creek. My only job here is to make sure you go free. Nothing else matters. Remember that. No matter what type of questions they ask, no matter how personal or mean they get, remember- you will be *free* when this is all over with. You'll do fine. Just tell the truth."

The judge returned to the bench and court resumed with her asking if prosecution had any cross-examination for the defendant.

Fred stood up and informed the judge that his assistant, Irene, would do the cross- examining, if it pleased the court. The judge nodded her approval.

Walter, meanwhile, was silently worrying. The jurors were watching the scene raptly; no sound was heard except the rustling of clothing. He was thinking that he had never lost a case, at least not since his post-graduate days, before he'd become the powerful name he was today. Would this be his first? He sincerely hoped not. Not because his reputation as a shark would be dampened, but because this case had become personal to him. He wanted to prove his client innocent. For her.

Irene waddled up to the stand and issued a 'Good afternoon' to

Judy. Judy murmured a reply, her voice almost a whisper. Irene then asked Judy to tell the court her full name and where she resided.

"Judith Lynn Larson. I live in Seattle, on Lakeside Avenue, not far from Green Lake."

"Do you go by any other names?"

"Not officially."

"Please explain what you mean by 'not officially,' Ms. Larson."

"Well, for my driver's license, passports and other documents, I use my given name. For parties and things related to business, I use other names." She crossed and uncrossed her legs nervously, knowing how that sounded to the jury.

"You use other names? Why is that?"

"People sometimes try to misuse my name, or call me in the middle of the night. This way, they can't track me. I'm safer if they don't know my real name."

Walter was pleased with her response, thinking it made her sound very smart and cautious. He started to feel more confident about her testifying on such short notice.

"So, that is why you have so many alias'? So many names on these business cards that were found in your purse?" Irene picked up a stack of papers from her spot at the defense table. "I have here several photocopies of the various last names used by Ms. Larson. If you would please pass these out to the jury?" She handed a stack of them to the bailiff, who passed them out amongst the jurors, while Irene handed a copy to the judge, Judy, and one to Walter.

Studying the paper, he saw that it was made up of business cards, laid out in rows of three, each bearing the same first name, Judy, but followed by a different last name on each card. The phone number was the same on each and he recognized it as the one belonging to Life Style Designers.

"As you can see, the first name is always the same, but the family name is different on each card. Explain why you did it this way."

"Like I said before, it protects me from trouble. The clients can't trace me if I use different names."

"So, lying is your way of staying out of trouble?"

Walter quickly intervened. "Objection! My client has done nothing illegal here. This is not relevant to the case."

"Oh, but I disagree. I will show you, in affect, that this is *very* relevant to the case, your Honor."

"Objection overruled. Proceed."

Arnie was listening closely, hoping her answers would show that she had, indeed, been telling him the truth all this time.

"It says here you work for Life Style Designers. Will you tell the court what you do there?"

"I'm a consultant."

"Ms. Larson, I'm a bit confused. Can you tell me *exactly* what you do as a consultant for Life Style Designers?"

Walter jumped up to protest. "What my client does for a living has nothing to do with this case, your Honor! We are trying to decide if she murdered someone, what she does for a living is irrelevant!"

Irene rubbed her belly. Walter was sure it was all for effect for the jury. "I believe I can show you that it *is* relevant. If you will let me continue, you will find this out!" she snapped. Irene leaned on the stand, trying to ease some of the pressure off her aching legs. She hoped Fred appreciated her martyrdom for this case!

The judge, sympathizing with the assistant's discomfort, having gone through three pregnancies herself, was still not going to let her condition sway her opinions. But she wanted to hear what she had to say, and let the question stand.

"Answer the question, Ms. Larson."

"I do consulting work. I go out and check on the latest fashions, purchase clothing for the company or clients, and arrange meetings to go with them to parties and such."

"But," Irene gleefully corrected, "that is not your main job at Life Styles, is it?"

Looking very uncomfortable, Judy threw a panic-laden call for help at her attorney. Walter knew he couldn't object again, that she would have to answer the question. He nodded his head at her, as if to tell her 'Remember what I told you, tell the truth.'

Taking a deep breath, Judy steeled herself for the worst. "No, you're right. I am a paid companion for the company. An escort."

"Are you a hooker?" Irene asked brashly.

"Objection!" Walter almost screamed, tipping his chair back in his haste to get to his feet.

"I will re-word the question," Irene quickly said, knowing the jury had already made an opinion about the suspect after her sly use of the harsh word, just as she and Fred had planned.

"As a *companion* then, what exactly do you do?"

Feeling like she needed to defend herself and her reputation, if she had one left, she thought, Judy sat up straighter and faced it head on. Walter, seeing her sudden change in body language, gave a silent hurrah. "As a consultant, I am available to escort men and women to posh parties, public events, private functions, wherever the client needs a friendly face instead of attending alone. My clients are wealthy, looking for a woman with grace and beauty that would be worthy of their attentions." She added this last as a dig to the overly pregnant, awkward assistant.

"Your company, Life Style Designers. Is it registered? Is it in the phone book? Do you have to be wealthy to be able to hire one of your girls?"

"No to the first two questions. We obtain our clients through word of mouth. And yes, you must be rich to be able to afford our services."

"Do you get paid for having sex with your clients?"

"No!" Judy replied abruptly. She didn't bother to expound on it.

Seeing Walter about to cause a commotion, Irene backed off. "So, the clothing you purchase is for the girls to wear to these fancy parties and all?" She unconsciously tugged at the hem of her maternity top, a smock tailored to resemble a suit jacket.

"That's right. If a man is going to pay a lot of money to have a pretty woman with him, she should be dressed in the finest we can provide."

"By all accounts of your luxury apartment and its contents, you must be making a lot of money in the escort business." She made the last two words sound dirty, just a hint of a sneer in her voice.

"Objection, your Honor!" Walter leaned on the table, trying not to jump up and wring the assistant's neck for her. He knew Fred had Irene handle this part of the dirty work because he figured a woman- a very pregnant woman, to boot- would be able to get further than a man in this type of bludgeoning of character. "There is no purpose to this line of questioning, your Honor. How much she makes and what she does with her money is beside the point!" He was livid. They had set this up to disgrace Judy's character, make her come across as less than honorable to prove she was the type of person who could carry out a murder.

Judge French was tired of what was going on. She called for a fifteen-minute recess, telling the attorneys, "and Mrs. Hill" to join her in her study.

The three went to the judge's chambers. They had barely sat down before Judge French nailed Irene with a hard look. "Just where are these questions leading?"

Before Fred could step in and defend his assistant, whom he had put up to this, Irene answered for herself, slightly breathless from the short walk. "I wanted to show the court that the suspect does not have a legitimate profession, and that her character is important in this case."

"You show her character through prior wants and arrests, and any other proof you have. You can't play with my client's rights this way. Unless she committed a crime where she works, you have no reason to be trashing my client this way!" shouted Walter.

The judge told him to calm down, and then she looked at Fred and Irene. "Do you have any proof that shows Ms. Larson has an unsavory character? A letter, a witness?" Irene shook her head. "Then, I suggest you stick with the facts and stop trying to lead the jury with speculation."

"Your Honor." Fred interrupted. "We believe we do have information that is pertinent to the case. Ms. Larson is related to another murder case. We'd like to continue our line of questioning, if we may." Fred gloated when the judge gave her consent, with a warning to stick to facts. Walter, not knowing the details other than the vague tidbits offered by his opponent, trailed behind, a worried look on his face. Willfully clearing his expression so he wouldn't spook Judy, he returned with the others into the courtroom as the trial continued.

Irene took a file folder out of her briefcase on the table. She lightly tapped it against her hand, trying to phrase the question in her mind. "Ms. Larson. Did you do any consulting work for a Steven Bloomington?"

Surprised, Judy nodded, then was reminded by the assistant to speak out loud. "Yes, I did."

"And is it true that he left you almost a million dollars in his will?"

There were gasps of shock and surprise. The room started to buzz with conversation until the judge reminded them they were in a courtroom and to keep quiet. Arnie realized his mouth was hanging open and closed it with an almost audible snap.

"Not a million, just $896,000. He left me one of his houses in Los Angeles and I later sold it for that much."

"Let the court note that Mr. Bloomington was killed three years ago, leaving his house to Ms. Larson in his Will. This is the first time I have heard of an escort inheriting a rich man's property."

Walter objected. "There is always a first time for everything. What has this to do with the case?"

Irene held up her hand, as if to ward him off. "Mr. Bloomington, according to the records we obtained from Life Styles – who, by the way, only let us have the information because he was dead – was a steady customer of Ms. Larson over a period of two years. It seems, as we see in these newspaper articles,"

Irene said as she pulled out photocopies to hand to the judge, "Our Mr. Bloomington died of suspicious causes. He was found dead in his house, no suspect ever found. Curious, isn't it?"

"Objection! Objection!" Walter rose from his seat and glared at the assistant. "Unless you can show that my client was prosecuted for his death, this is not related to the current case. I read that article myself, your Honor. Apparently Mr. Bloomington overdosed on his recreational drugs of choice. Case closed!"

"Stick to the facts, Counselor." the judge reminded Irene.

"I would like to point out to the court that Mr. Bloomington was a very wealthy man, he was killed without the suspect being caught to this day, and Judy Larson had been to his house earlier that day."

"Objection, again! There is nothing to suggest Bloomington was killed. This is not pertinent to our present case, your Honor. I'm sure my client knew many other people who have since passed on. That doesn't imply she killed them!"

"Let's stick to the case presently under examination, Counselor," warned the judge.

"Was Arnold Martin one of your... clients, Ms. Larson?" Irene asked, emphasizing the word 'client' by a slight hesitancy before saying it.

Arnie felt his heart slam to his feet. He wondered if he would start hyperventilating as it picked up speed and he broke out into a mild sweat.

"No! He wasn't. He's never been to Life Styles." Judy threw an apologetic glance his way.

"So, what was your relationship with the victim's husband? Were you lovers?"

"No! We were just good friends."

"Good enough to kill for?"

"Objection!" Walter's shout could barely be heard as the court broke out in pandemonium at her words. The judge banged her gavel several times before the room settled down. "She is badgering my client with speculative suggestions."

"Sustained."

Irene pursed her lips. Then she resumed. "Did you fall in love with Arnold Martin?"

Trying not to look over at Arnie, Judy looked over to the judge and replied, "That's a very personal question."

Judge French told her she needed to answer the question.

"Like I told you, we were very good friends. I liked talking to him, enjoyed his company. He's talented, interesting, funny," she shrugged. "He made a good friend."

"Yes or no, Ms. Larson. Are you in love with the victim's husband?"

Now Judy did look out and catch Arnie's eye, but only briefly. "Yes, I think I am." she murmured. Arnie felt his face turn red, the heat consuming him as several people who knew who he was turned to look at him.

Walter moaned. He could just hear the wheels turning in the juror's heads. Judy loved the husband, so she killed the wife so she could have him. Walter was not happy.

"Do you take any drugs? Sleeping pills, antidepressants, anything stronger than aspirin?"

"Judy shook her head no, then, remembering the court reporter had to hear her reply, she said, "No. Nothing."

"If you did want them, would you have access to any of these drugs through any of your clients, like, maybe a doctor?"

"No." Judy threw Walter a puzzled glance. She wasn't sure where this was going, but she knew it wasn't going to be good.

"Did Dr. Martin take any drugs? Or give you any?"

"No!" Judy protested. She was getting annoyed with this tank-sized assistant, and it was starting to show in her responses.

"Did you know that Mr. Bloomington also died with drugs and alcohol in his stomach, similar to Mrs. Martin?"

"Yes, I had heard."

"Do you think it's a coincidence that two people you had seen earlier, both died of similar causes?"

"Objection, your Honor!" Walter tossed the notepad he'd been scribbling on down onto the table in disgust. "Prosecution is implying my client killed this other person, while not dealing with the case at hand!"

"Overruled. I won't remind you again, Counselor, to stick to the present case."

"Did Arnold Martin tell you he would be gone for three days the week his wife was killed?"

"Yes, he did."

"And did he tell you the exact dates? His flight times?"

"Yes. Why?"

"So you knew when Dr. Martin would be gone and when he would be getting back home, is that correct?"

"Yes! But I didn't kill his wife!" she exclaimed.

"Order!" Judge French stopped the courtroom from bursting into talk with a single, sharp rap.

"Why did you go to see Mrs. Martin?"

"Like I told you before, she invited me, and I wanted to meet her. I wanted to tell her there was nothing to worry about between her husband and me."

"So, knowing you were in love with her husband, you decided to go visit her while Dr. Martin was away and, in the heat of the moment, you killed her?"

The courtroom surprisingly stayed quiet, waiting for Judy's reply.

"That's not what happened at all!"

"Then how do you explain the fact that you were the last person to see her alive? That within fifteen minutes after you left her house, Mrs. Martin was dead from a knife wound? And nobody saw anyone else enter the house or property after you left. How do you explain that, Ms. Larson?"

"I don't know!" Judy cried, in anguish. She had wrapped her arms tightly around her waist shortly after Irene started interrogating her. Now she pulled into herself even harder, trying to hold herself together.

"Did you kill Sondra Martin!" Irene spit out.

"No!" Judy wailed, bursting into tears, and burying her face in her hands.

"I have no further questions, your Honor." Irene said smugly, sure that they had the jury in the palm of their hands now.

In light of the emotional condition of the witness, the judge called adjournment until the next morning, when Defense would be able to cross-examine.

*   *   *

Arnie went home with a lot of questions on his mind about Judy. He wondered who she really was, and why she hadn't mentioned Bloomington and the thousands of dollars she received from his death. And what else didn't he know about her? He tried to analyze how he felt about Judy's public announcement that she loved him. It made his senses tingle, made him feel happy to know she reciprocated some of his own newly recognized feelings. While at the same time, it haunted him to have a remaining doubt that she may have actually committed the murder despite his deep desire for it not to be true.

He vaguely recalled reading about a millionaire's death, but he hadn't paid much attention to it. As soon as he got home, he booted up his computer and got onto the Internet to look up the case and try to find out the extent of Judy's involvement in it. He found the Bloomington articles and quickly scanned them to see if Judy's name was mentioned, then went back to the first article and read them more carefully. According to the news reports, Judy had been seen quite often with Steve Bloomington around the well-to-do circles for a period of two years or so. When he died from a heavy overdose of drugs and alcohol, not being one known to abuse either substance, it was investigated as a suspicious death, Judy initially in the forefront of the suspects. It was later proved that she was with a well-known actor at the time of his death, and was quickly cleared. No suspect was ever found, and the case was closed as a suicide. The Bloomington family, mainly his two greedy children, fought tooth and nail to reverse the Will, not wanting some little gold digger to get any benefit from their father's death. The judge, believing children should be taught to work hard for their lively-hood and not suck off their relatives, firmly denied the petition and told the "children," ages thirty-two and thirty-six, to be grateful that their father had been generous enough to leave them the other three buildings. One of which was a twenty-two-story office building in New York, and the stocks, bonds and the other four-plus million dollars that would support them for the rest of their lives. Case closed.

Arnie was happy to see that Judy didn't seem to have been involved in the millionaire's death, but it did bother him to read that the mode of death was somewhat like Sondra's, minus the knife, that is. And why hadn't Judy ever mentioned that she had all that money? That continued to gnaw at him until he was able to fall asleep, both of his girls curled up on either side of him, as they have since their mother's death weeks ago.

*   *   *

Walter was not a happy camper. He was losing his patience-with himself! He couldn't find any credible evidence on anyone that might help turn the case around. He hit the intercom and called Becca into his office to check if she'd been able to find out anything new.

"I did some more investigating on Laveen Chapman and her husband, but nothing. Zero. No records that show that either are anything but good citizens, the neighbors have nothing but praises for them, as well as the Martins, and no complaints or disturbances reported. In fact, that whole neighborhood is too good to be true! Nothing on any of them that would be worth dragging in. I even ran a check with the FBI, stuffy fellows that they are, and nothing there either."

"Thanks, Becca. What about Murray Evans?"

"I issued a subpoena to him yesterday, and we have delivered one to Arnold Martin today in court. That was easy, since he has shown up like clock work, so far." Walter nodded his approval. Becca turned to leave the office, then stopped long enough to wish him 'Good luck in court tomorrow" before heading out to her own desk.

"Yes, I think I'll be needing all the luck I can get on this one," he muttered to himself, back to staring out the window, trying to plan his next strategy. He grabbed the tapes he had recorded of his sessions with Judy, intent on finding something he could use. There had to be something he was missing that he could throw in tomorrow, a witness he hadn't thought of, a tactic he could use to divert the opposition. Maybe he needed to call for an extension, get more time to dig up information. But he knew that would be futile, that Fred would never let that happen, and he was getting too tired for all this fighting.

By the time he listened to all the conversations he and Judy had in the past few weeks, it was almost one in the morning, Becca had bid him an unheard 'So long' hours ago. He decided the best thing to do would be to go to bed and get a little rest. Maybe, if the gods were on his side, an idea would pop into his head in the form of a dream. He dared to hope.

Chapter 34

Arnie was driving to the court room and started to remember his visit to the house last evening. Leaving the girls with a friend Sunday afternoon, he'd taken his first trip to the house since the murder. There was a For Sale sign in the lawn, replacing the yellow police tapes that had previously stretched across the driveway.

Grabbing some empty boxes from the back seat of his car, Arnie cautiously approached the house. He stopped to stare at the oil stains left on the cement driveway from Sondra's old car. It had gotten to the point where they were adding oil to her old Honda every week. Sondra absolutely disliked dealing with salesmen, so Arnie took it upon himself to go out one day and buy her a nice, reliable car. Sondra wasn't real ecstatic over the Volvo wagon, but the kids loved it. And he felt better, knowing his wife and kids would make it home every day. Arnie swallowed the lump in his throat, caused by the memory.

Entering the house, Arnie avoided looking into the living room, afraid of what he might see. He kept his head turned away as he rounded the corner and went down the hall to the room he and Sondra used to share in happier times. He never told her that he had stopped sleeping with her because he felt like he was sleeping with a stranger.

He pulled bunches of dresses and blouses off the closet rod, and tossed them onto the bed. The room was a mess, clothing down on the closet floor, between the bed and the far wall, shoes thrown together in an indistinguishable pile. Arnie didn't see it. He sat on the bed, folding the garments carefully. Each piece bringing a hint of a memory, some good, some not so pleasant. Here was the elegant dress Sondra had worn to the last staff Christmas party. This was the blouse he had spilled beer on when they celebrated their tenth wedding anniversary. And this was the shirt she was wearing during their last argument, before he left for Los Angeles, before she got killed. Arnie buried his face in the shirt and wept.

*   *   *

Back in the courtroom before 9:00, Arnie noticed, for the first time all week, what Judy was wearing. It was the same dress she'd had on the first time they met on the flight from LA. He tried not to think of those times. It brought up too many delightful memories. He sure never thought it would end up like this!

His attention was caught by Murray Evans, strolling up the isle with his loose-jointed stride. Dressed in a black suit with a blue and green striped tie, he looked like he could be attending a wedding. Or a funeral, Arnie recalled, picturing Murray beside him that day, the image of a supportive co-worker. Arnie steamed. He couldn't believe his boss and his wife could do something like that to him. *And me so oblivious to it! What a fool!*

Murray acted like he didn't see Arnie there and sat several rows further up and to the left of him. Arnie hoped he could feel the hole he was burning in the back of his neck!

Judy was once again on the stand. The judge asked Fred and Irene if they would like to counter cross-examine the witness. Irene rose and said 'Yes.'

Standing directly in front of Judy, Irene began. "You said Mrs. Martin pushed you. Would you show the court exactly how she did this, Ms. Larson? You may come down here," she directed. Judy stepped down and stood in front of Irene. "Don't be afraid, you won't hurt the baby. Just show me where she placed her hands."

Judy thought back, then placed both hands near Irene's shoulders, just about below each collarbone. She lightly pushed against Irene when told to show this. "Thank you, you may return to the stand. Which hand was cut on Mrs. Martin?'

"This one, the right." Judy once again held up her hand and pointed to the finger that was cut.

Walter was pleased to see that this matched the bloody marks found on the left shoulder area of the dress Judy was wearing that night. He also noticed that Irene did not bother to point this out to the court, not wanting to help the defense in any way. Walter hoped the jury was smart enough to think of this on their own, and remembered where the bloodstains were on the dress they were shown earlier.

"Did you see Mrs. Martin actually cut her hand on the broken glass?"

"In a way, yes. She didn't have any blood on her hand until she started to pick up the pieces. At least I didn't see any blood until then."

"How could she have left so many bloody marks on the dress if she just got a little cut on one finger? Wouldn't it have left only a tiny spot?"

"I don't know. There was a little blood that was starting to run down her palm, I suppose she could have smeared it on her hand before she touched me." Judy made a wiping motion on her thigh, as if to rub off invisible blood from her own hand.

Irene, hearing this, grabbed at it. "You said earlier that she *pushed* you. Now you're saying she just *touched* you. Which is it, Ms. Larson? Did she push you or just lay her hand on you and you over-reacted and attacked her?"

Walter was waiting for something like this to happen, and was quick to jump to Judy's defense. "Objection! She's badgering my client and supposing events!"

With a satisfied smile on her face, Irene said she had no further questions, and Judy was allowed to return to her seat. Walter, realizing the prosecutors had just thrown doubt into the jurors again, seethed.

*   *   *

"You have a witness to call, Counselor?"

"Yes, your Honor," replied Walter. "I'd like to call Murray Evans to the stand."

Murray stood up with a small grin, enjoying the attention. Ignoring the very pregnant, therefore unavailable, Irene, Murray focused his attention towards Becca and the judge, who both chose to ignore the charming smile he threw their way. He swore the oath and sat down.

Giving him a hard look, Walter told him to state his full name and occupation for the record.

"Doctor Murray Samuel Evans. I am the head of the Science Research Department at the University Hospital in Seattle," he stated arrogantly.

"So you know why you have been called onto the witness stand?"

"Yes. To testify as to Arnold Martin's character, I imagine."

"Do you work with Dr. Martin?"

"Yes. I'm his supervisor, as well as to the entire research department."

"What can you tell us about Dr. Martin?" Walter was waiting for Murray to start talking badly about Arnie, a risk he felt they had to take, since he was the closest thing to a character witness they could find other than close friends, who wouldn't have lent half the credence as this guy. He breathed a sigh of relief when he didn't.

"Well, I can honestly say he's a good doctor and an excellent worker, often staying late to make sure a project gets completed on time. I believe he's a good father to his kids, too. He makes sure he goes to their concerts and teacher meetings. He's even had them up to see the lab a time or two." Arnie, listening closely, was pleased despite himself. He hadn't known Murray knew anything at all about his private life. But then he had a disparaging thought. *He probably heard about it from Sondra after a hot bout of sex! No wonder he was so eager to help me after she died. A guilty conscience?* He still wanted to deck the guy, now more than ever, knowing Murray was just sucking up right now, trying to impress the court.

"Did you know *Mrs.* Martin very well?" Walter emphasized the married title.

Murray's eyebrow rose in slight surprise. "Yes, I met her a few times." Arnie almost choked. *Liar! You apparently did more than meet her!*

"Did you have a special relationship with her, Dr. Evans?"

Murray was quiet for a moment, as if trying to figure out how to answer this. He finally said, "I was friendly with her, yes."

Friendly, my ass! Arnie hoped Murray would look out and see him so he could flip his middle finger up at him – be darned if he got thrown out for contempt!

"Did you have sexual relations with Sondra Martin – and I remind you that you are under oath, Dr. Evans."

For the first time, Murray didn't seem as sure of himself. He looked up and his glance happened to fall on Arnie, who had an angry expression very evident on his face. He looked quickly away again.

"Dr. Evans, answer the question," Judge French prompted. Everybody, including the aggrieved husband, was waiting to hear if he would perjure himself and deny it. A light sheen of sweat popped out on Murray's forehead. He could see no way out of this except to tell the truth.

"Yes," he finally replied reluctantly.

"So, you're saying you *did* have sex with the deceased. Is this correct?"

"Yes." Murray wiped his forehead with the crisp handkerchief from his breast pocket and returned it, not quite in such pristine shape as before.

"How long was this affair going on, Dr. Evans?"

"About two, three months, I guess."

"And this didn't bother you? Having sex with the wife of the man you claim is such a good person? And who *works* for you? Do you make a habit of sleeping with your co-worker's wives?"

"Hey!" Murray protested. "I'm not on trial here, she is!" He pointed to Judy, who glared at him in return. "And it wasn't *my* idea to have the affair in the first place."

"Explain what you mean, please. How did it start?"

Murray figured he could get off the hook if he played his cards just right. He started to feel a little more back in control now. "It was Sondra's idea. She was interested in me, always stopping and flirting with me whenever we met at a company party or she dropped into the lab to see Arnie. You could tell she wanted me." Arnie couldn't believe what he was hearing. He knew Sondra never dropped into the lab if she could help it, she thought what they were doing was about as interesting as watching grass grow. And he'd never seen her flirt with *anybody*, let alone *him!*

"Then she started calling me and asking me to meet her somewhere for a drink. Eventually I took her up on her offer." Murray shrugged. "Who wouldn't take the chance at a pretty woman who was throwing herself at you?" He ran a soft, manicured hand through his hair. He looked very smug.

"Are you married, sir?" asked Walter, trying very hard to keep his real opinion of this man from showing up in his voice. His one saving grace was that, when this jerk returned to work, he had a feeling his fellow scientists would have a different opinion of their boss – and their wives! Walter only wished he could be there when Murray's perfect world crashed.

"No, never."

"Why not, if I may ask? Any particular reason?"

"I'm just not ready for a long-term commitment. I'm too busy with my work and I don't have the time to start a family. I'm dedicated to my profession. Besides," Murray added, pulling his jacket lapel straight, "I'm still young and have a lot of ladies to meet!" He grinned at the jury, seeing several young women seated there. There was a young-sounding giggle from the audience, which immediately was rewarded by a very disapproving look from the judge.

Walter stood there quietly for a few seconds, making Murray nervous with his stern demeanor. After a length of time went by, Walter asked, "Did you, Dr. Evans, kill Sondra Martin on that October day? Perhaps to get rid of her once you grew tired of her? Maybe she was getting too close to you, and you don't want anything that hints of commitment or responsibility? Because then that would interfere in your lifestyle, your reputation with the ladies, wouldn't it?" There were several gasps of surprise at this attack. Murray's face turned red, his eyes got wide and immediately sought Arnie's in the seats before him. Seeing nothing but disgust there, Murray looked back at Walter.

"I didn't kill her!" he stated emphatically.

"You just told us she was pestering you all the time." Walter reminded him.

"She was. But it was a different kind of pestering, a come-on."

"Did you try to discuss this with her husband? Tell him what was going on? Have him speak to his wife about backing off?"

"No, I didn't."

"Did you tell Mrs. Martin that her husband was having an affair with a younger woman?"

"No. Well..." Murray attempted to find a more comfortable place on the hard chair. Walter, and even more so, Arnie, was glad to see him squirm. "When I went to see Arnie at the hospital, after his accident, Sondra, I mean Mrs. Martin, was there. She asked me if I knew anything about who her husband had been seeing the night he got hit by the car, and I merely told her it might have been the lady I had seen him with one day in a restaurant. It was her." He nodded his head over towards Judy.

"Why did you tell her it might have been Ms. Larson?"

"Because she's the only woman I've seen Arnie get all ga-ga over! He was so enamored by her that he couldn't concentrate the day we ran into her. And I saw them together a few times after that." This time he looked at Arnie with a little smile playing across his lips. Arnie didn't know if he was telling the truth and *had* seen them or if he was trying to place the blame on Arnie to get the focus off his own indiscretions – for once.

"Was the real reason you told her about Arnie and Ms. Larson to use it as a hook, to reel Sondra in so you could have an affair with her?"

"No, not at all. She came to me of her own free will. *She* sought *me* out, you'll recall!"

"Tell me, Dr. Evans. Do you have access to drugs, possibly where you work? Specifically ones that might alter moods, cause depression or assist with falling to sleep?"

"Yes. We have several different types of those drugs in our laboratories. They're used in various experiments, for research purposes only. We aren't allowed to remove them from the building, and we have to check them out when we want to use them. We keep a close record of all the drugs used and purchased on our floor."

"How about types of anesthetics."

"Oh, yeah. We need those when we have to take biopsies to check out skin lesions and assorted anomalies that are sent our way. Mostly they're topical – meaning we spray or rub them on the person's skin to numb it. Occasionally we have use for the kind you have to breathe in, but that's pretty rare. They mainly use that on the surgery floors, and we aren't into that kind of research in our lab."

Walter put his hand thoughtfully to his chin, his head tilted to the side as he studied Murray. "Are you aware that the victim in this case was given sleeping pills, then an anesthetic, before being stabbed to death?"

"Yes, I'd read about it in the papers."

"And you have access to these drugs?"

"I suppose we do, in the hospital somewhere, not just the lab."

"Where were you around two forty-five that day, Dr. Evans? The day your paramour was brutally attacked and killed?"

Murray gulped, finally realizing the seriousness of the situation he was in. "I was home sick"

"Really. Can you prove you were home sick that afternoon? Was anyone with you? Did you go to a doctor, perhaps?"

"No."

"Did you see or talk to anyone that day around the time of Mrs. Martin's death? Did you call the victim herself that day at any time?"

"No."

Walter saw just a hint of an expression flit over Murray's face, but it was too quick for Walter to recognize it. He decided to follow his instincts, just the same. "Dr. Evans. Let me remind you that you are under oath. If we find out you lied, that's perjury, worthy of jail time. Let me also remind you that we can check back over your phone calls and see who you chatted with that day." Walter went up to the stand, and leaning in close, he said, "Now, I'll ask you again, and I want you to think real hard before you answer. Did you call anyone, especially the victim, Mrs. Martin, anytime that day?"

Murray was in a panic. He wasn't sure if they could trace his phone calls or not. But he knew that if he lied, and they did find out, he would lose everything, including his high-paying job at the hospital. "Okay! I called Sondra that day!" It came out in a rush.

Walter tried to hide his euphoria at hitting the mark. "What time?"

"About one o'clock."

"Morning or afternoon?"

"Afternoon. I was feeling lonely and called her to talk."

Arnie doubted Murray called anybody just to *talk*. He would have felt better to know that almost everyone in the courtroom was of the same belief.

"Were you planning on meeting her?'

"Yes. But she told me she already had plans and couldn't make it."

"I thought you were sick? Not too sick to have a dalliance on the side?"

"I thought we could just spend some time together. Ladies like that stuff, you know."

"So, you got mad when she wouldn't meet you and went over there and killed her?"

"No! I did not kill her!" Murray insisted again. He wiped more sweat from his face.

"Who else did you call that day?"

"Another friend." Again that fleeting expression that something wasn't right.

"Tell us the name of your friend. Another hospital wife?"

Murray was quiet for several moments. Then he murmured, "Caroline. I called Caroline."

Before Walter could continue, Judge French called both sides to her bench. Fred joined Walter at the front. "Gentlemen, let's not make a soap opera out of this. Get the name and appropriate information from the witness after this session and you can verify it with me tomorrow. Continue."

They both returned to their previous places, Fred quietly informing Irene of what transpired after he was seated.

"What time did you call your friend?"

"After I spoke to Sondra, maybe about one-fifteen. And, before you ask, I didn't call anyone else." Murray opened his jacket and unbuttoned the top of his shirt.

"What did you do after you made your calls?"

"I met Caroline at a restaurant in town."

"Which one?"

"The Bai Tong. It's a Thai restaurant."

"Will the staff be able to confirm that you were there if we show them a photo?"

"Yes."

"What time did you arrive at the restaurant, and when did you leave?"

"We got there maybe at one forty-five and left close to four."

"That's a long time to be eating! And all the people involved can verify your story? Caroline included?"

"Yes." Murray sounded beaten, no longer the cocky young man he was when he entered the room. Arnie was happy to see this, although it didn't change anything. His wife was still very much dead. He wanted to believe that Murray had killed her. But it didn't look like that would happen.

"I think I'm finished with Dr. Evans, for now, your Honor."

Prosecution stated they had no questions for Dr. Evans, so Murray was instructed to give the full name and contact information of his friend so they could verify what he had said in court. He was then warned not to try to leave the area or a warrant would be put out for his arrest, as he may still be needed to testify. Looking straight ahead, Murray couldn't get out of there fast enough.

Court was set for the next morning and people filed out noisily, voicing their own opinion to each other of who had committed the murder. In their rooms, the jurors were doing the same thing. Judy would have been totally surprised to find out that the man she called the pit bull was defending her innocence against two of the other jurors, who were sharing a room with him.

Chapter 35

Arnie spent a miserable Thanksgiving holiday with his girls, trying to entertain them with games and stories. He even let them help him make a pie crust, getting flour everywhere and hopelessly burning the bottom of it. But they missed their mother on this first holiday without her, and the day was a failure. Normally they might have spent it over in Oregon with Sondra's sister, Libby, but things had been very strained between them since the murder, and Arnie didn't even bother calling her. Eating the dry turkey he had managed to cook, he was already dreading Christmas next month.

*   *   *

Walter, in his kitchen pouring himself another drink, had been glad that court was being held until after the holiday. It might give him some time to find another witness or two. Although, to be honest, he had no idea where to go from here. He still felt that Evans was the biggest suspect, but unfortunately, it sounded like he had quite a few witnesses saying he was where he said he was. He hoped the detectives could find something useful. Walter scratched his head absently. If he couldn't find something he could use, and soon, this might be the first major loss in his career. He returned to the living room to try to at least put on a show of cheer for his wife and relatives.

*   *   *

Judy was feeling as if all hope had been flushed down the toilet. Whoever thought she'd be spending the day of thanks behind bars. She poked the tasteless pumpkin pie on her plate. She'd been here far longer than even Walter Rodenberg had anticipated. She was going stir-crazy. On top of it all, she felt like Arnie had lost all respect for her. All the signs pointed to him believing she had done it, and that really hurt.

She thought about her mother and all she'd tried to do for her to make her life a little less confusing. Who would be there the next time her mother started calling out for her dad? She closed her eyes and tried to regain her faith in her own innocence. She should just give up, get used to this place. She pictured Arnie's face in her mind, heard his laughter, saw the twinkle in his eye when he told her something humorous. She felt a deep pain within her heart. Pushing her uneaten dinner away, she curled up on her mattress to pass another very lonely night.

*   *   *

With several days on his hands, Arnie decided to go back to the house after their pathetic dinner and pack up what he could, preparing for the eventual move. He hadn't accepted any of the job offers he'd found yet, but he was narrowing down his choices.

Leaving the girls with the neighbors, who had several young children they could play with, Arnie drove to his old house. He started in the girls' room this time. He hadn't noticed before now how neat the girls' room was kept compared to the one Sondra had used. He saw their names above each side of the closet, placed there a couple years ago by Sondra to keep them from arguing about what belonged to whom. He pulled clothes from the closet bar, hangers and all, and began the tedious chore of loading their things into his car. When that was done, he sorted through their toys and games, picking out what he figured they might consider important. They could go through the rest at another time.

Next, he pulled favorite books out of the shelves. He grabbed a drawing pad that Ashley recently got and several papers fell out, including one she had apparently taken from the garbage to draw on. Forever being told to stop this practice by her mother, Ashley continued to do so, wanting to recycle like her favorite teacher was always pressing for. Arnie stuck the papers back inside the cover of the book, a tight lump in his throat. He noticed that Sondra had made a list on the back, recognizing her rounded handwriting. But he refused to look closer at it. Even something as mundane as a 'To do' list would be too painful to read right now. He tossed the art pad into the box without another glance.

It was getting late, so he called it quits and took the load to his apartment. He would return later to go through more of the boxes and junk in the narrow attic and damp quarter basement.

*   *   *

On Friday, Becca informed Walter that all their leads on Libby Steel had washed out. And her FBI friend had found nothing on either her or Murray Evans. Walter decided to pay a visit to John Ward, the detective who was looking into whether Murray had been at the restaurant with his friend, Caroline. He set up a meeting with him for later that morning.

John Ward treated him to a friendly handshake and led him to his office. Walter came right to the point and asked how the investigation had gone. John pulled a file out of the stack on his desk and flipped it open. It was pretty thin, having only a single sheet of paper in it.

"Everything he said panned out. The staff remembers them because they were practically laying bets on whether they would still be there when the dinner crowd started to come in. I spoke to this Caroline chick. She denied it at first because she thought her husband had put a private eye on her tail. Apparently her husband is a very well known physician in the States. She's only twenty-four years old to his fifty-three, and knows which side her bread is buttered on. But, once I explained the problem, she was willing to

328

talk. She didn't seem like she was willing to put any effort into lying to save Evan's ass, so I believe her."

"Think it's worth trying to get her onto the stand?"

"Doubt it. I can't see her telling you anything more in this case. She's only guilty of being one of Evans' lovers, not the killer. I found out she has too many alibis for all the time surrounding the murder. Very popular girl with the salons and stores in the area. And just because Evans comes across as a total asshole, doesn't make him a killer, either, you know. Looks like your client is still in the running." John tossed the flimsy file on top of his desk.

"If you're trying to cheer me up, it's not working," Walter tried to joke. He left John's office feeling like he was letting Judy down.

*   *   *

Walter decided to go talk to Judy and run through everything one more time, even though he could practically recite her history by heart. He was running out of energy, hope and time. When Judy was led into the small attorney-client room, Walter could tell Judy was in a foul mood. She wore a defeated demeanor, shoulders slumped, no eye contact, but there was a resentful overtone in her greeting. Walter wondered if she was mad at him for not having this case solved yet, and he didn't blame her one bit if she was. She was definitely not going to be happy with what Walter was about to bring up.

"So, there's nobody else you can find to testify on my behalf? Does everyone out there think I did it?" she questioned angrily. "I might as well sell my apartment and call it quits! It's useless to keep trying." This last was made in a resigned voice. Walter was dismayed at how Judy seemed to be giving up, yet he had nothing to offer to change her attitude.

Then Judy started to cry, silently, her shoulders gently quivering. She did nothing to hide the tears that slowly rolled down her pale cheeks. Walter let her cry for several moments, then told her he needed to ask her something, and she needed to be totally honest and try not to get upset with him for asking it. Judy looked at him with a puzzled expression, drying her tears with her palms.

"Are you absolutely sure you were...of sound mind, when you were at Sondra Martin's home?" He held out a hand to stop Judy from saying anything yet. "Do you remember every second of what transpired there? No blank or fuzzy spot in your memory? Nothing to indicate something might have happened, even for a brief moment, that you are aware of?"

"You're talking about like my mother, aren't you? Do I have a mental illness like my mother?" Judy stayed surprisingly calm, having thought of this herself at one point. She shook her head in the negative and told him she was sure she could account for every second of that eventful day if he wanted to hear it. Walter shook his head, his last desperate attempt thwarted.

*   *   *

Arnie spent Friday stacking boxes against one wall of his bedroom, planning on starting to go through it and throwing away as much as he could before getting another load from the house. He would put the girl's things into a separate pile and let them decide what to keep or give to Goodwill. He would try to find a few momentos of Sondra's to give the girls, maybe when they were older.

He had spent the past few weeks trying to give the girls a normal life again. They had been spending time at parks, went to see a few lighthearted movies, and kept busy doing some of the local activities he found in the newspaper, like the Woodland Park Zoo and the Seattle Science Center. The girls were off until Monday, because of the Thanksgiving holiday, so Arnie packed them up later that afternoon and they spent some time at the little park down the street, playing catch. They stayed about an hour, enjoying their time in the cold sunlight, then headed home so Arnie could start dinner. He was getting pretty good at making simple dishes for the three of them.

He grabbed the mail out of the box on his way into the house and tossed it onto the pile of correspondence that he had all but ignored the past few weeks. A blue envelope slid out of the stack and caught his eye. Picking it up, he noticed it was stamped with a red 'Urgent. Immediate Reply Requested." *Oh, oh!* he said to himself, tearing it open and dreading what he would find. It was from a collection agency, demanding the $8,600 he owed them!

Holy crap! This has to be a mistake! He read the letter further. Sondra used to handle all the bills. What could she possibly have bought for that much money, a yacht? He couldn't tell what company it was from, the delinquent bill having been passed to the agency, which had a generic name. He would have to call them and get this cleared up as soon as possible. He grabbed the stack of mail and pulled out the bills and important letters he found, opening them one by one. Most were common household bills, but he also found three more letters referring to the exuberant amount they claimed he owed. He rubbed his temples in dismay. More problems to handle. He set it all asides and went to prepare dinner.

That night he tossed and turned. He was glad the girls had finally made the transition into their own beds because he would have kept them all awake. He'd noticed that one of the bills was for a cell phone in Sondra's name. He couldn't recall Sondra ever using one. There were quite a few calls on the bill, and he didn't recognize any of them. He had also found a bill showing that Sondra had visited a doctor he didn't know, several times in the past few months. He had spent the last hour or so going through all the things he had brought with him to the apartment, unsure of what exactly he was looking for, but not finding it. Tomorrow he would spend the day at the house and try to find Sondra's cell phone, as well as a few more answers to this puzzle.

The next morning, Saturday, Arnie got Heather and Ashley

ready and dropped them off at their friends' houses, giving them a big hug before they ran off. He then spent the morning visiting the bank, Sondra's doctor, plus taking care of several other things on his list. He ended his rounds at the house, a worried expression on his face as he stepped out of the car.

He tore up Sondra's closet, trying to find anything that would clear up some of the mystery. Nothing. Then he went down to the basement, a small, musty room that they rarely went in to. Boxes of out-grown toys, clothes and other mildew-laden items cluttered the small room. He wasn't sure where to start, so he grabbed the first damp box he reached and started going through it. He did this until he came upon an abnormally dry box, suspicious in it's lack of moisture. He hesitated, not knowing if he was prepared for what he might find inside. Then, picking it up, he carried it carefully up the stairs and set it on the coffee table. He sat there for quite some time before he ventured to open it up.

*   *   *

Sunday morning the girls were up and eager to start their day. They woke Arnie up with a squeal and attacked him, Ashley bouncing on the bed while Heather perched on his chest and demanded that he wake up. Having stayed up until the early morning hours, Arnie tried to force one eye open to look at his daughters, big smiles on their faces.

"Come on, Daddy!" Ashley insisted. She leaned over from where she'd landed, reaching out to pull the other eyelid open. "It's getting late! We want to do something!"

Arnie ran his tongue around his mouth, trying to find some hint of moisture. He felt like he'd been out on a bender instead of up reading all night. He shifted until his chest was propped up on his pillows and he could see the girls at eye level.

"What did you have in mind?" He yawned and stretched, knocking Heather off his chest in a fit of giggles.

They wanted to take the ferry to Victoria, something they

hadn't done in a long while. So, that's what they did. Bearing the chill wind and wet spray they stood on the deck of the white and green ferry, teeth chattering, then explored all the shops and parks on the other end. It should have been fun, but on the return trip, Heather summed it up for all of them, "The last time we came here, we had mom with us, and it was fun. I miss her so much! Why did she have to go!" Her pretty eyes tired up.

Arnie, feeling very sad, put his arms around both his girls. What do you say at a time like this? "I don't know why these things happen, but she's in a better place, now. You have to believe that. She would want us to continue on and have a good life, just as if she were with us."

"Are you going to get married again, Dad?" Heather looked into his face, a serious expression on her own.

"Let's not talk about that right now, okay? Mom just left us a short time ago. It's too soon to start worrying about things like that until it happens." Arnie treated the kids to dinner at Ivars Fish House after the ferry docked, and they were able to forget their sadness for a while.

Chapter 36

8:00 a.m. - Trial Day 6

Walter was laying all odds on Murray's friend, Caroline, denying that they'd been together that whole afternoon. So his dismay was twice as sharp when Becca broke the news to him.

"Even the restaurant remembers those two being there several hours. But I have some news that might cheer you up. Sondra Martin's sister, Libby Steel. Seems she had a bit of a tussle with her ex-husband a few years back involving a knife. Arrested for domestic violence. Husband was drunk, so he spent the night in jail with a cut hand. He didn't press charges, so they let her go the next morning. She was in Portland with her family, though, so..."

"Well, maybe we can find a connection to the Mafia or something! Look into it, would you," Walter exclaimed, knowing he came across as somewhat demented.

Thinking Walter was *really* stretching to want to find a connection to the Mafia, Becca just raised an eyebrow and left to go see what she could turn up. She placed a call with a friend of hers in the FBI. It was a place to start anyway.

*   *   *

It was Arnie's turn on the witness stand on Monday morning. His knees felt like they wouldn't hold him up as he started the long hike up the isle, feeling like an animal in the zoo as every head turned to follow his progress. It was a relief when he was able to sit down after all the preliminaries was taken care of. Until he looked out and saw all the people staring at him.

Walter coughed, then took a sip of water to clear his throat. All this talking had given him a dry throat. He asked Arnie to tell the court how he'd met Ms. Larson.

Arnie told how he'd met her on the plane coming back from LA, and some of their conversation during the trip.

"You're a married man. Didn't you find it uncomfortable being friends with a single lady?"

"I thought about it. But we weren't doing anything improper. A lot of people have friends of the opposite sex, married or not."

"Was your wife aware of this relationship with Judy?"

"Not right away. I told her later, after I had my accident." Arnie was afraid that sounded like he had been hiding it. He guessed he had been.

"How do you feel about your friendship with Ms. Larson now. Since your wife was killed?"

"I don't know," he said truthfully, not looking at her.

"Do you think Ms. Larson killed your wife?"

"I want to think she didn't," Arnie said quietly. He didn't really think she was involved, but where was the outstanding proof? It took him out of his comfort zone to think of Judy as a killer, so he chose not to think too hard about it at all. He wanted to wait until all the evidence had been presented before examining his true feelings about whether he believed her guilty or not.

"Fair enough. What is your general opinion of the young lady?"

"I think she's very attractive, bright, pleasant to talk to."

"Do you love her?"

Arnie had to think about how to reply to this. "I don't know. I liked her a lot, and liked spending time with her."

"And now? After the murder?"

Arnie shrugged. "I don't know. I'm too confused over the whole thing."

"Did you know your wife was having an affair with your boss?"

"No," Arnie replied gloomily. Not until I heard it in court."
Along with a hundred other people.

Walter tried to ask the next question as gently as he could, but
there was no easy way. "Do you think your wife was involved
with any other men, Dr. Martin?"

Startled, not having thought of that himself, Arnie started to
shake his head, then admitted he had no idea, since he hadn't even
known she was seeing Murray. "It's possible, I suppose." This
was said warily, not sure if he was about to be provided with a list
of her consorts.

"Just to clear the record, did you, Dr. Martin, kill your wife?"
As Arnie started to protest, Walter continued. "You found out
your wife is sleeping with the boss you dislike, you're having
marital problems, and you are very attracted to Ms. Larson, so you
decide to kill two birds with one stone, so to say. You have access
to all the drugs you'd need. Just a matter of covering up that
they're missing. *Did* you kill your wife, Dr. Martin?"

Arnie gave a choked cry. "No! I have two little girls who cry
every day for their mother. Just because I'm having some
problems at home, doesn't mean I'd... Why would I do something
like that?" Arnie was appalled. Was he a suspect again?

"I understand, but I'm here to find out the truth, so I have to
ask some nasty questions. Okay. Let's look at this in another way.
Was your wife depressed? Before the murder?"

"Off and on." Seeing Walter about to ask him to clarify this,
he anticipated it and said, "She's been showing signs of being
depressed for years. After our second baby, things got bad, but
then she snapped out of it and seemed happy again. Then lately,
maybe for the past year or two, she's been...was, moody, cried
easily, started getting angry at the smallest things. It was why I
didn't want to tell her about Judy at first. I never knew how she'd
act. It was easier to avoid it altogether." Arnie sighed, his
shoulders slumping. He stared down at the hands in his lap.

"So, as a doctor and concerned husband, would you say she'd
been depressed for quite some time?"

"Yes, I'd have to say that."

"Did she ever get diagnosed by her doctor, get pills for it?"

"No. She got mad every time I tried to convince her that she needed help. She thought she was just fine."

Walter decided he'd finished with the questioning and turned it over to Fred.

Fred got up and walked around restlessly. "Dr. Martin, are you sure your wife had no knowledge of your aff...*friendship* with the suspect?"

"I'm pretty sure, yeah." Arnie didn't like how he'd emphasized that word, as if it was a lie.

"Did you tell Ms. Larson you would be away between October 17th and the 20th?"

"Yes, I told her. We were going to get together for dinner when I got back."

Fred picked up the knife and showed it to Arnie. "Was this knife amongst the utensils in your household?"

"No, I've never seen it before Sondra...before it was used in the murder."

"And this bottle? Ever seen it before? Did it have chemicals in it at your lab, for example?"

"No. We don't use that kind at the lab. Clear bottles allow the chemicals inside to deteriorate. We usually store them in brown glass. We use different kinds of bottles, but none like that."

"Did your wife usually drink alcohol?"

"Sometimes she'd have a glass of wine with dinner. Or when we were out socially. She usually wouldn't drink hard liquor."

"Do you keep alcohol in your kitchen cupboards?"

"No. We don't keep alcohol in the house except beer in the fridge for barbecues in the summer, and a bottle of wine once in a while. Neither of us wanted to give the girls a chance to sneak into it, like you hear happens so often."

"Did you and Ms. Larson socialize in public? You know, parties, dinners with other couples, that sort of thing?"

"No, just a drink or dinner every few weeks or so in a

restaurant." Arnie was wondering where this was leading.

"Did Ms. Larson ever tell you she loved you? Do anything to let you think she loved you? Tell you, for example, that you should leave your wife for her?"

"No, we were just friends! How many times do I have to tell you people that!" Arnie stormed. The judge warned him to settle down, and he sat back and scowled at the attorney. This was getting old, fast.

"I have no further questions, your Honor."

Chapter 37

9:00 a.m. - Trial Day 7

Prosecution was looking pleased and confident, knowing the trial was coming to its final stage. Walter was basically sitting on empty hands, and Fred knew it. He would have felt a lot better knowing Arnie was sitting in stalled traffic, trying to get his valuable information to the attorney.

Judy was not looking very well this morning, somber and wan. She barely noticed as the jury filed in, also looking strained and not as made up as they had the first few days of their stint in the jury box. Tempers had flared and gotten shorter, and several members of the jury were barely on speaking terms this morning. The lady who usually wore a turban was without it this day. The Artist had found nothing of interest lately to occupy her pencil. Several were slouched down in their seats, eyes closed, waiting for the judge to enter so this day could get going. All were hoping this would be the end of the case so they could get back to families, social lives and even the jobs that weren't looking so crummy anymore.

"All rise!"

Court started off as usual. Walter requested that they be allowed to approach the bench. At the judge's nod, he and Fred met in front of the bench.

"I would like to ask for an extension, your Honor. I need more time to work on this case."

Fred shook his head. "I have a problem with that, your Honor. I have a meeting with the Attorney General at the end of this week, and a big case that will be going to court soon. Also, Irene, my assistant is going on maternity leave next week. I can agree to a few days stay in the case, but only if Rodenberg here is able to show just cause. What good will delaying the trial do? I'm willing to listen if you've got something concrete to offer." Fred, pretty sure that Walter was just trying to stall the inevitable, gave him a sly smile. "Well?"

Walter sighed. "I'm pursuing a couple of leads further, but I have nothing concrete, your Honor." Judge French ordered the trial to resume. Since neither had further witnesses to offer testimony in the case, they were directed to make their final statements. The jury members, seeing the end finally approaching, sat up straighter, giving it their full attention.

Fred got up and strode purposefully towards the jury. "Ladies, gentlemen. Let me start by reminding you that there are two little girls without their loving mother now. Some one made sure they would never see her again. I am going to show you that all the evidence you have heard in this court points to the one person who could have committed this heinous crime." He pointed his arm towards Judy. "That lady. The one you have seen and heard lies from these past weeks. We have substantial proof that she murdered Sondra Martin, and I am now going to list it for you." He dramatically held out a file he had carried with him. "Here, in this file, is the proof you have been hearing. The proofs that will send this murderess to prison for life, if that is what you, the jury, desire. But which would not even get *close* to making up for the agony and hurt she has caused this family. Let me now review the facts."

Opening the file as reference, Fred began to list the evidence that incriminated Judy in the crime. Nobody noticed Arnie slip into the courtroom and take a seat in the back. Being on the timid side, he was unsure of how to get Walter Rosenberg's attention without causing a scene by approaching him while court was in session.

"First: We have Detective John Ward going to the accuser's

340

apartment where she denied ever having met the victim. She clearly lied, as her own words later pointed out. Second: The taxi driver said she was acting unusual, like she was trying to hide the house number from him. And she later ran back to the taxi to leave in a hurry, forgetting even her coat on that stormy day. Third: Sondra's blood was found on Ms. Larson's dress, which she tried to hide by cramming it into a hamper. Blood stains, which appear to have gotten there under mysterious circumstances. You have to ask yourself if a small cut from a broken glass could actually have created enough blood to have left those prints.

"Then there is the fourth point, Ms. Larson's profession, which is rather unclear, having to do with escorting rich men around town. And she inherited a large amount of money from one client, who happened to die under suspiciously similar methods. Add to that my fifth point, that the accused admits to being in love with the victim's husband - who was in a strained, tempestuous marriage at best - and was in a questionable relationship with him before Sondra Martin's death."

Fred paced back and forth several times before continuing. "A sixth point is that she has mental illness in her family. Her mother, who has been residing in an institution for years now, was obsessed with her husband, Judy's father, after he walked out of the home and went to another woman. Instead of going on with her life, meeting another man, perhaps, her mother chose to hide out, deep within herself. Could there be a hereditary connection, with Judy Larson being infatuated enough with the husband of another woman to go to greater lengths than merely losing her senses, but to go out and kill the opposition?" At the stir this sentence caused, Fred smiled to himself.

"Then, point number seven, and most important of all, Judy Larson was the last one to see the victim alive, a matter of minutes between her leaving the house and the body being found. No other likely explanation has been found, no further suspects were in the vicinity, Ms. Larson's prints were found on all the crime scene evidence."

Fred, holding a captive audience now, paced back and forth in front of the jury. He tapped the papers he held, but had not needed to refer to, lightly against the leg of his smoothly pressed suit pants. This was the part of the trial he loved, when he had every ear of the court bent his way, hanging on his every word. *This* was law practice!

"Ms. Larson had the motive and the means in which to carry it out. She had the money to buy any drug or weapon she chose to use, whether through illegal means, such as the black market, or from more common resources, like buying out a doctor's service. Believing herself in love with *Mister* Martin, she had the desire to want the wife out of the picture, and have the victim's husband as her own. There is no other suspect in this case who would benefit from Mrs. Martin's death, not even the husband."

Judy, listening to him speak, found herself thinking that if it wasn't *her* the attorney was talking about, even she would be buying all that he was saying about her. She started to cry. Rodenberg, beside her, was upset with the reactions he was seeing on the faces of all who were listening to Fred Moor's closing arguments. If he couldn't say something clever to turn this around, he knew the case was lost. He wanted to comfort Judy, but there was nothing he could say.

After listening to Fred expound on Judy's guilt, Arnie decided he'd heard enough and moved quietly up behind Becca Simms. Tapping her on the shoulder, he handed her a note, which she read. They conferred briefly, then Becca turned to Walter and whispered in his ear, then gave him Arnie's note to read. Walter's eyes opened wide and a pleased expression crossed his face as he looked over his shoulder and gave Arnie a nod.

Walter stood up. "Excuse me, your Honor. I have had a serious matter brought to my attention. I would like to meet with you in your chambers, if we may?" He waved his hand to encompass Fred in the invitation.

They were in with the judge about nine minutes before they returned, a smug look on Walter's face, a displeased one on Fred's.

Judge French called a two-hour recess and left the room. Judy was escorted from the room, while Walter eagerly approached Arnie, making John Ward, seated in the front row, wonder what was up. He went over and asked if this was something he could be involved in, too, seeing as how he'd invested so much of his time on the case. Consulting Arnie first, Walter agreed and ushered his little group to a nearby conference room to talk in private. Ordering one of their gophers to pick up coffee and sandwiches, Walter got down to business.

Over an hour later they came out. "And you're one hundred percent convinced about this?" Hearing this, Fred and Irene exchanged puzzled glances. They had ordered lunch sent in so they could stick around and see what was transpiring, maybe hear something of what was going down. This didn't look good for them.

John Ward laughed and patted Arnie on the back before returning to his seat, saying, "You should apply to become a detective, Arnie! You'd be a great asset on my squad!"

"No thanks! *This* investigation is plenty enough for me!" Arnie retorted with a grin. Fred and Irene exchanged a worried look. This *really* didn't look good for them!

*   *   *

Walter rushed over to Judy, where she was kept company in a side room with two officers and a take-out lunch that had been brought to them. The conversation had been very minimal today, Judy not in a talking mood. She was curious about what Arnie had said to cause all the ruckus, but was feeling too withdrawn from everything to think about it. When Walter burst in, she didn't even wonder why he was so excited. Her guards left the two of them alone, waiting outside the door.

"Well, my girl, you really know how to pick your friends!" Walter said, unable to keep the grin off his face, making him appear younger than he had in days.

"What do you mean?" Judy felt herself reviving, his excitement contagious. "What did you find out?" She looked at him suspiciously, afraid to allow herself to begin hoping again.

Walter impulsively reached over and planted a warm kiss on Judy's cheek. "Just wait. You are going to be a free woman today Judy Larson!" He beamed.

"Why? Are you going to say *you* killed her?"

Walter laughed and said, "No, it's something even better. I have a big surprise for you when we return to court." He looked at his watch. "Almost time, we need to get out there."

Judy was left wondering if Arnie had confessed to killing his wife. No, he could never have done that, she knew. She was escorted back into the courtroom, wondering what was about to happen, and aggravated that Walter hadn't told her.

*   *   *

"Due to new information we have obtained, I would like to recall Arnold Martin to the stand." Walter Rodenberg turned towards Arnie and encouraged him forward with a slight smile.

Arnie approached the stand with trepidation. He wondered if the court could hear his knees knocking together in fear! He was reminded that he was still under oath and he took his seat, feeling the cool surface of the chair through his thin, khaki-colored dress pants. It matched the lack of temperature in his icy hands. He tried not to give in to the urge to bury them under his armpits for warmth, and instead, settled for lightly rubbing them together.

"I understand you have found out something about your wife, Dr. Martin. Tell us what you found."

"I have found some evidence proving that Judy Larson didn't kill my wife." There were many gasps around the room. Arnie, for the first time, turned his head towards Judy and really looked at her. He noticed the dark rings under her eyes, the pale skin, and her recent weight loss, which all lent her a fragile appearance. His heart tugged at the misery she must have been suffering, being in jail, knowing she would probably be convicted of a murder she never committed. She had her hand over her mouth at his news, eyes sparkling with unshed tears. He turned back to the lawyer.

"I believe, with the information I found, that Sondra killed herself." The court erupted into chaos. Judge French banged her gavel several times and yelled for everybody to be quiet or they would have to leave her court. The noise took several more seconds to actually get back under control so court could continue.

Arnold continued, but she didn't kill herself intentionally. Her plan was to just cut small on her hand and stomach to bleed a little and prove Judy tried to kill her. She didn't know some had a better plan. Murray Evans planned this to kill her. The court erupted into chaos again. Judge French banged her gavel several times and yelled loud for everybody to be quiet. The noise gets down to pin silence.

Walter was pleased with the commotion it had caused. "Can you tell us what led to this conclusion, Dr. Martin? Take us through the process you followed, if you please."

"Well, last Friday, I found a bill demanding a very large amount of money-$8,600! I got behind in my bill-paying, what with my wife's death, and...well, I looked back through the rest of the mail and found several more past-due notices for the same amount. I also found a statement and bill for a cell phone in Sondra's name, and I didn't recognize any of the numbers on it. I didn't even know she had a cell phone." Arnie supposed they all thought he didn't know much about his wife by then anyway, so he didn't care what they thought about this latest issue.

"The weirdest thing was that there were several bills for a doctor Sondra was going to, a specialist, plus others, like a radiologist and some lab tests. I thought at first that, maybe, the majority of the calls on the cell phone bill were to these places. So I visited Sondra's regular doctor the next day to talk to her and see if I could find out what was going on." Arnie took a deep breath, realizing he had hardly breathed at all through that speech.

"What did her doctor say? Did she send her to have these

extensive tests done because there was something seriously wrong with her?"

"Dr. Kim Henderson, would try to see me between patients. I asked to see my wife's file while I was waiting, and after telling the receptionist it would be okay because my wife was deceased and I'm her next of kin, plus a doctor, she allowed me to look at it. Dr. Henderson saw me with the file when she came out a few minutes later and wanted to know why I had it. She took me into her office so we could talk about it.

"I asked her what was wrong with Sondra, that I had found a lot of unpaid medical bills, test results from lab work ups, all negative. Dr. Henderson was surprised that my wife hadn't confided in me. Apparently, about two months ago, she'd been complaining about a lot of pain in her abdomen. She didn't find anything wrong on the preliminary assessment, but when Sondra went back two weeks later still complaining of pain, they gave her an abdominal CT scan and ultrasound. That's when she went to the specialist."

"And did they find anything wrong?" Walter stood in front of Arnie, and it seemed to help to have just one person to talk to versus the entire room. He wasn't feeling as nervous about going through with this as he was earlier.

"No. Because of the location of the pain, plus her fatigue and recent weight loss, they suspected pancreatic cancer. I think Sondra believed she had it, even though none of the tests showed she did. Dr. Henderson said Sondra had gotten mad at her and stormed out when she wouldn't confirm that she had it. She had it in her mind that she was very ill and would die from it."

"Is pancreatic cancer terminal, Dr. Martin?"

"Yes, it is. Mostly men over sixty get it. Only about 20% of the cases are operable. But she didn't have it! She just wanted to *believe* she did for some reason." Arnie looked down at the floor, he couldn't fathom why she wanted to think she was dying. Was life with him so impossible that she'd rather be dead? He looked back up when Walter asked him if he was all right to continue.

"Yeah. Let's get this over with," he said ruefully.

"Did you give her any medications, any pain killers?" Walter asked.

"No, she never mentioned any of this. She never gave a sign of being in pain, although maybe that explains the moodiness. I asked the doctor the same question. Because they didn't know what it was, and suspected it might be psychological, she was told to buy an over the counter med."

"Why didn't they tell you about what was going on? You're the husband."

"The doctor told me Sondra told them she had been discussing it with me and that I had been the one to suggest she had the cancer. Which is wrong, I didn't know about it. I guess she'd been lying all along about me knowing about it. It didn't occur to them to talk to me in person about it because she's an adult. Dr. Mohan told her to get a second opinion, and as far as she knew, Sondra had. They hadn't seen her for weeks before her death." Arnie tried to swallow the lump that rose in his throat at that last word.

Seeing his witness get choked up, Walter quickly moved on to the next question before it got the better of Arnie. "What did you discover about the cell phone, and all the unknown numbers?"

"After I found the bill, I spent a lot of time going through all the boxes of stuff we've collected over the years. I found the phone in a box in the basement. She couldn't have had it long, I only found two bills for it. I found an anatomy book with a page dog-eared to mark the place. It was a picture of the female body, the kind without the skin, showing muscles and organs. She had circled the pancreas. I don't know what she was thinking," Arnie sighed.

"Did you find anything else?"

"Yes. I came across her diary buried deep down in the box. She used to write in a journal for as long as I've known her. It never even occurred to me to look in it!" Arnie could've kicked himself once he found the diary. He could have saved a lot of grief if he'd remembered it. But it was a 'girl' thing, and he just hadn't been in the habit of worrying about what she'd written since the first couple of years when he used to tease Sondra about getting into it and finding out all her dark secrets. "She wrote in it almost on a daily basis, until two days before she was killed."

"Do you have it with you?"

Arnie took a small, novel-sized book out of the pocket of his jacket. It was about an inch thick, covered in pale green vinyl. Arnie had also found quite a few other diaries stored away, Sondra's legacy from years past. Maybe some day he would be able to sit down and read about her life. Maybe it would help him understand what led up to this, her death. He handed the journal over to Walter, who in turn handed it to Fred to quickly peruse before giving it to the judge.

"Does Sondra mention having an illness in her diary?"

"Yes. She was firm about having cancer, although she doesn't say how she came to believe this. She said she would be dead in a few years, maybe even a few months." Arnie lost the battle and gave a small sob. The room remained silent, respecting his sorrow. "She kept repeating this statement, that she'd die soon. It was like she had nothing else to talk about, that she was obsessed with dying. She also mentioned that she had to do everything that "M.E." told her to do. That it was the only way keep me away from Judy and so that our kids will be looked after she was gone. My God! Who would think to do that to someone!" Arnie was angry, which he preferred than coming across as a baby in court, no matter what the circumstances were.

"What did you decide to do once you found these items?" Walter pointed towards the judge's desk, where the diary sat.

"I thought it over a day or two, then I thought it best to contact you."

"I think you made the right choice, Dr. Martin," Walter said with a smile. "Why did it take you until today to bring it to my attention?"

"I tried to call you Saturday, but you were out of the office.

And nobody was answering the phones, either. So I spent the time trying to see if I could find even more proof of Sondra killing herself."

"And did you find anything else?"

"I found a list she'd written to herself to remember what she should do. I don't think she meant for anyone to see it, but my youngest daughter has the bad habit of pulling paper out of the garbage to use to draw on. I recalled some papers falling out of one of Ashley's books - that's my daughter.

So I went back through it and found it again."

"Do you have the list with you?"

Arnie started to hunt in his jacket pocket, then recalled leaving it on the defense table with Walter's assistant, Becca. Becca, seeing Arnie look at her and start to say something, grabbed a file and walked up to hand it to Walter.

Walter opened the file. "This list," explained Arnie, pointing to the top drawing of a horse in Ashley's childish scrawl, "shows that Sondra planned the whole thing to make it look like Judy try to kill her."

"You're saying she framed Ms. Larson," Walter asked, turning the paper over by a corner to read the words written there.

"Yes. I brought several other things in there, too," he said with a nod towards the file.

Walter took out the list and studied it. "Can you tell us a little about this list?"

"It seems to show the steps of what she was going to do to make her cuts look like they were caused by Ju...Ms. Larson." Arnie looked as if he was in pain.

Walter cleared his throat. "I would like to read this for the court, if I may." The judge nodded her assent. The list read as follows:

1) Get Arnie out of the house. ME to send him on a trip?
2) Take kids to Libby's. Leave them there.
3) Make sure to tell Libby that J. called me to arrange the day and time to meet.

4) Tell Laveen I'm expecting company so she'll be watching for J. and will know how soon she left. (This is important for the case witness part).

5) Pick up the drugs from ME. Make sure the bottles don't have any labels.

6) Check out pawnshops (outside of Seattle) for a knife. Longer the better to make sure it shows some one try to kill me.

7) Call J. and be friendly with J. and get her to come over. Be nice to her first.

8) Make her to pick up the drug bottle to get her finger prints.

9) Give her an alcohol drink and I should take a good drink and drink it fast.

10) Drop my drinking glass to break and cut a little on my finger.

11) Push J. and scare her enough that she'll run out suspiciously.

12) Make sure to get plenty of blood on her dress.

13) Hard part – soak the rag with pain killer and try to breathe it in while using the knife. Make two or three cuts on hand and stomach and cut enough to bleed. Dip the knife in the pain killer first. Scary, but I have to do this. No more problems with J. She will be heading to prison for a long time. J. is gone to jail and Arnie will be with my kids.

14) Call 911 soon after cutting.

As Walter read, he could hear the reactions of the people in the courtroom. "Oh my God!" "I can't believe it!" "How sick!" were but a few. Arnie was quietly crying, as was Judy.

"What motive do you think your wife had in incriminating Ms. Larson?" Walter asked.

"I think, when she believed she was dying, she realized that would free me to pursue a relationship with Judy, if I wanted to. I think she was a little crazy by then and didn't want us together even if she was dead in few years. So, with the help of Murray, she devised a plan to prevent that by framing Judy and sending her to prison for good."

Fred got up, silent up to now. "This is a clever fabrication, Dr. Martin. How do we know *you* didn't devise this plan, that it was *you* that brainwashed your wife into thinking she had a horrible disease, and that it was, in fact, *you* that killed her?

"I can't prove that I didn't do it," Arnie said honestly, surprising Fred. "But I *can* prove that Murray Evans was behind a lot of this!" He stated the name vehemently. "If you'll look in the diary, where I've marked it, you'll see a reference to Murray. Sondra says that 'M.E.' was helping her to get rid of Judy. She's very upset, seems to think highly of the jerk. She talks about how he had provided her with sleeping pills to help her sleep at night. Once the drug was mentioned here in court, and I found her diary, I read up on chloral hydrate. It causes mental confusion, poor judgment, irritability, and behavior disturbances – many of the things Sondra had been demonstrating these past months. I think Murray gave her the drug to get him off his back when he got tired of her!" Arnie spit out. "I think he was the one who told her she was dying once she started experiencing the affects of this drug he was giving her! He wanted to get rid of Sandra planning her to kill her by her self not knowing that she is killing her self. He planed it all out!" Arnie was standing up by then, shouting at the prosecuting attorney.

Judge French pounded her gavel, trying to restore order. She told Arnie, very firmly, that he had better sit down or be escorted out.

Arnie sat down, fuming. He wished Evans was present in the courtroom. He wanted to hear what he had to say about it.

"That's fine, Dr. Martin," continued Fred. "But we must first prove that Dr. Evans is actually the 'M.E.' referred to." Arnie shook his head in disgust. He *knew* it was Murray.

Walter decided to put a stop to the bickering, and asked the judge if he could approach the bench and have a word with her.

Both attorneys stepped up. "I would like to propose that we call a recess to allow enough time for us to investigate this new information, contact the doctors involved, bring Murray Evans in as a witness again, if need be."

"I agree, your Honor," Fred put in.

"Okay, gentlemen. I will call it for now. You have until Friday, December 1st, to gather your information. Let's not waste the taxpayers' money. Find your information as expediently as possible. Keep in mind that anything found to prove Dr. Evans guilty of assisting with her death, in any way, will need to go to a separate docket. Court will be dismissed until then." She banged her gavel and retired from the room.

Arnie stepped down from the witness stand, pausing long enough to look across the room. Judy was relieved. At last she might be found innocent. She sent Arnie a silent 'thank you' before she was led out of the court and the rest of the people were dismissed.

Walter made a list of his own. They would need to get an analyst started on Sondra's handwriting, since they didn't have much time. It had recently come to him that Murray Evans should not have known that an anesthetic of some type had been used, as this had not been released to the papers. Yet Evans had mentioned knowing this during his testimony. He had some serious talking to do to Evans, it seemed.

Chapter 38

Over the next two days, all those involved with the case were busy gathering new evidence, talking to witnesses, new and old, regarding the new findings. As information was verified, Walter had the ominous duty of trying to piece together the new information they now had with what they already had established.

John Ward had spoken briefly to Murray Evans about his involvement in Sondra Martin's plot, who immediately sought legal counseling. A handwriting expert was convinced to put a rush on the handwriting samples he was given, along with the note and diary of Sondra Martin. It was agreed that John Ward, as acting detective in the case, would testify as to the findings when court met on Friday.

*   *   *

9:00 a.m. - Trial Day 8

There was a buzz of excitement in the air as people packed the already crowded courtroom to witness first hand what was being called the 'Trial of the Year.' Arnie was glad he arrived there early to talk to the attorney, as he was able to have a front row seat instead of standing in the back like so many others. The jurors looked bright-eyed and fresh, as they did on the first day, anticipation apparent on their faces. Judy, once again studying them, noticed the 'Geek' staring at her, and returned his smile this time. The Turban lady was dressed in festive red and yellow. The 'Artist' was busy with her drawing of the full room, taking

353

advantage of the few minutes before the judge stepped up to her bench. The 'pit bull' surprised Judy by looking straight at her and giving her an unobtrusive nod. She guessed that was as close to a positive reaction as she would see from him, but it was reassuring. They all appeared to be full of nervous excitement, unable to hold still in their seats until order was called and court began. Only the gentle rustle of clothing could be heard from then on.

Walter was up, asking that the case be dismissed, that they had solid proof that Judy Larson was not the killer. Walter called Detective John Ward to the stand.

"Please tell the court your findings, Detective."

"We had a handwriting expert take a look at some of Sondra Martin's previous letters and her diary. Then he compared it to the list her husband found. Mr. Rodenberg has the sworn testimony from the expert stating he found them to be from the same person, Sondra Martin. He also notes that the later writings of Sondra Martin show a definite sign of emotional stress, her letters getting 'erratic and leggy,' as he puts it."

Walter handed the document to the judge. "What else did you discover?"

"When we got a search warrant for Murray Evans' office, we located some papers stating Mrs. Martin had signed up for one of his experimental programs. One having to do with alternate thought patterns and changing them through the induction of certain chemicals. It is, however, inconclusive whether or not this contributed to the victim's belief that she had a terminal illness.

"We did find out, though, that Evans gets a large amount of money to conduct these tests, whether he can show results or not. So, just the money alone could be a big incentive to do tests on people who really don't have anything wrong with them. Then he can "cure" them and get his name in all the journals." John allowed his disgust to be heard in his voice.

"Objection!" Fred said John was adding supposition, and had no way of knowing this to be a fact.

"Sustained," agreed the judge. "Please stick to the facts,

Detective."

"Yes, ma'am. Anyway," John continued, "We have several receipts we found in a file under the victim's name, showing she had been taking a couple of different drugs, one directly affecting your emotions, according to our lab tech, and a couple others that affect body functions." Walter handed this information to the judge also.

"The cell phone Dr. Martin found was registered under the name of Sondra Martin. The numbers on the phone bill belonged to Murray Evans' office, as well as a few other places, like the specialist she went to. We located the call Mrs. Martin placed to Judy Larson on September 7th, it was only about two minutes in length. Nothing between the two households after that. The majority of the cell calls were between Sondra Martin and Murray Evans, starting on August 4th, last call to him was the day of the murder, October 19th.'"

Arnie had stopped breathing. August? That was *before* his accident! Before he'd even told Sondra about Judy! That meant that Murray had been after his wife long before he'd given her a reason to go looking for revenge for his so-called indiscretions. He knew he'd have a lot of soul searching to do when this was over.

"We read over Sondra Martin's last diary, covering the past year. It seems she had a strong belief that she would die young, just like her mother did with cancer. Something her stepmother had apparently reinforced in her through her entire childhood. She occasionally wrote that she thought she had some illness or other, a classic hypochondriac, according to Dr. Mohan, who frequently treated her imagined ailments. Just like Dr. Nash in the movie, 'A Beautiful Mind.'"

Arnie was again taken by surprise. What else had he been oblivious to over the years? He felt like he'd been married to somebody he never even knew. He was a doctor, why hadn't he seen some of this happening? Why hadn't Sondra felt like she could confide in him, her husband, as well as a doctor? He rubbed his neck. The more he heard, the less he knew his own wife.

"The most distinguishable fingerprints on the list explaining what to do. Starting with send Arnold out.

"As for the knife, we checked out all the pawnshops within a fifty-mile radius, and were lucky to hit one fairly quickly in Auburn. A woman fitting Sondra Martin's description bought a similar knife several days before her murder. The owner remembers her because she was acting pretty high strung, asking if the knife was sharp and how she could make it sharper. He didn't want to sell it to her at first, afraid she was going to use it to hold up a bank to get drug money or something. But, money prevails in the end, and he sold it to her.

"In speaking with Dr. Evans, he admits that he arranged for Arnold Martin to take his place at the Los Angeles conference at the last moment in order to spend time with his new girlfriend. Something he made sure to inform Sondra Martin of so she would get the idea that it was over between them. According to him, she was still clinging to the fact that she could get him back. He called her the day of her death to tell her this, canceling a lunch date with her at the same time. He told me that Sondra was quite upset with the news. He denies encouraging her to take any of the sleeping pills he'd provided her with, given to her at her insistence, he made sure to mention. She claimed to be sleeping poorly, so he says he was just doing her a favor.

"At this point we have no solid evidence to prove that Murray Evans manipulated Sondra Martin in any way to cause her to create her own murder scene. But we plan on beginning an intense investigation."

"Thank you, Detective Ward. I have no further questions, your Honor." Walter stepped away from the witness stand and joined Judy. He patted her on the shoulder as he sat down, confidant that it was now over.

"Does the prosecution have any questions?" asked the judge.

Fred stood up, too impressed with the events leading up to the unexpected turnabout of the case to be upset that it wasn't going his way.

"No, your Honor. No questions."

"In view of the new evidence presented, I hereby call this case closed. Judy Larson, you are free of all charges and are free to go. Jury members, the court thanks you for your time, you may return home. Case dismissed." Judge French banged her gavel with a satisfied thud.

The court erupted in hoots and hollers. The jury members, anxious to return to their homes after such a long absence, nonetheless remained long enough to exchange a few words on the case. Two of the members, the young black man and the initially insecure Hispanic woman, traded phone numbers and walked out together.

Judy, laughing and crying at the same time, gave Walter Rodenberg a huge hug and thanked him profusely. Arnie was just about to go speak to her when he saw a tall, good-looking, and well-dressed man stand up and walk towards Judy. He hugged her and gave her a kiss on her cheek. He shook hands with Walter, and Arnie heard him introduce himself to Walter's assistant as Paul Malcolm, the President of Life Style Designers.

"I knew you would win this case – that's why I hired you!" Paul Malcolm joked with Walter.

Arnie noted that he kept his arm around Judy's waist, and she didn't seem to mind in the least. Feeling out of place, Arnie got up and started to leave the courtroom, wondering about the relationship between Judy and this new guy.

"Arnie!" Hearing Judy call his name, Arnie stopped and turned back around, a loving expression flitting briefly across his face before being replaced by sadness. She couldn't let him leave without saying anything. Not after all that had happened. Judy walked up to him, wanting to hug him closely, but afraid of his reaction if she did.

"I'm sorry all of this happened because of me," Judy said.

Arnie waved away her apology. "I'm sorry I was such a lousy husband that I didn't know what was going on under my nose," he replied, a bitter tone to his voice. "I could have prevented all of this from happening if I had paid more attention to my own wife!" He looked so dejected, Judy had to hold herself back from wrapping her arms around him.

"Don't feel that way, Arnie. It wasn't your fault. She had problems that she didn't want to tell anybody who was close to her, that's all. You can't blame yourself for how she chose to solve them." Judy placed her hand on his arm. "I won't ask if you believed in me, Arnie, but I do want to thank you. I know it was hard finding out all those things, maybe harder to bring it out in court. But I will be forever in your debt. I owe you my freedom. Thank you." She leaned over and gave him a gentle kiss on his cheek.

Before Arnie could reply, Walter came bustling up, a big grin on his face. He shook hands boisterously with Arnie and told him how much they appreciated what he had done. He also informed him that they had put out a warrant for Murray Evans arrest and the cops were now on their way to pick him up. Walter seemed refreshed, ready to go into this new battle. Arnie gave the appropriate responses and left as soon as he could

Epilogue

Arnie watched Ashley and Heather playing on the tire swing in the back yard of their new house. Two months had gone by since the trial and the move. The girls seemed to be adjusting well to their new surroundings. He had taken a job in Olympia, handling a lot of high tech equipment in a brand new lab. He thought he would be happy there once he got used to the routine, not too different from what he used to do in Seattle. He smiled and waved at the girls, then opened the patio door and went back into the house.

He picked up the morning paper. He had read about the up-coming trial, the State vs. Murray Evans, and wondered if he would be called in to testify against him. He hoped not, but he imagined he would be. He didn't even want to think about seeing Evans again so soon.

Arnie turned away, dropping the paper back onto the table. The phone caught his eye. Not a day went by that he hadn't thought of Judy. He walked over to it, wondering if he should give her a call, or if it was better to leave things as they were. Her phone number was still engraved in his memory. He picked up the receiver, dialed two numbers, then let it fall back in place. He stood there, staring at the phone, for a long time. Then his hand reached out again.

www.ingramcontent.com/pod-product-compliance
Lightning Source LLC
Chambersburg PA
CBHW030358030726
47497CB00002B/393